Eric Hoffmann's international adventure involves a PLO hitman, a ruthless CIA agent and the discovery of OPERATION DOVETAIL—a plot that could alter the course of history. The goal—the unification of Germany into its former glory, by nuclear skirmishing if necessary. Only one man can stop it. One inexperienced American suffering bitter losses and facing impossible odds.

THE
HOFFMANN
FILE

Brian Utermahlen

A DELL/EMERALD BOOK

Published by
Dell Publishing Co., Inc.
1 Dag Hammarskjold Plaza
New York, New York 10017

Dell ®™681510, Dell Publishing Co., Inc.

ISBN: 0-440-03657-7

Printed in the United States of America

First printing—December, 1983

"To this war of every man against every man, this also is consequent; that nothing can be unjust. The notions of right and wrong, justice and injustice, have there no place . . . force and fraud are in war the two cardinal virtues."

Thomas Hobbes
Leviathan, 1651

Prologue
WASHINGTON NOVEMBER 1963

The Capitol's half-mast flag snapped in the brisk breeze that whipped through Washington. Low, rain-laden clouds moved swiftly over the dome from west to east, occasionally obscuring the topmost point of the structure. The grass mall stretching out from the Capitol toward the Washington Monument and beyond to the Lincoln Memorial was strangely empty, except for two men who walked slowly along Independence Avenue. The city seemed dead.

"It's over for now," said the taller of the two, turning up the collar of his raincoat against the chill. His companion nodded.

The taller man was ruggedly handsome, with a deep, natural tan that was out of place when one considered that summer had long since departed the Middle Atlantic states. Women were naturally attracted to him—his athletic build, his chiseled looks; and he had known many of them through his college years at Nebraska and after that around the world. As a result of the hard physical exercise demanded by his latest field assignment for the Central Intelligence Agency, he looked younger than his forty years. Within the Agency's inner circle of power, he had a reputation as a man of intelligence, common sense, and loyalty to the Company. His tendency to ruthlessness was overlooked as an occasional necessity in an imperfect world. Bill Knight was being groomed for greater things.

"There's going to be hell to pay when this gets out," Knight's companion said, hunching his shoulders against the first few drops of rain.

"It won't—at least not all of it," Knight replied.

"Can we be sure?"

"Reasonably sure. I talked with the Director a little while ago. He's been with Hoover this morning, and got the Bureau to agree to keep things under wraps for us."

The other man lifted an eyebrow. The FBI had become increasingly uncooperative over the past several years, at the express orders of Hoover himself. "Interesting. How do they expect to do that when the President's been killed?"

"The FBI is running the investigation. They've had a little trouble with the Dallas sheriff's office, but they're taking charge—it's only natural. Hoover will be following every detail. He'll be selective in releasing any information, and he won't get any interference from the White House. He and the Texan are old friends. I understand both daughters regard him as a surrogate uncle."

"We ought to have somebody working with Hoover's people to keep an eye on things."

"No, that would be a mistake," Knight said. He'd already considered that possibility and dismissed it. "Our involvement would come out sooner or later. We'd have a rough time explaining. As much as we dislike it, we'll have to go along with Hoover."

"What are the chances the Texan will pick up the ball on Dovetail?"

"Essentially none. The timing's wrong. And, aside, from that, he was never let in on most of the foreign-strategy planning. The Director says he was never present at any of our briefings. Only the 'clan' was invited. Must be hell being the V.P." Now the underdog was on top: Knight wondered how many staffers were already packing their bags in preparation for the inevitable pink slips.

"There's another little piece of business to attend to— you'll have to handle this one," Knight continued, stuffing his hands deep into his raincoat pockets. "Hoover wants files developed and passed to him on two senators and a female reporter, in exchange for his cooperation."

"Who?"

"Rohde from Wisconsin, and Hammill from Arizona. The girl is Chrissy McLeod."

"Rohde and Hammill are cosponsoring a bill to set up an Oversight Committee on the Bureau, aren't they?"

Knight nodded.

"I can imagine how that sits with the old bastard. What does he want?"

"Tapes, mostly. And photographs."

"Why doesn't he take them himself? The senators are here in Washington almost all the time. So is the girl."

"He wants pictures of them together. In three weeks they're all going to the Philippines and some other stops in the Pacific on a fact-finding junket. Chrissy is going along representing one of the wire services. The idea is to get some compromising shots—he collects that kind of garbage, I hear. He also wants tapes of all their phone calls and conversations."

"That's bullshit!" The man glared at Knight, who continued staring impassively ahead. "We can't do that. You know what he's going to do. He'll splice and edit until it sounds like the three of them had a nonstop orgy all over the South Pacific."

"That's his method. And we can do it—the Director says we will."

"I don't like it. I don't like Hoover dictating terms to us."

"It's the price we pay for keeping things quiet. If word gets out that we know the President was killed by a Soviet, everything starts to unravel in a hell of a hurry and Dovetail is dead . . . for good."

"You're right. . . . Damn, I wish there were another way."

"There's not. Get the pictures and the tapes."

The men stopped at the base of the Washington Monument and looked toward the White House, about a half-mile away. The drizzle, combined with haze, all but obscured it.

"Ich bin eine Berliner," Knight said to himself. "He had a style we won't soon see again. He had the guts to make it happen. And the other side would have backed down again, just like they did in Cuba." He stood transfixed, thinking of what might have been.

"Let's get out of this damned rain," Knight's companion said.

The spell was broken, the moment gone. A time would come again when the scheme could be executed. For now, it would be locked away where nobody could find it, tamper with it, until history was ready for men with vision to breathe life into it again.

They turned and walked back toward the Capitol. At that moment, in Dallas, Lee Harvey Oswald died from gunshot wounds inflicted by Jack Ruby. A nation of mourning souls watched it happen and collectively reeled under the violence played out on television screens across the country. Some said Ruby acted on the orders of an organized conspiracy that feared what Oswald would reveal if brought to trial.

No evidence was ever uncovered to substantiate that theory.

Chapter 1

". . . and in another Watergate-related development, the Special Prosecutor announced this morning . . ."

Eric Hoffmann switched off the car radio. In the three months since Nixon's resignation, each day's news had been dominated by yet another startling development, to the point where it was becoming one long, unfathomable bore. He was sick to death of startling developments.

So, as he neared Silver Springs on the outskirts of the nation's capital, he surrounded himself in the comforting silence of the MG's neutral hum and thought about the events that had brought him to this Washington suburb on a dark Friday evening.

For twelve years, since his junior year in high school, he had sought out information on his dead father—a man he had never known, a casualty in the final days of World War II. But, strangely, a soldier about whom no record seemed to exist; an anomaly the son could not reconcile, especially in light of his own half-dozen years of military service, during which there seemed no end to the amassing of documentation on even the most trivial aspects of his personal and professional life. Yet of the father there was not a trace. Medical records, personnel files, pay records—all had apparently vanished as if Lieutenant Kenneth M. Hoffmann never existed.

Most of the men in his father's squadron had been lost in raids over Germany during the spring of 1945, and none of the survivors he had been able to locate was able to shed any light on the elusive young flight officer. Memories had clouded after more than two decades, and only a few men could even recall that an officer named Hoffmann had served in the unit, much less remember anything about him. It had been a desperate, frightening life as a member of a bomber squadron; one tended to get close to one's own crew, but not to many others—or so it would seem from those who had survived. Despite the deadends and disappointments, the frustrations and a growing sense of impossibility, the son persisted in his search through official channels and personal contacts. But he'd begun to realize he was wasting his time.

The dim bulb behind the MG's tachometer winked off and on, catching his attention before the gauge darkened. He tapped the glass cover several times before it illuminated, thinking the car was becoming another waste of his time—like the old farmhouse he'd bought nearly a year ago, after leaving the Army. Restoring the place had looked like an interesting challenge then, and maybe a way of turning a handsome profit in the bargain. But the renovation turned out to be more expensive than he'd figured, especially in light of the meager paychecks from the flying jobs at Tri-State Aviation. And nearly a third of that went to Barbara in the form of alimony. Poor Barbara.

She had never really understood him—at least she couldn't comprehend why he had extended his tour in Viet Nam for another six months. Somehow, she couldn't understand that he had found something he was really good at, and that he needed almost more than anything else the recognition of being the very best at something. Anything. Flying, especially the intensity of the experience in a combat zone, filled the bill.

The divorce came as a shattering blow, more so than he expected, and it took him long, soul-searching months to piece himself back together, re-sort his goals, his ambitions, and start over.

Now he was twenty-nine going on thirty, with the first lines beginning to form at the corners of his eyes. More than a hint of excess flesh kept creeping in at the waistline and took longer and longer to exercise away. He was beginning to feel old already, with nothing to show for his life thus far. Who really cared that he he could tune a foreign car and make it purr seductively, or that he was the best damned pilot in some small charter outfit? Where was the thrill in that? Aside from an occasional hop to New York with some obviously successful business types, the most exciting thing he did anymore was fly cancelled checks from branch offices in Lancaster and Harrisburg to the central bank in Philadelphia.

He'd told Phil Markowski that his greatest fear was of being hijacked by Polish bandits on one of these nightly runs. Well, at least he still had a sense of humor, though Markowski thought this debatable at times; and the sentiment found a partial echo from Tri-State's secretary, a pretty young thing named Cindy McDaniel, who had recently become the object of Eric's oblique but friendly overtures. So far she had succeeded in keeping their friendship at arm's length. Disappointing, but one could hope.

Still, the biggest frustration was the gnawing, nagging uncertainty concerning his father. Who was he? What was he like? Why was there no trace of him? The questions were endless, yet there were no answers. At times—especially in the solitude of the farmhouse while listening to old folk songs on the stereo bought during his tour in Germany—he could feel himself aching, wondering. There was a sense of being somehow adrift.

Earlier that afternoon, a phone call had changed all that in a moment of swift dread.

"You're getting very close to the truth," the caller had said at the outset, his words slurred and barely audible. He had identified himself as a retired general, Air Force. His name was Gregory. "Phillip Gregory, and I said you're getting close . . . probably too close to the truth about your father."

What the general was saying grabbed at his chest, and he felt as if some animate hand had squeezed the air from his lungs, bringing on a moment of dizziness, sending the half-finished cabinets on the far wall out of focus. The truth about his father! For long seconds he was aware of nothing except numbness and his own breathing. When he spoke, his voice betrayed the nervousness still gripping him.

"What truth, general?" he asked, the myriad of unanswered questions swirling and surfacing again in his mind. "What do you mean?"

"Just what I said."

"Sir, I'm not following. What is it you're trying to tell me?" He forced a calm into his voice that he didn't feel. After all these years! His first hint. He was on the brink of finally unlocking the mysterious puzzle that was his father. It was almost too much to hope for, too much to believe. "What is it?"

"I just . . . I just wanted to . . ." The voice trailed off, replaced by a heavy, labored breathing. The words were laced with anxiety, and Hoffmann suspected Gregory had been drinking, the reason for the almost imperceptible slur. *Damn you!* Hoffmann wanted to shout, torn with intolerant rage at the man's weakness. To be so close to finally learning—and dependent now on alcoholic old blue-suiter who probably spent most of his afternoons in the bottle reliving the good old days.

"General, did you know him?" I'll pull this from you word by word if I have to, Hoffmann thought, but he knew his connection to the general was tenuous at best. He could sense the man slipping away from him.

"Did I say that? . . . Yes, I knew him. Same squadron. England in 'forty-five . . . a few months before you were born. . . . I may have been the last one to see him alive. Him and his crew."

The statement sent a shock through him, a contraction of muscle in his arms and shoulders like the time he'd touched Sutter's electrified fence while clearing brush at the far end of his own four acres. The man knew!

"How did you find out I was looking?"

He heard the blunt, ugly laugh.

"A lot of people know."

"People? What people? Who do you mean?" A long, almost unendurable silence as he tried to understand, the meaning of the man's words eluding him like some shadowy wraith. "Sir, can we get together and talk?"

"No! Damn you, boy, all I wanted to tell you was that your dad was a decent sort, a credit to the service. Nothing more. I don't want to talk about it anymore!" The vehemence took Hoffmann by surprise, and the slur was gone, the enunciation clear and correct: an inconsistency that bothered him.

"Look, I'd like to meet you . . . somewhere, anywhere. Your convenience. Name the place."

"I said no, damn you. . . . Knew this was a mistake."

"General, this is important to me," Hoffmann said, casting about for some way to keep the man talking, knowing that he must not let the old soldier hang up without a clue as to how to reach him again. He felt inept, powerless, and this served only to heighten his frustration and nervousness. "I've been working on this for a long time. You've got to help me. If we can't get together, then at least promise me we can talk after today. Where can I reach you? What's your phone number?" He was instantly angry with himself for blurting out the question, knowing this was probably the last thing the man was likely to give him, no matter how much he'd had to drink. The response came as a total surprise.

"It's area code three-oh-one—" Gregory stopped abruptly. "You son-of-a-bitch! Keep away from me! I'm warning you . . . stay away. I won't see or talk to you. I won't admit this conversation took place. Do you understand? *Do you understand?*"

"General, I only—"

"Don't contact me!" Gregory was breathing rapidly, the noise on the phone rising and falling like the rushing sounds of electrical static. When he spoke again, his voice was low and ominous. "The word is out on you, young man. . . . They know."

"Who? What word?"

"They know."

The phone went dead. Hoffmann stared at it for long moments, aware of his own growing panic. *They know. . . . The word is out on you.* What had that meant? The familiar was hardly ever frightening, but the unknown . . .

Quickly, almost too easily, he located the caller's address through the information operator, wrote it on the back of an envelope containing last month's unpaid mortgage notice, and walked to the kitchen window. Outside, the late-afternoon sun cast a tawny glow on the fields beyond the barn. A peaceful scene, far removed from the brief, almost violent episode with Gregory.

The man had provided no answers—simply added to the number of questions. Who was it that supposedly knew about him? And what had he meant about the word being out? Nothing about the call rang true. There was something wholly wrong, out of place; maybe more than one something.

Hoffmann gazed at the phone number and the address he'd

written, still shaken but not wanting to admit it. He had spent countless hours in the service wondering about the sanity of the brass, questioning, poking fun. But none of them, in Gregory's place, would have been that stupid or gullible. The man had made it almost too easy to trace him.

He retained the murky, uneasy feeling that something was terribly wrong.

He reached General Gregory's address shortly after 9:30 P.M., his nervousness increasing the closer he got. Though he was eager to learn more, there was a dark, almost overwhelming foreboding that had shadowed him since the phone call.

The house was modest and sat surrounded by tall old trees in a quiet, respectable part of the town. Despite the late hour, no interior lights were visible from the street where Eric parked the dark blue sports car, debating whether he had made the right choice in trying to see the man tonight. At last, he walked up the driveway and quickly across the lawn to the small, covered front porch. When he knocked on the front door, it yielded, opening halfway.

"General Gregory? . . . Anybody home?" His calls went unanswered, echoing through the house. In the darkness, he blindly searched the wall with his right hand, found the light switch, and flicked it on. The soft glow revealed the center hall where he stood and a dining room off to the left, opposite a larger formal living room which created a mood of easy hospitality and warmth.

His own reflection in the mirror next to the doorway startled him, and he knew it was a mistake to have entered the house. Turning to leave, he noticed a thin shaft of light coming from beneath a door at the far end of the living room. Tentatively, he crossed the room and opened the door.

General Gregory sat slumped at the desk in his study, his back to the door, his hand clutching an empty glass. The room smelled heavily of stale smoke and liquor, the aftermath of several hours' overindulgence in both. Hoffmann gently shook the general's shoulder to awaken him, and heard the sharp gasp leap from his own lips, like the cry of a wounded animal, as the body slid from the chair and landed face up, revealing a large, ugly gash at the base of the throat. Blood trickled to the floor from the pool of red on the wooden desk.

Gregory was dead.

Hoffmann stood paralyzed over the corpse, angry and terrified, cursing himself for entering the house. The temptation to run was overwhelming, to put distance between himself and this place—at least until he had time to sort it out, he rationalized. Finally, he dialed the operator and asked for the police.

"Operations desk. Sergeant Morgan." The voice on the phone sounded weary beyond words, and Hoffmann could picture the scene: a crusty old cop, cigar in hand, reaching for a pencil.

"I'd like to report an incident," Hoffman began, his eyes still fixed on the dead man. His own voice sounded far away, strangely vacant, without depth. ". . . It's a murder."

"Go ahead," came the reply, the lethargic tone replaced now with a distinct ring of interest. "Where are you?"

"The address here is 1435 Baynard Road. Silver Springs. I think the man's name is Gregory, a retired Air Force general."

"Is this some kind of gag?" the officer asked testily, his voiced laced with anger. "1435 Baynard, right? Would your name be Hoffmann?"

Hoffmann stared at the phone in disbelief, as if some unseen hand had slapped him. His senses dulled.

"Look, friend, I hope this ain't some damned fraternity prank. The last time you called was exactly four minutes ago, and this is going to look pretty damned strange on my log.

There's a law against this, just like there is for yellin' fire in a crowded theater."

But the words were lost on Hoffmann, who barely heard the siren on the police cruiser as it slammed to a halt less than thirty yards away.

Chapter 2

Light streaming through a back window and the insistent ring of the telephone awakened him from fitful sleep. Glancing at the clock through half-closed eyes, Hoffmann saw it was almost 11:00 in the morning—three hours since he had finally dozed off.

The interrogation in Silver Springs had lasted well into the morning; four hours of constant repetition. The same questions over and over by a team of three detectives, until at last his body and mind could stand it no longer. His nerves frayed and his temper short, somewhere around 2:00 A.M. he had demanded to be charged or set free. That had apparently been enough for the police to let him go—at least for the moment. It had been a nightmare, one he could not shake on the drive back to Pennsylvania; or later, as he lay on the old fourposter bed willing himself to sleep, only to be awakened every few minutes by the sight of Gregory or the memory of harsh lights in the back room of the police station.

Wearily, he reached for the receiver.

"Good morning, Mr. Hoffmann. I take it you've had a rather full day already," The voice on the phone was cool, almost bored. "I'd like to talk to you about General Gregory."

Hoffmann was instantly alert, his mind racing, the pulse strong in his temples. "Who are you?" he asked after a brief pause. He knew his voice sounded shaken, hollow, the tone of one whose life has suddenly gone askew. He was irritated at himself for the loss of control.

"I was his aide for two years, and remained a friend of the family," the man was saying. "Don't worry—I'm not the law."

"Why should I be concerned about that?"

The offhanded laugh from the other end angered and frightened him.

"Nice try. Look, friend, I'm well aware of what happened last night, so we can skip the fencing. You're up to your eyeballs in the old man's death, with a very unconvincing story which we both know the police aren't buying. But right now that's your problem, not mine. So, why the call? Good question. Meet me in Kilkenny's Pub at noon."

"I still don't know who you are."

"But I know you . . . and so do a lot of other people now. You've earned yourself a certain degree of notoriety, shall we say. And, Hoffmann . . . don't keep me waiting."

The phone went silent, and Hoffmann replaced the receiver, his hands moist. He felt the fear feeding on itself, growing like some cancerous node he could not control.

The pub was one of his familiar haunts, a routine stopover after flying, where he could relax with a pint of the dark Guinness or a draft of Harp and listen to would-be tenors struggling with off-key ballads. It was a loud, raucous, freewheeling sort of place with a Republican tricolor flag out front. Inside, a long mirror behind the bar proclaimed KILKENNY'S IRISH PUB in bold green strokes; on the brick wall opposite this, Aer Lingus travel posters of Ireland's countryside and the mandatory dart board. What few offerings comprised the menu were scrawled in chalk on a square piece of slate next to the fireplace.

Hoffmann entered and walked quickly to the only occupied table; his footsteps echoed off the aged hardwood, the only sound in the room except for the chair scraping the floor as the man rose and extended his hand.

"Thanks for seeing me. Carle Landrum." He stood two inches taller than Hoffmann and looked more than that in the closeness of the room, with its low ceilings and small, clustered tables. Landrum's grip was firm and his smile disarming. "Nice of you to come."

"There's no way I could have said no," Eric replied evenly, wondering if he'd ever again think of this place as a retreat from the rest of the world.

"Sorry to be so cryptic." Landrum sat, motioned to the owner who was absently drying glasses behind the bar, and casually lit a cigarette. They were silent until the beer was in front of them and the bartender had gone. Landrum warily looked over his shoulder, then smiled again at Hoffmann, a smile rooted in scorn. "You really got yourself into one heck of a fix."

"I didn't need to come here to learn that. You said you were Gregory's aide. Why don't I believe you?"

"Because you're a skeptic. And right now you don't know who or what to believe. This little bit of bravado tells me you're probably scared as well. Like I said, I'm not the law, and we can dispense with the bobbing and weaving. I know most of the facts—a friend of mine is on the Silver Springs force, and I talked with him last night after Gregory's daughter called me. We were more than just acquaintances at one time, and last night she needed someone."

"And she thought of you."

"That surprises you?"

"A little. For a friend of the family, you don't seem especially upset by the old man's death." He said it to provoke a reaction, a defensive reflex until he could learn more about the man who seemed to know so much about him.

Landrum's face clouded for an instant, a transitory uncertainty replaced by a look of anger that came and went, as if he were forcing the reaction.

"I'll forget you said that, for the moment. But don't press your luck, flyboy. That old man, as you called him, was like a father to me those two years." He drank quickly and watched Hoffmann for long seconds, then said: "You're lucky I don't think you did it. . . . The State Department apparently doesn't think so either."

Hoffmann felt his breath catch. The State Department? A new dimension to the nightmare, a piece of information that, like the others, did not fit. He calmed himself with a deep breath, exhaling slowly. "I still don't know who you are," he said at last.

"An ex-general's aide, now with the State Department. In a rather mundane position with a very narrow career path ahead, if you want the truth." The condescending smile had returned; he looked to be enjoying their conversation—and Hoffmann's discomfort. "They sent me up here today to set up a meeting for you with a guy named Carnahan. On Monday."

"What for?"

"Police warrants aside, it's a matter of national security."

"So much for your apologies for being cryptic," Hoffman said, trying to sound breezy. But he was scared. Damned scared, without exaggeration, and the look on the other man's face told him it showed. "You're not being completely honest, are you?"

Landrum shrugged. "You won't know until you talk to Carnahan." He drank again and lit another cigarette. "All I know for sure is that State has been getting some pretty heavy flak, from places high up in West Germany, over a few old B-17's Gregory took an interest in a few months back. Somebody over there was damned touchy about it, and now the man who created the whole thing turns up dead. What makes it even more interesting is that one of those old crates was supposedly last flown by somebody closely related to you."

"And you expect me to believe that?"

"Actually, I don't care what you choose to believe. I was sent here to arrange a meeting. Nothing more."

"You could have done that by phone."

"Or stopped by the house, maybe?" Landrum laughed derisively and shook his head. "Your ignorance of the real world is refreshing. No wonder the police think you really killed him." He reached inside the coat, extracted a pad, scribbled an address, and slid it across the table. "Ten o'clock Monday morning. Don't be late."

"What if I don't want to come?"

Landrum rose and looked down at him. "Be serious. This is not an invitation." He tossed a five-dollar bill on the table and said, "Have another one on Uncle Sam. I'm on the expense account today. And remember . . . ten sharp."

Hoffmann watched the man walk quicky across the room and out the door, certain that most of what Landrum had said was a lie. The implication that his father's plane had been located after all these years was too convenient. Landrum's allusion to it had been transparent, maybe adlibbed on the spur of the moment. Why? None of it made any sense, and yet somebody was out there watching him, maneuvering him against his will and without his knowledge. The casual remark about national security had been a nice touch, designed, he was sure, to make the meeting sound more imperative. He felt like a man without sight suddenly adrift in a crowded, unfriendly room.

The need to do something—anything—was overpowering. To dwell on the hidden agenda behind Landrum's words was a certain path to ever-increasing anxiety, and he didn't need much more than what he now felt. He ignored the bartender's question about another draft as he walked to the pay phone in the back, dialed the number of a State Patrol barracks in Delaware, and asked for Ben Saxon.

"Ben? Eric Hoffmann." Saxon was another pilot he'd met at a local flying club soon after buying the house—someone to share expenses for a two-week trip to the Bahamas planned for the following summer. "I need a favor."

He outlined the events of the previous day, omitting the call from Landrum and their meeting. Listening to his own account of what had transpired, it sounded wild and unbelievable; something hallucinated.

"Can you find out what's going on with the investigation?" Silence answered. "If you're wondering if I did it, the answer is no."

"I'm thinking. . . . Damn, you ought to know I can't do anything like that. Tampering in somebody else's case. If they found out, I'd get cashiered out of here so damned fast—"

"Look, I didn't do it!" Hoffmann interrupted, exasperated and angry. His breathing came in rapid spasms. The injustice of it all! "Will you check into it for me?"

"I can't."

"Thanks, friend," he said sarcastically, and slammed on the hook. He walked quickly outside, feeling exhausted and impotent, sure of only one thing—Kilkenny's would never be the same to him.

Maybe nothing would ever be the same.

Saxon's call came in midafternoon.

"All right, I did some quiet checking on what you said. And I didn't learn much. Naturally they won't release any

info on the investigation, but one thing doesn't jibe with
their records: the two phone calls reporting the incident.
Their desk log shows it was only reported once."

"That can't be." The worry returned in a quick rush. "There
was a Sergeant Morgan on duty who said it had been phoned
in earlier. He knew my name! Can you locate him and check
it out?"

"Definitely not."

He was angry with the trooper, even though he knew
Saxon had probably risked his career simply by making the
call to Silver Springs—something he wasn't altogether sure
he would have done, had their roles been reversed.

"Morgan's dead," Saxon was saying. "His car went off an
embankment at about three this morning. You want some
advice? Get a good lawyer."

The drive to Philadelphia took longer than he'd expected,
heavier than usual Saturday-evening traffic and a missed exit
off the Interstate as his mind wandered, causing an irritating
delay. Hoffmann upbraided himself for the carelessness as he
drove the side streets, backtracking, stopping to read unfamiliar street signs. How many times had he been to Labruzo's
restored rowhouse on Society Hill without missing the turnoff?
For two days nothing seemed to have gone right.

Now was the time to turn that around.

It was difficult to imagine this small, unpretentious group
of dwellings as one of the most expensive and sought-after
areas in the city. Even now, as he stood outside the entrance
after pounding on the heavy brass knocker, he could not
imagine himself living in such a place. No open space, not a
single blade of grass. The asphalt jungle—expensive or not.

The door opened inward, bathing him in light. Framed by
a soft glow, there stood a tall girl apparently his own age, her
pretty features marred by acute agitation. This would be

Tony's latest, he thought, comparing her to the long string of attractive women his handsome friend had pursued.

"Come in. I was just leaving," she said, her eyes signaling that his intrusion was not welcome; her tone was ample confirmation. She looked over her shoulder toward Labruzo on the sofa, shirtless and drink in hand. "I'll probably be late tonight. No need to wait up." With a last accusatory glance at Hoffmann, she brushed past and hurried down the brick sidewalk.

"I don't think she cares for you," Labruzo said flatly, reaching for his shirt and pulling it on. "Your timing is pretty lousy."

Hoffmann stepped inside and pushed the door closed. "I remember a time not too long ago when you didn't think so . . . back when you were a grunt."

The lawyer stared back, also remembering. It had been four years ago, in the damp, oppressive heat of the jungle. His own recall of that day was of twisted sights and sounds; a montage of shattered scenes.

The firefight began as his platoon moved out after a brief rest halt and the unseen North Vietnamese opened fire all around them; the jungle exploded, the thunder of machine guns and rifles and grenades raging over them. And then he was hit, a searing, white-hot pain in his chest and arms that crushed the air from his lungs and sent him crashing against the hard earth. Consciousness came and went; with it the horrifying realization that he was dying. Sergeant Miles kneeling over him, sweat pouring down his black face, yelling into the radio for a medevac; the world tilting at a dizzy angle; numbness and nausea. Terrible moments of fear when they told him the medevac ship couldn't get in through the fire. Unconsciousness. Sight again, and sounds—the yammering of machine guns, the concussion of exploding artillery, the rasping that was his own breathing. Sounds of death. Then he was being carried to a helicopter, as if in a dream, buffeted by the swirling downwash of rotor blades. And then they were soaring above the trees, banking sharply. On the back of the pilot's helmet a name: HOFFMANN. The head turned in slow motion, a reassuring smile swam into focus, and the blackness closed in like a suddenly narrowing tunnel.

He awoke some time later, his body an aching mass beneath the clean white sheets of the Saigon hospital. His survival had been a close thing, the doctor told him. The convalescence would be a long one—but he would live. He learned the helicopter had been from one of the lift companies, and the pilot had dared to come in when the medevac ship held off.

Labruzo sipped his drink and motioned Eric in. "I remember," he said. "You've never been the one who brought it up before. This must be important."

"I told you that over the phone."

Labruzo nodded. "You look like you could use a drink. Your usual bourbon?" He stepped to the small bar in the corner, mixed the drinks, handed one to Hoffmann, and reclined in a large leather chair. "This better be good," he said, propping his feet on the coffee table. "I'd much rather spend the evening with Joyce than with you—I guess you know that."

Hoffmann drank several swallows of the stiff whiskey, feeling it burn down his throat. "I'm in trouble, and I need some help."

"You'll find my fee is fairly reasonable," the lawyer replied easily, flashing a jaunty smile. "Of course there'll be a little added surcharge for busting in on my social life."

"I'm involved in a murder."

Labruzo's mouth opened and he leaned forward, peering at him in disbelief. "You've got a weird sense of humor, my friend."

"It's true." They were silent for long seconds; the soft

background music from the stereo now seemed strangely out of place.

"Did you do it?"

"I didn't think that made any difference to you lawyers."

"It does to this one! Besides, you know damn well I don't get involved with anything like that—for reasons we're both aware of. Did you?"

"No. But somebody is trying hard to make it look that way."

Labruzo inhaled deeply and shook his head. "Sorry. I knew better than to ask. A knee-jerk reaction when somebody surprises the you-know-what out of me. How did you get involved?"

"It began yesterday afternoon about five, with a phone call from somebody claiming to be a retired Air Force general who knew my father."

The lawyer nodded in understanding, aware of what that claim would have done to Hoffmann. The pilot had shared the story with him in the months and years after their return to the States, when Labruzo made a point of locating him. They had grown close, almost like brothers; no wonder Hoffmann had wanted to see him, he thought, refilling the glasses. "Tell me about it."

Hoffmann took another drink and related the story—every detail, including the meeting with Landrum and the information provided by Saxon that afternoon. As he talked, the intensity and fear began to subside, leaving him drawn and tired. "I'm sure this Landrum was lying," he said at last.

"Why?"

"I just think he was. . . . The way he talked, how he reacted. I don't think I was imagining it."

"You're not in the best state of mind right now to be making those kinds of judgments." Labruzo weighed the information carefully, turning it over in his mind, trying to analyze how he might have reacted in the same circumstances.

Hoffmann was right—it all seemed too pat, too convenient. "What do you think of his remarks about the State Department?"

Hoffmann shrugged, more relaxed now after talking it out; the bourbon was beginning to have a calming effect as well. "I don't know. After these last twenty-four hours, I'm losing my ability to be surprised. At the time . . . well, I really don't know."

"Have you been charged?"

"Not yet. Does that mean anything?"

"Maybe. Until you're charged, there's not much any counsel can do for you, me included."

"Yes, there is." He wondered how the request would be received, knowing Labruzo's past, his family—the prime reason for enlistment in the Army years ago. "I can't simply sit back and let things happen, let people push and prod me. This thing is already driving me crazy."

"There isn't anything you can do. Besides, from what you've told me, it doesn't sound like they'd have much of a case in any event. I know that probably isn't much consolation, but you could be getting your bowels in an uproar over nothing."

"You don't really believe that."

The lawyer hesitated, staring at the ceiling. "No, guess I don't. Still, there's nothing you can do."

"I can find out about some of the people involved. Carnahan and Landrum."

"I wouldn't advise it. At least not now. How would you?"

"Through you." For the first time, Labruzo's face took on a hard set. "You have the connections."

"You mean my father has. Forget it. I won't ask him."

"It's not that much. Just ask him; tell him it's for me, not you. Damn it, Tony, I don't want to be locked away for something I didn't do!"

Labruzo looked away. He couldn't. Not after all these

years; not after the acrimony, mostly of his own doing, when he walked away from his father's "business" and all it stood for. The law degree was an atonement of sorts, for the sins of the father visited upon the son. "What good would it do?"

"I don't know for sure. Maybe just peace of mind. At least it would be something positive. . . . I just feel like I've got to do something; I can't sit back and do nothing. Alcohol-induced oblivion doesn't seem like a rational alternative."

Anthony Labruzo pondered the request, and debated. It would be going against everything he had declared that day when he left his father's house for the last time—even his sister had not been able to bring them back together, though she had never quite given up trying. But Hoffmann needed him; that was evident in his allusion to the events on some distant field. And in the desperation that was very near the surface when he spoke.

"For you, I'll do it. . . . But I still think it's a mistake."

"I've made enough already that one more won't hurt."

"You're sure?"

"Of absolutely nothing."

Chapter 3

Washington.

It seemed his whole adult life had centered around the capital in one way or another; barhopping weekends while at Maryland, unnumbered trips to various agencies in search of information about his father, the wild and barely remembered blowout after the final week of exams at the university. The proximity of College Park had made it a routine those four years. The city had always held a fascination for him, and not simply because it was a good party town, where it was an easy matter to pick up one of the young secretaries who frequented the myraid of night spots. There was a mystery and force about the place which was alive and almost animate. This was the center of power, and behind the walls of government, decisions were made that affected millions, changed the course of history. And now, behind some of those same walls, somebody was making decisions that would forever alter his own life—an added dimension to the monuments and sense of history that was his perception of the city.

Hoffmann's mind had been preoccupied and the miles passed quickly, but his attention returned to driving as he realized the next exit was for the beltway around the city. He took the South Capitol Street exit, passed Bolling Air Force Base, and crossed the bridge over the Anacostia. According to Landrum's note, the meeting was to be held in one of the old buildings near Fort McNair. An odd place, he had thought, but as he parked the car in one of the lots near Buzzard's Point, the location seemed no more strange than any of the other events since Gregory's call.

An Army sergeant inside the door of the building looked up from filling out a form. Behind him, the hall was alive with activity as military types and civilians hustled purposefully back and forth with that acquired look of being busy, the same atmosphere encountered in other official places over the years.

"My name is Eric Hoffmann. I'm supposed to have an appointment with a Mr. Carnahan at ten."

The soldier looked through a mound of documents. "Yes, sir. I'll need to see some identification."

Hoffmann produced a driver's license and his FAA pilot's certification. The sergeant looked at them quickly, made a note on the duty log, and handed them back before asking him to have a seat in the foyer while the call was made. The delay was irritating, as if it had been a calculated move to insure he knew who was and who wasn't significant. He had always hated these little power plays. Minutes later, a man of medium height and build approached the desk, then looked toward him as the soldier pointed in the direction of the waiting area.

"You must be Hoffmann," the man said as he approached, smiling and offering his hand. "Thanks for coming on such short notice. I'm John Carnahan." The smile was disarming, the greeting too friendly. Carnahan appeared to be in his early forties; his hair was stylishly long, and the clothes were tailored, expensive. "We'll be using the conference room midway down the hall. Care for coffee?"

He ordered service for room 118, then asked Hoffmann to follow him, keeping up a running commentary as they walked down the corridor. The idle chatter was slightly unnerving, out of place after Landrum's warning on Saturday. *Be serious. This is not an invitation.*

"How was the drive down?" Carnahan asked, after they had taken a seat at one end of the large mahogany table that dominated the small, rather austere room.

"It wasn't too bad. I missed the rush-hour traffic. But you didn't ask me down here to talk about driving conditions, did you?"

Carnahan smiled again. "No, you're right. I expect Mr. Landrum explained that to you."

"Actually, he didn't say much of anything."

The door to the conference room opened before Carnahan could reply. A matronly woman entered with a tray which held a pot of coffee, cups, cream, and sugar. Carnahan poured as he picked up a small white card on the tray. Glancing at it, he nodded almost imperceptibly toward the woman, then placed it in his vest pocket as she left, closing the door quietly.

Carnahan took a tentative sip from his cup and said, "Obviously, you're unaware of why we asked you to come down here today. Before I get into all that, I should tell you who I am, so you'll know by whose authority I speak. It's only fair, since we know quite a bit about you—I've had the National Security Agency run a top-secret check." He paused momentarily to let the words linger.

"I run the European Bureau of the State Department, with responsibility for monitoring developments—both Eastern and Western—in that area. I keep the Secretary, and the President, informed, and formulate our policies vis-à-vis the Warsaw nations—subject, of course, to their approval. In the matter we'll discuss this morning, I can assure you I speak with their consent."

"I don't see how that is related to what your Mr. Landrum told me on Saturday," Hoffmann replied, attempting nonchalance, but his stomach was a hard knot of anticipation.

"You will." Carnahan leaned forward and depressed a control on the top of a speaker box in the middle of the table. "Miss Webber, would you please bring in my file?" He leaned back and made a display of lighting a cigarette before continuing. "We've thoroughly researched your background, and find you possess a unique set of qualifications making you ideally suited for a certain job we would like you to undertake. It could be a great service to the country. I say that without exaggeration."

"This is beginning to sound farfetched."

"I assure you it's not. Quite the contrary. We've carefully evaluated the situation and all possible alternatives. This is a very serious matter with far-reaching consequences. Believe me, it is anything but farfetched. I think you'll see that as I explain."

"What does this have to do with General Gregory's death?"

"Perhaps nothing. But we can discuss that later on."

"I'd rather do it now." He was certain that everything that had happened centered on the old man's death, yet the government man was obvious in his attempt to skirt the issue. He could not let that happen. At the moment, nothing else mattered.

The secretary who had brought the coffee reentered the room, placed a large Samsonite briefcase on the table, and departed with a darting glance at him. Carnahan continued, ignoring the question about the general.

"The information in this file reveals some interesting facts—"

"Concerning Gregory?"

"No. But to answer your question, I will explain how that is related. Please, let me develop this logically . . . for my benefit as much as for yours. I think you'll understand why as we go along."

Hoffmann nodded.

"Good. This shouldn't take long. Now, near the end of the 'seventy-three Mideast war, the Arabs cut oil production by ten percent to show the West how dependent we are on their goodwill—a well-known fact, I think you'll agree. And, as we know, it had the desired result. Japan was severely hurt, as was Western Europe. We gave them some assistance; they did some belt tightening, as we did, and now it appears everything will eventually revert to the old status quo.

"There was another interesting fallout that is not so well known. At least, it hasn't gotten as much publicity as our own problems. The embargo—or more properly, the reduced production—hurt the Warsaw Pact every bit as much as it affected us. East Germany, Poland, and Czechoslavakia were importing most of their oil from the Middle East. Russia is virtually self-sufficient in energy and actually exports some oil to her Communist allies, but Eastern Europe was severely affected."

"I didn't realize I'd come here for a discussion of geopolitics. Frankly, you aren't making a whole lot of sense. And this doesn't have even a remote connection to Landrum's talk with me." The drift of the conversation was as unsettling as it was unexpected. Landrum had been blunt and malevolent; Carnahan, by his casual presence, seemed to be a greater threat.

Carnahan smiled easily, as if expecting the interruption. "Please, indulge me for just a few more minutes.

"What I'm about to disclose is classified as top secret. As you know from your military background, classified briefings often contain only a few passages that actually need to be classified. This one is no different. But I must caution you that all information from this point on is to be treated as top secret. Is that understood?"

Hoffmann leaned across the table. "I think this is the

point where I thank you for the coffee and leave you to continue by yourself." He looked at Carnahan's impassive features, more apprehensive now. The man showed no visible emotion, his eyes betraying neither surprise nor understanding. "All of a sudden this little talk we're having is beginning to sound like something I don't want to hear. Landrum said you wanted to talk about some old airplanes and how that might be related to my father—"

"You haven't let me finish."

"So far I haven't heard anything remotely related to that. You just called this a briefing; now you throw in top secret. What the hell are you trying to do to me?" He was angry—his normal reaction to any situation he didn't understand—and there had been too much anger in the past few days. Carnahan had known he would react this way. *They know.* Gregory's words, and at every turn they had been confirmed.

Carnahan relaxed, crossing his legs and lighting another cigarette. "Look, I'm sorry. It was a bad choice of words. I give dozens of briefings every day—it's a part of my vocabulary that too often finds its way into everyday conversation. The warning was simply a reminder—for both of us. I can wrap this up quickly, if you'll let me. The classified material is important to your understanding the whole picture."

Hoffmann stared at the man for a moment, saying nothing, wanting to walk from the room but feeling compelled to stay. Something about the way Carnahan looked at him told Hoffmann that leaving was not one of the options available to him. The bureaucrat blew a heavy cloud of smoke toward the ceiling and opened the briefcase.

"This photograph was taken by satellite, from an altitude of a hundred and twenty-two miles. The resolution is very good, as you can see." Carnahan pushed a black-and-white picture toward him; it was stamped TOP SECRET across the top in one-inch letters. "It shows part of a train pulled off on a siding, and you can also see the wreckage there in the last thirty or so cars where the following train impacted. You also might notice that most of the equipment is tank cars. That is significant, because the cargo is gasoline, diesel fuel, and heating oil."

"How . . .?"

"Can we be so sure? An easy matter, really. As I said, the resolution is extremely good, even from that distance. We can read the car numbers, and after that it's a simple procedure to match them to waybills, which are not really that hard to come by. Computer theft leaves no trails to follow. Other, less sophisticated means can also be used when that's not feasible." Carnahan produced several more photographs. "These show other signs of a deteriorating rail system—much worse than our own. There are many examples: overcrowded classification yards, other derailments, extensive repair work to the physical plant. All were taken of East German facilities since January 1974 and, taken as a whole, are pretty graphic evidence of a badly decayed transportation system—a system the Warsaw Pact relies on to maintain its armies in the field.

"With supplies from the Mideast interrupted and transportation problems further reducing imports, East German industry and military preparedness have steadily gone downhill. Recently we received fairly reliable reports that Russia is having its own problems with excessive water in the oil pumped from several of its larger fields. Our best estimates indicate that East Germany must import about thirty-one percent more oil than it is now capable of doing to reach 1973 levels of production. That is a bigger gap than was ever forecast for the worst-case industrial nation—Japan.

"Naturally, there are some very upset people at the upper levels of East Germany's government, and they're looking for a scapegoat. In a Communist country, that's the easiest of all hunting expeditions. Our intelligence boys figure they'll settle on this man. . . . His name is Heinrich Schellen."

Carnahan looked at the picture in his hand for a few seconds, then placed it in front of Hoffmann.

"He holds a position equivalent, let's say, to our own Secretary of Transportation. He was an SS officer in World War II, and at one time was the commander of a stalag at which over a thousand American and British POW's died during the course of the war. We have reason to believe that your father was one of them. I think that answers part of your question.

"We think Schellen has arrived at the same conclusion as our intelligence community—namely, that his days in power are drawing rapidly to a close. Several days ago, he contacted us through an intermediary. He wants out . . . now. And so, that brings us to your primary question."

Carnahan leaned forward, folding his hands on the table.

"We want you to go into East Germany and help Schellen escape to the West."

Words would not come; he was stunned beyond the ability to comprehend, to think, to utter anything except a low groan of disbelief. Everything except Carnahan's face seemed to go out of focus, as if in a mist.

"You're insane. . . . You can't possibly be serious."

Carnahan answered easily, with that same air of friendliness displayed upon introducing himself. "I can assure you I'm very serious. This is something none of us could possibly take lightly."

"I don't believe it." He felt detached from his body, dizzy and lightheaded. He means it! He really means it! The words rolled over him, repeated again and again until they no longer held any meaning. "You really are insane."

Carnahan smiled. "Not according to my psychological profile. They say I'm disgustingly well adjusted."

"To hell with your psychological profile. And to hell with your crazy kidnap scheme."

"You don't have to kidnap him. Like I said, he wants out;
in a very bad way, according to how it was relayed to us.
We're quite certain of his intentions. We're paid to be good
at what we do . . . and we are."

Hoffmann rose, feeling unsteady. "I'm not interested. I
won't do it—and you can be damned sure those are my
intentions."

"Maybe you'd be interested in this, then." Carnahan opened
another file inside the briefcase and slid a piece of paper
toward him. "It's the police report on General Gregory's death.
Another of your questions. It names you as the prime suspect,
puts you at the scene at the time of death, and is rather clear
about the murder weapon: a knife belonging to you."

"That's impossible!" His question to Landrum that Saturday returned, haunting him. Had they wanted him out of the
house? *Your ignorance of the real world is refreshing.*

"Nothing is impossible. Read it for yourself."

"You know this is false. I had nothing to do with Gregory's
death."

"I don't know any such thing. That's not my bailiwick.
But I've read the report, and my memory of an undergradu-
ate law course leads me to believe you've got big troubles."

"Were you the one who thought this whole thing up?
Damn it, if you're the son-of-a-bitch who—"

"Sit down!" The government man glowered at him across the
table, color rising in his throat; the outburst had charged the
air like the crack of a teamster's whip. "I don't care much for
your insinuations, but I'll let that pass for now. We can help
you with this little legal problem; the evidence can be made
to conveniently disappear, and the police report will never see
the light of day. And we both know that's not the only
problem you've got. You're on the verge of losing that house
of yours. Three months behind on payments, I believe. Or is
it four now? All in all, you've done a pretty lousy job of
managing your own affairs, even by the most liberal standards."

"I can handle that."

"Really? How are you going to explain being in the company of someone with known underworld connections the day after you murdered Gregory? Now that we've got all the dirty linen out on the table, why don't you knock off the histrionics and have a seat?"

Carnahan pulled another cigarette from the pack. "Think about it for a minute. You can do this the hard way if you'd like, but there are other, less painful approaches. We'd prefer cooperation."

The meeting had been carefully orchestrated; the plan was now clear, he thought. Carnahan had easily drawn him into conversation, glossed over the warning of classified material, and presented the damning police report to him almost casually. He had been led, quickly and professionally, into a position from which there was no returning, no room for maneuver. His eventual cooperation had been guaranteed days earlier; Carnahan must know that.

"We envision that you'll fly in, pick him up at some predesignated point, and return him to West Germany," Carnahan was saying.

"You can't be serious. That *really* is insane. Fly into some Communist country? Just like that?"

"It's been done—recently, in fact. By a young American working for an outfit in Austria. He crossed the border on three different occasions and brought a total of eight people out. Surely you've read about it, although I don't think it got much play in the national media."

He really means this, Hoffmann thought, staring at the impassive face in front of him. Worst of all, he was right about the rescues from Austria; one of the flying magazines scattered around the pilots' lounge at Tri-State had contained an article on it. He remembered laughing at the ludicrousness of the idea, and Markowski's offhand comments.

"If you're really serious about this, why don't you contact whoever it was that pulled those people out?"

"We considered that. But he has no desire to do it anymore, and can't—physically. He was wounded in the elbow, among other places, on the last trip and lost most of the mobility in the joint. Austrian officials have pulled his flying license and are watching to make sure he leaves the country as soon as he recovers enough to travel. After the publicity he's received, you can be sure the other side has him under surveillance for at least as long as he remains in Europe. If we approached him, they'd know it, and that's something we can't afford. We also considered using one of our own pilots. That, too, has its drawbacks. The skill is not a common one, and operatives in the CIA possessing it are rare—there just hasn't been much of a need. The ones we do have are committed in other areas. Pulling them out of South America or Southeast Asia and sending them to Europe would be suspicious."

"The Russians know who they are?"

"Very possibly. One acquires a certain degree of notoriety after a while in the community. Some more than others, and a person with an unusual skill or trait or specialty stands out."

"Why don't you use a military pilot—somebody in Europe, who's been flying there for some time?"

"We considered that also . . . and rejected it. Although military background and skills are desirable, there is a certain group-think mentality inherent there, either consciously or subconsciously, which rules them out. We need someone without any allegiance to some other governmental authority. Besides, pulling a military pilot would raise too many questions at different headquarters levels that don't have the need to know; simply raising the question is enough to scuttle this operation. You've been to Europe, so I shouldn't need to remind you of the terrible security problems in the service. Even the installation telephones have been tapped by East

German intelligence, and some careless talk about an unusual reassignment between a couple of personnel clerks would sooner or later compromise what we're doing. That's why we chose you—an outsider, unknown to any intelligence network, who possesses the requisite flying ability, who has lived and worked in Germany."

Hoffmann turned his back to the government man and walked to the window, peering through the panes at the half-empty parking lot and the ugliness of the electrical substation outside. Carnahan had anticipated his every question, every reaction. It was like playing chess against a computer—no matter what you did, what strategy was employed, there was no way to win.

They know about you. They know. . . .

"I'll need some time to think it over," he said at last, trying to postpone the decision. He needed to get away, clear his head, think rationally without this shadow of unreality stalking him. Carnahan was dragging him deeper into Gregory's death by offering the coverup. But the police report—true or not—was undeniably frightening. The specter of years in a small cell, living behind bars among the thieves and murderers and rapists, was terrifying. He knew he was not that hardened; behind those walls, he might not survive.

"Sure. Take a few minutes to think about it. . . . But I want your decision before you leave this room."

"I need more than that."

Carnahan smiled at him, looking serene. "Too bad. You don't have it."

"I don't have much of a choice, do I?"

The government man shrugged noncommittally as he pulled a typeset page from the briefcase. Without responding to the question, he said, "The first thing required is that you sign this confidentiality agreement. It's a standard form, and many government employees are required to, when working in sensitive areas.

"I'm sure you realize that divulging any information we've discussed thus far, or anything about what you'll be doing in the future, is punishable under the law. We do not deal . . . sympathetically . . . with those who betray a confidence in this line of work."

"I understand." Strangely enough, he did. The innuendo, the shades of meaning in Carnahan's words *were* discernible. But there was something unsettling about the man, beyond the words he spoke. The phrases used, the easy familiarity with what seemed like areas of intelligence that an assistant State Department secretary would not or should not know. But Hoffmann knew he was simply guessing, trying to find a reasonable explanation for inexplicable tension, trying to put shape and substance to suspicions seen through a distorting cloud. Nothing was ever what it appeared to be.

"Schellen is important to us for several reasons. We expect his absence will cause even more problems than the East Germans already have, because he really is an excellent logistician. More importantly—for us, anyway—he knows the details of the Warsaw Pact plan for a military takeover of Western Europe. We want that information. When Penkovsky defected in the early 'sixties, he gave us a lot of valuable information about their offensive strategy. Changes in organization, weaponry, and perceptions of our posture have altered much of that; at least we expect so. Schellen, who would be in a position to plan and execute the needed logistics functions, should have the most recent details. He intimated as much when he sent out this feeler several days ago. It's his major bargaining chip, one that we want very much—and he knows it.

"We also believe he still has connections to the underground SS organization that survived following World War II. Considerable fortunes were never recovered—enough to create a great deal of chaos in the Middle East, South America, or Europe. We want to keep ahead of them. Given suitable incentives, Schellen could be persuaded to assist us. And there are other reasons, none of which concern you."

"What about war crimes?"

"Ah, yes, the connection with your father. We feel there's still a case . . . and the Bonn government is anxious to prosecute." Carnahan laughed aloud, but the gesture was devoid of humor. "Naturally, he won't be told."

"I've read that the West Germans couldn't care less about bringing ex-Nazis to trial."

"That's a rumor being circulated. Believe me, it's just that." Reaching inside his coat for another cigarette, Carnahan quickly changed the subject. "Arrangements will be made for you. A suitable cover story has been arranged, information planted, appropriate people paid or persuaded to cooperate."

"You make it sound like this is already in motion."

"It is. Time is critical."

"Then you never had any doubt."

"That you'd agree? None. We're talking about the defense of Western Europe. There wasn't any time to worry about your preferences or sensibilities. This situation with Gregory was regrettable, and we don't care whether you did it or not. Either way, the timing was fortuitous for our purposes. Enough said. Let's move on." He glanced quickly at his watch, frowned irritably, then looked back at Hoffmann. "For the next three days, you'll receive as much training as we can give you. It will, of course, be handled by the CIA, as will your actual mission. As I said, time is critical. We would have preffered to take a month or more, but that's a luxury we cannot afford."

"Where?"

"A farm in northern Virginia. You'll be taken there as soon as we finish."

Hoffmann felt a quick rush of anger, a burst of outrage at the man's patronizing attitude, the indifference to the total disruption of his life. "Just like that?"

"If you're worried about clothing, personal articles, or the like—"

"Wait a minute," Hoffmann interrupted.

"No! You wait. We have neither the time nor the inclination to indulge your qualms. You were not invited here, you were directed—ordered. Future instructions are to be considered the same as orders. . . . You have been enlisted. We will train you; we will direct you in the accomplishment of this assignment. You will follow our orders—to the letter and without hesitation—for which you will be paid handsomely. I can assure that anything short of your full cooperation will be dealt with quickly and effectively. Can I assume that you'll cooperate, given those terms?"

Hoffmann felt engulfed; mists swirled around him, inhibiting rational thought. He was being threatened by his own government! They wanted him to do something wildly unbelievable, without question or hesitation. This had to be somebody else's nightmare.

"If that's the way you want it," Hoffmann heard himself say.

Carnahan leaned forward, his eyes hard and impenetrable. "It's not only how I want it, it's the way it will be. You no longer belong to yourself—you are ours. And you will not forget that without paying the penalty. And if that requires explanation, you're not as smart as we were led to believe."

Hoffmann nodded. Slowly, deliberately, he reached for the pen Carnahan was offering, and signed the agreement.

Chapter 4

The patrol leader surveyed the bleak Lebanese landscape through binoculars. Though it was only an hour before midnight, and there was almost no moon, the glasses magnified the available light and allowed him sight of the terrain not visible to the unaided eye. His sweeping search detected movement to the northwest, perhaps two hundred meters away. The enemy was coming the way he had expected. Their arrival was now imminent.

Akiva Ben Ari lowered the binoculars and let them hang by the nearly rotted leather strap around his neck.

He breathed deeply, calming himself; his pulse was rapid, the controlled anticipation brought on by a surge of adrenalin. The sensations were always the same, familiar and expected now after countless other episodes since his early youth, when he arrived in the Promised Land from a Jewish refugee camp on Cyprus. He had learned to control the fear early in his teens, and later the lesson had served him well, when others had needed his calm leadership: the pass at Mitla, the heights of Golan. But the fear was always with him, held under tight rein; a constant unfriendly shadow. He thought of Rabbi Solomon's words to him when he was a newly recruited soldier in the Palmach: "You must learn to live with it; there will be no peace in your lifetime." The prophecy had been fulfilled only too well.

Ben Ari pulled on the cord attached to his wrist. The immediate return pressure told him the mortar squad fifty meters to his rear was ready and alert. Next, he tapped the shoulder of the man in front of him, the signal to alert the patrol to the approaching enemy. They maintained fifty-percent security; half of his men would be asleep, weary after long hours in the fields, improving the defenses of the kibbutz—the continuous scratching for survival. Within minutes, Ben Ari felt a double tap on his arm, telling him the patrol was awake and ready.

The minutes dragged slowly.

Occasionally his straining eyes glimpsed a human torso silhouetted against the marginally lighter sky. Still, his best indication of the enemy's location was the noise they made; two miles inside Lebanon, the Arabs felt safe and paid little attention to noise discipline. They traveled a path of least resistance through the undergrowth, following a winding, narrow trail, strewn with rocks, which led into the killing zone of the ambush carefully laid by the Israeli patrol.

Ben Ari nervously fingered the plastic detonator switch in his hand, and placed the big police whistle between his teeth. The voices grew louder, words and phrases distinct in the otherwise quiet night. Dark forms passed in front of him, moving off to the right.

The explosion was deafening.

Ben Ari detonated the long bank of claymore mines at the same instant he blew the whistle. A heavy burst of grazing automatic fire shattered the night as the initial blast from the mines sprayed the trail with thousands of steel pellets, killing a dozen Arabs and creating instant panic among those still alive.

Sounds of the battle echoed through surrounding hills, rising and falling like distant thunder. In the kill zone, the roar of automatic firing continued; red tracers careered off at wild angles, whining and burning out in the darkness. The mortar squad pumped out a steady flow of 60-mm. rounds, one tube firing to the rear of Arab patrol, cutting escape along the path they had taken, while the other concentrated beyond the kill zone, blocking retreat directly away from the ambush. Those left alive managed to take cover in a shallow ditch on the far side of the trail away from their attackers, and began to return fire.

Ben Ari groped in the darkness, found the second detonating handle, and squeezed. Another bank of deadly claymores set up in the ditch ripped through the night. Resistance collapsed.

Still the murderous firing continued, and then Ben Ari shot a flare into the night sky. The green star cluster burst overhead, casting an eerie shadow on the scene as weapons fell silent, their hoarse staccato replaced by sounds of human misery on the trail. His ears rang from the concussions of battle; his night vision was destroyed by muzzle flashes.

Deciding that no further resistance remained in the area, he sent out two-man security outposts north and south along the trail, then took a four-man search team with him to pick up any intelligence information left behind, and to count the dead and wounded. They worked quickly, discovering nearly forty lifeless bodies and fifty-three weapons. Satchel charges in torn and shredded canvas pouches confirmed his initial analysis of the information passed that afternoon from his informants. The explosives had been destined for Yad-Il, where they would have written another bloody footnote to the twenty-year history of the border village. There had been a time when the carnage would have brought on a deep melancholy, a questioning of the purpose of it all. No longer. He gazed at the bodies without remorse, relieved that they were not Jewish, yet without a sense of triumph.

The search completed, his team retraced its path back to the main body. The squad leaders waited for him, rubbing cold hands together. One of them challenged him with the improvised password as he approached.

"Dov, any casualties?" Ben Ari asked, his voice a whisper, as it had been since leaving the kibbutz hours earlier.

"Two walking wounded in Zev's squad, and one in David's. I've redistributed ammunition among the squads, so everybody has about a hundred rounds for the trip back. Marc has the mortars broken down and ready to travel, with three rounds left for each tube."

"Good." He would save the compliments for later, when there was time. Dov was his second-in-command, barely twenty years old but already a seasoned veteran who reminded Ben Ari of himself in earlier days. This was his seventh patrol into southern Lebanon, and each one had gone without problem. Planning and execution. He could have written the after-action report before even starting out that evening. And much of the credit would go to the young second-in-command who had proven himself worthy of being placed in that position over older and more experienced men. "We move in three minutes. Reverse order of the move in, with one mortar attached to each flank squad."

Ben Ari took the hand mike from the radio operator and contacted his operational headquarters, submitting a quick report under prearranged codes requesting the planned artillery concentrations to cover the patrol's withdrawal. They started moving south as the first shells from Israel screamed through the night and tore at the land less than a half-mile from where they stood.

The entire ambush had taken only nine minutes.

* * *

The patrol arrived at the perimeter of Kibbutz Yad-Il shortly before 3:00 in the morning and was challenged by a youthful guard at the main gate, a boy not yet out of high school who had been disappointed at being left behind. They went directly to the meeting hall, which also served as military headquarters, where Ben Ari conducted his debriefing before sending them off to a few hours of sleep. With the coming of the late harvest, they would need all they could get.

It was an hour later when Ben Ari transmitted his report to Northern Sector Intelligence. The message-center clerk took the cipher without interrogating him, as he had on the last mission. Apparently the new man had learned. The word had been passed: the commander of Yad-Il was not to be questioned; his information was to be accepted as all-inclusive, his analysis of intelligence assumed correct. Relay his reports to the next-higher headquarters immediately, without delay or the need to obtain approval from local superiors.

He trudged back to the modest frontier dwelling, exhaustion finally overcoming him with the receding of tension. He sat on the edge of the bed, wearily pulling off his shirt and unlacing the field boots. The woman stirred.

"Praise God you're home," she said, touching his face. Her voice betrayed anxiety, and he knew she had not slept.

"You shouldn't worry," he replied. He had said it, to no avail, hundreds of times. He leaned over and gently kissed her. Magda was a good wife; a symbol of the nation's new breed of woman—hardened by the kibbutz life, independent. They had married late in life. Her ample frame had seemed perfectly suited to childbearing, and they had both wanted children. The birth of twin sons had nearly taken her from him, and now he would not let her risk another pregnancy, though she wanted more. He could not risk losing her, even for that.

"You know I'm always worried."

"Without reason."

"You checked the boys?"

"Both sleeping soundly," he said, slipping the undershirt over his massive shoulders and patting his stomach, still hard and flat despite his thirty-nine years. The transition from the fierce reality of the field to the calm, understanding role of husband and father always came as a shock. There was never enough time in between, and he wondered if Magda or the boys suffered from his frequent inability to cope with it. If they did, they had never mentioned it. Of all the things competing for his time, his attention, his loyalty, the family was the most important.

"A call came for you. It was General Trandau."

Ben Ari tensed in the darkness, the name sending a ripple of apprehension through him. "What did you tell him?"

"Nothing."

"Nothing?"

"I asked him not to call on you again. . . . Aki, you promised not to work for him again. These patrols are bad enough for me—and for our sons. I couldn't stand the other, not anymore. Please tell him no."

"Did you tell him I'd call?"

"I said I'd leave that up to you." She turned away from him and fell silent.

"I've got to return the call."

"As a courtesy?" Her voice was hard, accusation evident.

"He was the one who got me out of that rat-infested camp near Nicosia. He didn't have to. And I could have died there."

"How long must you go on feeling like you have to do whatever he wants because of that? Isn't there ever going to be a time when you stop?"

"Yes, there is."

"Now?"

"Yes. Now."

She turned back to him, running a trembling hand through his hair. "If only I could believe you."

"You can. I promise. But I've got to call. He deserves that much from me." He went into the next room and dialed the number in Tel Aviv. After several rings, the general came on the line; a deep, booming voice that rang with confidence and authority.

"Aki! Congratulations! The report just came through. Good work. Better to get them in the field than to fight them off the wire at the kibbutz, eh?"

"Yes, sir." An awkward silence followed.

Finally the general spoke. "Aki, we would like you to come see us tomorrow."

"General, I can't. We've been through that before. You gave your word to me, and I gave mine to Magda."

"This is important."

"So was the last time. Damn it, general, it's always important."

"Maybe more so this time."

"I've found a place here. This is more important."

"I know what you've done there, son. Probably nobody else in all Israel knows better than I. But I want you to come down and listen."

"Is that being phrased as an order?"

"It's a request. I need you . . . you are the only one I would trust." Ben Ari breathed deeply through his nose, angry at the man for playing on his sympathies. How many times in the past had this old warrior used the same approach on him? Always with success. Not this time, he thought. Not this time.

"Before you decide . . . we may have a chance to nab Schellen."

Ben Ari hesitated, wondering what he would tell Magda. "I'll be there."

"This is an opportunity that may not come again. But there are complications. Severe ones, I'm afraid."

"There always are."

"For you, personal as well as professional. My apologies to your wife."

"She'll be touched."

"I'm sorry, my son. But . . ."

"How soon can I get started?"

"Today, if you like. At least two days are required for briefing and logistics arrangements."

"See if you can't cut that in half."

"We'll see. I want to make sure everything is ready—including you."

"I've been ready for a long time, general. Thank you for calling." Ben Ari hung up, unsure if the anger he felt was directed at himself or the old man who had rescued him from Cyprus.

Chapter 5

Hoffmann slowed the rented Audi as he neared the Langenbruck exit on the northbound E6 autobahn out of Munich. He could see the small town off to the left, peaceful and quiet under leaden skies. Beyond the church spire and steeply pitched roofs of the village, rolling hills and farm fields spread out toward the horizon. The country had changed little from what he remembered as a brand-new second lieutenant of artillery.

The *gasthaus* sat on the right side of the road less than a half-mile from the autobahn, near the outskirts of the town. He parked near the entrance and went inside, taking a table in the back where he had an unobstructed view of the small room and the main door. Had they taught him that at the farm in Virginia, or was it a simple manifestation of growing paranoia? He couldn't decide. The three days of training had blended into a kaleidoscope of images and faintly remembered warnings; a confusion of bizarre details and abnormal behavior, admonitions and dire predictions. This was not his world—the nameless team had shown him over and over—he would be swallowed up by it.

He glanced at his watch. Almost 2:15; his CIA contact was late, and the uncertainty grew. Where was Leahy? They had told him the importance of being on time for the initial contact with the agent. Time was everything. Time was critical—the difference between success and failure. He searched the few faces in the room again as he drank from the half-litre glass of beer; none bore the slightest resemblance to the picture they had shown him that last night before the flight to Frankfurt. He ordered another drink. And waited.

Minutes later, the door opened and Sean Leahy stepped through, casually looking around with a sweeping glance that at last settled on Hoffmann. He walked directly to the table and sat with his back to the room.

"Welcome to Germany. Or should I say, welcome back?"

"Thanks, but the place doesn't seem the same." He had dreaded this moment; somewhere in the back of his mind was the unpleasant thought that once he met Leahy there was no possibility of turning back. The distant hope of a reprieve grew fainter now.

"Nothing is ever the same as what we remember." The young girl came over to the table and took Leahy's order, returning quickly with a ceramic mug of Hasen Brau. He drank tentatively until he was sure they couldn't be heard. "How is your memory?"

"Why?"

"I want to be sure I'm talking to the right person."

"Then that makes two of us."

Leahy nodded. "Three days ago you were taken to a farm in northern Virginia by two men whose names you don't know. There you were met by a four-man training team whose specialties range from weapons to demolitions to hand-to-hand combat. On the second day you attempted to qualify with four weapons: a Walther P-38, a .45 automatic, an

M-16, and the .38 Police Special. Your scores were ninety-one, ninety, ninety-four, and ninety-two, respectively; none of them passing marks."

"By whose standards?"

"It still bothers you, I see. They said you weren't too happy about it. Your scores on the quick-reaction course were equally low—the fourth and seventh targets were friendlies, and you shot them both."

"On the first time through. The second run was perfect."

"There are no second chances over here," Leahy said casually. "That should satisfy you. Now let's see if you can answer a few questions for me. Education?"

"Mechanical engineering. University of Maryland."

"Grade point average?"

"Three point seven."

"Military assignments? Chronologically from the beginning."

"Is this really necessary?"

"Damn right it is. Continue."

"Artillery Basic Course at Fort Sill. First Battalion, Seventy-seventh Artillery, Charlie Battery. Then flight school at Wolters and Rucker—"

"Dates?"

"October 1968 to June 1969. B Company, Two-two-seventh Aviation Battalion in Viet Nam from August 1969 to March of '71."

"Following that, you were returned to Fort Sill as an instructor."

"No. My orders showed as 'duty unassigned,' so they made me an action officer initially. There were too many officers in the Army by then, and they didn't know what to do with us. For the first four or five months I played a lot of golf and tennis."

Leahy looked at him over the rim of the mug, nodding in understanding. "During that time your divorce became final."

"While I was at Sill, yes. February tenth of the next year."

"All right, I'm satisfied. You got enough wrong answers."

"Wrong answers?"

"Enough to tell me that you're really Eric Hoffmann, a person with a normal memory. Certain things stick with us more clearly than others: the date of a divorce is remembered precisely, while something like the time period of flight school becomes hazy after a few years. Your orders covered the period of September 29 through June 12. If you had remembered those specific dates, I would have been suspicious and there would have been more questions until I was satisfied."

"Was that all?"

"There were other, more subtle hints. You said you were assigned to the Seventy-seventh Artillery without pointing out you were in Germany at the time—to you that was a familiar, redundant piece of information. To an imposter, it would be a vital fact, and one not likely to be eliminated." Leahy smiled easily and said, "You were also comfortable enough to round off a three point six two average to three-seven. A small deception, but revealing. It fits."

Hoffmann looked at the agent, letting his initial anger at being questioned recede. At first he had thought that Leahy was treating him with that same condescending attitude he'd found in Carnahan; the brief explanation now seemed sensible, even reassuring. The man was professional. And thorough. In a matter of minutes, both of them had had their doubts removed and were comfortable with the contact.

"Why were you late?" Hoffmann asked.

"I wasn't. In fact, I got here a half-hour before you. The package I got from Geneva was not very inclusive, and I had to be sure of what I was getting into. Nothing in the personnel file on you indicated any past association with this . . . business. Your actions confirmed my doubts: anyone with experience wouldn't have driven directly off the autobahn and parked out front without at least one pass by the meeting place to take a quick look. And you should have backed in—on the side of the building, not right next to the entrance. I'm surprised they didn't teach you that at the proving ground."

"Is that what you call the place?"

"Most of us do—those who have been through it. It's one of several, but certainly the toughest, and usually not one that a new man is sent to. I expect they were three very long and unhappy days."

"In the extreme," Hoffmann replied. They had taught him the basic skills of this new and bewildering world: breaking and entering without leaving a trace; picking locks; the most effective ways of turning a set of keys, an umbrella, a pencil, or a rolled magazine into a lethal weapon. Escape and evasion. Choosing clothes and changing identities. "Where do we go from here?"

"We meet tonight, after I get final instructions through Geneva. Like I said, my package wasn't complete enough, and I've asked for some clarifications. Do you know what you've signed on for?"

"Probably not. And I didn't volunteer."

"That's good."

"Why?"

"Because that really would have raised some questions—for me at least. There's too many already. But let me worry about that. For now, just go back to your hotel and wait for a call."

"We could have met there to begin with."

"Sorry, that was out. We didn't know where you would be staying, and there wasn't time to do a thorough recon of the area and check the room. On top of that, Washington set the place without my knowing it and didn't contact me until last night. That's one of the clarifications I'm waiting on. Because of it, we almost missed you at the airport when you flew in from Frankfurt at oh-dark-thirty this morning. Looks like you didn't get much sleep; do some catch-up this afternoon."

"Is that all?"

"For now. In a few days, you'll wish you had the time to rest. Starting tonight, you'll be on a very fast track that doesn't have an exit."

"Sounds ominous."

"It's more than that." Leahy's face seemed to go blank for long seconds, his eyes strangely vacant. "Without having all the details, I'd say your chances of success are one in ten; and succeeding gets you nothing. If you fail, there won't be one person in the Western world who'll ever admit to having made your acquaintance . . . including me."

The telephone rang as Hoffmann got out of the shower.

"This is Leahy. Just wanted you to know that it would be me knocking on the door in a few seconds. Are you alone?"

"Do you really think I've had time to pick up anyone since I got here?" The streets had been deserted that morning as the cab had brought him from the airport to the Esso Motor Hotel on Effnerstrasse, the only name he had been able to decipher from the listing near the transportation stand. After arriving, he had gotten a restless three and half hours of sleep before renting the Audi and driving to the rendezvous at Langenbruck; and despite Leahy's suggestion, he hadn't slept in the afternoon. "Where are you?"

"In the lobby. I'll be right there." The phone clicked dead.

Hoffmann opened the door when he heard the knock and recognized the agent's voice. Leahy entered and placed a small black briefcase on the bed, opening each of the three locks with different keys. Without a greeting, he pulled up two chairs and motioned Hoffmann to a seat.

"The information I requested—most of it, anyway—came through this afternoon, along with some surprising words of warning that carried a pretty high security code." He looked at Hoffmann warily and continued. "Until an hour ago, I was still willing to give you one chance in ten. I've decided to revise that. Downward. When they contacted me last night, I thought I had a basic idea of the operation. That got blown to rags when the courier arrived with this. I hope they're paying you a bundle.

"I've gone over the particulars they gave you in Washington and the more recent information on East Germany, the reason Schellen wants out. My job is to insure the logistics are set up. I was also counseled not to give you any advice—on your sanity or any other unrelated matter." He paused briefly, looking deep into Hoffmann's eyes. "When they first contacted me, the only thing I knew was that you were going to help an East German defect to our side. They didn't tell me how. Nor did they say who."

"You think it's too risky?"

"I think it's crazy as hell."

"You won't get an argument from me. But I don't have any choice."

"I figured that. We'll do our best to make things go as well as possible on this end. We've put you under surveillance; you'll never see or meet them, but they're there. The room was gone over this afternoon while we were up north, and it's clean—as we expected. And we didn't plant anything of our own. Depending on how things go, we may want to move you later, but for the time being you'll be safe here. Besides, it fits the cover story that's been developed."

"About being a charter pilot for some outfit over here."

Leahy nodded agreement. "They hadn't completed all the details when you were interviewed in Washington earlier this week. The file is here, and you have to memorize it before I leave. Get comfortable. This promises to be a long night. In the last two days, backdated résumés with your forged signature have been placed in several organizations in Europe—one in Switzerland, two in England, one each in France and Germany. All are charter services similar to those you worked for back in the States. All except the one in Germany have annotations that your request for employment was turned down."

"Who am I supposedly working for?"

"It's called Deutches Aero, located here in Munich and conveniently in need of another pilot. Nobody aside from one of the owners knows who you are. He's located in Bonn, and I'm not at liberty to disclose his name. That was one of the warnings I mentioned earlier; your knowing his name is not important in any case. Like I said, the details are in the file.

"Next item. This is the last time we'll meet here. Any future contacts will be made at 1503 Herzogstrasse, in Schwabing. 1503 Herzogstrasse." Leahy handed him a piece of paper with a phone number. "If you want to arrange a meeting, call that number and ask for Herr Falkenstein. Whoever answers will acknowledge by saying that Herr Falkenstein has gone to Schweinfurt but is expected back shortly. You reply that you'll call back later, and give a specific time—the time you want to meet me. Use the twenty-four–hour clock. We'll meet at the Herzogstrasse address then, unless you're contacted by one of my people. They'll do it in a way that leaves no doubt. Memorize the number—write it in your own hand if you need to, but I'll want to make sure that paper is burned before I leave.

"Next point. Heinrich Schellen. Copies of pertinent fact sheets from our dossier on him have been sent over, and you're to familiarize yourself with them."

"I remember you said something about this being a long night."

"And a fast track." Leahy smiled out of the corner of his mouth. "The file also contains seven fairly recent photos of him. Take as long as you like. Some kind soul in Washington was nice enough to prepare a summary sheet of what he thought were the important facts to be gleaned from the file. The style is crude and the syntax poor, but I think you'll find it a fairly good summary."

Hoffmann reached for the plain brown folder, and read.

SUBJECT: Heinrich Schellen
Occupation: Minister of Transport, GDR
Born: 12 November 1908
   Kassel, Germany

Heinrich Schellen was the only son of Gretchen and Hans Schellen. The father was a butcher by trade and by most accounts fairly successful prior to serving in WW I as an infantry man on the Western Front. He seems to have served the Kaiser with no particular distinction except to be badly wounded at the Battle of Verdun. After the war, he grew increasingly bitter over the nation's inability to control the rampant inflation and resultant hardships that eventually destroyed his business and the health of his wife. Young Schellen—a small, rather effeminate boy—was another disappointment in his life.

At age nineteen, Heinrich Schellen became associated with the growing Nazi movement in Nuremberg, where he had moved after breaking off relations with his father (five years after his mother's death). In 1929, he met Josef Goebbels, who put him to work writing and distributing an anti-Communist propaganda sheet in the Nuremberg area; he also wrote and circulated false but damaging papers on officials of the Weimar Republic who opposed Hitler. By the time Hitler came to power, Schellen was an established member of the Goebbels' staff, in the forefront of the Nazi movement yet far enough removed from the street-fight battle lines. He apparently had a hand in helping draft the denunciation that laid the blame on the Communists for the burning of the Reichstag, an accomplishment that cemented Hitler's control over Germany at that time. The years following show a steady, if unremarkable, climb up the bureaucratic ladder.

In 1939, Schellen, with Goebbels' assistance, managed a transfer to the SS in the rank of Sturmbannführer (U.S. equivalent: major). Eight months later, he was promoted to Standartenführer (U.S.: colonel) and served in several capacities in Poland, France, and Germany. His first assignment as colonel was as the commandant of the Dachau camp outside Munich. After fourteen months there, he became a member of Himmler's staff, responsible for upgrading plans for the "final solution" in Poland and improving transportation systems to insure the plan became a reality. In February 1944, he became commandant of Stalag 14, which housed captured British and American fliers.

By the end of June that same year, it became obvious to Schellen that the Allies would win the war, and he made plans to escape at the end of the conflict. He began by getting transferred to SS Headquarters—Berlin.

Arriving in Berlin near the end of February 1945, he began systematically removing his name from official documents and/or destroying them. It was perhaps the bravest act of his entire life, coming at a time when public hanging for defeatism was literally a daily occurrence in the streets of the capital. (One can only guess at the reason for these actions by Schellen, because he was in a position to know that every arm and agency of the Third Reich kept voluminous records, most of which were beyond his reach.) In addition, Post-War Military Government teams in Britain also maintained detailed dossiers of ranking Nazi Party members and complete lists of those of lesser rank for use after the war.

Schellen left Berlin approximately six hours before the first Russian soldier entered. He fled southwest disguised in civilian clothes, following an itinerary that led to Switzerland and then on to Rome, where a group of sympathetic Catholic priests would smuggle him to Spain and then to South America.

He was captured by the Russians twenty kilometers outside Leipzig, in the town of Weissenfels.

His next two years were spent in Russian camps. After that, for almost four years, no record can be found of his activities. He resurfaced again in 1949 as a minor clerical worker in the East German Ministry of Transport. The best theory for explaining his survival in the post-war Soviet zone is that the Russians were convinced his intimate knowledge of transportation systems in the area was of some value to them. But this is only supposition and remains one of the few inconsistencies relative to their treatment of other ex-Nazis.

The early 1950's indicate a conversion to Communism and a gradual advancement within the ministry. He is a skilled transportation manager, and this, coupled with an extensive record of hardline Communist politicking over the past two decades, appears to be the reason for his present position.

Hoffmann set the summary sheet aside and looked at the photographs. At sixty-seven, the man carried almost two hundred pounds on his five-foot, nine-inch frame; large, dark bags of flesh hung beneath his eyes, and the once thin face was almost round, the jowls puffy.

He read through the other documents in the file, some dated twenty years earlier. Most seemed lacking in detail, conclusions drawn not necessarily confirmed by fact. It took almost an hour, but by the time he handed the folder to Leahy, he had read each page.

"Is this what my file looks like now?" he asked the agent.

"Not exactly. The file isn't quite as thick, the pictures are better." Leahy reached out and took the folder. "Monday morning you'll report to Deutches Aero, to a man by the name of Hans Gerber, who serves as chief pilot. He'll give you instructions and probably an orientation flight in the area. You'll be turned loose when he thinks you're ready—like any other newly hired pilot. We hope that will be in a matter of days."

"How much does Gerber know?"

"Essentially nothing. They had need for another pilot, and, while he has a say on whether or not the man is suitable, hiring and firing decisions are made by others. You'll be paid normal scale."

"Which is?"

"More than what you got at your last job, which is part of the reason you sent out so many applications. The story ties together pretty nicely. You'll see when you get to reading it. We don't expect you'll be around long enough to pick up that first paycheck anyhow—the Schellen flight should be in less than two weeks."

Leahy removed another file from the briefcase and handed it over. "This is the complete cover story: dates, names, places. You'll have to know it as well, maybe better than you know your own life story, although it tracks your background. If you get into a position where you need information that's not covered in there, do and say what comes naturally. Whatever you do, try to be yourself—not what you think the Agency might want you to be. That's the best advice I think I can give.

"In the next few days we'll be arranging final details with Schellen. Until then, your days will be spent at the airport or in this room. That means no night life or wandering around—

sorry, but we don't want you making our job any harder than it already is." He stood and stretched, then went to the window and peered outside. "Why don't you get started on the cover story? I want to take a quick look around outside and check security for a minute. When I get back, we'll start going over it."

Leahy let himself out as Hoffmann began leafing through the report. He had read only a few pages when the knock came at the door, accompanied by Leahy's voice. The tone was strident, the words anxious.

"Let me in. Quickly, damn it!"

Hoffmann stood back as the agent entered, his breath coming in short, rapid gasps. His eyes betrayed confusion and fear.

"I had two men watching the main entrance, and another team in the back parking lot. Now they're gone, and I don't know why . . . but I damned sure don't like it. My orders were too damned specific to be misunderstood. Something's haywire, and I—"

"What do you mean you don't understand it?" Hoffmann cut in. The agent's worry was infectious. This was not the same man who had calmly briefed him a few minutes ago. Old doubts and fears surfaced, crowding his mind.

"*No way* they could have found out so soon," Leahy mumbled aloud, then looked at Hoffmann, his face contorted, eyes wide with alarm. "Don't move out of this room until I personally contact you. Clear?"

"What the hell's going on?"

"I don't know. I *don't* know!" Leahy quickly picked up the briefcase, replaced the papers, and handcuffed it to his left arm. Walking to the door, he paused, listening. Slowly, he opened it and looked cautiously in both directions down the hall. Turning to Hoffmann, he said, "I can't see any way that anybody could have gotten on to this so soon, but the possibility exists. Remote, but we can't rule it out."

"When are you going to contact me?"

The agent ignored the question and walked out into the hallway.

The small comfort he had enjoyed for a few hours after meeting Leahy had been shattered; in seconds he had gone from the relative relaxation of knowing that the man he was working with was a professional, someone who could offer at least some security, to a state of almost total fear. The transition had been too abrupt, the change too monstrous to believe. There was nothing, no one left. Leahy's promise had been hollow, without sincerity or substance. Now he was without any lifeline. He picked up the phone and asked for the overseas operator.

The call took almost twenty minutes to complete; after long delays and repeated requests, he heard the ringing of a phone on the other end. Tony Labruzo answered.

"Where the hell have you been for the past five days?"

"Virginia. Germany."

"*What?* Are you out of your mind? I went out to the house two days ago and it was boarded up, like it was abandoned. What the hell are you messed up in?"

"I don't really know. Not exactly. I couldn't tell you anyhow. But I need help. I need to be able to reach you."

"From where?"

"Germany."

"You really are there?"

Hoffmann breathed deeply to calm himself before replying. "Yes . . . I am. Don't ask me how or why—you probably wouldn't believe it anyway. I'm not sure I do myself. Nothing is making any sense. Not one damned thing."

"You probably won't want to hear this, then."

"What?"

"I checked up on those two names you gave me. The State Department has only one Carle Landrum on its rolls. He's a month away from retirement, and he's confined to a wheelchair.

Has been for almost ten years, since a boating accident on the Chesapeake. That doesn't sound like the person you described."

"That's got to be a mistake." He didn't want to believe the words, the implication was too awesome.

"It's not. And there's something else. Carnahan doesn't exist either. Neither one of them does."

He looked at the phone for long seconds, stunned. Labruzo's voice was a far-off murmur, a sound in a deep, damp cave. The lawyer was asking him something—a phone number, an address. Without conscious thought, he gave them and hung up. He quickly grabbed a jacket from the closet and keys from the top of the dresser.

Then he was walking down the hall toward the hotel entrance, aware of the faces, seeing them as if distorted through a wide-angle lens at close range. He had to run, to put distance between himself and room, to get away from the madness.

Carnahan doesn't exist. . . . Neither one of them does.

It couldn't be. Carnahan had been there in Washington. Had coerced him into doing this.

Carnahan doesn't exist.

Hoffmann ran through the night, toward the darkness of the parking lot. From the shadow of the building, a lone figure watched him get into the Audi and pull into the traffic in front of the hotel.

Chapter 6

The outer office was richly appointed; thick-pile carpet, large leather-covered sofas along two adjoining walls, heavy brass lamps on the end tables. Limited-edition prints of scenes from the American West hung on the walls in special conservation frames.

The man looked at the pictures and smiled to himself, wondering if they had been placed there with conscious thought: a statement of the psyche of the man in the inner office; a declaration that those in his line of work had replaced the cowboy in the hearts and minds of the public.

"Mr. Knight will see you now," the secretary said, looking at him from her station next to the door, which she seemed to be guarding. No one entered the inner sanctum of the CIA Deputy Director's downtown office without the approval of the old woman. She was a legend among those who had any dealings with William F. Knight; an acerbic old biddy who thought and acted as if she actually ran most of the clandestine operations, allowing her boss the privilege of thinking he was actually in control.

"Thank you, Bernice," the man said, rising and walking to the door. He could see the look in her eyes, a glance that told him he had crossed into dangerous ground with her. Nobody, not even the Deputy Director, called Miss Beeson by her first name. Without returning her stare, he entered the office and took a seat in one of the chairs facing the immense wooden desk.

"Everything is going according to plan. The first inquiry was made on Hoffmann about an hour ago."

"Good." Bill Knight grunted without looking up from the papers in front of him. He scribbled brief notes on several sheets before looking at the agent. "Have all the files been doctored?"

"Yes, sir. The computer at AmerIntell was fed information that makes it look like he was used by the Company for a minor job shortly after he left the service in 'seventy-three. The charter company he worked for never asked for a background check when he applied there, so it's impossible for anyone to know the information was recently entered. The programmer who entered it was employed by us until two years ago. His silence is guaranteed. The records at the Army Reserve Center in St. Louis were also changed to show an unexplained gap in his Viet Nam service—the first three months of 1971, so it corresponds with shutting down Paladin and the evacuation from Muong Sen."

Knight stared at the man, showing no sign of pleasure or satisfaction. Paladin. At least some good had come from the operation after all these years. Damn them. If MACV hadn't interfered, he could have made it work. When the evacuation was ordered, they were just beginning to get the organization to gel; the Thai mercenaries were starting to bring in good information on North Vietnamese troop movements down the Ho Chi Minh trail through Laos. But somebody in

Saigon or Washington had gotten cold feet. The movement out of Muong Sen and Ban Kavak had gone badly; most of the Thais and two Americans had to be left behind. Worst of all, his own record of success had been marred by the incident— not officially, but personally. He would never forgive them for that.

"Who made the inquiry?" Knight asked.

"A private investigator of questionable sanity from out of Atlanta. We've run into him before. He's got a bad case of *Mission Impossible* Syndrome—the usual symptoms."

"Engimatic glances and a penchant for Tae Kwan Do classes."

"Yes, sir. Something like that."

Knight smiled. "Who's he working for this time?"

"KGB."

"You're certain?"

"Reasonable so. He met one of their people at a bar in Underground Atlanta the day after the word *somehow* leaked out about Hoffmann's mission. They don't know we're on to him. He told AmerIntell he was running personnel background checks on several different people for Boeing, and Hoffmann was being considered for placement as a test pilot on the program to develop a new utility helicopter for the government. The cover story was good; all the facts were correct. The only fallacy was the inclusion of Hoffmann."

"Hoffmann . . . What do we have out of Geneva?"

"Leahy met him as planned and later briefed him on details."

"Did the message get sent through Comm II?"

"Yes. The transmission appears to be secure. But the conversations in the office should have been monitored. We detected activation of the Harmonica bug several times during the course of the day. We think it's being operated from Bern, but there's no way to trace it. Even so, it should be able to transmit, probably as far as Prague. Geneva has been warned not to be too obvious—the device is still important to sending other false signals. At least for the next few days. Tuesday morning, McArdle will find the Harmonica and counter it; that way, it won't look suspicious.

"The phone in Hoffmann's room was tapped, and we monitored his first call to Labruzo about an hour ago—three-thirty our time. He now knows that I don't exist, at least not as a State Department employee named Carnahan. The effect on him is unclear, at least from what we could tell on tape. Leahy's report should be coming in sometime around midnight, we expect, and that should give us what we need to know."

"Leahy bothers me. I never trust anyone suffering from a terminal case of altruism. How do you read him?"

Carnahan shrugged, not wanting to commit himself on the evaluation of an agent in the field. Especially this one. He knew that Leahy had been involved in some way in Paladin, and that Knight had the impression that the agent was partially to blame for the eventual dismantling of the operation. The foray into Laos had been Knight's plan, a piece of turf to be protected. Leahy's questioning was intolerable, and when the mission was scrubbed, Knight was sure that part of the reason could be laid at his doorstep. But Carnahan had worked with him before, in Argentina, and found him to be a cut above most of the men he had worked with in other areas of the world.

"I asked you a question," Knight was saying.

"It's hard to say, since I haven't worked with him in a half-dozen years or so. He was pretty good then, but people change."

"They do." The Deputy Director appeared satisfied with the response, reaching for a pack of cigarettes on the desk and offering one to Carnahan, who he knew was a chain smoker. He had held off lighting up himself, knowing the man wanted one. A small, insignificant gesture, but the signal would not be lost on the agent.

"Is there any chance the Schellen plan will be called off?" Carnahan asked, changing the subject.

"Doubtful. We know the Russians are behind it. The timing is unfortunate. Couldn't come at a worse time, as far as I'm concerned. The others agree, and they support the action we've taken so far. If all goes as planned, we'll be able to hold things together for another five or six weeks, and that buys us enough time."

Enough time. The words sent a shudder down Carnahan's spine. It would happen; sometime in the next two months. His knowledge of the overall plan was minimal, a conscious decision of the man in front of him. At the moment, he found that agreeable. Others, much more highly placed than he, carried the weight of responsibility for things at which he could only guess, though he had some guesses. Knowing Knight, he was sure it revolved around extending American hegemony or maintaining some semblace of nuclear parity in the world. The Deputy Director thought and acted on a global scale, as if he had been personally charged with nothing less than preserving Western civilization.

Knight looked back at the papers cluttering his desk, shaking his head and uttering a barely audible curse. "As if I didn't have enough damned problems."

"Anything I can help with?"

"Not unless you can get our new Director to stop shooting off his mouth about our operations to every congressional committee and reporter who gives him half a damned minute. He's given away more inside information on us than Dean ever thought of spilling about Nixon." Knight picked up a note from another pile. "And this thing from Personnel is almost as big a headache. You know what Watergate did to our recruiting? It tripled the number of applications— from a lot of high-powered schools, too. It seems that every Yalie wants to get involved. Exploding seashells, and dart guns with deadly toxins. Where do these kids get those kinds of ideas? This *patriotic backlash* is is worse than what we suffered through on the campuses in the late 'sixties, when you couldn't buy a minute from any school in the country." He tossed the note on top of another pile and looked at Carnahan. "One of these days we'll get somebody in Personnel who can make a decision without calling five committee meetings. But that's my problem, not yours. You stick close to the story on Hoffmann. Keep me informed . . . on everything. Day or night."

"I'll do that, sir." Carnahan rose.

Knight leaned back in his chair, staring at the ceiling. A look of contentment spread across his features, in conflict with the harsh words of the previous moment.

"It's beginning to come together . . . after all these years. Debts will be paid, dreams will be realized. It can be done." He looked back at Carnahan and said, "I want to know everything Hoffmann does. Everything. In a few days, I expect, we'll learn what his breaking point is. I hope, for our sake, his threshold isn't too low."

"What about his sake?"

"For his sake, too . . . of course."

"Of course, sir."

The car behind him turned off onto a side street and Hoffmann breathed deeply, shaking his head and exhaling angrily.

He had reconstructed the conversation with Leahy over and over, gradually eliminating the feeling that it had been laced with statements pregnant with double meaning. The atmosphere surrounding him after the agent's quick departure and Labruzo's revelation had been like a drug-induced hallucination: a series of events heightened by his own romanticism perhaps, an imaginary sense of danger. Yet each time he convinced himself of this self-delusion, doubt crept in—a memory of a disturbance on the telephone line while talking to the lawyer conjured up visions of a third presence; a car in the rearview mirror that seemed to be there too long to be coincidence.

Running from the hotel had been irrational, an act of fear. But it had given him time to think, to sort out to some degree of satisfaction what was going on around him. There were still too many unknowns, the decision on whom he could trust still open. He had become privy to a secret, and with that had been caught in the intrigue of it against his will, without the experience or background to cope with unknowns. His first reaction had been survival, to run from whatever it was and try to protect himself.

He had done that. What next?

Return to the room and await a call from Leahy? The agent was his only real contact with—with what? Going back to the hotel was not a comforting thought.

Lights from a following car reflected off the mirror, causing the old worries to resurface for long seconds, but he fought off the tension and returned to deciding his next move. *Call Labruzo. Have him send enough money for passage home, and worry about sorting things out on familiar territory.* Sort things out with whom? Carnahan? He didn't exist.

Call the number supplied by Leahy and set up a meeting at the address on Herzogstrasse.

Could he trust the voice on the other end of the line? Could he trust Leahy? Unknowns. Everything unknown.

He turned off the main street, entering a narrow, one-way avenue of dark houses and cars parked here and there along the curb. The car in the rearview mirror followed, closing the distance rapidly until its headlights disappeared below the line of the Audi's trunk.

The impact sent him out of control on the wet cobblestones, twisting the steering wheel from his hands for an instant, long enough for the car to jump the curb and sideswipe the brick wall. The sound of tearing metal; sparks, bright and red-orange in the darkness. The car door was open and he was running without realizing he'd gotten out of the machine. He stumbled on a brick protruding unevenly from the sidewalk, losing his balance and catching himself with an outstretched hand.

In that instant, he heard the first shot.

A round cracked over his head, a distinct splitting of the air only inches away, then a whining ricochet in a stillness broken only by the sound of a racing motor. The wall behind him spit out shards of rock and mortar as other shots were fired. He was on the ground, rolling toward a parked car, trying to find some cover between himself and his attacker.

Hoffmann's mind raced, searching for an escape, knowing there was none.

The car screeched to a halt. Cautious footsteps echoed off the cobblestones in the now quiet night. A sound of metal against metal reached him, the insertion of a clip, a round chambered.

Another car entered the street, its lights playing off the houses as it swung around the corner, bathing him in the bright glare for an instant. Hoffmann heard the sound of footsteps, running now and moving away from where he lay half underneath a parked Volkswagen. A car door slammed as the sedan sped down the street, disappearing from sight thirty yards away at an intersection.

The second car stopped abruptly only a few feet from him.

"Hoffmann!"

The voice was unfamiliar, the tone full of anger. A dark shadow appeared in front of him, moving quickly to block his path. Light reflected off the barrel of a gun that was swinging in his direction. He dove forward toward the crouched figure, aiming at the knees, knocking the man off balance.

He swung at the head, feeling a jolt in his forearm that traveled through to his shoulder. As the man went down, Hoffmann heard the expulsion of air and a muffled cry of surprise. An arm came from nowhere, grabbing at his legs, pulling him down. He was grabbed from behind and wrestled to the ground, his coat torn, and a knee shoved harshly into the small of his back. A steel cylinder was jabbed into the base of his neck, punctuated by the cocking of a hammer that sounded thunderously loud in his ears.

"Get up!" Rough hands pulled him to his feet and propelled him unceremoniously toward the open rear door of the car. He was pushed into the back seat as the driver gunned the engine and the car lurched off into the darkness.

"That was the most ignorant move I think I've ever witnessed. By all rights, you should be dead."

Sean Leahy turned toward him, his features indistinct in the darkness of the car.

"I'd like to hear an explanation—especially since I thought my instructions were pretty damned clear about staying put until you were contacted!"

Hoffmann looked away, stung by the agent's accusatory tone. It had made such good sense as he rationalized his actions before the incident. Now he felt foolish.

"No answer? Doesn't surprise me. Nobody in his right mind would have pulled a dumb stunt like you just did. Maybe somebody in Washington is trying to send me a message: 'Send Leahy the misfits and incompetents, and sooner or later he'll get the idea we don't want him anymore.' Is that what it is, Hoffmann? Are you supposed to be testing me?"

"No, damn it!"

"What is it, then?"

"I don't care much for the sarcasm." His pulse was still rapid, the memory of debilitating fear still clear. He had made a mistake, but that didn't give the agent a right to talk to him as if he were some obstreperous child. "It was your mistake that started all this. Where was the damned security you promised?"

"They got pulled off . . . by a small glitch in procedure. It won't happen a second time. And don't think that gets you off the hook."

"You have small glitches, but I'm the one who makes the big mistakes?"

Leahy was silent for a minute before replying. "Do you remember the procedure for SMLM sitings from your days here in the Army?"

"Soviet Military Liaison Mission? I remember."

"There was a sighting near where you're staying, outside the zone where they're allowed access. Military Intelligence couldn't respond quickly, and a dispatcher contacted our people for assistance. One of our operatives who hadn't been briefed yet on your mission pulled my team, because we have a letter of understanding with the Army where SMLM is concerned. If we had had time to bring everybody up to speed on your presence here, this wouldn't have happened. Like I said, it won't happen again. You can count on that.

"One of my men will arrange to take care of the car, repair the body work or whatever is needed. We'll have it back in the lot tomorrow morning." Leahy's tone had softened as tension drained from him. "We'll start checking on who took the shots at you and why. Security will be doubled until we find out. Depending on what we learn, we may need to move you; I'll decide in the morning. If you've been compromised— and that's what I'm thinking right now—that shelves the operation, in my opinion."

The car turned onto Effnerstrasse, eased into traffic, and minutes later pulled into the parking lot behind the hotel.

Leahy leaned forward and spoke to the men in the front seat as the car stopped. "Check out the room before he goes in. I've got a few more things to cover with him, so give us about five minutes."

When they were alone, the agent turned to him.

"I didn't tell you everything a while ago," Leahy said, his

voice a whisper. "And I'm glad you didn't ask for a lot of explanation. Sorry I had to come down on you like that—it's part of the role."

"For their sake?"

"Maybe. I told you before there were a lot of strange inconsistencies about this thing. I could be reading this thing all wrong . . . I hope so. But the way we finally found you was too much of a coincidence.

"When I found out what had happened on that sighting, I tried to call you but didn't get an answer. I put out a message on you in hopes that one of our people could pick you up before anything happened. It wasn't hard to construct what you had probably done; finding the car missing was somewhat confirming. I really don't think you've been compromised yet."

"But—"

"I know that's what I said. Let me explain. Sighting the Soviet mission car wasn't unusual—it happens all the time. They test us; we respond. It's a damned nuisance game they play—after almost thirty years, they know exactly what their geographic limits are. And they know that special license plate sticks out like a neon sign. I'd worry more if a week went by without some G.I. calling in a report.

"It took me twenty minutes to track down the dispatcher who contacted us, when it should have taken two. That was suspicious at first, but strange as it sounds, he was on break and hadn't mentioned the call to us to the guy who took his place. It sounds unbelievably stupid. It was. But I've seen it happen before. Handling a sighting has become so routine, none of us thinks too much of it anymore.

"We drove around trying to find you for about an hour, without a clue of where you might be, and then I made a call to home station from a pay phone. Nothing. Shortly after that, we found you—just in time. Doesn't that strike you as odd?"

"Should it?"

"I think so—especially in light of a lot of questions I still don't have answers for from Washington. Every time I think I've got all the details nailed down, another question crops up, or somebody drops something on me that doesn't fit. Small details, but I'm the kind of person that doesn't like any loose ends. I've seen some really good agents—most of them better than me—get caught by a detail they should have checked out but didn't because it seemed insignificant. And I don't trust anybody."

Hoffman listened, trying to fit the agent's words into his own perceptions of what had happened. Leahy's acknowledgment that he didn't know whom to trust made him more trustworthy, his candor more reliable. He decided Sean Leahy was telling the truth.

"Don't make a move out of your room this weekend until, and unless, you hear from me personally. I was serious about that."

"What if I don't hear from you by Monday? I still don't know what my cover story is for Deutches Aero."

"That will be the least of your worries. And I'm serious about that, too." Leahy reached inside his coat pocket, then held out his hand toward Hoffmann; in it was a small automatic. "You weren't supposed to be armed, but I'm going to override those instructions. Nobody knows you have it except me. If you have to use it, don't let that middle-class reluctance to shoot somebody slow you down."

Hoffman looked at the gun, then back to Leahy. In the darkness of the street less than half an hour before, he had felt naked without some way to protect himself, had cursed the agent for not giving him a weapon. But that had been in a moment of terror, when it looked like a very real possibility that his life was over. The finality of the act of stepping off into eternity without so much as an attempt to defend himself was emasculating. Yet now, he wondered if it were possible for him to point this gun at someone and pull the trigger. Once the weapon was accepted, the choice might be out of his control.

Hoffmann reached for the automatic, felt the impersonal coldness of the metal, and quickly put it in his pocket.

Chapter 7

Ben Ari looked at the three people seated around the table in the dimly lit back room inside the house on Lieberstrasse in Munich.

They had worked together for only two operations; once in 1969, and again in '72. Only two men outside the group knew of its existence—General Trandau and the Israeli Prime Minister. The team had never been acknowledged in official circles, their names unlisted on any documents. An old forger, an ex-commando, and a dark-eyed girl in her late twenties. Each different, but complementary. Seventy-two hours before, the innocuous classified ad was printed in a Munich daily and read by the people now gathered in the room.

"The target in Heinrich Schellen," Ben Ari said, pausing briefly to gauge the reaction on their faces. Only the old man, Simon Levin, had known what the announcement would be. He had met the Israeli major near the airport soon after Ben Ari's arrival, and arranged the needed room and transportation. The room where they met was located in one of three houses maintained by him for such occasions: two in different sections of Munich, and one on the outskirts of Ulm.

Ben Ari noticed the absence of reaction, as expected, and continued. "It's an unusual opportunity . . . and worth the effort, if we can pull it off."

"Do we kill him, or make him a present for the general?" The question was accompanied by a blue-gray cloud of cigar smoke exhaled toward the ceiling by the man in his mid-forties.

"They want him in Tel Aviv, Aaron." An almost imperceptible raising of the eyebrows was Edelmann's only reply. Ben Ari thought how deceptive the man's outward appearance was: despite the massive size of his midsection, the ex-commando sergeant was as agile as a gymnast. His expertise with weapons and demolitions was unsurpassed.

"Wiesenthal?"

"Not to be contacted, unless we absolutely need him, and then only at the last minute. He's watched too closely by the underground SS, and he's too set in his ways. Old age, I suppose . . . no offense, Simon." The white-haired man dismissed the comment with a wave of his hand. "The operation calls for maximum flexibility. Here's what we know so far.

"The Americans have developed a plan to help Schellen defect to the West, based on what appears to be a request from Schellen himself. Apparently he is under fire for transportation problems of substantial proportions, and wants out of East Germany. The reasons are not critical; his arrival into an area less denied to us is. Our chance comes when he's in West Germany, before they transport him to the United States. If he reaches America, political realities make him virtually untouchable."

Edelmann rotated the cigar in his mouth, looking directly at Ben Ari. "Political realities don't make the new Germany much of a hunting ground either. This is not exactly Brazil, or Argentina."

"The government is well aware of that. Several possible scenarios have been developed—one, or a combination of many, could be used to explain the fallout of our action. The general was not at liberty to disclose details, but they center around shifting the blame to a number of highly placed officials in the Bundestag who have known Nazi backgrounds. The idea I suppose, would be to show how they wanted Schellen silenced so their own pasts were not revealed. A Communist plot to assassinate a defector would not be outside the realm of the possible. But that's for the politicians. Our job is somewhat different.

"We must kidnap Schellen from the Americans."

"Forgive me, Aki." Levin's voice was soft as he interrupted. "But this is obviously a CIA operation, and while they have intentionally planted stories from time to time that make them look like amateurs, we all know that is not the case."

"True. But this time they *are* using an amateur. For some reason, they have chosen someone named Eric Hoffmann for the assignment. That's a name you haven't heard before. Until five days ago, he was a pilot for a small company in the eastern United States. His only qualification seems to be that he is very good at flying helicopters—which is how they plan to extract Schellen. Our people in Washington are trying to learn more about him, but all indications are that he has not been involved in any other operations of an intelligence nature."

Edelmann crushed out the cigar, grunted once, and looked at the major. "Military background?"

"Decorated several times for valor in Viet Nam; extended an extra six months. The general thinks he was a good choice—for the Americans, and for us. If we have to deal just with him, or with him and one or two others soon after they arrive in West Germany, it could make things easier. The route they have chosen may be their only option. Recently, Schellen cancelled a trip to the West on short notice, which may indicate that his superiors were afraid he may attempt to escape, even though he is heavily guarded by an entourage of secret police. The bodyguards are one reason we weren't able to get close to him in Bonn last year, or in Paris the year before that.

"General Trandau thinks the American plan has a good chance to succeed. So far this year, two of their Army helicopters have flown into Czechoslovakia during bad weather, landed, and returned unnoticed after realizing their mistake. The Iron Curtain is not as solid as they would like us to believe. Going into East Germany may not be as easy, but it's not impossible. We don't know what their time schedule is yet, so that means a close watch on what Hoffmann does. He arrived in Munich about eighteen hours ago; Monday he goes to work for Deutches Aero, and I suspect he'll use one of their aircraft for the mission. Aaron, pull together a briefing for me on the way they function."

"I'll have it by this time tomorrow."

"Now, as for Hoffmann. I'll take him for six in the morning until ten at night, starting tomorrow. We'll meet back here at the same time tomorrow evening, and I'll have a schedule worked out."

Turning to Simon Levin, he said, "I'll need four passports, two for me and two for Schellen. German nationals with visas for Greece and Egypt. Two identities for each of us, with complete personal papers: driver's license, credit cards, laundry receipts, memberships."

"For you, no problem. But for him it will take a day for pictures and working up the passport. Can you afford that?"

"I'll have to. Arrange a safehouse for us outside Munich."

Ben Ari at last looked toward the girl, her dark features silhouetted by low lighting off to her left. She wore no makeup, but the face needed none to accent her high cheekbones and delicately formed nose, her long-lashed eyes. "The last thing I'll need is a weapon."

"You'll want the Beretta, naturally," she said.

"Yes. You remembered."

"I remembered much more than that," the girl said, tossing her head so that the long, dark hair fell across her shoulder. She spoke as if flinging a challenge at him; her eyes flashed defiance. "I will bring it to where you are staying tonight. Simon has given me the address."

Edelmann covered his mouth with a large, beefy hand, masking his amusement. Ben Ari's studied avoidance of Deborah Mueller had not been lost on him. He wished he could be there to see what he knew would be an interesting confrontation, a test of wills which he sensed was already under way as the two of them stared at one another across the table.

"Something bothers me about what the Americans are planning," the ex-commando said, lighting another cigar. The girl looked away, releasing her hold on Ben Ari's eyes. "I sense it bothers you as well, my friend. Why are they risking such an important and delicate operation on an unknown quantity like this Hoffmann?"

Ben Ari spoke, his gaze still on the girl. "With his abilities, he has as good a chance as any of their hired agents to make it work. If he fails, they can easily disallow him, saying with some degree of truth that he was never employed by the CIA, that he was on his own. He may very well die. In contrast to the general, I expect he will."

Ben Ari looked at Edelmann and said, "My only hope is that he is able to accomplish moving Schellen to the West. Beyond that, his living or dying means nothing."

Ben Ari left the house alone, turning up the collar of his coat as he walked down the sidewalk in the shadow of the buildings. The street was deserted.

Schellen had provided a purpose to the group, a purpose

much like the last one that had brought Ben Ari to the city, a few short hours after the airport at Fürstenfeldbruck had erupted in gunfire and claimed the lives of most of the Israeli Olympic team. The year had been 1972. One of the charred bodies on the tarmac was a friend from the kibbutz.

Jossi Sorensen. A young giant transplanted from the United States in the mid-1960's to Yad-Il; people came from as far away as fifty miles just to watch him train for the games. Ben Ari had introduced him to the girl he was to marry upon his return. But the wedding had been shattered by Arab explosives in the darkness, in a land that had seen the death of many Jews. Ben Ari thought back to the night less than a week ago when part of his debt to Jossi Sorensen had been repaid in southern Lebanon. It had been dark then, too.

He drove from the meeting place, searching randomly for a telephone booth after assuring himself that he hadn't been followed. A mile from the house on Lieberstrasse he found one on a poorly lit corner, stopped the car, and stepped inside.

"Daniel has returned to the lion's den," he said when the answer came on the other end.

"Daniel! It's nice to hear from you again," came the reply. The voice betrayed uneasiness behind a thin veneer of informality, as if the call had been expected but unwelcome. "Where are you calling from?"

"I'm at the best café in all Munich, perhaps all of Bavaria. You remember that, of course."

"Certainly . . . who could ever forget? Will you be in town long? Magda will insist on having you for dinner."

"Another time. I have an appointment in an hour, a business engagement that can't wait. Just wanted you to know I was in the area. I'll call when there's more time."

"As you wish. Goodbye, Daniel."

"Goodbye."

Ben Ari hung up and walked back to his car; in twenty

minutes, he arrived at the small nightclub around the corner from the Hofbräuhaus. It was one of many he knew in the city, and he had chosen it on the spur of the moment during the phone conversation. He drove by slowly, and minutes later parked on a side street out of sight from the establishment. He walked around the block and approached from the opposite direction, crossing the street and entering quickly by the front door. He located an empty table near the rear exit, away from the crowd clustered around the bar. Loud talk, punctuated by laughter, filled the room. No one paid any attention to him as he took a seat and ordered a glass of house wine; the absence of reaction came as no surprise. His appearance was Aryan, his clothes nondescript. To the casual observer, he could have been any one of thousands of other factory workers in the city stopping for a drink on the way home from the evening shift.

Minutes later, another man entered, weaved his way through those at the bar, and took a seat at the table. "Shalom, Aki."

"Shalom, Petar. You're looking well. You seemed surprised to hear from me when I called."

"I wasn't expecting you until next week."

"The timetable has been accelerated."

"Your decision, I suppose."

Ben Ari nodded. "What do you have for me?"

"Hoffmann is registered at the Esso Motor Hotel on Effnerstrasse, under his own name. He's driving a rented black Audi with this license number." Petar pushed a scrap of paper across the table. "This afternoon he drove to a small town near Ingolstadt and made contact with a man named Sean Leahy—he's CIA, connected with the American consulate but operating through Geneva. Tonight, about four hours ago, they met again in Hoffmann's room."

"Security?"

"Three teams, rotated at six-hour intervals, from what we've seen since Hoffmann's arrival. Except for one instance, it has been extremely tight. Shortly after Leahy's arrival this evening, the surveillance team departed."

Ben Ari gave the man a questioning glance. "Is that significant?"

"We don't know for sure. Leahy left a little later, leaving Hoffmann alone. Shortly after that, Hoffmann himself drove away. It may mean nothing, but it seemed unusual that they would put him under such tight surveillance and then remove it for no apparent reason. I mention it only because it doesn't follow any pattern we've seen from them."

"Where did Hoffmann go?"

"We don't know." He saw the Israeli's harsh look and responded with a shrug accompanied by an open-handed gesture of resignation. "The fault is mine. I was not prepared, and he had vanished in the traffic before we could react." Petar glanced away, embarrassed at the mistake, expecting an outburst from the man opposite. Ben Ari's temper was short and violent, as he had seen first hand on other occasions in the twelve years he had known him.

"Tomorrow morning, pull your people off the American. I'll take over personally, and you'll revert to being my communications link. I don't want you or your organization anywhere close to him."

"I'm sorry. It was a momentary lapse."

"It was a momentary lapse by your predecessor two years ago that allowed the suicide squad into the Olympic village. I will handle this myself."

Petar looked at the man, saying nothing, understanding. The general had told him Ben Ari preferred working alone, that this assignment would most likely be handled that way. "You will need help."

"I need nothing other than for you to send the code that I have arrived and am proceeding. Beyond that, I will contact you as needed . . . if needed. Except for the twice-weekly code, you will not be involved. I will handle the operation by myself." He said the words easily, the lie coming as naturally as if it were the truth; another layer of deception. Should anyone other than himself be forced to reveal what he knew, the picture would be distorted, the organizations in Germany salvageable. Petar would not like it now, nor would the others if they knew. But their feelings meant nothing. His loyalty was to someone more important. More important than the man who had sent him.

Ben Ari glanced casually around the room. Rising, he said, "I'll leave first." He retraced his circuitous route back to the car and checked it quickly for any signs of tampering before starting the engine.

This would be the last mission, he thought, as he pulled out of the side street, checking the mirror. After this, there would be no more satisfaction in his revenge, no more burning need. The lies and deceit would be over, the debts paid. Maybe then he could return to Yad-Il, to his Magda, and find his own peace.

There will be no peace in your lifetime.

Rabbi Solomon's words came to him, a mocking prophecy.

"I'll prove you wrong, old man," he whispered. "I have it in my power now."

The light was dim in the hallway outside his room, but instinct sharpened by years of experience told him someone had disturbed the door in his absence. And he was certain it had not been by accident.

The apartment was one of three on the top floor of the building. Other than his, the rooms were vacant, verified earlier as he planned the escape routes. There were no steps to any attic, and it was unlikely that any of the tenants on lower floors would be wandering the halls at this late hour; more unlikely that the maid had come in four days early. The small drop of wax he had left protruding from the bottom of the keyhole and the fine thread on the inside of the doorjamb near the floor had not been disturbed by some casual passerby.

"Don't be afraid to come in, major. I've been waiting for you."

Ben Ari opened the door quickly and saw the barrel of a weapon pointed at his stomach. "Damn you!" he said, grabbing the pistol and tossing it on the bed.

"I see you still have the same bad temper as when you left." Deborah Mueller faced him like an adversary, her jaw thrust forward, her voice defiant. She pulled away from his grip and turned on the light next to the only chair in the small room.

"If you'll remember, it was you who had the bad temper that night."

"Actually, I don't remember that at all. Until now, I thought I'd done a rather good job of forgetting that you even exist. I think most of us have a way of blocking out unpleasant memories. And memories of unpleasant people."

Ben Ari looked at her for a long moment, knowing that she was not telling the truth. She was more beautiful than when they had first met. And she was part of the reason he had been reluctant to return to Germany, perhaps even more of the reason than his hatred of this country that had killed so many of his people.

"There's your weapon, as I promised." She continued to stare at him with dark eyes that matched the color of her hair. "You can see I always keep my promises."

"Thank you."

"Is that all? No other words of explanation?"

"I have no reason to explain myself to you."

"No reason! You forget that two and a half years ago we shared much more than some quiet conversation and a few evenings together. Maybe we said a lot that night, but we didn't communicate. There is still much that needs to be explained." She sat in the chair, crossed her legs, and looked at him expectantly.

"There's nothing to explain," Ben Ari replied, turning his back to her and hanging his coat on one of the wooden pegs along the far wall. Her defiance could prove disastrous to the mission, the one small hitch he could not afford. Handling her properly would not be easy, but it was important enough that he dared not dismiss her as he would a reluctant recruit. When he turned around, she was still staring at him.

"What happened between us?" she asked, her voice softer.

"It wasn't us, it was me. I told you that night. It had to end. I was a married man with two sons still in infancy. When I came to Munich that time, it was in hopes of saving the life of a friend, a man who was like a younger brother. But decisions had already been made by the German police before I ever arrived. I needed your help in tracking and destroying the remnant—which you gave. But I was wrong in thinking that we had fallen in love, despite what I said."

She rose from the chair and went to him, looking deep into his eyes in the same way she had many times before. Her arms circled his neck; the invitation had been made. Deborah pulled him down to her waiting lips, trying to fill the void left by his departure. Long seconds passed before she released him and stepped back.

"What we did was wrong," he whispered. "Starting it all over again would compound the error. You're still the most desirable woman I've known, but I can't let it happen again. I won't be your lover."

In one lithe, violent movement, she slapped him with her whole strength. The anger returned to her eyes. "You pig!" She pulled her wrist from his grip and cursed him through clenched teeth. "My lover! I never wanted that from you— then or now. Don't flatter yourself, Major Ben Ari. All I wanted was an explanation."

"And now you have it."

"Or so it would seem." She drew away and walked to the door, grasping the handle. Turning quickly back to face him, her long hair swung around, partially covering her face. "We have worked together before, and I'm sure we're both professional enough not to let personal feelings get in the way. But this will be my last mission for the general. Tell him that. I've got my own life to live, and I won't have it interrupted at your convenience, or his." She breathed deeply, aware that his features had gone slightly out of focus, knowing it was caused by tears forming in her eyes. "We could have made each other very happy," she said softly, then slammed the door behind her.

Chapter 8

Most of the hotel's breakfast crowd had already departed, leaving behind a half-dozen busboys cleaning tables and changing linen for the noon meal. Clinking glasses at the waiters' stations echoed off the high ceiling, drowning out conversation at the few tables still occupied.

Eric Hoffmann drank from a mug containing the last of his coffee, casually observing those who still remained.

It was a game, brought on by the boredom of inactivity: guess the background and hidden agenda of those around you. The day before—Saturday—had passed without incident, except for Leahy's return for another few hours of memorizing the cover story Washington had developed. The terror of the preceding night grew fainter. Except when he slept.

He waved at the waitress and motioned for a refill of the mug, using the gesture as an excuse for another glance toward the table occupied by three young girls. They sat next to the ceiling-high doors, beneath an abstract painting whose subject he could only guess. One of them, the blonde, looked his way, and he averted his eyes, embarrassed that she had caught him again. Her amusement heightened his feeling of foolishness.

"Herr Hoffmann?"

The voice of the desk clerk intruded, and Hoffmann turned toward the German standing next to the table.

"Yes?"

"A message, sir." The man stood militarily erect, his heels together, and Hoffmann thought he detected the slightest bow as the words were spoken. "The caller said it was extremely urgent." He produced a slip of the hotel stationery with a handwritten note.

Call Falkenstein.

"That was it?" Hoffmann stared up at the man.

"His exact words, sir."

"Nothing more?"

"Nothing, sir. He said you would understand." The man's voice betrayed his weariness at having to deal with the public.

"Yes, of course. Thank you." Hoffmann reached for the bill, looking at the total and quickly converting it from marks to dollars. Realizing the clerk had not made a move to depart, he handed the man a tip and mumbled a thank-you as he tried to calm himself.

Call Falkenstein.

Why had Leahy used that phrase? It was a departure from what he had been told the day before, something that didn't ring true with agent's obsession for following established procedures. He paused, certain that the method of contact held some hidden meaning. What was it they had told him at the farm? By breaking the rules of their agreement, Leahy was telling him something, expecting him to respond in an equally unexpected way. But what? How?

He left payment for the breakfast, walked quickly outside, crossed the lobby to a pay phone, and dialed the number.

"Herr Falkenstein, please," he said when the connection was made.

"Herr Falkenstein is no longer here. May I take the message?"

For a moment, he was unable to reply. Leahy's voice was laced with anxiety. The expected wording had again been altered.

"When is he expected to return?"

"Are you calling from the room?"

"No. The note said immediately. I'm calling from a pay phone. What the hell is going on?"

"Good boy. I hoped you'd understand." There was a hint of relief in the voice, but only for an instant. The agent continued: "Don't say anything. That phone might be tapped also. Listen closely, because I'll say this just once. I've gotten some of the clarifications, and they tell me you're in deep trouble. Your phone was tapped against instructions, and the incident the other night was orchestrated in conjunction with some of my own people—people I thought I could trust. Don't return to the room. They'll kill you."

"Your men?"

"Damn it, listen! Their orders are coming from elsewhere. And I think I know, but I can't say over the phone. Meet me at the address I gave you that first night."

"How?"

"I can't say in the clear. Use your head. Read the messages." The phone went dead.

He looked at the note. Two words. *Call Falkenstein.* What hidden message was contained in it? And Leahy had used the plural. There had to be more than a single meaning, yet nothing came to him. Three days had not been enough time to learn all the nuances that must be second nature to Leahy. His confusion grew, and with it anger.

Messages.

Damn Leahy. There was only the one . . . and it meant nothing beyond what he had done already. The call had been made, the frightening revelation alluded to in part. He replaced the receiver on its cradle, read the note again, and returned to the desk.

"Hoffmann. Room one twenty-seven. Are there any messages for me?"

"I'll check, sir." The man turned, searched the pigeonhole marked with his number. "Nothing there. Let me check the other desk." He moved to another location, looked through a stack of papers, and returned empty-handed. "I'm sorry, sir, but there doesn't appear to be anything."

"There must be."

"I'm afraid not."

Use your head. If Leahy used the plural, he had to have left another note somewhere. The room? Not if the warning about returning there was real. Where else in the hotel could he gain access? Nowhere. Every other place was off limits except to the staff; every place except the room, where all he owned was now beyond his reach. His clothes, papers, log book. The weapon. The only thing he hadn't left there was his passport, which Leahy had told him to put in the safe.

"Could you check the safe for me?" Hoffmann asked.

"For a message, sir?"

"No. For my passport."

The clerk entered a back room and returned moments later with the document. Clipped to it was an envelope. Hoffmann crossed the lobby to an empty chair. Inside the small folder he found a set of keys and directions to a car parked several blocks from the hotel. Relief and irritation comingled. He cursed the agent for not having told him earlier, for leaving him to guess at the cryptic meaning in the phone call. Or had he? Leahy did say something about using hotel safes as a drop. But that had just been in passing, yesterday in the room as they were going over his cover story.

Now he had to get out of the hotel, rapidly, and unseen by the security. They would be watching the main entrance and the rear; others were in a sedan near the Audi parked on the south lot. He returned to the dining room, driven by panic, watching the main entrance.

He neither saw nor heard the girl as he turned the corner and stepped into her path.

His arm grazed her shoulder as he hurried past, propelling her into the door. A cry of surprise and pain erupted from her lips as she looked at him, wide-eyed. Eric's first impression was that she was attractive, pretty in a natural way that avoided the use of all but a trace of makeup. Her hair was stylishly long with a hint of curl on the ends.

"Sorry," he mumbled absently, touching her arm and looking at her deep blue eyes.

"Sorry! You ought to be!" Her expression grew angry and she drew away from him, twisting her arm from his grasp.

Hoffmann started to apologize, checked himself, and turned away. He felt exposed; prolonging the confrontation with the girl would only delay him and possibly draw more attention. Attention he didn't need. She was an obstacle, something to be avoided if he were to escape from the hotel without being seen. From the corner of his eye, he saw her look of indignation as she turned to leave the room.

A quick glance around the dining room told him the brief encounter had gone unnoticed by the hotel staff, and he walked quickly to the large swinging doors leading to the kitchen. None of the waitresses paid any attention as he looked through the small panes of glass. The room beyond appeared vacant; large stainless pans were piled in a sink on the far wall, and the door to the freezer stood half open.

He slipped through the entrance and located several lockers in a back room that exited to the parking lot. One of the gray metal lockers opened when he tried the handle, and he searched through it. A set of cook's whites hung on a hook behind street clothes. Hoffmann pulled the trousers on over his clothes and reached for the coat. A shadow on the floor at his feet startled him; he turned to face the large, imposing figure of the chef.

The chef stared at him, his eyes darting quickly to the open locker, then back. Hoffmann saw the satin finish of the cleaver in a beefy paw.

"I'm not trying to steal anything," he said, gauging the distance between them. "All I want to do is borrow this set of whites for a few minutes."

He couldn't tell if the man understood or believed him. He looked at the meat cleaver again and thought he noticed a tightening of the grip around its dark handle. If the man were going to use it as a weapon, the first movement would have to be upward, a fraction-of-a-second delay that might give him the time he needed, unlike a quick thrust from a butcher knife. The thought surprised him.

Their eyes met briefly again, and Hoffmann saw the movement of the chef's arm. His own arm lashed out in reflex toward the silver blade, covering it with the stained jacket, feeling the hard jolt of the flat metal against his wrist as he stepped forward and crushed his fist into the side of the man's face. His trailing foot arced downward into an instep, and he heard the guttural moan leap from the chef as he staggered sideways. The cleaver clattered to the floor. Hoffmann swung again, this time toward the solar plexus, connecting with yielding flesh as the chef fell to his knees, then rolled to his side gasping for air.

Eric stood over him for a second, shocked at what he had done. His action had been instictive, born of desperation and executed with a savagery he could not explain. The chef was laboring in his attempt to breathe, his eyes rolling up in their sockets.

Hoffmann quickly pulled on the white jacket and went into the kitchen. He located a trash can and picked it up, retracing his steps through the locker room. *Act natural. Become part of the background.* The guiding words from the farm echoed in his ears, forcing him to slow down as he walked toward the far side of the parking lot, where a line of refuse cans stood in the corner beneath the trees. Less than a dozen cars, all unoccupied, sat on this side of the building. He deposited the can, looked around casually, then slipped around the chain-link fence. After shedding his disguise, Hoffmann ducked into a back alley and headed toward the car, his relief at getting away tempered by the memory of the means used.

It took him more than an hour to locate the address on Herzogstrasse among the unfamiliar streets of Schwabing.

He drove by the house, remembering Leahy's warning from their first meeting, and parked two blocks away. The buildings were clustered together in an arrangement that reminded him of the rowhouses in Baltimore, many of them built by German descendants. From across the street, he surveyed the house and decided not to try the front door; an alleyway between buildings appeared to offer access to the back.

His knock at the rear entrance went unanswered.

At last, he broke the pane of glass near the door handle, using a piece of discarded brick from next to the porch. Hoffmann unlocked the catch, and the door swung in.

The house was clean, orderly, without the normal signs of habitation. Glass crunched beneath his feet, sounding thunderously loud to him as he walked across the kitchen. The dining and living rooms were equally devoid of life, and only the faint aroma of tobacco gave any evidence of recent occupation. Intruding this way gave him an uneasy feeling, reminiscent of the night at Gregory's house, and he realized that his chest had grown tight.

"Leahy."

The word echoed in the quietness. No answer.

A stairway led to the second floor, its wooden steps worn and badly in need of refinishing. The boards creaked beneath his feet as he slowly climbed to the upstairs landing. Cautiously, he approached the first door, fighting the overpowering desire to run from the house.

The sound of protesting hinges echoed in the hallway as he pushed the door open. A round wooden table stood in the middle of the room, beneath a bare bulb suspended from the end of a frayed cord; four chairs were scattered in disarray around the table. Eric approached the closet door, hesitated, then opened it.

Staring back at him were the unblinking eyes of Sean Leahy.

Hoffmann's gut tightened; a gasp of revulsion was born, and cut off.

Over the agent's left eyebrow was a small, round wound; running from it, a dried rivulet of blood. The corpse toppled forward onto the aged hardwood.

The floor swayed beneath his feet, as if rocked by the hand of an unseen force. He staggered back, his eyes fixed on the body. *They'll kill you.* The words returned in a rush of fear. Leahy's words. Only an hour ago. A prediction given and fulfilled. But Leahy had died, not he. What had he learned?

His senses returned, and he realized he was on the street, walking away from where he had parked the car. The minutes after finding Leahy were lost behind a veil of panic and disjointed memories of terror-filled flight from the house. He felt detached from what had happened. It was another part of the nightmare, more acute because the agent was the one he felt he could trust. Now he was gone.

Why? Who had killed him? Why had he been allowed to find the body?

The questions swirled through his mind, haunting him. What was known was rarely frightening—but the unknown . . .

He circled away from the house, down unfamiliar streets, cautiously watching the faces of people he passed. The route he took was circuitous, but it led back to the car, his only hope now of leaving the city. He would drive north, to Heidelburg, or maybe west to Augsburg; anywhere away from Munich. There were U.S. Forces in both places. He would locate some high-ranking Army officer and tell his story—names, places, dates. Everything. And hope that some-body would believe him, that somebody would help. It seemed now like the only avenue of escape. He would run away from the unknown, and hope to find refuge in a world that was familiar.

He saw the black sedan approaching as he neared the car.

The blue light on the top and the gray lettering on the door caught his attention as the vehicle came closer POLEZEI. They were slowing, looking at him. Words were exchanged between driver and passenger, and the cruiser stopped.

"Herr Hoffmann."

The officer spoke after closing his door, walking directly toward him. He held what looked like a riot baton, the leather thong around his wrist wrapped tightly through his palm. His voice indicated he was not questioning, only confirming the identification.

"Herr Hoffmann, you will come with us." His partner stood by the front of the sedan, his hand resting on the open flap of a holster.

"What for?"

"More than one violation, according to the bulletin. It will be easier if you don't resist." He looked at Hoffmann and shook his head. "There will be time enough for explanations. I'm afraid you'll be a guest of the German government for a long time."

Chapter 9

"Very strange. . . . Most unusual. Wouldn't you agree, Herr Hoffmann?" The policeman in the right front seat turned and gazed at him through narrowed eyes. "Six hours ago, the hotel chef gave us a perfect description of you—even supplied your name. Now he can't recall exactly what his attacker looked like. Do you find that as hard to believe as I do?"

Hoffmann looked at him, shrugged, and returned to watching the flow of traffic.

He had said nothing during the long hours spent at the Munich police station, giving only his name and vital statistics for the record. With his arraignment scheduled for Monday, he had resigned himself to spending the night in a dark, damp cell barely larger than the single cot whose mattress reeked of old vomit and body odor. His release came as a complete surprise—the officer had been right about that—though his relief was overshadowed by anxiety brought on by another unexplained event.

"Strange, too, that you left your car at the hotel," the officer was saying.

"I was just out walking."

"So far from your hotel?"

"My own personal *Volksmarch*. I believe the government still encourages it." He had not wanted to tell them about the car, or finding Leahy's body; that would only raise more questions, for which he had no answers. Retrieving the car now was out of the question. Whoever killed the agent must know about it, and even if he didn't, he could not develop a story that seemed to have the slightest chance of being believed by the policeman who had arrested him.

The police car turned into the hotel parking lot and stopped at the main entrance. The officer on the passenger side got out to open the rear door.

"We apologize for the inconvenience," the German said flatly, peering at him from beneath the glossy black bill of his cap. "Mistakes sometimes happen. . . . You should remember this."

"Is that a warning?"

"Perhaps. But I would not want to ruin your stay in our country." He touched his cap with a finger, a casual salute, before stepping back inside the car.

Hoffmann watched the car disappear into the evening traffic, then went inside, stopping to look around the lobby. He had come full circle, in the process losing contact with the only man he knew in Germany—a man who had learned something terrible, which had cost him his life.

Full circle. He was certain his return had been by design, the retraction of charges by the chef part of the plan. Whoever it was knew he would not return to the car arranged by Leahy. And the police had brought him here without asking, on orders given by the watch commander. They could have released him at the station, leaving him to find his own transportation. But they had insisted, too forcefully. One of them had to be part of the plan.

But the source control was someone close to Leahy, of that much he was sure. The agent's brief warning had been only too clear. *People I thought I could trust.*

Hoffmann had no intention of returning to the room; beyond that, he had few ideas. He was not a professional—cold, calculating, and totally objective. At the farm they had told him to use that to his advantage, to do the unexpected. Verbiage. They had fed him a diet of platitudes without the staple of experience, wasting their time and his.

He recognized the girl speaking to the hotel clerk.

"Hello. I think I owe you an apology." He stepped toward her as she turned from the desk.

She looked at him with uncomprehending eyes, her expression a mixture of surprise and caution.

"I was in a hurry this morning when we collided outside the dining room. Really, I'm sorry . . . I hope you weren't hurt."

Recognition crept into her face, and with it a hardness that flawed her features. "Oh? You could have said that this morning."

"Something unusual was happening, and I was . . . well, like I said, in a hurry."

"Life or death, I'm sure," she replied, her voice laden with sarcasm.

"Something like that. But I do owe you an apology. When you stepped in front of me, I didn't have time to stop. It was clumsy of me."

"At least *that's* honest enough! But I didn't step in front of you. One doesn't usually expect to encounter a jogger when coming from the dining room." Her voice was strident, pitched higher than normal conversation, and it brought stares from those in the lobby who stood in groups waiting for the announcement that dinner was served. Under most circumstances, he would have found this unutterably embarrassing. That morning she had been an obstacle to be avoided; at the moment, he needed a shield, and her stentorian tirade provided it. No one would risk moving against him while they were the center of attention.

But that would not last long. Already, the girl was snapping her pocketbook closed and hiking the long strap over her shoulder, a gesture that signalled the end of their conversation.

"Could I talk with you a minute? Privately?"

"Why on earth would I want to do that?"

"Because I'm an American, like you, and I'm in trouble. You might be the only one who can help."

Her look held both scorn and disbelief. "That's a novel approach."

"It happens to be true."

"Does this have anything to do with the police? I heard some of the hotel staff talking among themselves this afternoon, after the ambulance arrived. Something about one of the cooks being attacked and beaten."

"It was self-defense."

"And you retaliated by putting him in the hospital?" She drew back from him, her eyes alarmed. "They say his foot is broken, and his jaw may be as well."

"I can explain. But not here. Please, all I want is a couple of minutes. Could we go to your room?"

"My room? Not likely! You *are* crazy."

"The dining room, then." A waitress was swinging the doors open, and people were beginning to move out of the lobby, some of them still casting glances at Hoffmann and the girl. In a moment, the lobby would be emptied, except for the clerk behind the marble counter who was now leafing through yellowed sheets while talking on the phone cradled between his head and shoulder. "Let me buy you dinner."

"I don't even know you. And I don't want any part of whatever trouble you're in."

"You won't be involved, I promise. It costs you nothing to listen. If you decide to help, it may cost you the price of a telephone call. Nothing more. There's two or three dozen people in there, and I'd be a fool to try anything in front of that many witnesses."

The girl looked at him with a trace of the same amusement that had been in her eyes, when she caught him glancing at her during breakfast. "Why should I believe you?"

"I don't know."

"Neither do I. . . . All right, I'll let you buy dinner, But no commitments beyond that."

"Agreed."

He asked the hostess for a booth in the back. It was removed from the other diners, with a view of the entrance into the spacious room. He summoned a waiter and ordered.

"Chateaubriand for two?" the girl said as the carafe of house wine arrived. "This must be some favor you want. That, or you're independently wealthy."

"Wrong on both accounts." Hoffmann sipped the Rhine wine. "I don't even know your name."

"Maggie Reynolds."

"Derived from Margaret?" She nodded, looking at him over the top of her glass. "Maggie seems more appropriate. It has a ring of independence, and . . . self-assurance. You're a college student, or a grad. Outspoken. Probably political."

She smiled amicably, a slight upturning at the corners of her mouth. "You're fairly close." Maggie drank again. "And you?"

"Eric Hoffmann."

"Very pedestrian."

"I'd prefer normal."

"Then why are you so nervous? You've looked over my

shoulder at those doors twenty times in the last three or four minutes."

"It's a habit—looking around. I'm a commercial pilot, and it's something I do all the time while flying."

"You're a very poor liar. Does it have anything to do with this trouble you're in?"

"Yes, it does," Hoffmann replied, watching her eyes. He could not tell her everything; but to gain her cooperation, some of the truth would have to be revealed, tempered with fabrication. "I'm trying to locate my father, or information about him. He was a bomber pilot in the big war, and he disappeared a couple of months before it ended. A few weeks ago I uncovered information that indicated he's still alive, living somewhere in Bavaria—a small town south of here called Murnau. I came to Germany to see if I could find him."

"Why would that cause trouble?"

"Because somebody doesn't want me to locate him. I don't know why. I don't have any idea why he would stay in Germany all these years. And somebody is trying to make sure I don't find out. Since I got here Friday, I've received two warnings—a note and a phone call. This morning another message—from the chef who tried to end my trip with a meat cleaver."

Her eyes rounded. "Go to the police."

"They won't listen. I'm a foreigner, an American. And they've had their fill of grief from G.I. troublemakers over the years. This afternoon, when I told them what happened, they laughed it off. They may even be involved with whoever it is that's been threatening me." He glanced around the room again, and saw the hostess looking at him from near the door. Another couple entered the dining room, and the woman seated them near the far window.

"If they didn't believe you, why aren't you in jail?" Maggie asked after a long minute.

"Because the chef dropped all charges. They wanted me

back on the streets; they wanted me here. Now can you see why I asked you to help?"

She stared at him, the aloofness of the previous moment absent. "You're really serious. This isn't some wild and woolly line." Maggie fell silent, averting her eyes briefly. Then she looked back at him, without kindness. "You said I wouldn't be involved. But I am. Just sitting here with you means I am, if what you say is true."

"You're not, really," he said, knowing it was a lie. Out of desperation, he had brought this girl into circumstances from which he might not be able to free her. He had approached her with only self-preservation in mind, and now the look on her face compounded his guilt.

"You had no right! I should have driven up to Nuremberg today with the others. . . . I won't help you. We agreed: no commitments."

"All you have to do is make a phone call," Hoffmann said, a controlled tone masking his uneasiness.

"Not even that. I thought you might need to borrow some money, or maybe wanted a ride to the American consulate. But nothing like this." He saw the tension on her face, heard it in her voice. She had been playing with him before, outside, but the game had changed, and the rules were now unacceptable. She studied him in silence, her eyes no longer angry, but frightened. "Why did you pick me?"

"Because you're an American. The fact that you spoke to me in English this morning didn't register at first, not until after I left the hotel.

"And this evening?"

"Chance."

"Or my bad luck."

"You won't think so when the dinner arrives. Of course, you could get up and leave now. That's always an option."

"I should."

"Maybe."

"You don't think I will."

"I'm hoping you won't. The longer I can keep you here, the better my chances that you'll help. I want that help. I need it. But I'd be lying if I said that was the smartest thing for you to do." He picked up the wineglass and shrugged, looking directly into her eyes. By saying the words, he had assuaged his conscience, leaving the decision with her.

"That's patently offensive."

"What is?"

"Putting it that way. Leaving it up to me. If I walk away now, I'll always wonder whether or not you're telling the truth. I'll never know if I could have stopped something dreadful from happening to another human being by making a simple phone call. Damn you, that's unfair."

"You still have a choice. Like you said—no commitments."

The kitchen doors swung open, pushed aside by a serving cart propelled by the waiter who had taken their order. He positioned it next to their booth and spooned soup from a deep ceramic tureen, but Hoffmann's eyes were on the hostess who was approaching the table. Anxiety written on her white, powdered face which contrasted in a striking way to the dark, floor-length gown.

"Miss Reynolds?" She asked. "There is a phone call. From California."

Maggie's face drained of color, her hand tightened around the napkin. "My father?"

"The desk clerk will direct you to a phone." The woman darted a quick glance at Hoffmann, then back to the girl. She hesitated a second, as if about to speak, then turned abruptly and walked away.

Maggie looked at Hoffmann. "I was afraid this might happen. He had bypass surgery a month before I left, and there were complications. I wanted to stay, but he insisted. He said I'd probably never get to Europe if I didn't go now." She shook her head from side to side. "I *will* be back."

Before he could reply, she slid out of the booth. Hoffmann tried to stand, but his way was blocked by the waiter who was placing the small bowl on a placemat in front of him. Soup spilled on the cloth, followed by an apology, distracting him. The man reached out with a cloth to absorb the brown liquid.

"Listen closely," he said, the words spoken just above a whisper, the accent gone. Hoffmann saw the automatic, its short barrel swollen with a silencer. The waiter positioned himself, shielding the gun from other diners. "Keep your hands on the table. Everything up front. Your first movement will be your last. Follow my directions without question . . . without hesitation. There are others." The voice carried an unmistakable tone of authority, indicating its owner was accustomed to being obeyed.

No! he wanted to shout, his mind on the girl who was disappearing through the doors. "She's not involved."

"We know. When I tell you, we're going to walk out of here, through the lobby, and down the hallway toward your room."

"I won't."

"Yes, you will. If you give me any trouble, it will trigger a sudden commotion across the room. A spilled tray. Broken china. A loud, irate customer, and confusion as other waiters move to help. It will last only a few seconds—more than enough time. In the most unlikely event you get by me, you'll find the only clear avenue leads to the kitchen. It will not offer you an escape route this time."

Hoffmann looked past the man and surveyed the room. It was true.

Waiters' trays had been located strategically in the aisles, a maze completed when the man served their appetizer. Two others on the staff moved toward him, straightening silverware on nearby tables; they were isolating him. Silently, efficiently, the trap had been drawn taut.

The waiter stepped back, replacing the weapon. "Get up slowly and walk to the first aisle, and then to the entrance. I'm right behind you. Don't stop for anything or anybody. And don't turn around."

Hoffmann rose and followed the directions, watching the path silently and unobtrusively cleared. In his peripheral vision, he could see the carefully orchestrated movements confirming the earlier warning. A glimpse of a profile at the far corner table removed any doubt. He had seen the face once before, for a fraction of a second, less than five days ago. In Virginia.

The lobby was empty.

"We've got less than a minute," the waiter said, his voice louder and more relaxed when they entered the hall. "Continue to the exit."

"Where are you taking me?"

"You'll find out soon enough."

They turned down an adjoining corridor; the door at the far end stood open, revealing a nondescript sedan parked at the curb, its motor running, the smell of exhaust fumes more pronounced as they drew closer. He passed the final doorway, and Hoffmann recognized the driver—one of Leahy's men, from the security team that had picked him up that night and driven him back to the hotel.

People I thought I could trust.

Hoffmann's body tensed an instant before he stopped, coiling to drive his back into the wall and turn on the man behind him.

In that instant of hesitation, he felt the stiff arm blow between his shoulder blades, jolting through his back and sending him off balance. The rear door of the sedan opened, and he was pushed inside. His head snapped sideways against the cushion as the sedan sped from the lot.

*   *   *

Rain beat a steady tattoo on the roof and ran down the windows in streams, blurring the scene outside the car, distorting the lights of other vehicles and the eerie shadows cast by streetlamps. The man in the back seat with him finally spoke after they left the main thoroughfare, slowing on a narrow residential street.

"Relax. It's over. You've had a hell of a scare these past few days. Sorry, we didn't have any time for long explanations." A match flared in the man's hand and was replaced by the full glow from his cigarette. "You're with friends . . . Roy Locke. I think you know Edison and Renzetti."

"I thought—"

"You didn't know what to think. Leahy counted on that. It was designed to increase the confusion."

"Increase . . . ? Why?"

"Leahy was a mole. He worked for us—at least it appeared that way. His orders actually came from the East Germans."

"You knew that?"

"Suspected. A few of us, anyway. Kind of a gut feeling we couldn't nail down. And that was only in recent days, except for one man in Washington who hasn't trusted him for years. The night before last was the confirmation—he engineered the incident with one of their operatives."

Hoffmann looked away, trying to make sense of this astonishing revelation, attempting to compare it to what he remembered of the agent's actions. It was impossible. He was certain of Leahy's nature; he couldn't have been wrong, not that far off. He *trusted* Leahy.

"I don't believe you," he said finally.

"That's understandable. He fooled us for a long time. He was smart, and he was discreet. Exceptionally. Leahy had the best cover around, a cover he developed and continually perfected. I expect they'll be using his example for a long time, now that we know." Locke reached inside of his coat and pulled out a weapon. "Yours, I believe. Number

115623—they still teach you to memorize your weapon's serial number in the Army, I expect. We found it in your room before the police searched."Locke worked the action, chambering a round. "What you probably don't know is that it doesn't work. The firing pin has been filed just enough so it won't."

A metallic click followed. Locke repeated the sequence twice more, with identical results.

"If you think they're dummy bullets, check for yourself." Hoffmann gazed at the end of the rounds, illuminated by Locke's match. The primer caps were unmarked. "He fed you a false sense of security, one you would have carried with you to Herzogstrasse. It was another edge for him in case something went wrong."

"But he was dead when I got there. Was it you?" A vision of Leahy's face as he'd last seen it came and went. He was sitting with the agent's executioners, and the thought was as sickening as it was frightening.

"We didn't do it. Not directly. I told you his cover was the best; in the end, it was his own cover that got him.

"Leahy set himself up as a gun dealer almost four years ago. Smuggling. Black market. And he was good at it. It also allowed him to travel alone, to disappear for days. He arranged sales to African governments and private interests. He knew most of the for-hire military types on the continent; a year ago he got in the middle of a feud between two French mercs. Got them bidding against one another for a consignment of Heckler and Koch submachine guns. Then he made the mistake of shorting the winner on ammunition when the shipment was made. Nasty business. Today, he got paid back." The cigarette glowed and was tapped out in an ashtray. "We supplied the location. If that bothers you, just remember that it would have been you instead of him. Sobering, isn't it?"

"But not necessarily true. You could have rigged the

weapon yourself. And I don't have any way of checking the story you just gave me." His initial shock had worn away. He would *demand* evidence this time.

"Let's go back to the beginning, then," Locke said. "The first contact with him at Langenbruck."

"Further back than that. Back to Carnahan and Gregory. Who is Carnahan? Does he . . . exist?"

They passed through a quiet intersection, beneath a lonely streetlamp which momentarily illuminated the back seat. Surprise was etched on the agent's face.

"What do you mean, does he exist? You met him."

"I met somebody who claimed to be Carnahan. There's nobody by that name in the State Department running our European policy."

There was silence.

"Who told you?" Locke's tone turned accusatory, ominous. "Leahy?"

"Yes," Hoffmann lied, still cautious.

The driver glanced into the back seat, using the rearview mirror. "He would have known. The two of them worked together once in South America."

Locke nodded, apparently satisfied. "Another layer of confusion—he could have told you they worked together," he said. The agent lit a cigarette and continued. "Carnahan used to sit at the right hand of power. He's been moved, set on the shelf—a tiny Caribbean island. State set up a flap when they found out he was using them, and our organization didn't like his excesses. Gregory was one of them. The old man was hiring ex-pros for training Moslem extremists; there were other ways of dealing with him. I guess Carnahan was pretty proud of how he recruited you. Most of us who know, weren't. That's all you'll get—and it's probably more than I should have given.

"Back to Leahy. He personally checked your room the morning of the first contact instead of assigning it to one of his team. Not altogether unusual, but it became one of many question marks when Edison found a device on your phone later. What do you remember about the first contact?"

"He told me I should have driven be the *gasthaus* before stopping, and that I should have parked along the side. But I'm sure he said somebody else was checking out my room."

"Was he late?"

"About fifteen minutes."

"He was late because *he* checked your room and left a bug."

"But he saw me drive up and walk in."

"He guessed. If you had actually done what he later suggested, he would have claimed mistaken identity. Remember, he'd never met you. My guess is that you beat him there because you drove twice as fast as you normally do back in the States. How fast does an Audi travel? I'm sure you knew by the time you got to Langenbruck. Leahy couldn't catch you."

"I could have started out early and stopped somewhere."

"In that case Leahy would have been on time. We can belabor the point more if you like, but the answers will be the same. Let's move on to that night. Renzetti arrived from Washington with instructions, and they went over it together with Edison. It was the first time Leahy knew the whole picture; from then on, he was accompanied by one or the other of them except when he was with you. During the briefing, he left the room and was gone for ten or fifteen minutes."

"He said he was checking security."

Locke shook his head, exhaling a cloud of smoke. "Why? Because he couldn't trust them to follow simple instructions? Edison."

Again, the driver looked into the mirror, adjusting it so he could see Hoffmann's face this time. "I was at the end of the hall. He could see me from your door. When he came out, he said he'd gotten a call about an SMLM sighting. Things just happened after that, but yesterday afternoon I checked. Nobody had anything on record."

"Then after the shooting that night, he did—or failed to do—two things that convinced us something was really off," Locke went on. "He didn't place a man in your room with you. And he didn't move you. Doesn't it stand to reason that, if somebody was close enough to find you on the streets, they were close enough to know where you were staying? He was setting you up."

"If he wanted to kill me, he had any number of chances."

"None that offered a sure escape after the first contact. He wasn't suicidal."

"Yet you want me to believe he was this morning," Hoffmann countered. Was he trying to defend Leahy because he still didn't believe what he was hearing? Or because he couldn't admit his judgment had been so poor. "It doesn't make sense. Why would he take the chance?"

"Because he knew we were on to him. His options suddenly narrowed—and he also knew the stakes. We know he never got the chance to pass along what he learned about your mission. It was a last-ditch effort; predictable, I think, when you put yourself in his position."

Hoffmann leaned back in the seat, closing his eyes, suddenly tired by the mental exercise. Leahy had tried to talk him out of carrying through with the mission, the most convincing and compelling reason for trusting him. Confusion—the agent had been the source of it all along. The subtle hints had been there, he saw clearly, feeling mocked by his inability to understand them before. "I should have known. It was right in front of me."

"Not necessarily. Like I said, we weren't sure—positively sure—until yesterday, and we had more information than you. Nothing's been compromised, the situation is stable.

We continue from here. You're checked out of the hotel. Your belongings are in the back."

"You arranged for my release?"

"Hospitalization costs and a substantial punitive payment for the chef; a small bribe to the police. The form said you had an aptitude. I think you corroborated that to a certain degree today, although not totally. Using the girl wasn't bad—as far as you went; but it didn't go far enough. When you stopped, it gave us time to organize and move. The dining room was one of several contingencies. If you had kept the situation fluid, we had others."

"She doesn't know anything."

"The girl? What did you tell her?"

"That I was in Germany looking for my father. I told her I'd received some threats from people who didn't want me to locate him, and the chef was one of them. She didn't want to get involved."

"Did she buy it?"

"I don't know."

Locked breathed deeply, shaking his head, thinking. "We can't completely disregard her, but I doubt any harm's been done. If we're lucky, she'll forget it after getting over being stuck for the check. When she gets home, it might make interesting conversation at a cocktail party."

"How did you arrange the phone call?"

"There was none. Our man saw you talk to her this morning. We didn't know how she was related. A quick background check was made, and the information became part of a scenario. As it turned out, it was useful." Locke rolled down the window and flicked the cigarette butt into the street. "You're still a little confused, uncertain. There are other questions running around the back of your mind that we haven't answered, at least not to your satisfaction. I don't know that we ever will."

"But the mission is still on?"

"Yes. The East Germans know nothing."

Hoffmann looked at the agent's face, only an outline in the darkness. "You're sure?"

"Absolutely."

Chapter 10

Berlin. Eastern sector. A gray pall hung over the city.

From where the man stood, gazing out of the fourth-floor window, the streets appeared deserted. A trolley wound its way around the corner two blocks away, rocking slowly from side to side, then stopped as a single passenger descended to the cobblestone street, still wet from the drizzle. The city seemed forlorn, a marked contrast to the first time the observer had seen it. But that had been many years before. He had been young then.

Hitler was conducting his intensive political campaign in the summer of 1932, outshouting all other campaigners. It was a time of freewheeling politics, charges and countercharges, torchlight parades. Six months later, Hitler was Chancellor. Celebration. The first of many.

The Thousand-Year Reich was born.

More victories followed. The Sudetenland. Austria. Poland. Greece. Crete. The Sixth Army marched through the streets of Paris, beneath the Arc de Triomphe.

Berlin celebrated.

But finally the celebrations ended.

Even before the Russians entered the city, it died. By day, the Americans came with their precision patchwork bombing; by night, the British. The once alive and beautiful city shuddered, groaned, and was still, Der Führer's suicide the final punctuation. Now there were two Berlins, divided by a grotesque wall, separated by ideology.

The man at the window continued to stare at the scene below, his hatred of those victorious nations a festering sore which had never healed. Germany—his Germany—would someday be whole again. It was his one remaining dream.

Heinrich Schellen turned from the office window and looked at the Russian who sat on the sofa across from his desk, drinking a brandy that had not been offered. Yuri Kasimirov. Schellen knew him as one who had long ago retreated from individual conscience or thought, a man who no longer knew the difference between right and wrong, good or evil. He knew only the State—and its will.

"*Nein!*" Schellen said angrily. "I will not do it."

Kasimirov said nothing. He enjoyed watching the pompous German squirm, having made a career of doing the same to others, though usually of lesser stature than the East German Minister of Transport. Kasimirov knew the German hated him, a realization from which he derived even greater pleasure.

"You can tell the minister that I will not do any more than I have done already," Schellen continued. "And you are out of order to come here, especially under false pretenses, and even suggest such a thing."

Kasimirov casually swirled the dark brown liquid in the snifter. "Are you saying, then, you won't cooperate with the Soviet Union as directed by your government?"

Schellen stopped pacing and eyed the Russian coolly, weighing his response to the carefully phrased question. "I say no such thing," he replied. "You seem to indicate that my government has not cooperated with the Soviet Union. Three decades of history prove you wrong."

"Your grasp of history is commendable," the Russian said with feigned courtesy, raising his glass in a toast. "But the case at hand is not your government's actions; rather it is yours."

"I have always followed the directions of my country. My record speaks for itself."

"Then why do you hesitate now?"

"Because you are not my government."

"Yes, true. But Herr Gessler assured us of your total cooperation from the beginning. Now you say you won't do what is necessary . . . and it is such a simple thing."

"If it is so simple, employ a double. The Americans are easily fooled. There is no reason for me to be at the pickup point. I am a busy man, especially now, and there is much to be done."

"We must be sure, though. Nothing can be left to chance."

"Even if they weren't fooled, you have lost nothing. You said yourself that if the plan failed, nothing could or would be used by the West."

"Yes, but that was two weeks ago," Kasimirov countered. "Comrade Brezhnev is becoming more concerned over U.S. relations with the Chinese. He wants to be able to use this as a bargaining chip. It is important that the Americans not be scared off."

Schellen moved to the small bar and poured himself a drink. The Russian was well prepared, and although he hadn't threatened to go to Gessler, the warning had been neatly inserted in the conversation, so it could not be discounted. And Gessler was an enemy to be reckoned with.

"I will consider your proposal," Schellen said finally, his back still to the other man. "I will give you my answer tomorrow."

"Fine," said Kasimirov. He rose. A smile of satisfaction creased his face. "You know how to contact me. We can meet in my office at the embassy."

Schellen turned to face him. He disliked Kasimirov's superior manner; more than that, he distrusted him. He wanted to meet in familiar surroundings, where he could control the atmosphere, a placed removed from Russian recording devices. Years of experience had made him cautious. "No, you will come here tomorrow. One o'clock."

"Meeting here is agreeable, if that makes you more comfortable." The condescending tone held. "I'm sure you'll make the right decision."

Schellen offered no reply. His eyes followed as Kasimirov turned and left the room.

Heinrich Schellen began to pace. He knew he was being maneuvered into a position from which there was little chance of escape. From the beginning, when he had been ordered to contact the Americans to stage a supposed defection, he had seen it as a plot to remove him from power. Permanently. And Berthold Gessler was behind it; of that, he was certain.

Even now, the government could have him before a people's court and brand him a traitor. A "confession" could easily be obtained; the public trial would seal his fate. He knew, because it was a sequence he had often used himself.

The Russian was right, Schellen thought. The answer to Kasimirov's question was a foregone conclusion. They had told him he must complete all the arrangements and follow them through to the very last minute, including being at the pickup point.

The Russians were pleased. They would have their incident, and eliminate him for Gessler at the same time.

Maybe.

Schellen had not survived for twenty-nine years simply by luck. He poured another cognac, then sat in his favorite overstuffed chair to contemplate. There was a way to survive.

It would mean the end of a three-decade old dream, but that was now secondary. He would have to call in many old debts, and making the arrangements would entail great risk. But it could be done.

The only problem was time.

Berthold Gessler waited in Kasimirov's austere office for the Russian to return.

"What did he say?" the East German asked when Kasimirov entered.

"He said no, which is what I expected. He's been around long enough to be able to see things very much as they really are. Your scheme is quite transparent—any fool could see what you're doing." He hung his coat on a rack next to the door, walked behind his desk, and sat in the big swivel chair.

"I'll have to apply more pressure, then."

"That shouldn't be necessary. He wanted some time to think it over. In the end, he'll agree to do it. There's no other choice for him. We meet again tomorrow at one o'clock. I'll have his answer then."

"It is important that he be caught in the act of defecting. He still has some powerful allies, and they must be given no way to refute that Schellen is any enemy of the State."

"Don't worry, our plan is sound. And it was nice of the Americans to choose a helicopter pickup. It's an easy matter to follow the aircraft route once it's inside your border. Just be sure your arrangements are thorough."

"They are, believe me. The site will be ringed with automatic weapons, and extra fighters will be on alert. We've already begun to reinforce the border outposts—very quietly, of course."

"You see," Kasimirov said, gesturing expansively, "it is really very simple."

"I hope so. We should all be much better off within the next two weeks."

Kasimirov leaned back in his chair and stared at the ceiling as he lit a cigarette. When this assignment was over, he would surely be due a promotion, and he hoped it would provide him the leverage to secure a transfer to his native Georgia. These Germans, he thought, were a disgusting culture to deal with.

It was nearly midnight when Schellen arrived home. A damp chill was in the house, and he shivered as he stacked wood on the hearth in his bedroom. Moments later the embryo of a fire licked at the logs, cracking and popping, until at last he had a warming blaze started. He rubbed his hands over it, then threw the heavy coat and bearskin hat on the foot of his bed, and walked down the hallway to the kitchen.

He descended the stairs leading to the wine cellar. The musty smell of damp wood and concrete permeated the basement where he stored a private stock of only the best wines, his compromise with a higher standard of living. Though not allowed to the working masses, it was not unusual among government officials.

Schellen carefully removed three dozen bottles from two shelves on the right wall. Heavy layers of dust covered the wine rack, but after a careful search he located the wooden plugs hiding recessed screws by which both shelves were connected to the upright. These he removed and placed in his pocket.

Using an old screwdriver, he removed the screws and placed them in his pocket also. Next, he lifted the empty shelves slowly and carefully, trying to disturb as little of the accumulated dust as possible. Then he removed a two-foot—square section of the heavy wooden paneling which served as the backing to his wine rack, exposing an aged brick wall.

The exertion winded him, and he was forced to rest.

Despite the relatively low temperature, beads of sweat glistened on his forehead and upper lip. The moisture rolled down the back of his neck, wetting his shirt collar. It took several minutes before he was ready to continue.

With the screwdriver, he wedged out the mortar around four of the bricks. Painstakingly, he pulled them from the wall and laid them on the floor. Taking a handkerchief from his pocket, he again wiped perspiration from his face and neck before returning to his task.

He reached into the wall cavity and retrieved a package wrapped in a waterproof liner. It represented more then two decades of painstaking work in compiling a list of former SS members still living in Eastern Block countries. This, he hoped, would be his passport out.

After unwrapping the package, Schellen took out a small pad and a pencil. For two hours, he methodically poured over the lists, stopping occasionally to write a name with its address and serial number. His work completed, he neatly folded the papers and returned them to the waterproof container, reversing the original sequence of dismantling the rack. In thirty minutes the wine bottles were again on their shelves, all traces of the night's work carefully concealed.

By the time the German crawled between the sheets of his bed, it was just past 2:30 A.M. Monday morning. The Minister of Transport slept the sleep of a tormented soul.

Chapter 11

"Schellen owns a cottage just east of Heiligenstadt on the Leine River, several miles inside the border. That's where he's to be picked up."

Hoffmann drank from a large gray ceramic mug as he listened to Locke's explanation, watching the agent circle the location on a map. They sat in the small kitchen of a house in Karlsfeld, north of Munich, only a few miles from what remained of the Dachau extermination camp. It was ten minutes before eight, and outside the evening sky was dark, as it had been the previous night when Locke brought him to the cottage.

"Schellen always takes an early-morning walk when he's there," the agent was saying. "He's a creature of habit." Locke glanced up from the map, paused, and said, "You haven't heard a thing I've told you. Tired? We can do this later if you want to take a break."

"No. Let's keep at it."

The briefing had been going on for more than an hour,

since his return from Deutches Aero. He had explained in
detail his first day, answering the agent's questions, summa-
rizing his impressions of the air-charter company and the
man who ran it. Gerber had wasted little time on idle
conversation, reducing their first meeting to a few sentences
on policies and pay scales, followed by a tour of the operation
which sat diagonally across the airport from the main terminal.
Following lunch, they took off on an orientation flight south
of Munich in the direction of the snow-covered Alps, with
Gerber pointing out local landmarks used by the tower for
traffic control. The day had passed quickly, each step run
with what Hoffmann guessed was typical German precision.
Although the chief pilot had not been unfriendly, he had
been aloof, wary of the outsider.

"He always walks his dog, a big shepherd," Locke said.
"When you pick him up, he'll be wearing a bright red
hunting jacket and smoking a pipe. You've seen recent photographs of him in the dossier."

"I need to know exactly how the area is laid out—fields,
roads, houses. What about maps?"

"We've got a packet for you. One to fifty thousand scale
military versions. Air Force intelligence provided some low,
oblique aerial photos that our Imagery Analysis section had
enhanced. Our biggest concern is the weather."

"Morning fog."

Locke nodded. "Visibility is usually less than half a mile
until midmorning. But I guess you know that."

"What time is the pickup scheduled?"

"Nine-thirty. Ten days from now. Thursday of next week."

Hoffmann stared across the table at the agent, aware that he
hadn't felt the full significance of what he was about to do
until this moment. Ten days. He'd have to memorize the
routes in and out; a visual reconnaissance from the air needed
to be made. Heiligenstadt was over three hundred kilometers
from Munich, according to Locke's map, and that meant a

refueling stop before crossing over. How? Where? His mind filled with questions; too many unknowns. Ten days—closer to nine now—and he needed volumes of information. Border strengths. Antiaircraft sites. high-performance aircraft in the area. The whole crazy idea took on the form of a military operation. A secret war.

"I don't know if that's enough time," Hoffmann said at last.

"That's all you've got."

"Are we absolutely sure Schellen will be at the pickup point on time?"

"Within reason. Like I said, his actions are predictable."

"You mean you're not sure?"

"I didn't say that."

"What are you saying? He's got to be at a specific point where I can set down, at an exact time. You're making it sound like the whole thing is being ad-libbed."

Locke cut him off with a withering look. "We know what's required. There won't be any surprises." He reached for his briefcase, a black metal container next to the table. "Everything is in here. The Missions and Programs staff has been working on it since Schellen first contacted us. I'd be surprised if you had any questions after looking through the packet. . . . And none of it is ad-libbed." The agent handed over an unmarked binder, then sat back and lit a cigarette, watching as Hoffmann scanned the pages.

"You're right," Hoffmann admitted. "It's thorough. I'll need time to study it."

"Memorize it," Locke corrected.

"If I can."

"You'd better. That's the only copy in existence; even the typewriter ribbon was destroyed. That file doesn't leave my sight, and I'm not going to be with you every waking hour."

A car pulled up outside the back door, and Locke's hand went inside his jacket, reaching for the automatic in the shoulder bolster. Motioning to Hoffmann, he crossed to the door, turned off the light, and pulled the curtain aside. Seconds later, the door opened and Edison stepped inside.

"There's been a change in plans," the agent said. "It just came in. Schellen changed his mind."

Hoffmann and Locke worked under the harsh glare of a table lamp in an upstairs room. The clock on a scarred bureau showed it was almost midnight.

"Why the hell did he do that?" Hoffmann asked, throwing his pencil down in frustration after locating the town on a map. Zdikov. A small village in Czechoslovakia. He disliked it immediately. "It's almost twenty miles inside the border. At least double—maybe triple—the flying time. At sixty knots, I'm inside the border for more than half an hour."

"Our people are working up another brief on the area." Locke got up, walked to the window, and peered outside, then lowered himself onto the bed by the wall, stretching and stifling a yawn. "There's bound to be a good reason."

"Are they on to him? Why else would he move the location and set the day up to next Tuesday?"

"We don't know—yet."

"Something's wrong. I don't like it."

"Neither do we," Locke said grimly.

"But you're not the one who has to pick him up." Hoffmann looked back at the map and shook his head. "Flying in the mountains is another level of difficulty. Compared to this, the other plan was simple."

The spot elevations showed mountain ranges that rose to more than four thousand feet, long ridge lines describing narrow valleys—low-lying areas to trap and hold the dense mountain fog. And there was always the unknown of electric cables or telephone lines stretching between peaks, unseen, and deadly for what they wanted him to do.

"Can it be done?" Locke asked, leaning toward the table

and crushing out his cigarette, smothering stray ashes that sent up tiny spirals of smoke.

"Are you giving me a choice?"

"Only asking a question."

"I don't know." He was about to say that anything was possible, given the right circumstances. "In this case—with the prevailing weather and damned little time—I'd say it's not promising. If you want the truth, I think all of you are part of the lunatic fringe." Hoffmann rubbed his eyes, feeling drained. How long had it been since he'd had a decent night's sleep? When he looked up seconds later, the agent was peering through the window again.

"Two cars," Locke said absently, pulling the curtain aside.

"What two—?"

The sound of automatic weapons firing and tires screeching drowned out the remainder of his question. Downstairs, glass shattered. Locke ran from the window toward the bedroom door.

"Move!" he yelled at Hoffmann. They ran out into the upstairs hallway.

Edison appeared at the foot of the stairs. "Firebomb. Through the front window. Half the downstairs is on fire."

"Anybody hit?" Locke yelled to make himself heard above the hoarse bark of automatic weapons.

"Renzetti. In the shoulder. Not bad."

Locke took the steps two at a time, with Hoffmann close behind. He looked through the shattered front window, then moved away at a crouch. "You and Renzetti cover me," he said to Edison. "I've got to get Hoffmann out of here."

They reached the kitchen, and Locke took a quick look outside, then threw the door open as he dove to the ground, rolling toward Hoffmann's Audi, which Edison had retrieved late Sunday night. He pushed himself up on a knee and looked over the hood.

"Come on," the agent yelled.

Eric ran from the house, bent over low from the waist.

"We'll have to walk out," Locke said. "This way."

Together, they ran across the field behind the house into a stand of trees a hundred yards away. Ten minutes later, after battling through undergrowth and low-hanging tree limbs that cut at their faces, they came to a stream.

"There's a road off to the right that leads into Munich. We'll try to find a phone booth so I can make a call and get a car out here to pick us up."

Hoffmann said nothing as he tried to catch his breath. He turned and looked back in the direction of the house, where the brightness of the fire reflected off a low cloud cover. In the distance was the mournful wail of sirens, their warbling tones piercing the now quiet night. He saw Locke move, then followed the agent through the cold, ankle-deep water.

They paralled a road for another half-mile. A phone booth sat on the corner of a crossroads beyond a small open field. They approached it cautiously. Locke slipped inside, leaving the door open so the interior light stayed off. Minutes later, he slid back down the enbankment to where Hoffmann was waiting in the shadows.

"We'll have a car here in ten minutes," the agent said, cupping a match as he lit a cigarette.

"What about Edison and Renzetti?"

"They can handle themselves."

"My car?"

"We'll square it with the police and the rental agency. Cold? You're shivering."

"Damn right. But it's not just the temperature. What's going on?" His breath came out as small clouds of condensation; a wave of nausea came and went, a reaction to functioning on nervous energy.

"Must be Leahy's people. What's left of them. It's conceivable, anyhow."

"But you don't know."

"No. But we have ways of finding out. We'll know before sunrise. In any event, we won't let you out of our sight. . . . Except, of course, when you're flying."

"You *are* mad. I won't do it. Not now."

"You aren't in a position to refuse," Locke said.

"And you aren't in a position to make me go through with it. Not after this. The whole thing could blow up in your face. What if they *know?*"

Locke breathed deeply, then said, "We'll talk about it in the morning. You've been under a lot of pressure."

The words had a ring of finality.

Bill Knight sat at his desk. As usual, it was neat and orderly; the wood glistened beneath a freshly applied coat of wax, a single file the only work before him. It was after 10:00 P.M., Washington time, but not an unusual hour to find the Deputy Director of the CIA at work. Knight listened attentively as the voice on the telephone, thousands of miles away in Germany, continued the explanation.

"How is Hoffmann bearing up?" Knight asked curtly.

"Better than we expected, but he's exhausted, confused, and scared."

"Stay on top of him."

"We are, sir."

"Keep me informed directly. And another thing . . ."

"Yes, sir?"

"Don't be afraid to make the decision if you have to. I don't need a mess on my hands because some agent in the field lacks guts. Understand?"

"Perfectly."

"I knew you would." The Deputy Director placed the phone on its cradle, then closed the file and stared at it for a moment before locking it in the bottom right drawer.

The file was marked with a single name: Lieutenant Kenneth M. Hoffmann, U.S. Army Air Corps.

The Deputy Director left the office shortly before 11:00 P.M. But instead of heading toward his Alexandria, Virginia, home, he pointed the big Pontiac northwest. He hadn't bothered to call his wife, Carolyn, to tell her he'd be late; not that it mattered. The marriage hadn't really been one for six years, since his return from the last field assignment in Viet Nam; their living together was now an arrangement of convenience. She liked the social life Washington offered, and, as the wife of a high official, many doors were opened to her. That she had had a string of affairs was no secret to him, though it was never mentioned. His only demand was that she not flaunt them publicly; aside from that, he couldn't care less.

Bill Knight used the Washington office as his excuse for never being home and as a cover for his own affairs. Although the Agency's headquarters were at Langley, he rarely worked there, preferring the office on Pennsylvania Avenue because of its close proximity to the decision-making machinery of government.

More than once he had been able to head off trouble with quick personal visits to the lawmakers before events got out of hand. He got an unsolicited reputation as the Agency's lobbyist because of his frequent visits to Capitol Hill, and rumor in certain Washington circles held that his attendance record at roll-call votes was better than that of half the Democrats in Congress. But most congressmen respected his opinions on foreign affairs, and this had saved the Agency from some possibly embarrassing situations on a score of occasions. What people didn't know was that most of these visits were made out of desperation, to save himself from the personal embarrassment that disclosure of CIA activities would cause. Lately, the visits had become more frequent.

As he left the city, his thoughts were on a recent meeting with the Senate Subcommittee on Assassinations. Someone had resurrected long-forgotten tapes of the presidential motorcade in Dallas—tapes he knew would show beyond doubt that shots had come from a grassy knoll as well as the Book Depository. Senator Billingsworth had a new lawyer looking into the evidence, an earnest young man recently graduated from Harvard Law School who was out to make a name for himself. It was an irritating development, especially now.

Knight took the Hyattstown exit from the Interstate and turned south toward the Potomac, navigating the winding road with a sure hand. This was not his first excursion to the estate near the Maryland foothills. Seven miles farther, he turned onto an unmarked road, slowing as he negotiated the winding gravel path strewn with potholes and fallen limbs. After another mile, a wrought-iron gate barred his path. Knight inserted a plastic card in a receptacle and waited for the barrier to swing open. Six hundred yards later, he stopped in front of a dimly lit mansion protected by towering maple and oak, and walked into the house. He was twenty minutes early for the meeting.

One by one, the other four men who had been summoned arrived at the antebellum estate, each driven by a chauffeur trained at Camp Peary in southern Virginia. These were the men who had inherited Dovetail. Their survival was insured by the assignment of handpicked bodyguards, including one who wore the uniform of an Army captain on whom records had never existed in the Pentagon.

Only one of the attendees was familiar to the general public—the senator from New Hampshire, F. Douglas Emory. His lined face and striking white hair cropped up constantly on network talk shows, and he was an oft-quoted spokesman for liberal causes in his home state as well as on the banquet circuit. Surprisingly, his voting record was only marginally left of center, an inconsistency known to few.

The next to arrive was General Harrison Shockley, familiar to a generation of G.I.'s as "the Shocker," a trim man of fifty-four years who looked as if he were still capable of leading a tank battalion in combat as he had done under Patton. Shockley's unit had been the first to relieve the beleaguered garrison at Bastogne, a war story that surfaced after his first half-dozen shots of Old Grand-dad during officer's calls at the club. The Army's Deputy Chief of Staff had a reputation as a hard drinker.

The third man was responsible for presidential security. He was a middle-aged ex-Marine who still wore a flat top, as he had while playing linebacker at Clemson, and he appeared to be a coiled mass of tension ready to explode. His life was tedium punctuated by moments of terror; it was generally agreed that Gordon Upshaw's job was the most thankless in Washington.

Last to arrive was Clifton Redwood, who acted as principal counsel to the Senate Foreign Relations Committee, to which Senator Emory belonged.

The living room served as a conference room during the rare meetings of these five men. They sat around a large coffee table in leather-covered armchairs, saying nothing, as Shockley poured himself two fingers of bourbon from a crystal decanter at the bar. At last, Douglas Emory spoke.

"I've called this meeting because I'm concerned," the senator said, looking at the other faces around the table. "Tell me where we are on the schedule, each of you. Mr. Deputy Director? You first, I would think."

Knight loosened his tie and began. "We should see the first signs of unrest inside Poland by next weekend. Food strikes are expected to begin on the following Sunday, when the factories are shut down. My agents there say—"

"Yes, what do they say?" the lawyer cut in. "You keep alluding to them, but I'm still not convinced the Polish Secret Service hasn't coopted your whole network."

Senator Emory silenced Redwood with a disapproving stare. "We've heard you voice that before, Clifton. The Deputy Director has explained—at least to my satisfaction—that the stories we've been told on the subcommittee were intentionally misleading. The Poles had not bilked the CIA of millions in gold. Please continue, William."

"Thank you, senator. It will begin slowly and gather momentum the following week. Job actions. Strikes. Food riots will reach a peak by the middle of next month. It will be one of many diversions, and it will coincide with increased border activities by the Chinese."

"General?"

"Confirmed," Shockley replied, sitting heavily in a chair at the end of the table, facing the large fireplace. "The slopes are moving ten divisions up line, reinforced with unusually large concentrations of tanks and artillery. Nothing the Russians can't handle, but they won't ignore it. The satellites show movement of troop trains along the Trans-Siberian heading in that direction. I think we'll see a lot of ass-kicking on both sides."

"Very graphic, General, as always," Emory replied. Shockley shrugged and took a long pull on his drink, unbuttoning his uniform blouse.

"The guerrilla movement in the Ukraine will also be activated," Knight added, looking at Redwood, who left the statement unchallenged. This was another of the attempts at covert action in the late 1940's that was generally regarded as a failure. Almost none of the equipment, funds, or operatives infiltrated behind the Iron Curtain on the mission had been heard from since before Korea—but that had been by design. The network, though small and operating in a closed society, was still very much intact. The time had come to use it. Once overt, the organization would fall prey to the Soviet Union's all-pervasive internal security in short order, but it would serve its purpose. The operation—for those involved—was expected to be exciting. And brief.

"You're convinced the timing will coincide?" the senator

asked, smoothing his long mane of hair with a manicured hand. Knight's only reply was a quick nod.

Emory turned to Shockley. "The garrisons in West Germany?"

"The Germans will seal them in the early-morning hours. Our forces will be coming off a major exercise two days before; a natural letdown after weeks in the field. There's always a certain amount of confusion on an installation after an exercise, and the fact that we're going on a Sunday evening is in our favor."

"You seem to find this disagreeable," Emory offered.

"You would too, in my place. Thirty years ago I was strangling Germans; now I'm helping the bastards pull a fast one on our boys. Damn right, I don't like it." Shockley downed the last of the bourbon and got up to pour another. "Most of the senior commanders involved don't like it either."

"But as we've said time and again, our Army must be kept out of it. I might also remind you this would be unnecessary if the country had listened to your former mentor. General Patton's predictions have certainly been proven correct."

Knight exchanged looks with Emory, aware the senator was also worried about this phase of the plan. Invoking Patton's name seemed to mollify the general. "Can we assume the cavalry regiment will also be taken out of the picture?" Emory asked, watching the soldier pour himself another drink. Shockley had just returned from a NATO tour, ostensibly to shore up allied confidence in the American commitment to European defense. His unscheduled side-trips and private conferences with selected U.S. commanders had been the real reason for the trip.

The general replied, "The Second ACR will be pulled off the border for the exercise, replaced by a panzer grenadier regiment. After that, they'll take a stand down in Aschaffenburg. General Hart will publish the orders in two weeks. His G-3 has already completed the draft. When the two Germanys move, there won't be an American within fifty miles of the border."

Douglas Emory paused for a moment, nodding almost imperceptibly. "I assume the President's plans remain the same. We haven't seen anything in the press so far, Gordon."

"Normal procedure," the ex-Marine replied. "The announcement will be made six days before his vacation. We expect to be able to keep him from the news for thirty-five to forty minutes. A private dinner has been arranged at the ski lodge, hosted by an old friend; the senior aides and critical cabinet members will be in attendance. The agents guarding the lodge have been selected, and I'll be there myself. I can assure you of a half-hour—but that's it."

"That should be sufficient," Emory replied, then looked questioningly to the lawyer.

Redwood opened his briefcase and extracted a single sheet of correspondence, which he passed to the senator. "Your participation has been confirmed by the network, scheduled halfway through the evening news. They've put a reporter on special assignment to develope a five-part report on the food-stamp program. Your live interview that night will start it off."

"Excellent. I expected much more difficulty."

"The program director owes me for six or eight exclusives out of the committee. Being an unnamed reliable source finally payed off. The news should hit there a few minutes before air time, and since you're also on the Foreign Relations Committee, I'm certain they'll opt for your views of the German situation and leave the welfare story for another night. Maybe drop it altogether." The lawyer produced a thin binder from the briefcase. "I've drafted a statement for you, with the content we discussed last week."

Emory reached for the document and said, "I'll read—and destroy—it before leaving. This is the only copy?"

"Yes, sir. Typed it myself."

"Thank you, Clifton. But it was unnecessary, really. I've had many years to develop my remarks."

"Do you still plan to formally recognize United Germany on behalf of the government? That's quite a leap, even for you."

Douglas Emory smiled paternally, as if soothing the hurt feelings of an obstreperous child, telling him not to worry about his indiscretion. "At that moment, I will be speaking not just for our small fraternity here, but for the country. As General Shockley might say, we're tired of getting our backsides kicked. I think they'd welcome a bold stroke, given the present national malaise."

"But the President—"

"—Will not be entirely disposed to countermand what I say. He can't, really. If the two Germanys can hold together for forty-eight hours, we have an entirely new set of circumstances. The debate on recognition will take time . . . but, it will give our friends in the Kremlin something to chew on." Emory gave them a broad, toothy smile, leaving unsaid the consequences if the Russians were able to render the new European state impotent. "This is our best chance; there will not be another."

Without a formal announcement, they knew their meeting was at an end and began to leave. The senator caught Knight's eye and asked him to stay behind.

"What is this I hear about Schellen?" Emory asked when they were alone.

"He came to us with a request to defect. We're sure the Russians are behind it."

"Now? How does this affect us?"

"Only a minor problem. Gessler has been involved since the beginning, and he'll make sure Schellen is eliminated at the proper time. The Deputy Minister of Transport is prepared to step in and seal off the eastern borders and close down the airports. Other than that, there will be no changes.

We've developed a suitable action plan—it's being run by one of my best resettlement teams, headed up by a reliable bureau chief. They report directly to me."

"No complications?"

"None."

"I shall sleep much better tonight, in that case." F. Douglas Emory relaxed, a smile of satisfaction creasing his face. "It's a comfort to know you've again handled things with such attention to detail. I didn't expect there would be any difficulties with you at the helm."

"No, sir. In fact, this development has allowed me to take care of a number of minor problems." Knight smiled to himself, thinking about the folder locked safely away in his desk.

No problems at all.

Chapter 12

Shortly after Bill Knight left the building for the evening, the guard at the main entrance made an entry in the log, with the time—10:56 P.M. Forty-seven minutes until the next shift came on.

Two other guards patrolled the four-story building, one in the east wing and one in the west. Harry Pike guarded the main entrance from behind a console of bright lights and toggle switches. He knew that at 11:00 P.M. sharp one of the other guards would check the main desk; it was a routine. Rounds took twenty minutes, and were staggered so that the front desk was checked every ten.

Pike watched the eight closed-circuit TV monitors. The exact time in hours, minutes, and seconds was displayed across the bottom of each screen for possible reference later. All screens were taped and each tape maintained on file for a minimum of seven days.

The guard covering the east wing arrived as expected.

"Eleven o'clock and all is well," the man said. He was

Fred Kelly, a forty-eight-year-old ex-policeman. "You playing those skin flicks again?"

"No, nothing worth looking at tonight, unless watching empty hallways turns you on." Monitor number four showed the west-wing guard, Bill Schaeffer, walking slowly down the second-floor corridor. "That monitor has been acting up a little tonight. Hope it holds out until the next shift comes on, so they have to fill out all that damned paperwork instead of me."

Kelly threw him a halfhearted salute and departed. As soon as he was out of sight, Pike got up from his desk, checked monitor number four, and walked quickly to the stairwell. Taking the steps two at a time, he arrived on the second floor and went directly to the locked janitor's closet next to the stairway. Key control in the building was rigidly enforced, but for this night a key was not needed. Reaching inside his brown uniform jacket, he extracted a set of lock picks. Thirty seconds later, the door yielded quietly. A glance at his watch told him he still had eight minutes left.

Pike set up the ladder he found in the closet beneath the camera that scanned the hallway, being careful not to come into its field of vision. From atop the ladder he could just reach the cannon plug at the back of the metal box. This he unscrewed.

Retracing his steps, he returned the ladder and arrived at his desk with three minutes to spare. Monitor number four was blank.

"Son-of-a-bitch!" Pike said aloud as Schaeffer came into view.

"What's wrong?"

"That damn monitor on the second floor. It's been flickering for the last fifteen minutes or so and finally quit. I'll be here past midnight filling out those friggin' reports."

"Maybe it's the panel."

"Checked that as best I could. I don't think so—leastwise, as far as I can tell."

"Don't we have a maintenance number to call?"

"Yeah. Guess I ought to do that—as if something was gonna happen. You know those S.O.B.'s ain't gettin' outa bed for this. Listen, could you watch the board for me? I'd like to go up there and give that thing a look. May be just a loose connection or something."

"Maybe you oughta wait."

"You're not the one that's gotta fill out the damn forms. Let me borrow your key to the janitor's closet so's I can get a ladder and take a look. It'll take five, maybe ten minutes. Who's to know?"

"Okay. I'll watch the tubes for you. It'll be nice to sit down for a change, anyway." Schaeffer handed over the large keyring containing about three dozen keys.

Pike took the ring and walked to the stairwell. Once out of sight, he took the stairs as fast as he could, almost stumbling at the top in his haste. He opened the janitor's closet with his lock pick, knowing that was faster than trying to locate the right key. Seconds later, the ladder was in place.

He walked quickly to the entrance of the Deputy Director's office, wasting two precious minutes in locating the right key. He let himself into the outer office, closed the door, and turned on the light. Another minute passed before he found himself inside Knight's office.

Pike sat behind the desk and unlocked the middle drawer with another lock pick. Then, reaching in and halfway down the drawer, he tripped an electric switch, disarming the first of two alarms. Next he unlocked the left-side drawers in a prearranged sequence: three, one, two, four. Only then could the two right drawers be unlocked without setting off the second alarm. The bottom right drawer opened, revealing a small safe. Pike checked his watch. Four minutes remained of the ten he had allotted himself; after that, both guards would be at the main desk, and one of them would surely come looking for him. He was already more than a minute behind schedule.

Pike controlled his nerves, surpressing the desire to call it off and leave. With deliberate speed, he massaged the dial through four digits. The door opened.

Inside, a file drawer yielded two folders. One he expected—that of Lt. Kenneth M. Hoffmann. The second he also extracted, though he had no idea of its importance. It was marked with a single word: DOVETAIL.

He spun the dial on the safe and quickly locked each drawer, being careful to reverse the sequence exactly, thus resetting the redundant alarm system. His training and attention to detail had paid off.

Nine minutes into his self-imposed time limit, he stood at the top of the ladder, rescrewing the cannon plug. The ladder was returned to its place, and the door closed behind it. Both folders were placed midway down the stairs. He returned to the main desk. The files could be retrieved at the next opportunity.

"Looks like you got it," Schaeffer said, pointing at the monitor as Pike walked toward the console. "What was it?"

"Just a loose plug in the back."

Pike leisurely took his place as the other man yielded the chair.

"How 'bout that. Well, it's nice to have somebody around who knows what he's doing."

"It just takes practice." Pike smiled. A lot of practice . . . and an inside knowledge of security systems.

Chapter 13

Afternoon dispatches from Langley sat in Knight's in-box, but he hadn't touched them; nor had he scanned the morning briefing file worked up overnight by the communications section. His calendar had been cleared, appointments rearranged, a luncheon with the Majority whip rescheduled for the following week. The Deputy Director had more pressing matters, his attention divided between the man seated in a chair across the room and thoughts of the chaos that would be loosed if he couldn't retrieve two missing files.

"I've checked the travel agencies, and Pike didn't go through anyone in town to make arrangements," Phillip Decker said.

"Check the ticket counters at National, Dulles, and Friendship."

"No need to."

"Why not?"

"I checked Washington National and learned he took a flight to New York and made a connection to Frankfurt."

Decker's personality grated on the Deputy Director. The personnel man from the Directorate of Management and Services had an irritating inability to get to the point, a tendency to make every statement a drawn-out affair. Every important detail had to be pulled from him. Germany? The significance was clear, the identities of those behind the theft clouded.

"When did he leave?"

"Twelve-fifteen A.M. to New York, with a one forty-five special charter to Germany. He went under an assumed name, but the ticket agent remembered his face."

"Is that his file?" Knight asked, looking at the brown folder cradled in Decker's hand. "Let me see it."

The contents were not unusual. Background checks appeared normal, the routine tests of loyalty and reliability successfully accomplished under careful monitoring three years earlier. Annual lie-detector tests had been negative, and Knight placed heavy reliance on the findings of the polygraph.

"Do you think it's possible for somebody like this Pike—or whatever his name is—to beat the black box?" Knight asked after carefully reading the file.

"It's possible. We all know that. The specialist who ran the test would have been gauging it on an American, somebody expected to be straightforward and relatively predictable. It's not hard to isolate somebody who's not up to our standards."

"Damn it! Answer the question!"

Decker blinked back his surprise, unaccustomed to being the target of the Deputy Director's anger. "Yes, he could beat it. If he's a foreign agent, and the operator didn't allow for cultural differences, he'd be tough to read. Or if he's a psychopath, a congenital liar, or out for money to satisfy some private vice, he could beat the box. You can't gauge the morals of somebody like that. But his record is good."

"Too good. It's excellent."

"I don't think the Office of Personnel can be held accountable for that."

"No, but you can. Damn it, there's no excuse! I want the operator who screened him out of here by the close of business. And I want a complete review of polygraph procedures— investigated, summarized, and on my desk by tomorrow night, with recommended improvements to preclude a recurrence. If it doesn't do anything for me, I'd suggest you dust off your résumés."

"Understood, sir."

"I knew it would be." Knight tossed the folder on the desk and watched Decker leave the room, then dialed out on his private line. The phone rang twice and was picked up.

"Locke?"

"Good evening, sir." The agent's voice was distinct, the connection unusually good.

"Execute phase three. We've had a minor problem," Knight said in even, measured tones that masked his nervousness.

"Five days early?"

"I know the timetable. Yes. Five days early. Use your own initiative, and call upon completion."

"May I ask why?"

"Negative."

"All right, sir. I understand."

"You're very perceptive."

"Thank you, sir."

"Locke. One other thing. I appreciate the way you handled that business with Leahy. It could have caused some very real problems if you hadn't found out what he was up to . . . and where his loyalties were. I've got a spot for you at Langley when this is over."

"I'm looking forward to it."

"I thought you would."

Knight rung off, his thoughts on Eric Hoffmann in Germany, where it was early evening.

*   *   *

Hoffmann reached into the refrigerator and retrieved a ceramic-topped beer bottle, then sat at the table beneath the light of a single bare bulb. He was tired.

He had spent a second day flying with Gerber; more maneuvers in the morning at Munich, followed by a cross-country to Regensburg in the afternoon. The chief pilot had been more distant than the previous day, his critiques biting, as if he were building a case for not hiring the new pilot. He had intimated that Hoffmann needed extensive retraining—perhaps a week or more—before being allowed to fly passengers. It had come as a shock, made worse because he was nearly exhausted, and he knew his reaction had not done anything to ease the personality conflict between them. He would have to talk to Locke about the problem—the pickup was now less than a week away. Hoffmann closed his eyes, the weariness all but intolerable.

He wanted more than anything to sleep, but Edison had told him they were flying in a man from Berlin—Schellen's contact—who had the details of the revised plan. Hoffmann doubted he had the energy to remain alert. He finished the beer and closed his eyes.

"No rest for the wicked," Edison's voice intruded. Next to him stood a middle-aged man of medium height, with high cheekbones and a long nose above curiously thin lips.

"Where's Locke?" Hoffmann asked.

"Should be here in a half-hour or so, I guess. We'll do the briefing without him. He can play catch-up when he arrives. This is our man from Berlin."

"I met with Schellen this morning," the man said, without offering a name or handshake. "I don't have much time before the courier flight back. Can we get started?" He appeared nervous, exceptionally so for someone who had many years of experience in clandestine operations—at least according to what Edision had said earlier.

Hoffmann replied, "Any time you're ready."

"All right. Let's look at the layout of the area." He placed a military map on the table. "Has anybody shown you where the border outposts are? No? . . . Okay, we'll start with that. This area is a national park which butts up against the Czech border for a stretch of about fifteen miles. Guardposts are located about every half-mile, with vehicle patrols in between. That's an area to avoid."

The agent made a tic on the map just south of the national park and traced a line southeast along the border to a place where he made another mark. "From here to here, there are only five guardposts, and they're about two miles apart. I've got a list of the coordinates, which I'll give you so you can plot them on the map. Three barbed-wire obstacles parallel that stretch, with tank traps in between. Again, vehicle patrols run between guardposts on irregular schedules."

"How about wires?" Eric asked.

"None above ground anywhere in this sector. All commo wire and power lines between outposts are buried. The highest manmade obstacle is the electrified fence, which is fifteen feet in most places, and most of the trees have been cut for visibility between guard towers.

"Between the border and the Vitava River, which parallels it in this section, there are no houses. But there are some high-tension power lines along the river on the border side. Beyond the river are some small towns and a few dispersed farmhouses. Hopefully, the map is correct on the locations; it should be, but we haven't field-checked it, for obvious reasons. Questions so far?"

Hoffmann had none, so the agent continued.

"There are a number of routes you can take into Zdikov—I leave that up to you. Zdikov is small, its population between five hundred and a thousand. Zdikovec, the town about a mile to the north sitting on the crossroads, is slightly larger, with a population of about two thousand. The closest military installation is at Horni Vitace, some twelve or thirteen miles directly south, or eighteen road miles. That's where the central headquarters for the sector is located."

"How many troops?"

"About a hundred and seventy total. Half of them are always on the border—that's one company. The post is manned by two companies."

"Antiaircraft weapons?"

"Yes. Each company is equipped with three thirty-seven—millimeter antiaircraft guns, radar controlled. The guns are vehicle-mounted and roam the border, again on an irregular schedule, as far as we know. Sorry we can't tell you where they'll be at any given time. I know you'd like to have that information."

Hoffmann nodded. "Tell me about the units manning the border outposts. When they change guard, how long the shifts are, how long they've been pulling this duty."

"The guard is changed every eighteen hours. One company relieves the other at the twelve o'clock or six o'clock mark. A company going on at six in the morning is relieved at midnight; that company goes back on duty at six o'clock the next evening. Normally they pull this duty for thirty days at a time. We don't know how long these particular units have been doing this, but since it's close to the end of the month, my guess is they've been on it for probably three weeks. I'll check on it for you, but I can't promise an answer by Tuesday."

If the soldiers manning the border outposts had been on that kind of schedule for the three weeks, they would be tired, inattentive. If he crossed the border early, between six and eight in the morning, chances were only one in four of going over when the guards were in the first few hours of duty and thus at their best.

"I convinced Schellen an early-morning pickup is best," said the Berlin agent. "He'll arive in Zdikov tomorrow night.

The following morning, he'll take an early walk to Zdikovec and back. It's not unusual for him to do that; it's his only form of exercise anymore. Each day he'll leave Zdikov at eight; by eight-ten he should be halfway between the towns. Before returning, he'll walk around Zdikovec and depart there, so as to be at the halfway point at eight forty-five. That gives you two times as possibilities."

"I assume the vegetation shown on the map is correct. Most European maps are accurate in that respect."

"This one is, according to Schellen. Both sides of the road are cleared farmland. You could land anywhere near him next to the road."

"What if the weather is so bad I can't make it either time in the morning?"

"We considered that. He'll take a walk Tuesday afternoon, with pickup times of one-ten and one forty-five. One of those times should be suitable. If the weather picture is still bad, everything gets set back twenty-four hours."

"Is there a way to contact him if we want to change any arrangements, or if he comes up with a change?"

The agent shook his head. "What we have is locked in."

The man from Berlin next explained the intelligence summary of the soldiers on duty along the border. Both companies in the sector near Zdikov were experiencing low morale brought on by prolonged periods of inactivity, accompanied by an excess of disciplinary problems.

"Possible air defenses," the man continued, opening a plain black binder.

Beyond the kitchen, a door opened, followed by muted conversation near the main entrance, hidden from view. Seconds later, Locke entered the room, his topcoat soaked. He looked at Edison, inclining his head toward the living room. "Briefing's over," he said.

The agent from Berlin frowned. "I haven't briefed him on the air-defense setup in the sector."

"Is it in the book?"

"Yes, but—"

"We'll handle it."

The man glanced at his watch, furrowed his brow, and said, "I've got time."

"Your flight was pushed up. Weather's coming in. Berlin is expected to close down in less than two hours, and we can't afford to have you missing in the morning. Edison and Renzetti will take you back." The agent hesitated for an instant, gave Hoffmann a quizzical sidelong glance, then followed Edison through the house and out the front door into the wet night. Locke removed his coat and threw it over a chair in the corner.

"What was that about?" Hoffmann asked when they were alone, aware that Locke's arrival had abruptly changed the atmosphere in the house, charging it with electricity.

"A change in plans. I just got it from Washington."

"Another one?"

"This is the last—you can be sure of it. We're moving to phase three . . . earlier than expected." Locke reached inside his coat, leisurely extracted his service revolver, and pointed it at Hoffmann's stomach. "We hadn't expected to do this until Sunday, but for some reason you've become a liability we can no longer afford. You're not going to pick up Schellen . . . because phase three is where we terminate your participation.

"That—by the way—carries the connotation of extreme prejudice."

Chapter 14

Hoffmann barely grasped the agent's words; outside stimuli were obstructed by a clouded lens, obscuring color and sound. He stared at Locke, not wanting to believe.

"You've probably figured out what's happening by now," Locke remarked calmly.

"You're not with the CIA."

"Wrong. . . . Don't be too surprised. The fact is, you've been used. We never intended for you to pick up Schellen—everything was staged for the benefit of our friends across the border."

"This whole thing was a charade!"

"Exactly."

"Why me?"

"Let's just say you fit the bill." The agent sat across the table from Hoffmann, keeping the weapon in front of him.

"What happens now?" Hoffmann's mind raced, looking for an escape, remembering the officer at Fort Benning with the bulldog face who had said the best time for a prisoner to break away was right after capture.

"Tonight you'll have an accident on some back road in southern Bavaria. The highways are in bad shape from the steady drizzle, and accidents are not uncommon in Germany." The finality of the agent's words tore at Hoffmann's gut. "You'd be amazed at how easy these things are to fix. There's a few loose ends, but nothing that can't be handled in a day or two. Your behavior here has been erratic, strange. The police will eventually get to most of the people you've come in contact with, and the story they'll get is one of a tired, often irrational person—an accident ready to happen."

He saw that Locke had been setting the stage all along. The constant movement. Late nights. Never enough rest. And all the time there was the shadowy fear of unknown assailants trying to kill him. The killers had been with him the whole time.

"Leahy wasn't killed by a French mercenary, was he?" Hoffmann asked, watching the agent search through his coat pockets for a cigarette. "My guess is that none of what you told me that night has so much as a nodding acquaintance with the truth."

Locke smiled, cocking his head slightly. "Maybe not."

"I don't understand."

"You don't need to. Yours was a very minor part in a much larger play; but an important role. We don't want Schellen—at least not now. He did come to us for help, and we had to make it look like we were responding, strictly for appearances. You were chosen because you had a requisite skill, but not one that we couldn't have gotten elsewhere. We've got one of the biggest fleets of airplanes in the world—complete with crews, men who could have easily done what we proposed for you."

"Then why?"

"I'm not entirely sure myself. But your selection was specifically directed."

"By whom?"

Locke gave him another harsh smile and said, "Of course I can't tell you . . . and, if you're thinking you can distract me, or delay the inevitable, by talking—forget it. Renzetti and Edison will be back in twenty-five or thirty minutes, and then we'll go for a ride. Any attempt to escape will only accelerate what is going to happen anyway."

"And you have a contingency plan."

"Several."

Hoffmann fell silent, his own breathing loud in his ears, his pulse a constant drumming at the temples. There was no way out; he would die thousands of miles from home, on a mountain road in some strange land. And no one would know why; not even himself. It was madness.

He started to rise from the chair. The agent gestured at him with the weapon. "Don't."

"Not even for a cup of coffee?" Locke was lighting his cigarette, holding the matchbox with two fingers. He struck the wooden stem twice against the striker before it flared. Hoffmann averted his eyes, glancing quickly at the stove, then back—a sudden look of surprise and fear. "Gas! Smell it?"

The agent's eyes darted toward the stove, the match shaken out; the indecision lasting only a split-second.

Hoffmann seized the sliver of time to heave the end of the table upward, pushing it toward Locke in one quick movement, his eyes riveted on the gun barrel. He pivoted to the side as the weapon fired, feeling an icy incision in his upper left arm. Two more shots shredded the plaster wall behind him. The table floated toward the agent, an insignificant weight propelled by the strength of Hoffmann's desperation. In one quick step he was on top of Locke, blocking the pistol to the side with an open hand while driving a knee into his groin.

Locke's eyes rounded. The cigarette fell from his lips as he swung a clenched fist that struck Hoffmann a glancing blow above the left ear.

Grasping the hand holding the weapon, Hoffmann pressed forward, keeping the agent off balance. Three times in rapid succession he hit Locke with solid left fists aimed at the sternum. The last caused a loud expulsion of air, a muffled groan. Hoffmann's hand clawed at the face, then grabbed the cloth of the jacket, yanking it sideways. Locke's eyes rolled up in their sockets as he was slammed into the wall and his head crashed into solid plaster. The gun clattered to the floor, and Hoffmann grabbed the man's lapels. Locke looked up at him through half-closed eyes, struggling to remain conscious, feebly attempting to fight back, his punches landing without authority.

Hoffmann swung him around and drove a clenched fist into the man's face that carried the full force of his weight. Locke's nose erupted in a shower of red, splattering both of them. Hoffmann felt teeth break beneath the blow; the agent's knees buckled, and he slumped forward. Hoffmann pulled him upright to deliver another crushing right, which caused the object of his rage to crumple on the floor. Hoffmann stood over him, his fists still clenched, breathing hard, trying to control the urge to continue beating the unmoving body.

He rolled Locke over on his back, straddled his chest, and pulled his head up off the floor. Blood poured from the nostrils.

"Can you hear me?" Hoffmann hissed, shaking him roughly. "Damnit, don't drop out on me. Can you hear me?" Locke moaned and half-opened his eyes.

"Who's outside?"

Locke turned his head and spat out blood mixed with pieces of a broken tooth. "One man," he mumbled through rapidly swelling lips. His eyes closed, and his head started to slump forward. Hoffmann shook him again.

"Don't pass out yet, damn you! Who is it?"

"Duncan."

"I don't know Duncan. What's he look like? What's he wearing?"

"Your size, black hair . . . We'll get you, Hoffmann . . . nowhere to run."

"Maybe not," Hoffmann replied, his face only inches from that of the agent. "I want you to remember this night. If I ever see you again, I'll kill you. Understand that."

He had no idea where the words originated. This was not him talking; he'd never threatened to kill a man before. The words and the rage that spilled out frightened him, his uncontrollable ugliness sending a shudder through him.

"I have nothing to fear from you." Locke was barely able to speak, his words slurred like those of an aged prizefighter. "You're a dead man already. You're worthless . . . like your father."

Hoffmann put all his strength into the blow that knocked the agent unconscious, causing his head to strike the floor with the sound of a sledgehammer meeting concrete. A bolt of pain shot through his arm, beginning at the fist and traveling deep into his shoulder blade. He winced in pain.

He buttoned Locke's jacket, turned him on his stomach, then roughly pulled the jacket down over his shoulders as far as it would go. He stood up, unsteady, fighting for balance as nausea swept over him. Moments later, he walked out the front door, spotting the man described by Locke.

"Duncan, I need the keys to the car."

"Where's Locke?"

"Inside. He and I are going for a ride."

"You sure?"

Hoffmann gambled. "Didn't he tell you about it before he came in?"

"Uh, sure. But . . ." Duncan's eyes searched beyond Hoffmann, toward the house.

"Which car is it?"

"This one."

"Give me the keys. Damn. I want to get out and back so I can get some sleep."

"Maybe we ought to wait until Roy comes out." Hoffmann could tell the man was suspicious, and he wondered if Duncan could see the torn cloth of his shirt or the bloodstains in the dim light.

"Okay, have it your way." Hoffmann shrugged and started to turn away. Abruptly he turned back and caught the man high on the cheekbone with a solid left hook that spun him around and sent him spread-eagled over the hood of the car. Hoffmann was on him, driving his knee into the small of the back; then, grasping Duncan's hair, he smashed his face into the fender. Hoffmann held on and searched through the man's pockets and found the keys, then pulled him from the car and propelled him toward the house, watching him stumble to his knees, head down.

The car was unlocked, but Hoffmann wasted precious seconds fumbling with the keys in his nervous haste before finding the one that fit the ignition. Shoving it home, he started the sedan, turned on the lights, and sped from the curb.

Rain pelted down with intensified ferocity as he careered through the streets of Munich, following signs to the E6 autobahn leading south out of the city. Minutes later, with the speedometer registering 160 kilometers, he left the city behind.

The E6 parallels the Starnbergersee for a distance of twenty kilometers. But Hoffmann could not see it in the dark and wouldn't have paid attention to the passing scenery had it been daylight. His eyes were riveted on the road, his thoughts jumbled now that he was out of immediate danger. Locke had taken him to the brink of death, and he had somehow survived. He was vaguely aware he was headed south as he focused on the road as seen through the driving rain. By sheer willpower, he forced himself to concentrate on anything but the night's events. Later he could sort out what it all meant; for now, he had to put distance between himself and the city. The autobahn ended near the town of Ohlstadt, where he turned south on Route 2, following roadsigns for Oberau and Garmisch-Partenkirchen. He was aware that the mountains were getting higher, their mass looming over the two-lane valley road. In the mirror, a car was following him—it had been behind him for the last fifty kilometers, exactly the same distance away each time he looked. He fought down panic, trying to convince himself it was impossible for it to be any of Locke's people.

Hoffmann slowed the car as he entered Oberau, but remained well above the posted speed limit. On impulse, he slammed on the brakes, sending the rear end of the car sliding dangerously to the left. Fighting for control on the wet pavement, he negotiated a right turn onto the side road. A sign flashed by in the periphery of vision: OBERAMMERGAU 15 KM.

Oberammergau. He'd bought a woodcarving there about six years ago. The town was famous for them. What had the shop owner said it was called? The town crier? The night watchman? He couldn't remember. His thoughts drifted. His eyes stung from trying to see through the sheets of rain.

He was brought sharply back to reality as he glanced into the rearview mirror and saw headlights swing left to right and then back again behind him. The car to the rear of his was fishtailing—it had taken the turn at high speed.

It was following him!

"Can't be them," he said aloud, but there was no confidence in the statement. He continued to watch the lights in the mirror; they were gaining.

After negotiating a turn in the winding road, he checked the mirror; each time he looked, the lights were closer. He dared not push the sedan any faster—as it was, he lost control momentarily on every turn. Increasing speed was a sure way of sending himself off the road into darkness.

He flashed through the small town of Ettal and the road turned north, straightening out; the forest closed in on both sides. Hoffmann pressed the accelerator to the floorboard. The other vehicle was only fifteen or twenty yards behind, gainly slowly. Finally, the headlights disappeared below the trunk of the sedan—a frightening memory of a dark city street came and went—and he felt the first bone-crunching contact.

Hoffmann fought to control the machine, but it wouldn't respond—nothing he did with the steering wheel had any effect. Once, twice more, the car behind slammed into him, pushing the sedan further out of control. He held the wheel in a death grip, paralyzed, afraid that anything he did would only make matters worse.

The sedan made a slow left turn, its nose pointing almost at right angles to the direction of travel. Reflex reaction forced Hoffmann to slam on the brakes just before his left front tire blew out, sending the car shooting off the road and down an embankment. The right fender struck a solid object, causing the rear end to whip around savagely. His last conscious memory was his own scream.

He had no idea how long he had been lying in the wet grass with the rain beating down on him. His head ached, and when he tried to push himself up, a searing pain knifed through his left shoulder. Struggling to his feet, wavering on the edge of unconsciousness, he saw the outline of his car twenty yards away, its one remaining headlight throwing a beam upward at a crazy angle through the downpour. He stumbled toward the car and fell against it. The driver's door was crumpled forward, attached by a single hinge.

A car stopped on the embankment above him, only its outline visible; the engine went silent, and a door opened.

Hoffmann staggered away, slipping on the wet mat beneath his feet, overbalancing as he tried to run through dense foliage. He had no sense of time or direction. The wavering, obscure form of the forest seemed impenetrable, his path undergrowth and finally came to a trail. His breathing was the absence of caution. Hoffmann fought through the tangled undergrowth and finally came to a trail. His breathing was, labored, and he paused for long seconds to catch a second wind before running down the path, still staggering on rubbery legs that would not obey his commands.

A beam of light directed into his eyes startled him, and he stopped, trying to fill his lungs with air.

"Nice try." The voice belonged to Edison, who stepped in front of him in the darkness, his face shielded by the glare of the flashlight. "But not good enough."

Hoffmann said nothing. He was beaten, and he knew it.

"I almost lost you at Oberau. That was a good idea, only you were a little slow on the execution."

"How . . . ?" Hoffmann coughed from deep within his chest, exhausted. He wanted to plead for his life but couldn't find the words.

"How did I pick you up? Just luck. Our man from Berlin left his briefcase. We were coming back for it and got there just as you took off. It's always the simple little things that catch up with you. All right, lace your fingers behind your head. On your knees." The agent moved behind him, and Hoffmann felt the rough hands probing his arms, legs, pockets. "On your feet," Edison said, stepping back. Hoffmann turned to face him.

The sound of the shot was muffled by pouring rain. He felt nothing, only sensed the encroachment of blackness on his vision. A beam of light, swaying. He was falling; the ground rushed up to meet him, and the smothering pain enveloped his chest. The smell of decayed vegetation invaded his senses.

There were voices above him. They made no sense.

A dark shadow moved toward him, grabbed his arm, and pulled him upright. He struggled against it, his protest verbalized in a harsh, gutteral sound, his strength no match against the formless body. The light was oscillating, playing across Edison who lay at his feet, face down, arms twisted at unnatural angles.

"Can you hear me?" The question came from far away. "Can you walk?"

"Yes . . . who are you?"

"A friend. Explanations can wait. Nothing will happen to you."

Hoffmann lurched to the side, balance gone. Huge hands steadied him. *I must know.* "We were alone. . . . Where did you come from?"

"A kibbutz called Yad-Il. My name is Akiva Ben Ari."

Chapter 15

A lone figure stood on the small bridge of the gunboat, peering into the darkness. The dull throb of diesel engines washed over him, then carried out to sea on a chill wind and dissipated in the blackness of the Mediterranean night. Ahead, only ten miles or less by now, lay the coast of Israel.

His name was Kareem Abu Sharif. A devout follower of Islam and a well-known figure within the Palestine Liberation Organization, he was one of the men charged with carrying out the PLO's grand scheme of destroying the Jewish State. As such, it was his duty to plan, organize, and execute raids within Israel.

Behind and below him, the five-man team huddled over their equipment, nervously fingering weapons and checking magazines for the hundredth time since departing from Sidon on the coast of Lebanon six hours before. They were silent, each alone with his thoughts. Sharif knew each of them intimately. He had personally selected each man months before and had supervised his training from the beginning, growing more pleased as the weeks went by. They had surpassed even his expectations. Two days before, these men had performed the normal ritual of making out wills and having their pictures taken singly and as a group, so that family and friends would know they had gone into battle eagerly, in high spirits. Now, as they closed on the Israeli shore, the bravado disappeared, replaced by the somber realization that by the next sunset all of them would be dead.

Sharif knew this also. It had been his only promise to the group.

It was unusual for Sharif to accompany such a mission, and it had taken Policy Council agreement to allow him to board the vessel. Normally, he monitored the raids from one of several command posts inside Lebanon, following developments as reports were received by radio. But this mission was different; the target was specific, and one that he had a personal interest in seeing eliminated.

As a boy, he had grown up in a small village that now sat deserted less than a kilometer from a Jewish kibbutz called Yad-Il. His family had been forced to leave in 1950 as the Jews moved in and began reclaiming the land. His mother had died shortly after, unable to stand the rigors of refugee life. But the compelling reason for Sharif's preoccupation with Kibbutz Yad-Il was even more personal.

He wanted Major Akiva Ben Ari dead.

The Jewish commando leader had been responsible for an assault on a camp nine months earlier that had claimed the life of Sharif's daughter, a pretty child with her mother's eyes and an unbounded happiness with life. Sharif had been inconsolable for weeks; nobody dared approach him in his grief. Following the mourning period, he set about with grim determination to strike back—exactly four weeks to the day after his daughter's burial, he began his recruiting program. The Israelis had called their attack a limited strike to neutralize a known terrorist headquarters; Sharif did not plan to limit his revenge in any way. Ben Ari was the prime target, but his squad was under orders to continue their slaughter of Jews until they themselves were killed. Escape and evasion had never been mentioned or considered. They would die gloriously for the cause of Palestine.

A change in the throaty pitch of the engines indicated they were near the drop-off point. Black-clad figures, their faces smeared with dark green camouflage stick, began to stir on the afterdeck. Wordlessly, they moved with practiced deliberation, slinging weapons across backs, then moving the six-man rubber assault boat toward the port side. The gunboat slowed, then turned parallel to the shore and stopped dead in the water, rolling gently with the waves. Sharif descended from the bridge.

He shook hands firmly with each man. Not a word passed between them; the time for action was now at hand. Action that Sharif was forbidden from joining, though he would have gladly traded places with any one of them. He would have to enjoy the killing of Ben Ari far removed from the scene.

The rubber boat was lowered into the water, and secured fore and aft by ropes held by two members of the squad. A third man sat in the boat, quickly securing demolition equipment as it was lowered to him. Finally, after less than three minutes, all five men were aboard. They began rowing toward the dark coast two miles away. The captain of the gunboat quickly got under way, fearing possible detection by an Israeli patrol boat.

Sharif went below for a cup of hot coffee and an attempt at sleep. The trip back would be a long, tedious one.

The sun was just beginning to lighten the eastern sky as Kareem Abu Sharif jumped to a small dock erected in the sheltered cove. There to greet him was Youssef Behzadnia, an old friend who was now a staff officer in Sharif's planning section.

"Seddik is here to see you," Behzadnia said as they walked down the dock toward the Citroën parked next to a wooden hut that smelled of dead fish and rotted bait.

Sharif offered no reply. It would be like the PLO leader to show up in grand style to claim as much credit as he could for an operation such as this. Now that all the work had been done, their leader would be very much the center of activity at the command post, making historic pronouncements, pretending to hang on every word as reports came in. Whether it was in the dreariness of the refugee camps or on the glitter of the world stage, Hossein Ali Seddik had to be the center of attention. And he usually succeeded.

Sharif entered the single-story dwelling just as Seddik launched into one of his many diatribes against the Jews. He stopped speaking abruptly and crossed the room to hug his top general. Holding him at arm's length, he smiled broadly.

"Kareem, you have done it again. A masterful stroke. I received the first report only an hour ago from one of our border outposts that is now in contact with the team."

Sharif looked past the man to the radio operator seated in front of a bank of radios with his headset on. "What has happened so far?" he asked, directing his question to the young Arab at the desk.

"Even more than I expected" Seddik replied before the operator could speak. "They breached the defenses unnoticed in the darkness and set the charges on the fuel-supply area. Then they cut the communications lines and put the radio out of commission before being detected. They've blown the fuel dump and claim twelve kills already."

Sharif could easily picture the scene. It was exactly how he had planned and rehearsed it dozens of times. "What about Ben Ari?"

"The only thing that disappoints me is that they did not

get the ammunition point," Seddik continued, ignoring the question. "At least twelve killed and more than twice that number wounded, they say. Do you think that American woman will interview me now?" At this, he threw his head back and roared with laughter.

The four men in his entourage joined in. Sharif's men smiled nervously, noting that he stood impassive, almost glaring at the PLO leader. Their thoughts mirrored Sharif's own: was this all the certain death of five soldiers meant? An interview for American television?

"What about Ben Ari?" Shariff persisted.

"Ben Ari?" Seddik stopped laughing. "Well, they will not get to him, unfortunately."

"What do you mean?"

"We have learned that Major Ben Ari is not at the kibbutz."

"Not there! How do you know?"

"We learned he left Israel five days ago."

Sharif turned and walked away, seething. Not there! All the time, the work, the training for nothing! "When did you learn this?"

"Yesterday," Seddik answered matter-of-factly.

Sharif faced the man, glowering. "You let me go ahead with this mission—knowing its primary purpose—without telling me that the man we were going after had gone?"

"I make the decisions," Seddik replied, matching Sharif's menacing tone, "and I make them based on what is best for the Palestinian people. Our personal feelings must be put aside until our people are returned to the land that is rightfully theirs. This includes your revenge on Major Ben Ari."

Sharif had heard these words many times before, the same pompous oratory used to brush off any disagreement. It would not work this time.

"Where is Ben Ari?"

"He is not in Israel."

"Where?"

"Our sources say he is in Germany."

"Then I will go to Germany. He will be an easier target there." The two men stared at each other across the short distance between them. After what seemed an interminable pause, while others in the room held their breath, Seddik smiled.

"Of course you will," he said, like a king bestowing a great reward on one of his subjects. "I grant you that privilege. You have worked hard—and accomplished much, I should add—and are in need of a rest. When you return, we will talk about your future within the organization."

It was done. The leader had diffused the situation by the granting of a favor, a magnanimous gesture. And had, in the same breath, told him that his part in the movement had come to an end. So be it. Sharif strode from the room without a word.

Inside Kibbutz Yad-Il, sporadic firing continued. Five Arabs held off an entire armed town from the strategic location of the meeting hall. Communications, both wire and radio, had been severed as reported. All other reports had been overly optimistic.

The fuel supplies had not been completely destroyed, as originally thought, despite the rising column of black smoke. Half of the total quantity was in a buried tank on the opposite side of the kibbutz. The exact number of wounded would later be determined to be seven; two were dead, not twelve.

It was an hour after sunrise, and Dov Tober, with his 90-mm. recoilless rifle and two rounds, had finally worked his way into a firing position. He aimed at the side of the meeting hall about two feet above ground level, sighted through the small lens, and squeezed the trigger. The blast of the weapon crushed in around him, a deafening roar whose concussion was lost a split-second later within another, louder, explosion as fifty pounds of TNT inside the building detonated.

The Arabs died knowing they had killed the one man they had come for.

They were wrong.

It was instead Magda, his wife.

Chapter 16

Visions of bright orbs paraded across Hoffmann's subconscious; twisting, turning, rushing rapidly toward him and then disappearing. In the dream, he grabbed two long, obscene shafts of light and controlled them for a moment; then slowly they pulled him down a dark, endless corridor. He resisted, tried to let go, but couldn't. The corridor became a narrow ledge bounded by a blank abyss on either side. Suddenly he was falling, unable to stop himself. Looking up, he saw a huge shadow descending upon him, and then it enveloped him, squeezing the air from his lungs as he continued to hurtle through the bottomless pit.

Hoffmann awoke with a start and sat up. The pain in his left shoulder forced a gasp from his throat and made him dizzy. His heart pounded, and he was wet with perspiration.

Soft hands lowered his head to the pillow and brushed his hair to the side. "It's all right," a gentle voice said. "It's all right. You were having a nightmare." The voice was familiar. The face came into focus slowly. Maggie Reynolds.

"Why—?" His voice had a distant, hollow ring; the word floated, hanging suspended.

"You're in Bad Tölz. It's almost one A.M. They brought you in about four hours ago and deposited you here after dressing a nasty looking-cut on your left arm. They said you were in a car accident." She moved slowly, as if afraid of jarring him; her left hand gently stroked his wet hair. "There was blood on your clothes, but the cut on your arm was the only wound. Your knuckles are swollen, and some of them are gouged. It doesn't look like anything is broken."

"Who are these people? How many of them?"

"Four that I know of—all Jewish, one of them from Israel."

"Akiva Ben Ari, Kibbutz Yad-Il." His mind was beginning to function, throwing off the last vestiges of sleep. So many questions. Locke had answered some, surfaced more. The appearance of a shadowy figure from Palestine brought him to another level of confusion. Maggie Reynolds' presence made the situation indecipherable. He had to *know*. Hoffmann sat up, resting his back against the headboard, grasping both her arms above the elbow.

"Why are you here?"

"I don't know," she said, her eyes suddenly filled with alarm. "They thought I was associated with you."

"They said that?"

"Yes. . . . Please, you're breaking my arms! You said I wouldn't be involved."

"I know."

"You lied."

"I hoped you wouldn't be. I'm sorry."

"That's precious little compensation." She pulled back from him, staring deep into his eyes. "That night you said you were in trouble. These past few days have convinced me, but I think you understated it. Somehow you're wrapped up in something terribly sinister—something beyond just searching for an unknown father. You're a practiced liar. Frankly, that scares the life out of me."

"I lied, but it wasn't practiced. And I *did* need help. You wouldn't have believed me if I told you the truth. If you had known, it would have been more dangerous."

"You used me!"

"I had to. You drew attention, and that provided some measure of protection."

"Protection! You say that so easily, like you're accustomed to using people." Maggie stopped suddenly, the silence accompanied by a short gasp. "They said a man died tonight—because of you. That's the reason for the blood on your clothes, the wound . . . You're a thief, a—"

"No!"

"—a murderer." She grabbed his hand, turning it over to expose the knuckles, then released it quickly, as if it were a venomous reptile. "You fought with someone, then killed him." Maggie stood, walked to the far side of the room, and stared off into space.

"That's not true!"

"Prove it."

"I can't."

"It's true, then." She turned and looked at him; the dim glow of the small lamp reflected off her gold hair, imparting a softness to her features. "We didn't meet by accident—you planned it. You talk and act with deception and violence. Like you were trained for it."

"A trained killer wouldn't have left the hotel chef alive to identify him to the police."

"Maybe. Maybe not."

"Nor would he have been foolish enough to allow himself to be arrested. I'm not a professional."

"Which implies you're something else, but somehow related to it."

"Distantly. But not by choice. Damn it, I *want* you to believe me!"

"I'd like to, but—" She stopped in midsentence, breathing deeply, clutching her arms across her chest and shivering as if the room had been invaded by a cold blast of air. Her eyes searched his face, an imploring look that wandered to the large gauze bandage on his arm.

The door opened, startling her, and a tall, powerfully built man stepped in. An aroma of freshly brewed coffee filtered through the doorway. "We heard voices." He motioned Maggie toward the door.

"She stays," Hoffmann said.

"I think not," Ben Ari replied. "We must talk . . . alone."

"Not before we establish certain conditions—conditions that affect her. She remains here until they are agreed upon."

The man looked at him for long seconds, nodded, and closed the door. "State your conditions."

"The girl will be protected."

"She is already."

"I don't know that. She could be a hostage."

"She is not. Your next condition."

"Arrange safe passage back to the U.S. for her—today."

"Agreed. But not today. There are more important matters, and my resources are limited. The two of you will return together next week, when we have finished our business."

"Heinrich Schellen?"

"Yes."

"Then we have nothing to discuss. If you have the resources to know about that, you have the capability to arrange the other—unless she is to be held as insurance for my cooperation. Your method makes you untrustworthy."

Ben Air stood motionless, his eyes narrowed and leveled at Hoffmann. "Your continued existence is dependent on cooperation. Beyond that, we need no insurance."

"Then the girl is unimportant to your proposal."

"Correct."

"She remains outside the scope of any proposition."

"Her knowledge—though limited—involves her already."

"Indirectly, yes. I want your promise she won't be required to participate directly; without it, we are at a stalemate." Hoffmann held his breath, aware of oppressive silence in the room, wondering if the man knew the words came from desperation. At last Ben Air spoke.

"You have stated the conditions. Now we will talk."

"We haven't reached an agreement."

"True. But we are not at an impasse. Your negotiating position is a weak one. Hopefully, Miss Reynolds is suitably impressed with your concern over her welfare, so we can put that aside. Her presence here makes your anxiety moot: she is in no danger. She should be listening to some tour guide in Füssen explaining why Neuschwanstein was never completed, or perhaps having her picture taken by the fountain in the garden of Hohenschwangau. Your carelessness brought her here; your solicitude will not protect her any more than what we have already done. If you really care for her safety—and yours—you will cooperate.

"If not . . . I think you know the alternatives."

"You should have stitches," Maggie Reynolds said, removing the blood-soaked pad and pulling the lamp close to the edge of the night table. She doused a fresh dressing with alcohol and patted the open wound, wincing as if the pain on his face were her own. "It's going to leave an ugly scar if you don't."

Hoffmann watched her face. She was more beautiful than he remembered from the hotel. "I'm sorry."

Maggie silenced him, placing a finger on his lips. "Quiet. You're consigned to bed rest for the next twenty-four hours. You've been through quite an ordeal . . . I understand that now."

She had sat through the past hour on a chair at the foot of his bed, motionless, without interrupting as he told his story to the Israeli. By inference and example, Ben Ari had proven knowledge of the events leading to their meeting in a forest near Oberammergau. Locke's attempt on his life was the final confirmation.

"No wonder you were having a nightmare," Maggie said, applying the last strip of adhesive.

"But it should have been mine, not yours."

"I didn't have to accept the dinner invitation. You seemed nice enough, and the story was intriguing. It was . . . a bit of excitement. A strange man. A foreign land. The stuff of romantic fiction. And it struck me at the time as being something outlandishly old-fashioned, like the car running out of gas. I didn't believe you . . . not at first."

"When?"

"That phone call during dinner. The desk clerk said it had been transferred to the room. When I got there—nothing. It took me maybe fifteen minutes to reach home, and my father was fine. You were gone by the time I got back, and I didn't know whether to be angry or not. Last night I went to the Hofbräuhaus, and when I left, the cab driver took me to the railway station instead of back to the hotel, picked up another passenger, and forced me to go with him. After transferring cars, he drove me here. His name is Simon—and he works for Ben Ari." She paused, shaking her head at the memory. "He said I was being followed."

He took her hand, and squeezed it gently. "You probably were. The man who tried to kill me knew about you." *We can't completely disregard her.* Lock had her shadowed, and probably intended to make sure . . . The thought caused a shudder, and he started to raise himself up. Her hand touched his chest, a silent order accompanied by a disapproving look.

"Bed rest, remember?"

"I'm a lousy patient."

"I've observed. You also talk a lot in your sleep. Most of the names make sense now, though, except one. Barbara. You don't wear a ring—I always check. Your wife?"

"Ex. Our parting was somewhat civilized."

"You think about her a lot."

"More than I should."

"Which says you loved her very much—or you don't like to fail."

"Equal amounts of both."

"And I'm prying." His silence corroborated the statement. "You *are* sentimental; I'm beginning to see that. You were serious when you made those demands on Ben Ari."

"He made a fool of me."

She laughed softly and shook her head. "He listened. I think you two share a certain anger, perhaps frustration, about this Schellen, and your sense of equity or justice struck a responsive chord. . . . Psycology major, UCSB. Two years ago. See, I'm qualified."

"You're trying too hard." He saw the eagerness leave her eyes as Maggie bit her lower lip, and he was instantly angry with himself. "I shouldn't have said that."

She looked at him, blinking back tears forming in the corner of her eyes. "You have this disgusting habit of being overtly apologetic and not really meaning it. It's not spontaneous—very shallow and self-serving. No wonder she left you." Maggie stared up at the ceiling for a moment, then back at him. "Now I'm contradicting myself. . . . None of this is making any sense. Nothing."

"It will, I promise."

"No, it won't!"

She was terrified. He had stripped away the mask of serenity with one callous phrase. Why? "You can't allow yourself to believe that. I don't."

When she replied, the softness in her eyes had vanished. "Then what you have is a form of insanity."

* * *

Ben Ari left by the rear exit, walked behind the row of houses to an alleyway, and crossed the cobblestone street. Deborah's apartment was on the third floor of a building housing a bakery at street level, next door to a restaurant. It was still hours before first light, and the dark green shutters were tightly shut. An inscription above the restaurant's entrance read GRÜNERBAU 8 in two-foor letters. White lace curtains hung in all the windows of the five-story structure, and the exterior walls were adorned with four large paintings, three of which were of religious themes; the fourth, a butter churn decorated with flowers, seemed out of place. Ben Ari wondered if during World War II the people of Bad Tölz had followed the Christian principles they now so proudly displayed on the exterior of the building.

He walked west, downhill, toward the end of a concrete island which separated the two-way traffic before the street reached a bridge spanning the narrow Isar River. His car was parked in an alley just on the other side. His inspection revealed all the nearly invisible signs he'd left on the car were in place. Ten minutes later he was speeding north on Highway 11.

He stopped in Königsdorf, parked around the corner from the public phone, and placed a call to his communications contact. Their conversation lasted a scant three minutes and consisted of prearranged codes, one of which could only have been issued from Tel Aviv. Ben Ari returned to the car and drove toward Munich and the unwanted meeting with Petar.

Norwegen Import, A.G., was located on Erhardstrasse in Munich, on the banks of the same Isar River that ran through Bad Tölz. Despite its name, the firm's actual volume of trade with Norway was limited. Its primary function was as an arm of Mossad, a point of contact for Israeli agents operating in West Germany.

Petar greeted him in the outer foyer, then ushered him

through the deserted hallways to the inner sanctuary which was his office, closing the heavy wooden doors behind them. Pictures of ocean vessels adorned the walls; the office was furnished with a formal, almost austere collection of Scandinavian furniture. Ben Ari chose a seat next to the sofa.

"A drink?" Petar asked, crossing to a small bar.

"No, nothing. It's too early—and you drink too much. I have a lot to do, and you didn't invite me here to socialize. I know the general issued the message, so it must be important. Let's get it over with."

Petar took a sip of his drink and sighed. "The news is not good. A drink will help."

"If the news is not good, nothing will help."

The man shrugged and sat on the edge of his desk. "I wish I were not the one who had to tell you this, but it is better to come from a friend." He paused, groping for words. "Ben Ari, there has been . . . there was a raid on the kibbutz. The news is about your wife. She was among those who were killed."

"No!" His anguish filled the room.

"I'm sorry."

"By the prophets, no!" He was on his feet, his huge hands grasped the cloth and flesh of the other man at the base of his neck, shaking him violently. "It's not true!"

"Ben Ari, please. The general himself confirmed it."

Anger, frustration, guilt washed over him. He was oblivious to everything around him for long seconds. Finally the outburst passed. He released the other man and sat, staring at nothing.

"When?" Ben Ari asked, after a moment.

"Twenty-four hours ago."

"The PLO?"

"Yes."

Rage boiled within him. He wanted to reach out at anyone, anything, and destroy. "My boys?"

"They are alive and well. The general is looking after them. A nurse has been hired, and they are staying with him in Tel Aviv."

"It will take them a lifetime to forget, if they ever do."

"They are young. Their memory will fade quickly."

"The young do not always forget." For an instant he was back at a rail siding outside Auschwitz; the year, 1942. He was ten, and the little girl clasping his hand was four. Colors were not vivid, nor had they been that cold, gray morning. He forced the scene from his mind. "Tell me . . . everything."

"There were five of them. They infiltrated before dawn, and blew up the fuel and cut communications. It was a suicide mission; they held out for almost two hours before it was over. All of the attackers died in the meeting hall. Two of our people were killed and several, I don't know exactly how many, were injured."

"It was never in the news?"

"I haven't seen it."

"Nobody cares. They come, they kill, but nobody cares." The shocked anger receded, replaced by aguish and despair. "History repeats itself, and nobody cares."

Petar looked at him but said nothing. To speak would be to provoke, and to provoke would be to interrupt the man in his attempt to purge his soul of torment.

"She begged me not to leave this time. The only thing she ever asked of me was to stay with her, to give this up . . . this endless search for the vermin that were the Third Reich. And she was right. We'll never find them all, and even if we do, who will care? It's over. The world wants to forget. If I had listened to her, she would be alive now. It is my fault."

"It is your job. It is not just for you, but for all Israel."

"Israel is not worth it."

"Yes, Israel is worth it, even this."

Ben Ari turned, a hint of madness in his eyes. "Don't you tell me about Israel," he thundered. "You have not been there. You don't know the constant fear, the worry, never knowing if they will come in the middle of the night to snuff out your life. Germany today is not the same as Kibbutz Yad-Il. Don't preach to me about Israel!"

"I would gladly trade all of this for the privilege of living there. It is not my choice to be here. I serve Israel here because I must, just as you must serve in your way. The Lord sends hardship to make us stronger, not to break us."

"You speak like a rabbi."

"There is a little of the rabbi in all of us."

Ben Ari turned and gazed out the window. In a few hours people would be walking the streets, huddled in animated conversation, oblivious to murder and hardship, because they did not touch them. For that, he envied them, because he had never known any peace in his lifetime—and now Magda was gone. His only anchor, his only link to any kind of normal existence, and now she had been taken from him.

"Have arrangements been made?" he asked, still looking out the window.

"Yes. Everything has been taken care of."

"I will return home for my children."

"The general prefers you stay here."

"Hang the general."

"There are reasons."

"None good enough, I assure you."

"Listen to them before making your choice."

"I will listen, but it will make no difference."

"Your children are being well cared for by the general. You are like a son to him, and the boys like his own grandchildren. They will want for nothing until you return." Petar opened a desk drawer and retrieved a large envelope. "Last night we received this; it was taken from a safe in Washington. The contents are frightening—when you read it you'll understand. Until now, capturing Schellen was important only in that it would settle an old score. Documents in this file cause us to reevaluate objectives. The desired result is still the same, but his removal from East Germany is now more imperative.

"There is also another development for you to consider. We have been made aware of the arrival of Kareem Abu Sharif in West Germany. He was undoubtedly the one who set in motion the raid on Yad-Il. We can only assume he is here because you are; the coincidence is too great to be chance. We learned of it through an intercepted cipher from Lebanon transmitted in a code we had broken three weeks ago, a code they knew we had. We think they were sending us a message concerning Sharif's future."

"You're sure he's here?"

"He has not been sighted yet."

Ben Ari was not normally given to indecision. He would stay. "Let me see this file of yours."

Petar offered it to him.

"Seddik wants us to do his work for him. . . . This time, for once, we will not frustrate his plans."

Chapter 17

"Who is he?" Hoffmann asked the dark-haired girl. "He said nothing about himself except that he came from a kibbutz called Yad-Il."

Early-morning sun filtered through white curtains, shading the dining area in a sandy color like well-tanned skin. The apartment consisted of two small bedrooms, a bath, and kitchen, each with old but functional furnishings. The style was nondescript, the theme spartan. Deborah Mueller's eyes held neither welcome nor hostility as she poured coffee from a scarred percolator.

"Have you known Ben Ari long?"

She looked at him with strangely cool eyes and said, "Long enough. We do business sometimes."

"Then you should know. Tell me."

"He is a major in the Israeli Army . . . sometimes. Most of the time he is a farmer on a kibbutz near the Lebanese border. Until two years ago, he was a member of the Special Commando Group, Unit 269, the Saiyeret, You may remember the Sabena airliner hijacked to Israel two years ago. The terrorists held the passengers and crew hostage on the ground at Lod airport to negotiate ransome until commandos disguised as mechanics got on board and killed three of the four hijackers. He was the first one in. He killed two of them."

"Now he's a farmer?"

"And commander of defense forces there. Last year, during the war, he led an infantry batallion on the Golan Heights before resigning. Now he is in the reserves, but, like all of them, he is on call."

"What else?"

"The rest he will have to tell you himself," she said, cutting off further discussion. "Give me your hand."

The knuckles were barely distinguishable in the bruised and swollen flesh, painful to the touch. She wrapped the hand tightly in an elastic bandage and secured it with a strip of white surgical tape, then went into the second bedroom, leaving him alone. From outside came sounds of the village coming to life: a dog barking, wooden wheels on the cobblestones, a woman talking loudly to a neighbor as she swept the sidewalk. He finished the coffee, and poured another, his thoughts on Maggie Reynolds.

What have I done to you?

She had lived in southern California all her life, a surfing fanatic by admission. An indifferent student through four years of Santa Barbara who became a political activist, first as a diversion and later for reasons of honest commitment. She gravitated to radical fringes, fell in love with a charismatic senior in poli sci who would change the world by force or guile or the supernatural. It became too much. He turned out to be a superficial world-beater, shallow and uninspired. Power corrupts, she learned, almost too late. His reshaping of the world order died in a narcotics raid on a coastal bungalow; the girl with him was arrested as well.

She tested the working world and found doors closed to

women—the truly important doors leading to the corporate boardroom. If one was to be corrupted by power, why not make it absolute? A master's in business beckoned from Northwestern, and after that perhaps economics.

As she talked, he saw the animation covering her fears, but this time he didn't shatter the thin veneer. He listened; and was consumed by her.

What have I done to you?

A key was inserted in the lock, and the door opened. Ben Ari moved to the table and sat facing the window. He wasted no time on pleasantries.

"Picking up Schellen has taken on added importance. What we do in the next few days may determine the political future of your country, and therefore mine. You will have to be prepared to do whatever I tell you, instantly, without hesitation, regardless of what is is."

"I'm not sure I want to."

"Your desires, and mine, are of no importance. I can apply the necessary leverage and whatever force is required to make you comply with my demands, but that could be cumbersome at times—maybe fatal to both of us."

"That sssumes I'm willing to work with you, something I haven't agreed to."

"Then you are a fool. You won't be alive this time tomorrow if I let you loose in Germany tonight. Already the net is drawn throughout the country. They will not let you live. But your life and mine don't matter unless we work together, very closely, and you follow my instructions."

"What are you talking about?"

"I'm talking about this." Ben Ari tapped the folder on top of the table. "This file contains the plans to reunify Germany by military force. We—you and I—have less than a week to stop it."

*   *   *

The contents of the file lay stacked in neat piles on the table. Ben Ari had briefly outlined what it contained, and the American had scanned it.

"You're sure this is real?" asked Hoffmann.

"Yes. It's existence has been rumored for many years. Enough of the rumor is contained in those pages to convince me and others in our organization."

"But it's so ridiculous . . . incredible."

"Which may be its strongest asset."

"Why don't you just go public with it? Tell the world."

"That was considered, but with today's political climate, it's not a viable alternative. The United States just went through one of the worst political crises it ever faced, almost as bad as your Civil War. This revelation could create havoc in your government, chaos in others."

"That's reaching."

"Maybe. But would you want to be responsible for making that decision . . . taking that chance? I grant you it's a remote possibility, but not so remote as to be totally disregarded. There's also the Soviet Union to consider. U.S.–Soviet relations are not as good as one might suspect, primarily because of the American overtures to China. The problems in NATO are significant, also. The alliance is probably in as much trouble as it has been in since it began; a unilateral decision by the U.S. to help reunite Germany would shatter it."

"And this file indicates the U.S. is going to attempt it?"

"Yes. And if it does, your country would never be trusted again. The resulting power vacuum in Europe without NATO might be too much for the Russians to resist. We know the Russians are capable of taking Europe faster than Hitler ever dreamed possible, using conventional forces and selective chemical warfare. The question is: Would the U.S. use nuclear weapons to stop them? That's a subject I'd rather see argued by professors in the relative safety of the classroom."

"You're convinced the United States plans to go ahead with this anyway?"

"Not the government; certain individuals within the government. Most of the responsible people in your country know that the time for using force in Europe is past. But there are apparently some—unfortunately, some with a certain amount of power—who disagree. The greatest danger to the world lurks in covert plots by men of zeal, well-meaning but without understanding."

"But what's the point?"

"To shatter the Eastern Bloc, of course, and thereby seriously weaken the Soviet Union itself."

The idea of such an unrealistic endeavor scared him. Hoffmann picked up the staff study. It was awesome in its simplicity. The man who had written it, or the man for whom it had been written, had not been given to extensive prose.

EYES ONLY

Chairman, Joint Chiefs of Staff

1. PROBLEM: To effect reunification of the German State through armed intervention

2. FACTS BEARING ON PROBLEM:

   a. U.S. holds 4–1 numerical superiority in strategic nuclear capability (Annex A)

   b. U.S. holds 3–1 advantage in nuclear throw weight (Appendix 1 to Annex A)

   c. U.S. holds 2.5–1 numerical superiority in strategic-bombing capability (nuclear) (Appendix 2 to Annex A)

   d. U.S.S.R. holds 2.5–1 numerical superiority in ground forces under arms (Annex B)

   e. U.S.S.R. holds 4–1 advantage in number of armored forces within intended battle area (Appendix 1 to Annex B)

f. U.S.S.R. holds 1.5—1 numerical superiority in ground forces under arms vis-à-vis North Atlantic Alliance (Appendix 2 to Annex B)

g. Mobilization and deployment times, Communist forces excluding East Germany, exceeds 17 days (Annex C, Appendices 1–5)

3. ASSUMPTIONS:

a. U.S. ground forces under arms will decrease as projected, U.S. Army DCSPERS (Annex D)

b. Soviet Bloc forces will increase as projected, CIA Special Study Delta, Extract (Annex E)

c. East German populace will not institute significant guerrilla activity in the event of armed conflict, Phase I Insurgency Operations

4. DISCUSSION:

a. Numerical superiority in strategic nuclear weapons can be used to preclude massing of enemy forces

b. Nuclear throw weight advantage will deny enemy access into battle area and eliminate pre-positioned logistics (Annex F)

c. Air supremacy cannot be achieved. Local air superiority can be expected over 95% of the battle area for H + 18 hours; thereafter, over 60% of area. Strategic bombing capability can be employed through H + 18 in a tactical nuclear role; thereafter, in strategic role

d. Enemy superiority in number of ground forces negated through H + 18 due to air superiority and mobilization delay time

e. Enemy advantage in armored forces will be reduced from 4–1 to 1.5–1 due to technical superiority of U.S. equipment (first-round kill probability 96.5%—U.S.; 63%—U.S.S.R.). Advantage further eroded when calculation adjusted for supporting artillery comparison (Annex G)

f. Forces outside intended area of operations not a factor considering mobilization 18 days or greater (Appendix 6 to Annex C)

5. CONCLUSIONS:

a. Introduction of U.S. forces into East Germany is desirable and feasible, with acceptable loss rates

b. Current comparison of opposing forces dictates commencement of operations within 180 days, not later than 365 days

c. Operational command and control should be delegated to Commander, U.S. Army Europe (USAREUR)

d. Theater control should be retained at Joint Chiefs of Staff level

6. RECOMMENDATIONS:

a. Recommend conclusions in paragraph 5 above be adopted and acted upon

b. Recommend all pre-positioned equipment in Western Europe be brought to C-1 status

Attached as part of the staff study were ninety-two pages of annexes—graphs, charts, maps, each with detailed explanations and evaluations. Hoffmann was overwhelmed by the scope of the document. This was not the work of a junior officer rushing to place on paper hurriedly assembled and disjointed facts for submission to a military-school instructor. It was an exhaustive research effort matched with an equally impressive military analysis.

Hoffmann placed the document in front of him on the table and sat back, awed. "It's frightening. Do you know who wrote it?"

"Our best guess is Major General Phillip Gregory, who was a colonel at the time."

General Gregory! Was that the reason for his death? Was he becoming irrational in his old age and therefore a threat to

. . . to whom? The questions generated by this new piece of information were endless.

"I knew him, or at last spoke to him just hours before he was killed. I may have been the last person to talk to him."

"Which could be the reason you were singled out to be sent over here."

Your selection was specifically directed.

"But if somebody wanted to know what the general told me, he could have found out."

"Chances are that they realized, during the interview with Carnahan, that you hadn't learned anything from Gregory. You fit nicely into their plans because you had motive—to learn about your father—you were expendable, and you were qualified to do the flying part of the assignment. They planned to eliminate you before the scheduled pickup in a way that didn't arouse Russian suspicions. That way, it would look like they had tried to help Schellen escape, and Schellen could stay in East Germany."

"But this staff study . . . it seems possible, but not all the pieces fit. You say a military plan won't work, and that most of the people running the country realize that—"

"Our best guess is that the study was written sometime around 1954. That's based on a quick review, so we could be a year, maybe two, off. The other documents contain revisions to the study made over the years as the military balance shifted. Eisenhower was probably the reason it was never executed in the early 'fifties, because he cut U.S. military strength drastically during his administration. The plan was resurrected again in 1959, according to one of the documents, revised, and proposed as an answer to Khrushchev's demand that the United States pull its troops out of West Berlin. There was not enough time to execute it then—the balance of power had shifted to the Warsaw Pact.

"Then came a new administration in the early 'sixties, flexing its muscles and rebuilding the American military.

Look at the Cuban missile crisis. And who backed down? Worldwide, U.S. forces still held an edge over those of Russia, and American strength was on the rise. Kennedy made that speech in Berlin, pledging to unite a divided Berlin and a divided Germany. How do you think that looked to the Russians? If they didn't have a copy of this paper, they had a good idea that something like it existed, and they saw a president who might possibly follow the recommendations you just read. John Kennedy didn't live long after that."

"Are you saying it was Russia who had Kennedy assassinated? That's ridiculous."

"Nobody to this day knows who really killed him. Oswald had a part in it, but it's strange he never got to trial. The Kennedy investigation will never be closed."

"So let's assume the Russians did know about the plan. If that's true, then surely nobody could think it'll work now."

"It won't work as originally conceived, but some of the documents in the file indicate how the plan changed. It's no longer strictly a military operation. Britain, France, Italy, Canada, and West Germany became involved at one time or another in the mid- to late 'fifties because the original planners knew the U.S. couldn't accomplish it alone. Some very important people got drawn into it, most of them out of fear over Soviet expansion. Several of them still hold key positions in their governments. When Kennedy died, so did the scheme for German reunification—or so they all thought. Even the Russians thought it had finally been dismantled."

"But you insist it hasn't."

"This file confirms it. The original idea, as captured in the Gregory study, did pass from existence. The United States got mired down in Viet Nam for a decade, wasting its military resources and depleting the small standing army in Europe even further. Western populations tired of the rigors necessary to blunt Communism and tranquilized their governments. Now the scenario has evolved into one in which the Germans accomplish the reunification for themselves while American forces are immobilized by their own leaders. And the plan must be executed now, spearheaded by the older generation who remember the glories of a united Germany. Younger Germans lack their vision, and the leadership knows it."

"I don't see how it can be done."

"On paper, it looks possible. The combined force of the two Germanys is an impressive array of firepower. They have had more than ten years to set everything in place. Russia is the big unknown. We think she will use maximum force to keep the plan from succeeding. And we don't think the Russian leadership will accept the smokescreen that West Germany kept the American Army from interfering—paranoia is a national pastime in the Soviet Union. To them, it will look like an American show from beginning to end."

"That means a nuclear confrontation."

"The same conclusion we came to. And if that happens, we will be witnesses to the end of our planet."

Hoffmann stared at the man across the table from him. Ben Ari had answered every question, dispelled every doubt, countered each objection with arguments so persuasive as to eliminate disbelief. Suddenly, he felt insignificant.

"What can you and I do to stop something like this?" Hoffmann asked, noting the discouragement in his own voice.

"We can take out a key link—Schellen. His job, according to the file, was to shut down Warsaw Pact access into East Germany and open it up to the West. He can close rail lines and airports as well as highways. Of course, he'll work with the Army on that. His major contribution will be in clearing railroads and highways, so that equipment can be rushed in from West Germany to assist the East German Army. That is no small logistical problem."

"You really think that removing Schellen will make a difference?"

"For a while . . . until the ones who are behind the plan can be located and stopped. We know some of them, but not all. If we can delay their timing, there's a chance of discovering the identities of the decision-makers and removing them. They are enemies of your country and thus of mine, because our future is dependent on American strength and stability."

Ben Ari folded his hands; he sat silent for a long moment. "We can let nothing stand in our way," he said finally. "That is why I must have your absolute and unquestioning cooperation, willingly. There will be no accolades if we succeed; no acknowledgement of success—or failure.

"Rewards and punishments have no significance."

Chapter 18

"I checked the border dispositions, and our sources confirm what he told us," Edelmann said. "Each detail matches, down to the changing of the guard. In every respect we can verify, the briefing appears accurate."

Ben Ari nodded silently, took a deep breath, and looked at Hoffmann. "What do you think?"

"If the arrangements were actually made, there's a chance—maybe. I don't think it can be quantified."

The table was covered with a map supplied by Edelmann, one of several extracted from a cardboard tube with American military markings. An hour after lunch, Simon Levin had taken photographs necessary for the passports and departed, followed by Deborah and Maggie, who had gone in search of a traveling wardrobe for the girl.

"Are you sure this man from Berlin said they couldn't contact Schellen between now and the pickup?"

"That's what he said. How true it is, I don't know. He was genuinely surprised, disconcerted, when Locke cut the briefing short. I don't think it was an act."

"Then we go with it basically as planned. Schellen will be expecting you Tuesday morning, and we won't disappoint him."

"What about Maggie?"

"She will stay with Aaron and his wife in Landsberg until Wednesday. Her passage is being arranged."

Hoffmann stared at the Israeli, a question forming. The timing seemed convenient—was Ben Ari insuring his cooperation through the girl? He wasn't sure he wanted to know. Edelmann was pulling a weapon from the rucksack in the corner of the room next to the table; a light coat of oil covered the metal.

"Are you familiar with the Uzi?" the man asked, tapping a long ash from his cigar. He handed it to Hoffmann. "Six hundred and fifty rounds per minute, maximum rate. A reliable weapon—your own Secret Service carries them when guarding the President."

Eric held the submachine gun in both hands, surprised at the weight. "Heavier than I expected."

"Nine pounds. It's out of the lightweight class. The major can explain the use of it later—it's a weapon he carries often." Edelmann inserted the long clip and switched on the safety after chambering a round. "There's one for each of you, with ten clips of ammunition apiece."

"Grenades?" Ben Ari asked.

"Eight of them. Our own Number 14's." The weapons expert placed two on the table. "Five inches long and made of laminated paper with sheet-metal ends. Twelve ounces of flaked TNT, activated by a five-second delay fuse. They're produced here in Germany under the nomenclature of DT11B1. There's a shipment leaving Bremen tonight short by one case—I hope Dayan won't be too upset when the inventory fails to match the shipping papers. Deborah will have to contact Richter for the sniper rifle."

Ben Ari saw Hoffmann's quick glance. "It may be necessary,"

he said simply, then motioned for Edelmann to replace the equipment. The logistical details were falling into place, despite the sudden departure from his original plan; his greatest concern was the operations phase, and Hoffmann's unspoken skepticism. "How do you propose to get us to Zdikov?"

"Here's the course that looks best to me," Hoffmann said, tracing a light pencil line across the multicolored sheet. "The initial point starts at Mauth, and follows the road north to Finsterau, the town closest to the border. From there, it's one and a half kilometers to the crossing point. From ten miles south of Mauth until we're back out, we'll stay at or below treetop level."

Ben Ari nodded as Hoffmann continued to trace the flight path.

"The heading out of Finsterau is about zero-two-zero degrees for nine kilometers. That should put us at the point where the Vitava River crosses the road. It's a good checkpoint, and we'll be able to correct easily enough if we're off a little." He circled the point on the map, labeling it CP1.

"From there we pick up a general heading of three-fifty-five degrees and follow this valley until we hit the next road. That's our second checkpoint." He laid the pencil next to the line and marked the distance with his thumbnail, then compared it to the scale at the bottom of the map. "Seven point five kilometers."

Hoffmann turned the map slightly and drew another line. "From the second checkpoint, we turn right to a zero-one-five heading up this next valley. That puts us at Zdikovec, where we turn right and follow the road south to Zdikov until we see Schellen. The total distance is twenty-four kilometers from Finsterau—just about all of that inside the border."

Ben Ari looked at the route. He was pleased. Hoffmann had chosen a path that was simple, short, and took advantage of the terrain. There were only two small changes of direction, so navigation would be relatively simple.

"The alternate route begins here at Finsterau again," Hoffmann continued, "and goes on a heading of about thirty-five degrees to this point where the river makes an abrupt bend. Then we follow this valley straight to Zdikov, just about due north. I don't like it—it's close to this village of Novy Svët, and we'd have to overfly Zdikov on the way in."

"I agree. The first route is better."

"The return trip should follow this valley southwest of Zdikov to the road, then through the draw on a heading of one-nine-five until we hit the next road, then due south. If worse comes to worst, I can always pick up a heading of one-ninety from Zdikov and go straight for the border. That should bring us out about the same place. Can you navigate from the air?"

"I have in the past . . . on the Golan. But I'll want to study it in more detail."

"Let me figure out the exact timing at different airspeeds so we hit the checkpoints on time all the way through. I want to doublecheck the headings."

"You're very thorough."

"What I have is a form of insanity."

"Your Miss Reynolds told you that?"

"All she did was provide the confirmation." He looked back at the map where the colors blended together into a multicolored blanket. A shroud. His.

"What's this?" Maggie asked when they were alone in the bedroom, her face an amalgam of suspicion and trepidation. "In other words, you're shipping out the excess baggage."

"A precaution," Hoffmann replied. "They've used this place for twenty-four hours, and there's been an unusual amount of traffic in and out. Odd hours. Strange people. It's for your own safety."

"How long?"

"Only a few days. Until next Wednesday. By then they'll have arranged to get you back to the States."

"And you'll stay here . . . you agreed to work with them!" She spoke as if the idea were a sudden, mystical revelation. "After everything that's happened!"

"It's the only way."

"No, it's not! These people don't care about you. You know things they need—I heard some of them last night, and it frightened me just to hear what you've been through. It scared me more than I ever believed I could be. But it's only a prologue to what's ahead if you go through with this idea of . . . It's reality turned inside out. You're doing this because of some antediluvian sense of honor—because of me. I won't allow it!"

"The decision isn't yours."

"Whose, then? It can't be yours either—despite the way you're acting, you're not certifiably insane."

"It goes behond me. Beyond Ben Ari and his people." He remembered the Israeli major's words; they had brought on an overwhelming feeling of insignificance, suffocating him.

"Let them handle it. They're equipped for it—you're not." She hesitated, then continued in a subdued voice. "If you try this, you won't come back. Walk away from it."

"I can't."

"Then it's only because you don't want to. This Ben Ari is not the type to simply throw you back to those people who tried to kill you, despite what he said last night."

"I know that, too."

Maggie would not look at him, letting her eyes stray to the bag of clothing on the bed, next to the open suitcase which had been her first evidence of an impending departure. "You're a study in contradiction."

"You said as much last night."

"And you prove it again now. Does this have anything to do with your father?"

"Partially."

"And the rest?"

"I can't tell you."

"You mean you won't."

"Both."

"At the very least, you owe me a reason."

"I owe you the assurance that you won't become more involved. Telling you the why or how nullifies that."

"You're very convincing," she replied without conviction, again looking at him. "Where am I going?"

"To Landsberg. With Aaron."

"Will I ever see you again after today?" Her voice carried a resignation absent until now.

"I'd like that very much." He reached out, placing his hands on her shoulders which now seemed so narrow, so slight. Slowly, he guided her to him, finding no resistance; her kiss was the singularly exciting thrill he had envisioned that morning in the hotel, when he watched her from across the room. He released her and turned toward the door, not wanting to let her go, afraid that by staying he would only make the eventual parting more difficult. For the first time in years, he felt himself caring deeply, unselfishly, for someone else. "I wish things had been different." Before she could reply, he left the room and quietly closed the door.

Yuri Kasimirov remained standing in the presence of his superior. He had not been offered a seat, but dismissed the lack of courtesy. Anatoly Kusheloff was not normally a courteous man.

"So, the Americans have decided to change their plans," Kusheloff said, tapping the end of his pencil on the desk behind which he sat.

"That is what Schellen told me, yes."

"When did you learn of this?"

"This afternoon, about six hours ago."

"And you are just now informing me?"

Kasimirov weighed his answer carefully. Kusheloff was nominally his superior in East Germany, but in fact had no actual authority over him. Kasimirov's instructions came directly from Moscow, a fact that rankled the older Kusheloff. Kasimirov's only responsibility was to keep the other man informed; operational decisions were made by others—men in an obscure building on the Prospekt Kalinina, six blocks west of the Kremlin.

Kasimirov replied, "There were many details to attend to in a short period of time. It could not be helped."

"In the future, I will expect you to keep me better informed. I should have known about this as soon as it happened."

"This time it could not be helped. I will endeavor to do better."

"See that you do." Kasimirov bristled under the rebuke. Kusheloff was one of the major reasons he hoped to return to Russia soon; the man was impossible to deal with. And incompetent, a failing he tried to overcome with abrasiveness. "Explain to me why the Americans changed their minds," Kusheloff continued.

"According to Schellen, they wanted to make the pickup in a more remote setting. The area around Heiligenstadt is highly populated, and there are several military installations in the vicinity."

"I am well aware of military dispositions in that area," Kusheloff interrupted, testily. "Continue."

Kasimirov brushed aside the affront. "Supposedly, the Americans were wary of that and the fact that the terrain is relatively flat, allowing for early radar detection. This is a logical assumption. As a matter of fact, that area of the border is well covered by our radar and troops—I should say by East German radar and troops."

"A minor distinction."

"In any case, these factors are known to the West, even though their knowledge of details is sketchy. They wanted to move the pickup point to an area less heavily defended and opted for a place in Czechoslavakia suggested by Schellen. A town called Zdikov, one hundred and twenty kilometers east of Regensburg."

"Why there?"

"Schellen convinced them it was a place he could use without raising suspicions over here, and it was near a border area that is lightly defended. Both statements are true. He has stayed with friends there before. I'm told the fishing in the mountain streams is quite good, and he has traveled there four times in the past several years."

"Have you insured that this new area is adequately protected?" Kusheloff asked.

"Yes, that's what I've been doing this evening. I've worked out the details with our people in Prague. They have assured me the area will be adequately covered."

"What have you arranged?"

"There are many details. I don't think there's any need to go into them."

"Ah, but I do," Kusheloff said, smiling, enjoying the obvious discomfort of the younger man. "Explain them to me."

"The pickup is scheduled for just after eight o'clock next Tuesday morning on the road between Zdikov and a town about two kilometers to the north. Early Monday morning, four men will arrive in Zdikov and take up residence there. They will keep an eye on Schellen and be there when the pickup is attempted Tuesday."

"Monday is too late. Have them there Sunday," Kusheloff said, asserting his authority.

"Monday is better. The pickup will not be until Tuesday, and I don't want to arouse any suspicions."

"How can that possibly happen? Send the men in on Sunday."

"I will see what I can do," Kasimirov replied, not wanting to concede the man's authority.

"I am sure you will do your best," Kusheloff said, his voice laden with sarcasm. "You may continue."

"Monday night, after sunset, an antiaircraft company will be deployed in the woods west of the road linking the two towns. At the same time, the border area will be reinforced along a forty-kilometer stretch with an additional eight companies of soldiers armed with individual antiaircraft weapons. They will supplement the border outposts already in place. This is being done at night, at the last minute, to keep from alerting the Americans. Even if they are detected, there will be delay in analyzing what it means and communicating it to the proper people."

Kusheloff weighed the information. This much was true. Those running the operation would probably learn of the troop movements hours after it was too late to change anything. By that time, the incident would have already occurred.

"The Czech Air Force will be on station continuously with a squadron of Fitters, starting at six in the morning on Tuesday," Kasimirov said. "They will be the third line of defense in case all else fails, which is unlikely."

"How will this be coordinated?" Kusheloff asked.

"I will personally run the operation from Zdikov. Radios and extra telephone communications will be installed tomorrow at the house where Schellen is staying. I will be with him throughout. After the helicopter is shot down, he will be arrested and turned over to the East Germans."

"All very neatly done, but I should not want to be in your shoes if something goes wrong."

"Nothing will go wrong. All possible situations have been evaluated and covered."

"For your sake, I hope so."

"Thank you for your concern, comrade," Kasimirov said, without meaning it. "I have to leave now. Schellen is on his way to Zdikov. He left six hours ago and is probably already there. I don't want to let him out of my sight from now on. If I leave now, I can get there by midnight—one in the morning at the latest."

"You may go. I will expect a telephone call twice each day to keep me informed."

"Yes, I will do that if it is possible."

"Be sure that you do." Kusheloff dismissed him with a gesture of his hand.

Heinrich Schellen stopped the car in front of the small brick house in Zdikov. He was not used to driving himself, and the long hours on the road had taken their toll. He unlocked the trunk of the car, retrieved the single large suitcase, and trudged toward the house. Inside, the lights were on.

"I see you made it with no problems," the man answering the door said. "Let me take your suitcase." Schellen entered. It took several seconds for his eyes to adjust to the light.

"Have you been able to contact everyone?" Schellen asked, collapsing in a cushioned chair in the small parlor.

"Not yet," the man answered. "Your message arrived only this afternoon, but arrangements have been made for taking you out Monday night, as you asked. Would you care for a schnapps? You look like you could use some."

"Yes. Thank you, comrade."

In a moment, the man returned with two glasses, handing one to Schellen. "*Prost*," he said, lifting the glass.

"*Prost*." Schellen took a long drink, the liquor warming him. "Now, tell me what you have done so far, Josef. We have only a little time. I expect I will have visitors within a few hours."

"To begin with," Josef Hersch said, "I have contacted

about half of the people on the list. I think you made a tactical error in threatening them; most would have helped willingly."

"It was necessary," Schellen said flatly. "I had to be sure they would cooperate, and quickly. I haven't much time. Men who think their comfortable little worlds may be shattered are more easily convinced to help."

"I still think it was unnecessary. They were angry that you would even consider exposing their SS backgrounds. To their minds, you have broken the oath."

"To hell with what they think. If they help me, that is all that counts. Willingly or unwillingly, it doesn't matter."

"Maybe not. Anyway, a car will pick you up Monday night at the church on the south side of the town. Stangl will be with whoever is driving the car. Be there at exactly nine o'clock with the dog; that is how they will recognize you. The recognition signal will be the 'Horst Wessel' song. They will give you the second line; you answer with the next to last."

Schellen smiled, "Very appropriate."

"We thought so. From there you will be driven about ten kilometers and change cars for the next leg of the journey."

"Where is that?"

"I can't say. For everyone's protection, it is best that you don't know all the details, just in case."

"Agreed. What else?"

"There will be several such changes during the night. I've set it up so that each driver knows only where he is to pick you up and where to drop you off. That way no one person knows the whole route, or more than two people who are involved."

"Very good, Josef. You were able to accomplish all this in one afternoon?"

"Yes. We have used the same basic scheme several times before. It was a matter of selecting different drop points, that's all. You will be taken to one of four crossings on the Austrian border where the guards are easily bribed. Once inside Austria, things become much easier. You will be taken to the town of Ried im Innkreis, where you will be given a complete new identity: passport, photos, and a new history. After that, there are several alternatives, including South America, which is what I would suggest. But that's up to you."

"It appears you have done well. Thank you."

"Is there anything else you need?"

"Not at the present. It's unlikely that I can get away to contact you later, because I'm sure to be watched closely. But just in case, how can I get a message to you?"

"Go to the butcher shop in Zdikovec. The butcher's name is Doubrava. Give him the message—say it is for Hersch—and he will see that I get it. If an answer is required, he will have that, too."

"Fine. Now I think you should go. My friends should be along shortly to make sure I'm following their orders."

Hersch rose and started toward the door. "There is one final thing you should know," he said, pausing with his hand on the door. "Things have changed in South America. The Jews are no longer taking prisoners, as they did with Eichmann. There have already been half a dozen killings there this year, and Bormann himself is in hiding, along with Mengele and others. I expect they will also come after you once they learn you aren't in East Germany. It might be wise to carry a cyanide capsule; it's been rumored they're using some of Eichmann's methods on our people. . . . Enjoy your trip, *mein herr*."

Chapter 19

It was nearly dark when Deborah Mueller eased her Fiat to a stop next to the white rail fence surrounding the small cottage on the edge of a woods near Kreuth. The setting was peaceful. The house was immaculately maintained, from the sparkling white shutters and freshly painted trim to the scrubbed flagstones that formed a winding walkway. Only one thing was out of place here: the owner, Eduard Richter.

Richter was a gunsmith, one of the finest craftsmen in Europe, though unknown outside a small circle which included some of the most wanted men and women on the continent. His clientele was small in number because he preferred it that way. Each paid well, far in excess of what the average gunsmith ever dreamed of demanding. The weapons he produced were unequaled in craftsmanship, but it was his method of doing business that earned him the privilege of charging exhorbitant prices. In seventeen years, he had never been linked to anyone with whom he dealt, because he followed two basic principles: never question a customer for name or motive; and supply only specially made, handcrafted, and therefore untraceable weapons.

His weapons were always individually tooled and produced at the client's request; he maintained no stock on hand. Each rifle or pistol was designed to suit a particular need and set of circumstances described by the buyer. To his knowledge, none had ever failed to perform as promised.

Deborah Mueller was one of his clients and, like the others, an infrequent visitor to the cottage. He opened the door quickly to her knock. Silently, they climbed the stairs to the attic workshop. She thought his glasses looked thicker than before, a stronger prescription probably due to long hours of close work.

"What can I do for you?" he asked, once inside his shop.

"I need a sniper rifle with scope. Seven point six two millimeters, with an effective range of six hundred meters."

"How soon?"

"In four days, by Sunday night."

"I'm sorry, it can't be done. Even without other work, it would take much longer."

She hated the inevitable bargaining that always accompanied any transaction with the man. "It's important. I'm prepared to pay an additional five hundred marks above the normal fee."

"That is unnecessary. I'm already working on a project for someone else." He indicated a barrel clamped in the bench vise, next to it a modified folding stock.

"If you can't do it, I'll have to go elsewhere."

Richter shrugged his shoulders. He didn't like Jews anyway; losing her business would not be a major tragedy, though he doubted she could find someone else.

"Would an additional thousand marks speed up development?"

"The money has nothing to do with it. My work takes time, and you have come during a busy period." He glanced at the clock above the workbench. "You must go now. I'm expecting another buyer. And please, next time call before coming here. It may save us both some time and . . . embarrassment. You were lucky I didn't already have some-one else here."

She reddened under the rebuke. "I'll try to remember, Herr Richter." Deborah wanted to remain and convince the old man to take on the job, but he gently took her arm while motioning toward the stairs. She let the gunsmith show her to the front door, then walked quickly to the Fiat and drove off. In her anger, she failed to notice the car parked half a kilometer east on the side of the road, barely hidden by the trees. It pulled into the spot she had just vacated.

A lone figure emerged and walked to the cottage. He had had it under surveillance for twenty minutes, and had seen the girl enter and depart. She was known to him, though she was unaware of the fact.

Richter opened the door shortly after the man knocked. The German was unable to hide his astonishment when he looked at the man's face, but quickly regained his composure.

"Are the shells ready?" the man asked.

"Yes, exactly as requested. Hollow tip, mercury bead insert. Please come in."

Kareem Abu Sharif followed the gunsmith inside.

The apartment was empty when Deborah returned at 8:30. She looked for a note, but there was none. After placing the armored vests in the spare bedroom, she put water on for coffee.

A soft knock on the door interrupted her thoughts; thoughts of Ben Ari, their affair, and the awkward love—hate relation-ship that now existed. Without hesitation, she opened the door, expecting him, hoping he was alone. She was ready to reconcile their relationship; the words, the setting, had been rehearsed in her mind after dinner. The emptiness of the .

hallway greeted her. Then a figure emerged from the shadows of the staircase several feet away.

The man was alone. But it was not Ben Ari.

"You're Deborah Mueller," he said flatly, his accent pronounced, the origin Arabic.

"I am. And you?"

"My name is not important." He looked beyond her into the apartment.

Fear transfixed her for an instant.

The man raised the pistol in his right hand and pointed it at her stomach, pushing her back into the apartment, then closed the door behind them. "Where is Ben Ari?"

"I don't know anybody by that name."

"Yes, you do. Where is he?"

"I told you I don't—"

"Tell me!" He grabbed her hair, twisting it viciously with his left hand until she winced in pain, forcing her to her knees. "Again, Where is he?"

"He's gone. I don't know where."

"When will he return?"

"He won't be back." She struggled as the man continued to apply pressure.

"I don't believe you." He released his grip on her hair and slapped her with a full swing of his left hand, catching the side of her nose, causing it to bleed freely. "Where?"

"Please . . . I don't know."

The second slap was delivered with greater force than the first, and she slumped to the floor on hands and knees, looking at the blood dripping to the carpet. She felt herself being pulled roughly to her feet. The next blow, a closed fist, struck the side of her head, causing her ears to ring, bringing more tears of pain to her eyes. She prayed for unconsciousness but it would not come, though her eyes closed involuntarily as she lay splayed on the floor.

She sensed rather than heard the metallic click only inches

away. Opening her eyes, Deborah saw the gleaming blade. A scream was born deep within her chest, only to be cut off as blackness enveloped her.

The wooded areas of Germany are well manicured, proud domains of local *forstmeisters* who know every tree, every animal. The pride is shared by the local populace, and it is not unusual on Sunday afternoons to see families walking briskly along the hard-packed dirt paths beneath the trees, a tradition passed from generation to generation. The woods hold a strange fascination, near worship, for the German people, a relationship that traces its origins to mythical figures of a distant pagan past.

Ebersberger Forest was such a place. It was there that Ben Ari took Hoffmann when they left Bad Tölz.

The cottage was an architectural hybrid of stone masonry and English Tudor design, more like a vacation home than a residence. The lower half had been built of large, irregularly shaped stones that were not quite gold—almost rust-colored—though flowing patterns of steel gray appeared throughout. The mortar was a dull white. Above the stone foundation, which extended to a height of four feet, the Tudor influence took over, with dark timbers set at angles in off-white stucco. Each window was made of small diamond panes. Although the cottage was not in the deep woods, several large pines grew in the front yard, offering a measure of seclusion.

Inside, on the first floor, the house contained a kitchen, bathroom, two small bedrooms, and a large living area dominated by a stone fireplace on one wall. There were no rooms above the living area, where the ceiling extended to the top of the cottage, making the room seem much larger than it actually was. Upstairs was a large, open sleeping loft overlooking the living area.

Upon entering, Hoffmann felt a chill and got the impression the cottage had not been used for a long time. Ben Ari stacked logs in the fireplace and soon had a blazing fire going. Warmth filled the house as Hoffmann sat watching the flames dance crazily from the logs, lighting the first floor, the blue-and-yellow wisps of color forming a myriad of ever-changing designs. Occasionally, loud pops came from the fireplace as the heat grew more intense.

He felt his shoulder being shaken and awoke with a start. Ben Ari stood over him.

"I've brewed coffee, if you want some."

"How long have I been out?"

"About thirty minutes. Your body is still recovering from lack of rest. Let's take another quick look at the maps and then get some sleep."

Hoffmann spread the maps on the drop-leaf table. Next to the routes he had sketched in pencil were printed the distances and times for each leg at thirty, sixty, and ninety knots.

Ben Ari looked at them closely, mentally checking times. The first three he calculated agreed with what Hoffmann had written, and he accepted the others as correct. Together, they traced each route slowly, with Hoffmann commenting on significant elevation changes they would encounter en route. Twenty-eight minutes and two cups of coffee later, they were finished. Hoffmann stood, rubbed his burning eyes, and followed Ben Ari to the kitchen.

"It's all an exercise in futility, isn't it?" he asked, feeling hugely, inordinately fatigued.

"You lack patience. An ingrained American malady after too many years of expecting immediate and positive results. I wouldn't be here if I thought we couldn't carry it off."

"Then you delude yourself. What you propose isn't plausible."

"You were willing enough to believe it before."

"I was coerced. There was no recourse except to do what I was told. My cooperation was guaranteed by force and fraud."

"Cardinal virtues."

"Hardly. But you employ them yourself."

"One must—at times. This is not one of them. You've seen the Gregory staff study and know the consequences of inaction. Your agreement was without hesitation, although I suspect your motivation is not entirely altruistic."

"And yours?"

Ben Ari leaned forward, his face contoured in harshness. "I would not weep if both Germanys vanished from the face of the earth. The roots of Hitler's Reich are deeply imbedded; new shoots resurface with growing frequency, reported with more openness and less discrimination in the German press. The world has a short memory."

"And you want to open all the old wounds."

"I want justice."

"You want revenge."

"That, too." The nightmare of a rail siding returned, and Ben Ari paused.

"We have a plan," Hoffmann was saying, "but no way of accomplishing it."

"The means are being arranged."

"How?"

"You don't have to know. At least not now." The Israeli rose and went to the telephone. Three times he was frustrated by a busy signal.

Finally, on the fourth try, the phone rang.

"Please . . . please let him go!" The woman's voice cracked. She was near hysteria.

"Magda?" Saying the name dredged up punishing thoughts of his own wife.

"Magda, this is Daniel." A faint change in background pitch warned him someone else had lifted an extension.

"This is Daniel," he repeated quickly so she wouldn't speak his name by mistake. "I must talk to Petar."

"I thought it was them again."

"Calm yourself. Slowly, now . . . tell me what is wrong."

"He is gone . . . they kidnapped him."

"Who kidnapped him?"

"They say they are part of Baader-Meinhof."

"When did it happen?"

"Tonight . . . this evening . . . the man with him in the car is dead, they say . . . but Petar is alive . . . they have been calling all night . . . the same question, again and again . . ."

She was close to total panic. Baader-Meinhof. It didn't make sense. Before he could ask the next question, a male voice cut in.

"What is your interest in this?" The heavy German accent came as a surprise.

"He is an old friend. Who is this?"

"That is not your concern at present. Why are you calling?"

Ben Ari ignored the question. "Magda, listen to me. When exactly—"

One extension clicked dead, and the German asserted himself.

"This is a serious police matter, I assure you, so it would be in your best interest to cooperate with the authorities. I must insist you identify yourself and come forward if you know anything concerning this case. If you want to help, and I assume you do, I can give you my personal assurance . . ."

The officer was being too friendly: a trace had begun. Ben Ari hung up.

Petar kidnapped. It couldn't have been Baader-Meinhof. A minor figure in an export firm of little consequence was not the type of hostage they would choose to make a political statement, or to bargain with to obtain the release of other gang members. Someone else, with a different objective, had executed the kidnapping and claimed it for the terrorists.

His greatest immediate concern was their exposed position in staying at the cottage. Of equal importance, Petar had been arranging for the machine that Hoffmann would fly when they picked up Schellen. Losing that vital link was a telling, possibly final blow.

"Grab the maps and whatever else you brought in," Ben Ari said, without explanation.

"Bad news?"

"The worst. I'm cut off from my home station. And we don't have transportation to pick up Schellen."

"Then it'll happen, won't it?"

Ben Ari was moving quickly and silently to the kitchen window, turning off the light above the table. "Quiet," he commanded in a loud whisper. "There's somebody outside. Do you have a pistol? . . . Get it, and keep an eye out front."

Hoffmann retrieved the weapon and stationed himself beside a front window. The blackness outside was impenetrable.

Several minutes passed.

"Can you see anybody out front?" Ben Ari asked.

"I can't see a damned thing."

"All right. Come here . . . our man is about thirty meters beyond that closest pine and to the right. Keep an eye on him. I'll got out the front and work my way around to his rear. After I'm gone, shoot anybody who tries to get in here. When I come back, I'll use the front door. The signal will be two knocks, followed by a single knock, then three more louder than the others."

Hoffmann repeated the sequence, then took up his position beisde the window, still unable to make out any human forms in the woods.

Ben Ari was swallowed up by the forest so quickly that someone only ten feet away would not have seen him. The absence of undergrowth made the going quieter and more rapid than he expected. A light southeast breeze offered a measure of background noise and helped cover his movement. Still, he was careful of his foot placement for fear of treading on a random fallen branch. Every three meters he stopped and listened, each time pausing for a different length of time, so as not to establish a detectable pattern.

Thirty minutes later, he was in position, as close as he could determine by pace count, placing whoever was watching the house between him and the cottage. He stood immobile. Listening, Watching. Finally he located his target.

Barely twenty meters ahead, almost hidden, the man shifted position and cleared his throat, the total duration less than a second, all the Israeli needed to fix the exact location. Ben Ari inched forward at a crouch, attempting to avoid low-hanging branches. He stopped for each step to listen before transferring his weight to the other foot. The pace was excruciatingly slow.

He was within three meters before he was detected.

A red beam stabbed through the blackness half a meter to his left, followed immediately by shots that shattered the heavy quiet of Ebersberger Forest. Ben Ari dove to his right as the shaft of red traversed the night air toward him. He rolled to his side, then to a prone firing position, and squeezed off return fire toward the source of the light.

A muted cry of pain came from the figure as the flashlight fell to the ground, its beam penetrating upward through the trees. The man crashed through the forest toward the house. Ben Ari was on his feet quickly, warily stalking his unseen prey in the darkness.

Inside the cottage, Hoffmann heard the shots and the cry that rung out almost simultaneously. Seconds later he saw the shape of a man moving toward the front door. He went opened the door and turned on the outside spotlight.

Surprise registered on the man's face as he was caught in the brilliance of the light, and for an instant he froze, staring at Hoffmann from beneath heavy, dark eyebrows. Then, recovering, he brought his weapon up and fired.

Hoffmann saw it unfold in slow motion, as if it were a dream, then felt himself fall backward into the darkness. As he did, he saw the man turn away and disappear.

Seconds later, Ben Ari entered. "Are you all right? Why didn't you take him out?"

"Buck fever. I couldn't move. Seeing him again—"

"Who was it?" Ben Ari demanded.

"Gerber . . . the chief pilot at Deutches Aero."

"You're positive?"

"He was right there! Why?"

Ben Ari ignored the American, his mind working feverishly for answers that would not come. If they had broken Petar and learned about the cottage, other sanctuaries could be compromised—even those unknown to the contact. Now nothing could be assumed.

Ben Ari dialed the phone; on the seventh ring it was picked up.

"Deborah?" No answer.

"Deborah!" He repeated the name several times, but heard no reply. Finally the dial tone cut in. He slammed the phone down and picked up his jacket, alarm etched on his face. "Collect all your gear. Maps—everything."

Hoffmann hurriedly filled the rucksack with their few belongings. "She didn't answer?" Ben Ari's eyes narrowed as he shook his head.

"I hope we're not too late." As they sprinted toward the car, a voice in Ben Ari's subconscious told him that time had already run out on the girl.

The tires never stopped their squealing protest as they plunged through the black countryside at a velocity well beyond the headlight's range, but Ben Ari maneuvered the car like a man born to Grand Prix racing. They arrived on the eastern outskirts of Bad Tölz and parked in a back alley. Ben Ari took off down a darkened side street at a fast jog, Hoffmann matching the pace with long, easy strides.

A back entrance to Deborah's building was open, and they entered quickly, with weapons drawn. The hallways were empty as they silently climbed the stairs and stopped outside the apartment door. Ben Ari tried the doorknob, found it unlocked, and in one rapid movement flung the door open and dove to the floor. The expected fusillade never came.

The room was devoid of life.

Hoffmann had seen many horrors in Southeast Asia, but he was unprepared for the sight of the crumpled, lifeless body of Deborah Mueller. She lay by the phone pulled from the small stand near the front window. Only four hours earlier they had been sitting around the table eating dinner. Now, it was covered with her blood.

"Get out!" Ben Ari hissed, turning on Hoffmann, pushing him toward the door. Then he turned his back and looked at the girl.

She had been beaten severely, and one arm lay at a skewed angle. Several narrow gashes were evident at the base of her throat and below the eyes, which were swollen shut. She was barely recognizable.

"Let me help you," Hoffmann said, as Ben Ari knelt to pick her up.

"No. I can take care of her," he replied quietly, with a sadness Hoffmann could only begin to understand. The Jewish agent picked her up gently, as if he were handling a precious, delicate ornament. Without a word, he carried her into the bedroom.

Hoffmann searched the room, looking for any signs of the intruder, and finally found it: half of a broken wooden match. It had not been carelessly tossed on the floor or accidentally left on a cushion; it was almost as if it had been left as a calling card by the person who had been there.

Ben Ari came out of the bedroom and closed the door slowly, silently, as if not to awaken the girl.

"I think I know who it was," Hoffmann said as Ben Ari crossed the room. "It was Locke." He handed over the small matchstick. "How long does it take to get from here to Aaron's place?" Eric asked.

"A little more than an hour." The implication of Hoffmann's question snapped him back to another level of awareness. The Israeli picked up the phone and dialed; it was answered almost immediately and the situation explained in less than a minute. He went into the second bathroom, which over-looked the street. When he returned, the automatic was in his hand.

"There's a car out front with two men in it, probably watching this place. This is what we do." He laid out the plan to Hoffmann.

They went downstairs together, then split up, Hoffmann leading through the back door they had entered earlier. He followed a path leading west behind the buildings for about seventy-five yards, to a point where it crossed an alleyway that connected with the street. Keeping in the shadows, he followed the passage until he found a dark alcove only a few feet from the sidewalk. When he was in position, the only sound he could hear was the beating of his own heart, a pounding at the temples due more to anxiety than physical exertion.

Exactly six minutes after Hoffmann was in place, Ben Ari came out onto the main thoroughfare, crossed to the opposite side, and walked west. The driver of the surveillance car remained behind the wheel; the man in the passenger seat got out and trailed Ben Ari on the opposite side of the street, about forty yards to the rear.

From his position in the shadows, Hoffmann saw Ben Ari stop, gaze into a shop window, then continue his leisurely pace. The tension in his stomach increased. He waited.

Thirty seconds went by. A figure passed him only an arm's distance away, the man's attention riveted on Ben Ari. He failed to hear Hoffmann's movement until it was too late.

"Don't move, or this thing goes off," Hoffman said too loudly, jabbing the gun barrel in the man's back before taking a quick step back. "Take two steps back, slower . . . and lace your fingers behind your head."

The man followed directions reluctantly as Hoffmann grabbed the entwined fingers, forcing them together, painfully immobilizing the man's hands. A grunt of discomfort came from the figure as Hoffmann pulled him farther back into the shadows. He forced the man to kneel on the rough cobblestones while maintaining his grip on the fingers, pushing him off balance against the wall.

Ben Ari entered the alleyway. "Who are you?" he asked, pressing his automatic to the man's temple.

"Go to hell." Ben Ari's violent blow almost caused Hoffmann to lose his grip. Again he asked the question.

"Pritchett," the man said, in obvious pain.

"Who's in the car with you?"

"Hawdon."

"Do you work for Locke?" No answer. Ben Ari struck the man a crushing blow, knocking him unconscious. "Keep an eye on him. I'll be back in a few minutes with the other one."

Before Hoffmann could reply, he was gone, down the alley toward the back of the row of buildings, moving silently. After what seemed like hours, a car pulled to a stop, blocking the street entrance as it backed in. Ben Ari got out and opened the trunk.

"Did you search him for a weapon?" Hoffmann handed it over. "Get in," Ben Ari said to the groggy figure. The man obeyed sluggishly, crawling in on top of his companion. The trunk was slammed shut.

"What are you going to do with them?"

"They'll be taken care of."

"You can't kill them," Hoffmann insisted.

"I could . . . but I won't." His furious eyes grew wide, a look of deep hatred, on the border of hysteria. "They are minor soldiers; pawns. When I find the animal who did it, he will not be shown such mercy. He is now as good as dead. and it will be a lingering death . . . as hers was. Even that is too good for his kind of filth." Ben Ari looked away. "Follow me in the other car; we'll leave this one on a back road and then find Deborah's killer."

"You're forgetting Schellen. What about him?"

"He is beyond our reach."

"There's another way. . . . I'll tell you later. We will help each other. First with Schellen . . . and then we'll decide what else."

Chapter 20

The *gasthaus* in Pfaffenhofen had only two rooms on the second floor, directly over the small open bar. Part of the building housed a barn: four stalls, a manure pile at the corner outside. A road wound past the entrance and disappeared into the surrounding hills between fields of hops, each laced with tall poles; heavy-gauge wires were strung in between to train the vines, absent now until spring. Through the single small window, Hoffmann could see the barren fields, most of the road, and a brooding sky promising rain.

It was almost noon.

"If we want Schellen, there's no other way," Hoffmann said, turning from the window. The idea had seemed ludicrous at first, even to him. But it was possible.

Ben Ari sat across the room on the edge of the bed, his fist clenched, tapping it absently against his chin. He had listened to the proposal, weighing alternatives and analyzing what Hoffmann had presented. "You can't be entirely sure.

Procedures change. The last time you were here was six years ago."

"Then we find out what they are. Aaron must have access—his maps came from American sources. I saw the packaging and labels."

"He can't be spared. Unless you've forgotten, he's guarding your Miss Reynolds."

"Then I'll do it."

"Not without running a very high risk of being recognized. The authorities will have been notified."

"It's a chance we'll have to take. Do you want Schellen?"

"Your question is redundant."

"As is your answer."

"Where would you steal this machine?"

"I repeat. Hohenfels. It's close enough to the border—just barely. The place is a major training area—thousands of troops there year around."

"You don't just walk into an installation like that and remove an aircraft."

"Someone did—eight months ago at Fort Meade, a flight-school washout who flew one away, buzzed the Washington Monument, and landed on the White House lawn. There's your proof."

"Which means that security will be tighter than ever. Such lessons are not quickly forgotten."

"That's why I have to find out what procedures are being used now."

"You can't do it."

"What? Learn the procedures? Or steal a helicopter?"

"Both."

"Then offer a better alternative, damn it!" Hoffmann paused, breathing deeply. Why was Ben Ari so obstinate? He had ridiculed the idea from its first mention, found fault with every facet, mocking him. "I say it can be done. Secrets—top secrets—are stolen every day from government facilities around the world more closely guarded. Properly executed, this would be easy by comparison."

"Agreed."

"But you say it can't be done."

"Then you haven't been listening. I said you couldn't do it. At least not from what I've heard so far. You offer a vague plan, based on more obscure assumptions, without a rational analysis of facts. What procedures will you need to learn? *How* will you learn them? From whom? And once learned, how will you employ this knowledge? Don't give me ambiguities based on the idea that you can't fail because of what some mentally unstable misfit did almost a year ago. Give me logic, not hostility. Facts; as you know them, and as you plan to use them to learn others. In detail. Leave the platitudes to the politicians."

Hoffmann stared at the Israeli, angered and frustrated. "I'll give you your damned facts—as I know them. You'll have to learn to live with the hostility."

"A small enough price to pay if it helps you perform."

Hoffmann bit back a response, calming himself before replying. "Augsburg is the first step."

They arrived outside Sheridan Kaserne a few minutes after six in the evening. Ben Ari parked the car two blocks from the main gate of the American post, on a side street near a trolley stop. Hoffmann walked down the wet pavement beneath the spill of streetlamps and approached a store twenty yards from the post's main entrance. The windows were cluttered with uniforms, patches, boots, insignia; a sign offered twenty-four–hour service on dry cleaning and overnight tailoring.

He tried the door and found it locked. Peering through the glass, he could make out a man in his late forties or early fifties seated behind the counter, counting the day's receipts.

Persistent knocking finally brought the shopkeeper to the door.

"We close at five o'clock," the man said irritatedly.

"I've got an emergency," Hoffmann replied.

"You Americans have emergencies all the time."

"I won't take long . . . and I'm willing to pay for your trouble."

"How much?"

"Let's say double the price of whatever I buy."

The man weighed this for a second. "What is it you want?"

"A complete new uniform."

The door opened wide as the man stepped back.

He selected a set of the new-style wash-and-wear fatigues, a hat, leather jump boots, and cloth insignia for the rank of captain and artillery branch. A counter on the far wall yielded the necessary unit patches and embroidered badges to round out the uniform.

"Can I get a cloth nametag made and have all these items sewn on?" Hoffmann asked when he'd finished.

"Nametags take five days."

"It's worth an extra fifty marks to me. The general will have my ass if I show up looking like last week's laundry. The name is Hoffmann . . . two N's." He pulled out a roll of bills and paid a hundred dollars on the counter.

The shopkeeper took the shirt and insignia, and disappeared through a curtain behind the counter. Seconds later, a heavy-duty sewing machine started up. When the man reappeared and handed over the uniform jacket, the work had been done to perfection. The shopkeeper took his money, then ushered him out of the shop and pulled the blinds.

Hoffmann returned to the car and changed into the uniform. The Israeli looked at him from the front seat.

"Your nametag!"

"I know. Couldn't be helped. My identification card had to match. . . . Let's go to Gablingen."

They headed north out of Augsburg to where the road cut through the flat valley farmland. Thirty minutes later, Ben Ari dropped him off near the airfield gate. A solitary guard shack sat beneath the glare of a spotlight. The Israeli departed, driving to the first curve in the road. He doused the headlights and made a U-turn, then parked near a farmhouse where he had clear sight of the entrance.

Hoffmann approached the guard station.

"Good evening, sir," the M.P. said, stepping from the shack and saluting. "Can I help you?"

"I need to get into flight operations."

"Flight ops is closed, sir. Won't open up until zero eight hundred."

"I know," Hoffmann replied, His mind raced, assimilating the knowledge, sorting it with other possibilities. A delicate balance between asserted authority and requested assistance was required—too much of either would raise questions in the normally suspicious minds of the military police. "Details like that don't seem to faze the brass from Heidelburg. What's the chance of getting in with the staff duty officer or N.C.O.?"

"Your business, sir?"

"The general decided to extend his inspection tour to include Austria over the weekend, and I need—I should say, he needs—charts. Plans on departing at oh-dark-thirty."

"May I see your identification, captain?"

Hoffmann pulled the green card from his wallet and handed it over, apparently uninterested as the private wrote his name on a form attached to his clipboard.

"Unit, sir?"

"HHD, USAREUR. The flight detachment in Heidelburg," Hoffmann replied, looking at his watch, frowning; an officer in a hurry. "These receptions are a pain in the ass. He'll probably raise hell because I'm late—no wonder everybody hates these no-notice visits. The brass burn us peons for trying to do our jobs, then think nothing of taking off on some junket to Kitzbühel because there's a good restaurant at some ski lodge they know. But I guess Rank Hath Its Privilege. Who did you say the S.D.O. was?"

"Lieutenant Rhodes, sir. I'll give him a call."

"Thanks. I appreciate it."

Minutes later, a jeep pulled up to the gate. The M.P. returned the ID card, and Hoffmann got in. They drove to a long, two-story building, a hangar built by the Luftwaffe in the late 1930's. Operations and flight planning were located on the second floor, in a series of rooms overlooking the cavernous work area where a dozen or more aircraft sat in various stages of disassembly. The upstairs hallway was painted a light green and decorated with a montage of unit insignia and photographs in flat black frames. Flags stood next to the trophy case outside the commander's office, and above it pictures of the senior officers in the chain of command. Hoffmann stopped momentarily to survey the contents of the glass case, a passing interest, his eyes wandering to the pictures, names memorized quickly. A counter next to the flight-planning table provided the needed publications.

"Do you have an SOP in here for the MTA's?" Hoffmann asked. "General Davis wants to stop en route back on Monday."

Rhodes shook his head. "Don't know, captain. I'm not assigned here."

"Mind if I look?" Hoffmann asked, glancing at his watch. "It's worth a few minutes to keep myself out of trouble. The Deputy C.G. has a memory that's frightening when it comes to things like that." He checked the row of black binders on the shelf next to a locked file cabinet, finding nothing on the installations. A unit roster was thumbtacked to the bulletin board; he skimmed it and found two familiar names—one more so than the other. Six years. The outline of the face was a distant memory. But it was enough. He wrote the phone number above the legend on one of the maps.

"Small-world department," Hoffmann offered in response to Rhodes's unasked question. "Thanks for your help. Now, if you could do something about the value of the dollar and my lost hold baggage, I'd get you a meritorious ARCOM." The sudden friendliness was too effusive, out of character for an angry officer running an errand at odd hours. An edge of scorn was on his voice when he said, "As if the brass really cared. I've got what I need. Can we go?"

Ben Ari picked him up on the road out of sight from the M.P. shack ten minutes later. Hoffmann changed clothes in the back seat as they drove toward the autobahn.

"Couldn't get everything," Hoffmann said as the Israeli pulled away. "A phone call should get the rest of what I need."

"Problems?"

"None. Neither one of them suspected a thing."

Lieutenant Vince Rhodes made another entry in his duty log:

> TIME: 1937
> SUBJECT Picked up classified dispatches and delivered
> to S-2 vault (SFC Hornberger)
> ACTION: Logged
> INITIALS: VJR, Staff Duty Officer

The dispatches were in a courier's pouch on top of the desk. A receipt inside indicated only seven messages he had signed for; two copies of the receipt remained. He would have Hornberger sign and give him a copy for the vault files, keeping one for attachment to the duty log.

Out of curiousity, he opened the pouch and extracted the computer-printed messages, looking through them to insure everything was there, an unnecessary motion since he'd already done it twice before. This time he pulled back the cover sheets and read through them quickly to see what they contained.

The third page caused him to stop and catch his breath. He read it again. Underneath the three-line heading of letters, numbers, and an assortment of different punctuation, all indecipherable to him, was a plain-text message classified secret.

    SUBJECT U.S. Army deserter—Eric Michael Hoffmann
    TO: Installation Commanders
        Installation Provost Marshalls
        USAREUR Distribution Alpha (-)
    FROM: Commander, USAREUR

1. Subject deserter Eric Michael Hoffmann, wanted by U.S. Army. Last sighted vicinity Munich. Subject armed and considered dangerous. Considered mentally unstable and unpredictable. Also wanted by civilian authorities in connection with civil crimes. Commanders are to apprehend, detain, isolate subject. Report through Provost Marshall channels directly to CDR, USAREUR ASAP pending Article 32 investigation. Installation interrogation is not, repeat, is not authorized.

2. Description: Age: 29
                 HT: 74 inches
                 WT: 190 pounds
                 Hair: Brown, light, short
                 Eyes: Blue
                 Disting. Characteristics: None

3. Dissemination: Provost Marshall, Military Police only
                                CDR
                                USAREUR

Rhodes blinked in disbelief. The man described in the message had been sitting across from him only a half-hour ago. Now he didn't know what to do. Reading the classified documents was expressly forbidden, an order made abundantly clear by Colonel Parker that afternoon. He could put everything back in the pouch and hand it over to Hornberger, and nobody would be the wiser . . . maybe. He debated which of two bad alternatives he should choose.

He picked up the phone and dialed.

"Colonel Parker, this is Lieutenant Rhodes, weekend S.D.O., sir. Something very important has come up you should know about. . . . No, sir, I think it should be done in person. Sorry to bother you, sir, but it won't hold until Monday. . . . In the adjutant's office . . . fifteen minutes? . . . Yes, sir."

Lt. Vince Rhodes, VMI, Class of '72, hung up the phone and wondered if there might be some way of salvaging his military career. He doubted it. One crummy little mistake in two and a half years, he thought, and they'd crucify him. He felt sorry for himself. And he hated Hoffmann for being the cause of it all.

He hoped they'd catch the guy.

Lousy deserter.

Chapter 21

Almost every efficiency report ever written on James Roberts included a statement about his ability to deal with people, his knack of getting others to like him and willingly do anything he said needed to be done. This was usually attributed to his genuine regard for others, and the fact that he just liked people. The man sitting on the chair across from him in the apartment was testing that reputation.

That man was Roy Locke.

"I can't accept that," Roberts said firmly.

"It's the simple truth. Your friend Hoffmann is a wanted killer."

"Impossible. I've known him for six or seven years, on and off. We aren't talking about the same person."

"I'm afraid we are. How do I convince you that Hoffmann is dangerous? He's wanted by the Army and the German police. In the past few days, he's destroyed a rented car, kidnapped a girl named Maggie Reynolds, and killed an officer who was trying to arrest him."

"I still find that hard to believe."

"Facts are facts."

"Even if what you say is true, and I'm sure it's not, I don't see how I could help."

"Look, we know he was here in Augsburg just a few hours ago. You've confirmed he called. All I want from you is his location. You don't have to be involved. We won't say where we got the information."

"There's a lot more to the story than what you're telling me, isn't there?"

"No—unless you want all the gruesome details. Just let me know where he is, and you won't need to be bothered with them."

"I don't know where he is."

"I think you do. This is an important investigation, and if you're not cooperative you can be charged as an accessory after the fact. I'm sure you understand what that implies."

"Damn right I do," Roberts replied angrily. "It implies a threat. And I don't like being threatened by you or anybody else."

"I'm not trying to threaten you, believe me, but I don't think you understand the seriousness of what's going on here. You say he's a friend, but ask yourself this: how well do you really know him? In the military you run across people you knew somewhere else maybe two or three years ago, and because they're a familiar face in a strange setting, they're automatically labeled 'friend.' How many close friends do you really have? And I mean people you know well."

Roberts thought about the question. The Army, with its constant movement and assignment changes, didn't make it easy to get to know people intimately.

Locke could tell he'd raised a doubt in the officer's

mind and pressed the advantage. "When was the last time you saw Hoffmann, before tonight?"

"About two years ago. Passing through Sill." It had been a brief encounter which Hoffmann had forgotten, barely remembered even after he'd mentioned it.

"Two years! And before that?"

"I don't know—maybe another four years."

"And that qualifies him as a close friend? Somebody you know well? I just can't imagine how. People have a way of changing, and your friend Hoffmann is no different. You're not exactly the same person you were two years ago. Did he tell you why he got out of the service?"

"He said it just wasn't for him anymore."

"A half-truth. He was assigned to Fort Campbell in 1973 and got caught messing around with a sergeant's wife. Apparently, it was an ugly scene when the husband caught them in his own house one night. Neighbors called the M.P.'s, and by the time the investigation was over, Hoffmann was forced to resign. They transferred the sergeant." Locke turned to Kate Roberts, who had remained silent, sitting next to her husband on the sofa. "He's a changed person from what he might have been two years ago. If you want to check this out, call the Munich police and they'll read you the arrest warrant, which includes assault and battery on a hotel employee, among other things. Just by knowing he's here, both of you are in danger. I don't mean that to scare you—it's simply a warning, for your own safety."

"Okay, maybe we don't know him that well," Roberts said.

"I didn't think so. He's used you, like he used the girl in Munich and others. You don't owe him anything."

"We still don't know where he is."

"Will he be back?"

"We invited him for dinner tomorrow night."

"Chances are he won't show, but we'll have people watching the place. What did he want to know?"

"We just talked, that's all. Mainly about the Army, and what Kate and I would be doing when we left here."

"Did he say anything about what he might be doing the next few days?"

"Nothing."

"Was there anything he seemed particularly interested in about Germany? A place, an event."

"Nothing outside Augsburg. He used to be stationed here himself. He didn't mention any other names that I remember. We talked about the Army, but that's not unusual. Hell, when you're in it, that's about all you *can* talk about."

"Tell me what you discussed."

"Flying, mostly. I'm an aviator and he is too—we went to flight school together—so we did a lot of talking about flying."

"Did he tell you about having a job with an air-charter company in Munich?" Roberts nodded. "Did he say anything about going back there?"

"No. Except he said he had to go to Munich tonight. He had a date there."

"Another lie, I'm afriad, but we'll check it out. Anything else?"

"That's all. He did mention he'd been down at Fort Meade shortly after that incident where some flight-school dropout stole a helicopter and landed it on the front lawn of the White House. He asked if we had felt the results of that episode over here yet."

"In what way?"

"Increased security. Locking up helicopters and installing ignition keys."

"Go on."

"Our helicopters never had ignition systems that required a key. They still don't over here, but, according to Eric, a modification is being made."

"You mean that anybody could just get in one and start it up?"

"All they'd have to do it connect the battery. Apparently that's what the kid at Meade did."

"And the doors aren't locked?"

"Not really. We've installed a thin strip of sheet metal that fits over the cargo-door handles and locks onto the front doors so that neither can be opened. I think that's standard throughout the Army now, but it's just eyewash. Anybody who wanted to could still get inside with ease."

"That's it," Locke said, half to himself. Knight's theory had been right; the American was working with Ben Ari. And they were going through with the plan to pick up Schellen by stealing an Army helicopter. Unbelievable. But desperation was the mother of invention. And, given the situation, it was a workable idea.

"What's it?" Roberts asked, breaking into the agent's thoughts.

Locke ignored the question. "Was he interested in any particular airfields?"

"No, he wasn't."

"In your conversation with him, did you mention any specific place where helicopters can be found?"

"No . . . except Hohenfels. I told him we were going there for a month's training, starting next week."

"I think I know what he used the two of you for. Now listen. If he calls you, don't disclose anything that we've talked about tonight and don't tell him I've been here. Can I have your word on that?"

"I guess so."

"No guessing. If we're to keep him from harming anybody else, it's important for us to get to him quickly, and I can't do that if he knows what we've discussed. You shouldn't talk to anybody about tonight. It could damage our whole investigation. . . . You've been a great help."

He rose and walked quickly to the apartment door, urgency propelling him. After thanking them again, he left quickly, almost running to the car. Two hours! Hoffman could be a hundred miles away. Several minutes later, he stopped at a pay phone, checked in with his office, then drove onto the E11 autobahn, headed east.

The autobahn ended on the outskirts of Munich. Locke drove to the building on Ludwigstrasse, arriving forty-five minutes after leaving Augsburg, and parked the car in a side street out of sight from the entrance. Inside the office, Renzetti and Duncan stood talking by his desk. They looked up from the files scattered on its top.

"What is this important message you told me about on the phone?" Locke asked, removing his coat and tossing it over a chair. He looked at the plain-text inscription on the computer sheet handed to him. It contained only seven words:

UNIFORM. REPEAT. G.W. TEXT. 22 NIKOS —14.
QUENTIN. DELTA ROMEO.

"When did this come in?"

"About nine forty-five. It's not a code we're familiar with."

"Who received it?"

"The commo section."

"Specifically."

"Snyder."

"Tell him to forget he ever saw it. You two do the same."

"Do you want us to hang around?"

"No. I've got to make a call. I'll ring if I need you."

Locke stared at the message for several seconds. He didn't like what he saw. In truth, it bothered the hell out of him.

"Quentin" was his code name for this operation, the reason Duncan had put out the message signal on the beeper. The

G.W. stood for William Goff; another code name, assigned to Pete Anderson for a joint operation they had worked on eight months earlier. Anderson was now in Langley at the Communications Center. Placement of address indicated use of Madras, a set of automatic switching terminals in Washington known to less than a dozen people in Europe and used only in certain extreme circumstances specified in standing procedures. Even the bureau chiefs familiar with it were forbidden to make calls through the system unless given specific priority approval by the Director of the CIA. Now Anderson was saying to use Madras to contact him between 3:00 and 5:00 P.M. Eastern Standard Time. And to do it immediately, without verification of approval. He didn't like the implications.

He picked up the phone, bypassed the overseas operator, and placed a call to Atlanta, Georgia. A phone rang twice on the opposite end, followed by a brief dial tone. Eight seconds of silence later, the sound of relays being activated came over the line, followed by another dial tone, then the repeated sound of electrical relays. He entered five digits, waited three seconds, then entered six more. He waited, knowing that someone at Langley was tracing the call to its origin. Finally the silence was broken. Pete Anderson's voice came on the line.

"Are you crazy?"

"The message said most urgent, and you placed it almost an hour ago. I couldn't waste time trying to find another phone."

"But calling from your own office?"

"This line doesn't go through our own board. Nobody's listening. Besides, if anybody checks Madras, I'm sunk anyhow; they'll know it was me. What do you have?"

"A hot message I've been sitting on for too long."

"Which is?"

"A memorandum with your name on it. I'm the only one

on shift with a code alpha-six, so Knight brought me the cipher."

"Read me the message."

Anderson recited the words. The memorandum meant only one thing to Locke: he had to locate Hoffmann and the Israeli quickly. Speed was paramount.

Locke asked: "Addresses?"

"Athens and Berlin, East."

"When are you going to send it?"

"I already have. But I wanted to get to you in person before it was on the wire too long—I owe you that much from Cyprus."

"Then I'd say we're even."

"So would I."

"Any reasons given."

"None. Knight has been going crazy around here. I don't know what it is, but he's pulling some screwball moves with the staff. I don't want to get caught in the middle. When I hang up this phone, it'll be like I never knew you."

"I understand."

The phone went dead.

Locke flipped the switch on the office intercom. "Duncan, get in here." Seconds later, the door opened. "Tell me what you've gotten from the files."

"Ben Ari has worked with five people in Germany that we know of," Duncan began. "What we have here dates back two years ago, to the 'seventy-two Olympics. Apparently, he got here just a few hours after the Israeli dormitory was taken over. He worked with these five people." A list of names was handed over: Aaron Edelmann, Klaus Grunwald, Werner Schmidt, Simon Levin, Frederick Evlom.

"Do we know where they are now?"

"Edelmann is living in Landsberg, of course. Grunwald and Levin are in Munich. Evlom is in Landshut. Schmidt was killed over a year ago near his home in Ingolstadt. The police report lists it as an unsolved murder—hit and run."

"What background have you been able to dig up?"

"Not much. What we have is pretty sketchy and probably more fiction than fact. It's being typed now; we'll have it for you in about twenty minutes."

"See if you can't speed that up. I've got to get moving. Pull that team off the stakeout on Edelmann's place in Landsberg; he won't be back there, and there's no need to waste the manpower. I'm going to be out of pocket for the next few days, but I'll call in from time to time. Tonight, I'm going to Bremerhaven, if someone needs to get in touch with me."

"Bremerhaven?"

"I got a tip in Augsburg he might be trying to get out by ship. It'll take me two or three days to work the docks. I'll let you know how to contact me once I get there."

"You want us to get hold of our man in Hamburg?"

"Not yet. If I need him, I'll let you know."

"Any special instructions?"

"Just keep the surveillance setup we have going now. And if anybody finds him, I want to know about it. Put it in code on the Armed Forces Network, during the hourly newscast. They're usually cooperative."

Locke reclined in his chair, lit a cigarette, and threw the broken wooden match in the ashtray. He wondered if Pete Anderson had sense enough to locate and destroy the voice-activated tape made every time the Madras intercept was utilized. Personally, it made no difference to him. Not now.

Chapter 22

A cold, clammy Saturday hung quietly over the countryside as Ben Ari negotiated the high-speed curves of the highway. He had barely spoken all morning, and now his mind was on his driving. Hoffmann concentrated on the disagreeable weather, knowing it would play the major part in the success or failure of their mission. What he saw was disturbing.

He had grown accustomed to analyzing the weather closely; his interests encompassed frontal movements and predominant weather patterns associated with them. Wind velocity, ceilings, and visibilities were the common items he looked at each day; temperatures, dew points, barometric readings—all had special meaning to him. If a strong front didn't push through before Monday, everything they had done so far was wasted effort.

Ben Ari braked hard and swung onto the ramp leading to the E5 autobahn just south of Regensburg. They entered the highway and turned northwest, following it for five exits to the Parsberg interchange. Hohenfels lay nineteen kilometers ahead.

The small town of roughly two thousand people looked like most others its size in Germany. Streets lined with small shops and residences were the rule. A calm, unhurried atmosphere prevailed.

"If my memory is any good, the main entrance to the post is down that road," Hoffmann said, indicating a street to their left.

They parked on the main road and waited. Only a few military vehicles passed them in the first half-hour. Finally, Hoffmann slipped into the fatigue jacket he'd purchased the day before in Augsburg and stepped from the car.

"I'll try to be back by noon." He walked a short distance from the car and a few minutes later hailed a lone jeep, which pulled to the curb.

"Hop in, captain. Goin' on post?" The southern drawl was thick, overemphasized.

"That's right." Hoffmann sat and swung his legs on board. The distinctive smell of wet canvas reached him, a familiar scent that brought back a flood of memories. The driver forced the transmission into first, grinding the gears.

"This damn ol' thing is always doin' that."

"It's called planned obsolescence. The transmission's only built to last five thousand miles. That's how they keep the civilians in Detroit employed."

The driver laughed too loud and slapped his knee. "That's a goodie. Ain't many officers got a sense of humor." He let out the clutch, and the jeep lurched forward, clashing gears each time they were shifted. Hoffmann noted the soldier was young, probably no more than nineteen; the bumptious insolence of the disparaging remark made him instantly disagreeable. The insignia on the collar showed he was a PFC, and from the rumpled look of the uniform and the proliferation of black grease stains on both jacket and trousers, Eric wondered how he'd even gotten that far. The private's hair was longer than his own and stuck out at various angles from the soiled cap that had once been green.

"You new here?" the driver asked.

"Just got in last night."

"Thought so. Had a feelin' you didn't know the rules about not goin' into town. The post commander is a pee-bringer and he'd 'a fried your butt if you was caught."

"I didn't know. Thanks for the tip. How come you're in town?"

"Me? I had to haul chow out to some guys at the railhead." He indicated a case of open C-Rations in the back seat. "C's. I won't touch 'em. Told the top shirt I refused to eat them damned things . . . and I don't."

The jeep crested the hill at the edge of the military reservation. Fifty meters ahead stood the stone guard shack at the post's entrance. Hoffmann knew from memory it was never manned, especially on weekends.

A tightness gripped his stomach when he saw a khaki-clad figure in a glossy black helmet step from the shack and motion for them to stop. He thought back to the staff duty officer in Augsburg. Was it possible an alert was out on him?

"Let me see your trip ticket," the M.P. said brusquely, standing next to the jeep on the driver's side, resting his weight on one leg and looking at them with an acquired air of superiority. Hoffmann could see it from his chest to his knees. The nametag on the heavily starched shirt read CRENSHAW; a buck sergeant's chevron of three stripes was neatly sewn on each sleeve. "Now the logbook."

The driver handed over the green looseleaf.

"Your dash-one daily isn't filled out. Is this your vehicle?"

"That's my mistake, sergeant," Hoffmann said, before the driver could reply. "I failed to check it before we left the motor pool this morning. I'll make sure it's corrected."

Crenshaw leaned over and looked past the private at Hoffmann, noticing the captain's bars on the hat for the first time. "Sorry, sir, I didn't see you were an officer." The tone had mellowed, retreating behind a veil of feigned deference.

"That's all right . . . sergeant," Hoffmann replied, emphasizing the rank. "It's hard to see this subdued rank sometimes."

"Yes, sir," Crenshaw said. "Good morning, sir." He handed the logbook back to the driver and snapped a precise salute which Hoffmann returned. The private shoved the protesting gearshift into first and they moved forward. Hoffmann drew in a deep gulp of air as they pulled away, realizing he'd been holding his breath for several seconds.

"What in hell was that?" the grease-stained private asked, twenty yards inside the gate.

"I just saved your butt," Hoffmann replied, slipping into a slight drawl himself.

"You did?"

"Sure. He was going to write you up until he realized he'd screwed himself by not saluting me. I never did like M.P.'s much anyway."

"How 'bout that. An officer playin' games with the po-leese. Man, you're all right in my book." The soldier gave him a toothy grin and then looked back to the road.

"Now you can do me a favor."

"How's that?"

"Drop me off up by Range Control. Do you know how to get this thing off post without going out the main gate?"

"C'mon, that's easy in a four-wheel drive."

"Okay. Pick me up in an hour."

"You goin' back into town?"

"You got it."

"Man, I wish you was our C.O."

"Thanks," Eric replied, concealing his dislike for the little Southerner. Aside from his unkempt appearance, he didn't know how to address an officer.

Hohenfels Range Control was housed in a small cinderblock building on the main post, amid a grouping of similar structures, out of the main traffic flow. A quick look around told Hoffmann it was unoccupied, so he tried the main entrance after the jeep departed and found it locked. The rotted wood of the door splintered around the hasp after a few seconds of force, and he entered.

It was typical of most centers set up to control the activities associated with military training. Several maps hung on the walls, indicating the various ranges used for weapons firing and their associated safety zones; acetate-covered charts showed available ranges, their map coordinates, and the units occupying them. Crumpled papers littered the floor around overflowing trash cans, and papers were spread in general disarray on desks that badly needed painting. A quick search produced copies of the previous week's range assignments. Two sheets had radio call signs scribbled in pencil next to several of the unit designations. A stack of message forms lay in a box on the corner of a table next to a radio mount, but they revealed nothing of interest.

Two desks in the room were unlocked, and in one he found a copy of the range assignment schedule for the upcoming week. He noted the unit assigned to the range farthest from the main post and wrote down the call sign, then put both schedules in his pocket. Several maps of the post lay on another table. He took one, carefully folded it, and placed it inside his shirt.

The search had taken only ten minutes but produced all the information he needed, including the FM radio frequency used for controlling activity on the post. With a quick look outside, he departed.

His next stop was the airfield, about three-quarters of a mile away. The route he took was circuitous, away from the main roads, keeping in mind what the jeep driver had mentioned earlier about the number of M.P. patrols. For some reason, they had been out in force since Friday night.

Hoffman was sure he knew why.

An hour after entering the Hohenfels training area, Hoffmann was on his way out, this time overland. The driver had taken the southwest tank trail and turned into the woods two miles down the muddy road. The bone-jarring trip over what had once been no more than a deer trail had Hoffmann holding on to the vehicle's windshield the entire way. Finally, after a twisting descent down a twenty-degree slope, they came out on the main road.

The soldier dropped him off on a side street near where Ben Ari was parked. He walked the remaining fifty yards to the car.

"Did you get everything you needed?" Ben Ari asked, as Hoffmann slid into the seat and removed his fatigue jacket.

"Everything. I've got an idea now on how we can do it." Hoffmann unfolded the map on the seat between them. "Let's go back up the east side of the reservation and check out these trails; two of them are close enough to put us within walking distance of the airfield."

"What about aircraft?"

"There's seven on the field right now. All of them are locked with the sheet-metal strips, but I figure we can get through them with no trouble. Do you have any tools?"

"Screwdrivers and pliers."

"That should do. None of the ships has the new ignition switch, and two of them have helmets left inside. I'm hoping they'll still be there Monday morning; if they aren't, we'll use the headsets Deborah gave you."

A small pack of wild boar trotted across the open field not fifty yards from where Hoffmann stood, just inside the treeline. They had parked the car nearly a mile away, next to a stream that prowled slowly through the floor of the valley behind them, then hiked through thick woods until coming to the edge of the reservation. Ben Ari knelt next to him, the map spread out on the ground as he oriented it to north by matching terrain features to the countour lines on the sheet.

"Doesn't look promising," the Israeli said, looking up. "We wouldn't get the car ten meters up this trail."

"How far is the next trail from here?"

"Two kilometers north."

"It puts us that much farther from the airfield if we use it. This might be the best entry." Hoffmann stopped at Ben Ari's side, scrutinizing the map. "It looks like about four hundred meters from here to this tank trail that cuts across the main post road. It's open terrain, and once we're on the tank trail we'll make good time."

"It's about five kilometers on foot, an hour's walk."

"Not too bad. We could still check out some other places closer to the airfield. If we can't drive the car up here, we might as well leave it closer to the field and cut down our travel." As he spoke, Hoffmann indicated points on the map with his finger, tracing a number of places where the terrain was not too steep.

They both heard the movement at the same time.

"No sudden moves," a voice barked. "You . . . next to Ben Ari. Take his gun with your left hand and throw it into the woods. Slowly. I am prepared to kill you both." Hoffmann did as he was told. "Now, both of you . . . kneel down. Hands behind the heads, and cross your legs behind you."

The man walked around to face them from ten meters away, the short-barreled shotgun pointed at Ben Ari's head. He was of medium height and slim build. With his dark black hair and dark complexion, he was obviously a foreigner to Germany. The man's penetrating stare fixed on Ben Ari only, excluding Hoffmann as if he did not exist.

"So, Ben Ari, at last. I have traveled many miles for this moment. It has been worth it."

"Sharif."

"I am surprised you recognized me." An icy smile began to form, then disappeared.

"I didn't. But your presence is not unexpected. Your leader let us know you were coming."

The cold smile returned. "I know. He is an old woman who will not remain long in power when he finds he can no longer balance all the different factions of the Palestinians. But that should mean nothing to you now. I am here, and soon I will settle the matter between us."

"You killed my wife."

"I did not know she was among the dead. Thank you. It pleases me."

"It's too bad you don't have the courage to accompany your suicide squads."

"I was not permitted."

"A coward's defense."

The grip tightened on the shotgun for an instant, then relaxed. "Certainty of death makes you a brave man. But killing children proves you to be the coward."

"Another PLO lie. But then your very existence is a continuous mockery of the truth."

The two men glared at one another. Hoffmann could sense the years of bitterness between cultures focused in these two enemies who faced one another hundreds of miles from the scene of their past struggles. Finally, Sharif looked at Hoffmann for the first time.

"You should be more careful when you choose your friends. Now you must share his fate."

Hoffmann's mind raced. "I don't know what you two are talking about."

"I am Kareem Abu Sharif. And I have come to kill this man for what he did to my daughter. He is a child-killer."

"I still don't understand."

"Many months ago this Jew led a raid on a refugee camp

in Lebanon near Sidon. When he was done, the village was destroyed and my daughter with it. She was not yet thirteen."

"Untrue," Ben Ari said. "When we arrived at the camp, everyone was already dead. You own men did it, because they could not take the weaker ones with them and were afraid of what they might tell us."

"You lie!" The sound shattered the forest calm. Sharif took a menacing step forward.

"How did you find us?" Hoffmann asked, diverting the Arab's attention.

"That is not your concern."

"What difference does it make?" Time. He just wanted time. He hoped that Ben Ari could do something. Anything.

"We located you in Bad Tölz and followed you to the house in the Ebersberger Forest."

"Gerber?"

"Yes. He was stupid . . . but still smart enough to follow you to the house and notify us."

"But how did you trace us here?"

"A simple matter once we had planted a homing device on your car. The Odessa has many resources, including people." Sharif relaxed a fraction. "Don't look surprised. We work with them very closely now. Their funds are available to us since they have given up on the Egyptians. We have bought and paid for our recognition in the United Nations with their money. They are laughable old men who spend their time pouring beer into their ponderous bellies and devising impossible plots. But we are more than willing to use their money and manpower."

Ben Ari's almost imperceptible movement did not go unnoticed.

"Do not try anything so stupid again," Sharif said, adjusting his grip on the weapon. "This gun has five shells in it, and I can fire three of them into you before you can blink. Be patient. We are almost at the appointed time. Enjoy your final minutes while you can."

Hoffmann's inner being wanted to cry out. They had come so far, endured so much to stop an insane scheme for reuniting Germany; a plan that would send the whole world into chaos. Now this Arab would become the unknowing accomplice of those who would attempt it.

"Do you know what you're doing?" Hoffmann blurted.

Sharif laughed, a low, mirthless chuckle devoid of humor; a demonic sound. "I have always known. My life has been guided by the surety that we would rid Palestine of the Zionists, more recently by the fact that I would see Ben Ari dead. The time has come."

The Arab swung the barrel of the shotgun from Hoffmann to Ben Ari and crouched forward, legs spread, breathing audibly through his nose. Pressure was being applied to the trigger!

Hoffmann saw the flash from the corner of his eye at the same time Sharif's right side erupted in a shower of red. The body contorted hideously as Sharif spun halfway around and the shotgun went off, its report a hollow echo rising and falling in the woods.

Roy Locke stepped from behind a tree, a .45-caliber service pistol in his right hand. He approached them as they got to their feet, and then for long seconds stood immobile, looking from one to the other.

"We've got to get moving before somebody comes investigating," Locke said finally. "I'm here to work with you. I figure we need each other."

"Did you kill Deborah Mueller?" Ben Ari asked.

"No. I got there after she had been worked over."

"Who did it, then? And why the surveillance team?"

"I don't know the answer to the first question, and I don't think we have time right now to talk about the second. Let's get the hell out of here and sort out details later. None of us can afford to be caught hanging around this place."

"How do we know we can trust you?"

Locke took the pistol in his left hand and tossed it at Hoffmann's feet. "You can use that if you want. There's still five rounds in the clip."

Ben Ari stooped over, retrieved the automatic, and aimed it at the agent's stomach. "Give me a good reason why I shouldn't pull this trigger."

"I said it before—we need each other. Life is a constant series of *quid pro quo*'s. If that's not good enough . . . you're the one who has to make that decision."

Ben Ari hesitated, then tossed the pistol back to Locke. "Where's your car?"

"Not far from yours."

"Follow us."

"Where?"

"Schmidmühlen. Ten kilometers north."

They sprinted back down the trail toward the partially hidden cars as the church bells just over the hill in Rohrbach chimed the noon hour.

Chapter 23

Ben Ari turned from the window and looked at the American agent. "Why do you want to work with us?"

"Personal survival."

"Your own people?"

"Yes and no. I was informed that the man I'm reporting to decided I'd become a liability he couldn't afford."

"I seem to remember you used the same phrase with me the other night," Hoffmann cut in.

"The same man ordered that. The reasons were never explained; it's part of the business we're in. It wasn't personal."

"That depends on where you sit. It sure as hell was to me!" He found it strange to sit in the same room and converse with a man who had recently tried to end his life.

"Continue," Ben Ari said to the agent.

"The message was a termination memorandum." He saw Ben Ari nod in understanding. "It was sent to one of our people in Greece and to an East German. I'm sure they're both on the way here now."

Hoffmann was now following. "What's a termination memorandum?"

"It's both a directive and a request. Within the framework of the CIA, it's an order for one operative to eliminate another, either because he's gone over to the other side or, for some reason, has become too dangerous to be left alive. The phraseology is always vague—intentionally. The meaning isn't. Between intelligence agencies, it's a request to eliminate an agent who's become a threat to both sides."

"You mean the CIA would kill a KGB man at their request?"

"And vice versa."

"Does it happen often?"

"Not very. I know of only one time. That's why I need you—to find out why the CIA would do this."

"Why should we need your help?" Ben Ari asked.

"Because without it you won't be able to steal the aircraft you need to get Schellen." Locke lit a cigarette and inhaled deeply, watching the other two closely. The Israeli remained stoic; Hoffmann's face registered complete surprise. "That was your plan, I believe."

"It might have been," Ben Ari replied.

"It was. Or is, I should say. In your situation, a good idea, really. Unexpected, at least. But there's an alert out on you," he said, looking at Hoffmann, "and when they find the body we left back there, you won't get within five miles of that airfield.

"And you can get us past the security?"

"I can draw them away with a diversion."

"By doing what?"

"Blowing up fuel storage. There's three or four different cantonment areas near the main post, and each has a motor pool. I'll set charges on a couple of fuel tankers in each one. A single fuel explosion would cause a lot of trouble for them; three or four would mean mass confusion."

"I could do that by myself," the Israeli said.

"You could. But that leaves Hoffmann to fly by himself . . . and we both know that picking up Schellen is a two-man job."

Ben Ari agreed with the logic but remained silent.

"How did you know to find us in Hohenfels?" Hoffmann asked.

"Through your friend Roberts. The European Provost Marshall channels notified my office that you had been at the post in Augsburg. I drove up there from Munich and talked to the lieutenant you conned into allowing you a look at the officers' roster, after I had Langley run a computer match. We patched into the Pentagon computer and ran an inquiry on officers now in Germany with assignments matching yours while you were in the Army. It yielded over two hundred names of people you could have come in contact with—seventeen of them in Augsburg. Roberts was the third one I tried. It didn't take long."

"He couldn't have told you anything. He didn't know."

"I walked him through the conversation you two had. He wasn't cooperative at first, but I convinced him you were a pretty dangerous character—we've established a well-documented case against you on a number of counts. Different things the two of you talked about tied together: your interest in locking devices and your questions about the training area. When he confirmed there were helicopters here, it all seemed to fit. Until then, I was working on the assumption you were trying to get out of the country."

Locke turned to Ben Ari. "Do we have a deal? You still haven't answered that."

"It depends on exactly what you want in return."

"Information. I want to know what you have on Knight."

"What would you do with it?"

"Use it any way I could to make sure he cancels the memorandum."

"We would have to put restrictions on it, then."

"What?"

"The information cannot be made public. If we do allow you to see it, you'll understand."

"I want something from you also," Hoffmann interjected. "Assistance for me and Maggie Reynolds when we go back to the States."

"What kind of assistance?"

"I want to make sure neither of us has to spend the rest of our lives looking over our shoulders."

"That may not be possible. I can try, but I can't commit myself until I learn what it is you have that has Knight in such an uproar." He crushed out his cigarette in the lone ashtray in the room. "We're back to square one. The question is still open. Do we deal?"

Ben Ari turned, looked out the window, and said simply, "Yes."

Papers from the file lay spread out on top of the bed. Locke read through another sheet. He had been absorbed in the contents for over half an hour.

"How did you come by this?"

"We were lucky."

Locke understood; the Israeli would not tell. It wasn't really important for him to know how the file had been obtained; knowledge of the contents was enough. "I agree this shouldn't go out, but if it got to the right people in our government, they could do a lot of housekeeping. Perhaps the 40 Committee."

"I'll leave that up to you when we finish with what we have to do here."

The agent lit another of the ever-present cigarettes. "What have you worked up so far?"

"First of all, we're going on Monday," Hoffmann said. Ben Ari's silence indicated agreement.

"A day early?"

"Yes. Unless you know some reason we shouldn't. There's always increased confusion at a place like Hohenfels after a weekend. It takes time, though not much, to get everyone readjusted. The range bulletin indicated a new brigade arriving early Monday morning as well. Do you think we can be reasonably sure of Schellen's schedule being the same that day?"

"Probably. He was supposed to set up a routine. From everything I was told, and everything I saw until this"—he indicated the papers—"the operation was a 'go.' It was all laid on. Only a half-dozen people in my office knew you weren't supposed to complete the mission, but other than that, it was being played out like the real thing on both ends. Your plan?"

"Ben Ari and I take the control tower at the airfield a few minutes after six o'clock, during the shift change, to give us time to steal the helicopter. It should give us thirty minutes' to an hour's head start on the search."

"If you're not detected."

"We won't be."

"What's your alternative?"

"There is none. I considered a deception with Ben Ari calling the tower by radio, faking a medevac request from a range at the far end of the post. But there were too many holes in it—locating the radio, counting on the tower operator not to doublecheck the unit designation. A deception worked once at Gablingen; I don't think it would work again here—especially now. We'll need as much of a diversion as you can provide. How will you do it?"

"Delayed explosives. I can get my hands on the needed equipment, from a dealer outside Frankfurt. He's safe—and he owes me from last year, when I destroyed part of a file and kept him in business."

Hoffmann listened, no longer surprised by any of the

information or the casual way the agent dealt with the truth. Locke lived in a world of lies, a world that Hoffmann was growing to accept. That was what alarmed him most.

"What's your flight time from here to Zdikov?" Locke was saying.

"An hour fifty-five, based on a ten-knot headwind."

The agent gave a low grunt, shook his head, then looked from Ben Ari back to Hoffmann. "There's no margin for error in that. You'll never make it back across the border."

"It'll be close," Hoffmann replied, "but not impossible. I don't expect much wind that early in the morning. Most of the year it blows westerly, and that means a quartering tailwind on the longest leg. In that case, it'll be a help rather than a hindrance."

"You can't be sure."

"No more than I am about you." For an instant, the agent's eyes glistened. The specter of an earlier night—in the kitchen of a house near Munich—intruded in Hoffmann's mind. He returned Locke's gaze until the agent looked away. "The risk is minimal in comparison to the alternatives."

"His capture means a great deal to both of you, doesn't it?" Locke asked after a minute, addressing Ben Ari. "It's more than just what's in the file. I can understand Hoffmann's reasons, but not yours."

"What made you think I was working with Hoffmann?" the Israeli asked, ignoring the question.

"Knight figured it, after Langley got a sighting on you two days ago. One of the communicators on shift put two and two together, and forwarded it to him. Otherwise, we might still be a few days behind you."

"How will your people react when you remain out of touch for an extended period?"

"I won't. They think I'm in Bremerhaven, following a lead at the docks. For a while, that should keep the situation static. But I'll have to check in periodically to keep it that way."

"One of us should stay with him," Hoffmann said, seeing the harshness return to the agent's eyes.

"All right, you've made your point," Ben Ari replied, silencing him with a stern look. Now was not the time for accusation; they needed Locke as much as he needed them, though he—like Hoffmann—was reluctant to put too much faith in the man's word, or his motive.

"I'll be back tomorrow morning," Locke said, getting to his feet and straightening his coat so the bulge of a shoulder holster disappeared. Momentarily he hesitated, looking at Hoffmann, then left without a word.

"You're very foolish," Ben Ari said when the agent was gone. "He's not the type of man to forget or forgive a personal slight."

"It's the truth."

"So it is. You're right, of course—he can't be trusted completely. But for now we'll have to use him. And remember, he could be valuable to you later. Don't antagonize him. He's a man who cares little for principles or abstractions—like honor or truth—which you seem to care for too much. But he cares dearly for his life. Use that to your advantage—to our advantage."

"I'm not that type of person."

"You are . . . more than you think."

The messenger, a Russian, was not a welcome sight to Anatoly Kusheloff; he was one of those people who carried the weight of authority from levels of the Kremlin so high up that Kusheloff hardly knew they existed. Such men never brought good news.

With an excess of uncharacteristic humility, Kusheloff greeted the visitor.

"Welcome to East Berlin, comrade. I have looked forward

to your arrival with great anticipation. It is an honor to have you here with us." The messenger, a man in his late forties, ignored the fallacious statement and sat in a chair across the desk.

His name was Dmitri Gagarin, and he was all but unknown outside the Tupelov Section of KGB counterintelligence, itself a closely guarded secret. There was nothing about Gagarin's appearance that distinguished him from other men his age. His slightly below-average height, thinning hair, and dark suit made him the type of person that one sees but never notices or remembers in a crowd. He preferred it that way.

His eyes darted around the room quickly. "You would not be so foolish as to have recording devices in here, I presume."

"Of course not," Kusheloff replied, almost pleading. He was beginning to sweat under his heavy wool suit, although the temperature in the room was lower than normal.

"The Premier is apprehensive about the operation surrounding Schellen. I am here to relay his concern to you."

"I share his anxiety. It would appear that Kasimirov has not prepared sufficiently for all possible contingencies. I have detailed my observations in a memorandum to my superiors in Moscow." Kusheloff had in fact written such a letter. Although it was dated two days previously, he had not sent it. It was his insurance in case something went wrong.

"What have you done to make sure all goes as planned?"

"I have made many suggestions, comrade, but I am afraid Kasimirov has not incorporated all of them."

"That is your responsibility. He does report to you."

"You may not be aware, but the man is not directly responsible to me." He was sure Gagarin had knowledge of the arrangement allowing Kasimirov to bypass him and deal directly with Moscow. But he knew he had to phrase his comments carefully: Gagarin might be the one who had made that decision.

"I should make it clear, then, that as his superior in the field, you are organizationally responsible for his activities."

"Of course, and I accept my responsibility. I have grave misgivings about the arrangements made thus far. A letter was sent to my superiors requesting permission to replace Kasimirov. However, I have not received a reply. When word came of your visit, I though you might be bringing the answer."

Gagarin saw this for the lie that it was—Kusheloff was typical of the mediocre bureaucrats in similar positions elsewhere. Like the others, most of his efforts were directed toward self-preservation. And this meant covering every possible situation with a blanket of requests and negative reports on subordinates, so he could never be held personally responsible for anything that went wrong. Gagarin would not let that happen this time.

"I have no such message, since I am not in your direct organizational line. My mission is to relay the concern of our leadership and return to them your personal assurance that nothing will go wrong."

"You have my word . . . if I am allowed to replace Kasimirov, or assume total control myself."

"Such a qualification would not be looked upon favorably at the level from which this assurance is sought. The Premier is not accustomed to being questioned by someone such as yourself."

"I did not mean to question. Please. I simply meant to relate to you my own uneasiness over the qualifications of the man making final arrangements in the field."

"Your reservation is noted."

"That is all I ask."

"Then you have no reason not to give me your unqualified assurance there will be no mistakes concerning this matter with Schellen."

"It will be taken care of without any problems."

"That is what I came to hear." Gagarin reached into his briefcase and retrieved a typed sheet which he placed before Kusheloff. "I have prepared this statement for you to sign. I will personally deliver it to the Premier. He will be pleased to know that he has your faithful support."

Kusheloff realized the trap had been sprung. As long as things remained verbal, he still retained some hope that his request to remove Kasimirov would support him should anything go wrong. The wording of the statement eliminated that possibility. Reluctantly, he signed just above the typed signature block.

For the first time, Gagarin smiled, though only briefly, as he replaced the sheet in his briefcase. "You are aware of recent developments with this Hoffmann?"

"Such as?"

"The events the Americans are staging to make us think he has decided not to attempt the pickup."

"Perhaps you could tell me, in case there is something which has not yet reached us."

"A few days ago, he parted company with the CIA operative Locke. That is what they would have us believe. They are trying to make it appear as if he decided not to go through with the plan. Now they have started a search for him all through West Germany."

"You think this is a deception?"

"We are positive. It is all very amateur playacting. They are trying to make it look like this Hoffmann escaped from one of their better agents, as if it were another mistake made by the CIA. They cultivate that idea of the Agency being some kind of comic opera, but we know it to be untrue. Washington has gone so far as to send out an order for Locke's death."

"You have analyzed all this?"

"Yes, of course. It indicates to us they are altering the original plan. They may have somebody already on the scene in Zdikov to take Schellen out another way, or their timing has changed. But I am sure you will be ready for any possible situation."

"We will be ready."

"I know," Gagarin said, patting the briefcase. He stood, tucked the case under his arm, and quickly departed.

Kusheloff had known nothing of the events related by the messenger, further proof that Kasimirov could not be trusted. He had yet to call in and report as instructed, nor had he arranged for additional troop coverage of the area before Tuesday's planned pickup. That worried him more than anything, especially considering Gagarin's analysis of recent events in West Germany. Kusheloff was determined to have the area around Zdikov saturated with troops before the weekend was out.

He picked up the phone and ordered his driver to meet him at the building entrance.

Chapter 24

"Edelmann's body was found in Ulm last night, according to the paper," Roy Locke said. Even in the dim light of the dining area, he could see the color drain from Hoffmann's face. Ben Ari's remained unemotional, totally controlled. "There was a woman with him when the police found the car. The report said they had been dead for less than two hours."

"His wife," Ben Ari said.

"The identity wasn't given; the mention of her was brief, almost an afterthought. Somebody wanted to make sure we saw it—I suspect the article was planted."

"What about this other announcement?" Ben Ari asked. "You said it was on the radio."

"It was the message I was expecting, although it came sooner than anticipated. My executioners are in the field." The report was typical of the filler pieces one expects from AFN on a Sunday afternoon, when nothing of consequence can be found. The story concerned recovery of a small fortune in artifacts from the excursion steamer *General Slocum*, lost in New York harbor soon after the turn of the century. References were made to New York's little Germany, members of St. Mark's Lutheran Church, and an inspector from the Steamboat Inspection Service held responsible for the sinking of the vessel. What he heard was significant—it was also false. "I called in after hearing the report, and Duncan told me they found Hoffmann this morning, about an hour before the broadcast."

"They know about the memorandum."

"I doubt it. Knight wouldn't allow dissemination. But the office was given some story. Maybe that I've crossed over. They'll be looking for me in Bremen, and that should buy me another day at least. Sometime tomorrow they'll figure out I know."

"To hell with your memorandum," Hoffmann said, his mind churning, able to speak now that the initial shock of Locke's revelation had passed. He realized he hadn't heard a thing the others had said for the last minute or more. "She's gone! Somebody's taken her—maybe worse."

Ben Ari's hand was wrapped around his forearm, a painful vise. His eyes flashed a warning. "Control yourself. You're drawing attention."

He tried to pull away, but the Israeli held his arm tightly, increasing pressure. Finally he relaxed, his rigid body going limp as he looked away. A soaring wave of despair crested over him. "I've killed her."

"We don't know that," Ben Ari replied, glancing toward the small bar, satisfied that the innkeeper showed no interest in a momentary disagreement at a corner table.

"I've killed her," Hoffmann repeated in a whisper. Everything that had happened was clearly his responsibility. There was no retreat from the condemning reality. *Your carelessness brought her here; your solicitude will not protect her* . . . He had invaded her life through fear, used her as one would a passive object, without discretion, she had forgiven him. Forgiven him!

He rose from the chair and walked slowly upstairs.

"Could it have been your people?" Ben Ari asked, looking at Locke.

Locke shook his head. "Very doubtful. We didn't have a line on Edelmann as of Friday, when I called off the surveillance on his house. And there was no reason to eliminate him in any event. It's not something we would have done—there was no reason."

"Any ideas?"

"Nothing concrete. It could have been someone associated with your friend from the Middle East."

"His mission was personal, a matter of revenge between the two of us. Restricted parameters, which wouldn't have included others."

"It included the Meuller woman."

"Perhaps."

"Or it could have been a German organization. Access to the news-gathering sources would indicate that possibility. There are rumors circulating. Veracity of the information is questionable but can't be ruled out."

"Something new?"

"The players are, but the roots go back many years, a mutation of the Hitler Youth. This time it takes the form of a strange alliance of young Germans in the universities and the military. We've heard it called by several names, but the most prominent is Der Zorn. Apparently it began in the Luftwaffe two or three years ago. From there it spread to the Army, although it still appears confined to small, isolated cells. An undetermined number of students are involved—as usual, the disaffected. To some, Hitler has become something of a cult figure. Publishers are having a difficult time keeping up with the demand for *Mein Kampf*."

"How seriously are you taking them?"

"Enough to try and get a line on them to keep the organization under surveillance. So far we haven't linked them to any overt action, even though one source indicates acts last year credited to Baader-Meinhof were the work of Der Zorn. It could be the reason neither has been solved."

"The Odessa never claims credit," Ben Ari observed. "And they're far better organized."

"Apparently this group shuns any contact with them. They look upon the older generation as incapable, enfeebled."

"You say this is all conjecture."

"For the moment. By the time we can confirm all suspicions, I suspect they'll be well organized and more of a force to be reckoned with in Germany, an insurgency of the far right. But this time its ranks will be filled with hungry, intelligent young men and women, not the street thugs who populated the Third Reich."

"They would be more dangerous."

"Definitely. But their cause won't enjoy a broad following as long as the German economy remains strong."

"Unless they can galvanize public opinion on some other major issue—nuclear arms, for example. It's a popular bandwagon for the young, although opposition to it would appear counterproductive. Other causes have been manipulated; ample precedents exist. The world should keep a close watch on what develops among the young of Germany. . . . Never again.

"But we are considering possibilities too far in the future," Ben Ari continued. "We should be thinking more in terms of the next twelve hours. You've said nothing about the explosives."

"Thirty pounds of C-4; det cord and primers. I left the car in a downtown Frankfurt garage in the long-term parking area and requisitioned an old Mercedes from the dealer. The exterior is the worse for wear, but the plates are German and the engine is oversized. I also picked up a bolt cutter to get us through wires, and you might need it later at the airfield."

The Israeli nodded. "You'll have to meet us once we're back inside the border. I'll show you on the map upstairs. From the pickup point we'll to a farmhouse in the Danube River Valley."

"What will you do with Schellen?"

"It shouldn't matter to you."

"And Hoffmann?" Locke pursued.

"The two of you can decide your next move after that. Once we reach the safehouse, our compact is over, the obligations fulfilled."

"He'll expect you to help him locate the Reynolds woman."

"Then he expects too much."

Locke pursed his lips, inclining his head to the side as he looked at the Israeli. "You ought to think it through before then; he won't be easy to handle."

"Hoffmann is the least of my worries. I suspect you'll have more trouble with him than I will. At some point he's going to demand an explanation of something you told him. It had to do with his being worthless—like his father."

"He remembered that?"

"Several times he's mentioned it."

"Part of the briefing I got from Washington." Locke wondered what the reaction would be. He had no intention of letting Hoffmann know the truth—at least until he secured the file from Ben Ari.

"His father worked for the Germans during the war. He was a traitor."

Chapter 25

Hoffmann felt the violent shaking motion; more asleep than awake, it became part of the nightmare. He awoke with a start, bathed in perspiration.

Ben Ari stood over him, a white ceramic mug in his hand. "Get up. It's nearly four A.M." The voice was calm and quiet. "I brought an immersion heater and some instant. I'll fix you a cup while you shave."

Hoffmann put on his uniform trousers and boots, then clumped down the hall in the darkness to the communal bathroom. Minutes later he returned to the room and shaved, using cold water from the pitcher. The coffee Ben Ari handed him tasted of chemical residue; the Danish had a texture reminiscent of old newspaper. As the American ate, Ben Ari rechecked the equipment in the rucksack, inserting a clip in each submachine gun before replacing it.

They left quietly by the back door. Locke waited for them beside Ben Ari's car, wearing khaki trousers and an old field jacket faded to gray-green. Soon they were accelerating through the narrow streets at Ben Ari's usually excessive speed. The American agent followed in the mud-spattered Mercedes.

A mile from the town, they turned onto a forest path. Ben Ari removed the few items in the car that might allow it to be traced easily, then drove it twenty yards into the woods; in ten minutes it was well camouflaged. It would be three days later by the time a local farmer named Erhard Schultz spotted the car, and more than a week until an overworked police staff traced it to a man in Munich who had absent-mindedly failed to report it stolen.

An early-morning fog lay in the valleys, restricting visibility to less than half a mile as they returned to the main road paralleling the Vils River.

At 4:48 they left the road and crossed a wooden bridge, driving west over a winding path into the woods before stopping on the side of a gradually increasing slope. Locke backed into the undergrowth, pointing the car downhill. In single file they began moving through the forest. Unseen branches whipped at their faces in the darkness. Undergrowth pawed at them, impeding progress, soaking them with moisture. The slope grew steeper for the first hundred yards, until they reached the top of the hill. As the terrain flattened out, the woods became less dense, allowing them to move more easily until they came across a rusted barbed-wire fence marking the reservation boundary. They crawled beneath the lowest strand, and ten minutes later stood at the edge of a woodline.

"This should be the maneuver area," Hoffmann said between breaths. "There's a path off to the left that leads to the south tank trail—about a mile and a quarter to the troop area near the main post." He glanced at the luminous hands of his watch. "Quarter after five. We've got some time to make up."

The path was narrow, barely able to support one-way jeep traffic. The surface was rutted and pocked with holes. Ben Ari led out, picking up the pace. They arrived at the intersection with the wide, hard-packed tank trail twenty minutes later and stopped inside the edge of the trees to rest. Almost three hundred yards away sat the motor pool, the outline of armored vehicles barely distinguishable. Beyond lay the concrete troop barracks, still quiet and dark except for an occasional light in an orderly-room window.

"If we stay inside the treeline and parallel the road, we can get within thirty or forty yards of the entrance," Hoffmann whispered. "We'll split up there, and Locke can set the charges. You and I have another hill to climb to get to the main post; once we pass the dispensary, it's open—too open. We'll have to stay close to the buildings on the opposite side of the main post road until the first charge goes off."

"Six o'clock?" Ben Ari asked.

Locke checked his watch. "Still a 'go.' " He ducked into the trees and walked at a crouch toward the vehicle park.

The high grass around the motor pool was saturated with moisture, and Locke's clothes were soaked through as he kneeled just outside the barbed wire that defined the entrance. A lone guard walked the circumference of the area, which held nearly a hundred vehicles of all sizes and descriptions, most of them tracked personnel carriers. He located the prime target: six 1200-gallon tankers of gasoline.

As the guard began another circuit of the perimeter, the agent made his move.

Locke covered the short distance toward the green-clad figure of the soldier quietly, in long strides. The blow to the base of his neck with the butt of the .45 was vicious, but meant only to stun; killing the soldier was unnecessary. He dragged the body and placed it out of sight behind a nearby vehicle.

The agent checked each tanker and the four smaller trailers. A valve was cracked open on the trailers, allowing several gallons to spill on the ground; a small but steady stream continued from each. Then he went to the tankers, opened the internal valves and then the bleed valves in each pump compartment to start a continuous leak. By the time he was done, a pool of thirty gallons of gasoline lay on the ground, growing larger every second.

He pulled the detonation cord and the box of blasting caps from the small satchel, then cut ten-foot lengths of cord and placed a cap on each, securing them with a crimper. With his knife, he cut a slit in the opposite ends from the metal caps, inserting four matches apiece. Blasting caps were placed inside the ten-pound bundle of plastic explosive wedged tightly between the pump and the bottom of one tank. Two caps were placed within the pool of gasoline. Finally, he struck a match and lit the ends of the cords. Small flares ignited as the match sets caught and started the powder inside the flexible detonation cord burning slowly toward the gasoline.

"What the hell you doin', man?" The voice caught Locke by surprise. He whirled to face the youthful figure—another sentry, until now unobserved. An M-16 was pointed directly at his stomach from ten feet away.

"What's it look like?" The agent took three tentative steps forward.

"Looks like you was plannin' to blow this place away."

"That's right."

"Man, you're crazy. You can't get away with this."

"Who's going to stop me?" Locke continued toward the soldier.

"I am . . . stop right there!" Fear crowded into his speech.

"But you can't stop me."

"Hell I can't."

"You and I both know they don't give you any live ammunition."

The guard turned to run. In his haste, he lost his footing on the loose gravel and stumbled. Locke was on him before he could cry out; the soldier slumped unconscious under the agent's assault.

Seconds later, he ran through the entrance to the parking area, toward the next cantonment site, a quarter of a mile down the tank trail. Locke checked his watch. The explosion and resulting fire would occur in approximately nine minutes, maybe sooner. Barely enough time. He picked up the pace to a fast trot. A Military Police jeep came down the hill, its headlights casting twin shafts through the fog. Locke dove off the trail and crawled through the tall grass to a culvert as the vehicle turned toward him. He remained motionless until it passed him and disappeared over the small rise behind him. He ran across the macadam road, jumped the drainage ditch, and was swallowed up by the woods ten yards away. Moving quickly, he recrossed the tank trail and approached the next barbed-wire enclosure.

Lights were mounted on telephone poles spaced at fifty-yard intervals around the motor pool. A guard stood at the gate, stomping his feet, occasionally checking his watch. Lights were going on inside the buildings beyond.

Locke cut two short pieces of det cord, crimped a blasting cap on each, and pushed them into one-pound blocks of the plastic explosive. Leaving the satchel, he worked his way to the rear, where jeeps were parked tightly side by side, backed almost to the triple concertina fence. He taped two additional blocks on either side of those with the blasting caps, lit the fuses, and tossed the charges beneath separate vehicles.

The first explosion came thirty seconds later, a thunderous rending of the silence.

Shouts came from the buildings as they emptied of soldiers

in various stages of dress. Locke ran toward the pushing, shoving throng, in the shadow of the shooting flames, moving into the darker area between the motor pool and the barracks. The milling crowd offered anonymity.

"Fire!" He yelled three times and heard the call echoed by other voices. The crowd surged toward him and he grabbed the first man, shaking him roughly. "Call the M.P.'s—quick!" He spun the soldier around and pushed him toward others spilling from the buildings. Five people rushed past him. "Call the post fire department! Get somebody—"

A second explosion ripped through the night.

Others surged past him, and he grabbed another body. "You! Get a squad together and bring all the fire extinguishers from the barracks."

"The vehicle extinguishers are locked up."

"Get somebody to unlock them! Move!"

A voice—an officer or N.C.O.—was calling out instructions over the noise, trying to bring order to chaos. Other shouted commands could be heard. The confusion was almost complete. Locke sent three more people to call the M.P.'s, another to call the fire department. "Get the dispensary to send an ambulance!" he yelled at a small group near an entrance. "Somebody get those fuel trucks moved before the fire reaches them!"

A soldier ran into him carrying a small portable fire extinguisher. "Weren't you the one I told to call post headquarters?" Locke demanded, angrily grabbing the red metal canister.

"No, sir!"

"Do it!"

The sirens were wailing at the top of the hill now as a vehicle sped toward them, its rotating light on. It stopped by the entrance to the motor pool, and Locke could see a shiny black helmet reflecting the light.

An explosion erupted a half-mile away, lighting the sky as a miniature mushroom-shaped cloud rose on a thermal column and disappeared into the low overcast. Locke partially discharged the fire extinguisher, then ran toward a group of eight or ten gawkers standing at the fence, looking on from outside. "You men! Come with me! We've got to move the injured." He melted into the crowd with them and entered the vehicle park, approached the fire for a brief moment, and turned back. Engines were being started; fuel tankers created a traffic jam in the close confines as he fought through the crowd and walked back outside the gate toward the M.P. who was talking urgently on the radio.

". . . Unit four, roger. A second one—"

"Sarge . . . I saw the guy who did it," Locke said breathlessly, wiping his forehead with a tattered jacket sleeve.

The M.P. turned toward him, taking in everything with a quick look.

"He dropped something over there," the agent said quickly, pointing. "A knapsack or a small suitcase." Together they searched in the darkness until the M.P. found the satchel.

"Here it is—explosives!"

Locke joined him, still carrying the partially discharged extinguisher. "Which way to the ammo point from here?" The soldier pointed over his shoulder. "That's the way he was headed!"

"You're sure?"

"Positive. . . . Take me with you—I can identify him."

They ran back to the jeep and pulled away as the first red pumper arrived. Behind it, two more were headed in the opposite direction, following other M.P. jeeps. The M.P. reached for the microphone hung between the two seats on the dashboard as they swung onto the tank trail.

"Unit four is enroute to the ASP . . . alert them to a

possible arson attempt." He started to replace the black plastic transmitter on its hook and saw the weapon pointed at his head.

"Request a backup if they ask, and turn toward the main gate. Is it open?"

"At zero six hundred."

"Then it should be by the time we get there. Turn on the lights and siren, and don't slow down going through. If you attempt to stop, or deviate in any way from what I think is normal, you're dead. Believe that: I can end your life in less than a heartbeat." Locke reached over, removed the .45 from the soldier's holster, and tossed it into the brush alongside the road. "The siren and the lights."

Behind them the chaos grew, feeding on itself.

Streetlights in the distance were surrounded by halos of luminescence as Hoffmann and Ben Ari crouched in the shadow of a building five hundred yards from the airfield ramp.

"The wind's come up a little," Hoffmann said, looking at the open expanse in front of them. The field was lower than the rest of the main post, making the fog slightly more dense. "But the weather's still lousy."

Two more vehicles passed them, headed toward the unseen fires whose bright glow reflected off the overcast beyond the hill at their back. They waited for long seconds, then ran across the road, sliding down the wet grass of a steep incline. There was no cover to protect them next to the parking area, and little concealment in the shadows. They stayed close to the side of the hill, stooped over as they moved. The last forty yards were a sprint across the hard, flat ramp to the base of tower. Ben Ari crept to the rear of the building, found the door, and went in.

A man in uniform sat at a long folding table drinking

coffee. He started to rise, then stopped halfway, his eyes frozen on the barrel of the Israeli's submachine gun. Without a word, Ben Ari crossed the room, grabbed the soldier's collar from behind, and pushed him toward the stairway, shoving the Uzi roughly into his back.

"How many in the tower?" he demanded.

"Two . . . the morning shift."

"How many?" The question was repeated, punctuated with a prod of the weapon.

"Two! I swear it!"

"Lead the way." They climbed to the landing and came to a locked door; next to it on the wall was a small speaker. "Do you have a key?"

"No. The lock has to be deactivated from the tower."

"Speak to them—and make it convincing. You've left something behind. What is it?"

"I don't know . . . my coat."

"Wrong. They'd have noticed it. What else?"

"A letter . . . I was writing a letter to my wife. I couldn't bring her over with me . . . the housing shortage for dependents."

The Israeli looked to Hoffmann; the American nodded.

"If you're not telling the truth, we'll have to blast our way in. If you're smart, all of you will be left alive. Talk to them."

The soldier pressed the button next to the speaker and related the story. Seconds later, they heard an electronic buzz and the door was unlocked. Ben Ari motioned for Hoffmann to cover the man, then pulled the door back and raced up the sharply pitched steps. A cry rang out and was quickly cut off.

"Hoffmann! Bring him up."

Both the operators stared at him with wide eyes as he entered the tower and pushed the hostage toward them. The tiny room glowed red, the color and low intensity needed to preserve night vision.

"What kind of weather are you reporting?" Hoffmann asked quickly.

"Four-hundred-foot ceilings with a half-mile in fog," one of the operators replied, wiping blood from a gash on his cheek.

"What is it in Nuremburg?"

"Last hour they reported nine hundred overcast with a mile and a half visibility."

Hoffann looked at Ben Ari. "It should be good enough there." He glanced at the clock above a bank of radios and said, "We've got to get moving."

The Israeli removed the rucksack from his shoulders and withdrew a large coil of rope, cutting three lengths. He tied their hands behind them, then forced two of them to the floor on their stomachs. After tying their legs, he tightly cinched their arms behind them, passing the running end of the rope through the counter legs and back around their waists. The last man was bound tightly and secured to a heavy wooden desk against the wall. Five minutes after taking the tower, Ben Ari and Hoffmann disabled the radios and telephone, locked the door, and headed back down the stairs.

Ben Ari turned off the light in the ground-floor room and looked through the open door before easing outside. They stopped at the corner of the building. The ramp was still quiet.

Hoffmann whispered, "Hurry. They may be cranking up a medevac soon."

"Which one?"

"Follow me." He started to move. Ben Ari touched his arm.

"Nuremburg is almost the opposite direction."

"They don't know that—"

The Israeli followed him through the parked helicopters to the outer row. Hoffmann turned on the flashlight and played it across the tail of the last aircraft in the line.

"They've moved it. We'll have to take this one. . . . Get the locks off while I remove the covers." He connected the battery, then climbed up on the roof, quickly removing the tailpipe and inlet covers, and tossing them to Ben Ari on the ground. A fast visual inspection followed, then he removed the canvas pitot-tube cover and climbed down. Fuel sloshed down the side of the fuselage when he removed the cap. After a rapid walk-around inspection, he swung the blade perpendicular and climbed into the right seat. Ben Ari was already strapped in as he handed over a headset and flipped on the battery switch overhead. Seconds later, switches were set and the throttle positioned for a start.

A whining turbine broke the silence on the ramp as Hoffmann eased the throttle to flight idle. Radios were turned on and cockpit lights adjusted as he keyed the intercom. "How do you hear?" he said into the boom mike.

"Loud and clear."

"Roger, same here." He ran through the ground checks rapidly, without benefit of the checklist, abbreviating or eliminating most of the items. With systems and flight instruments checked, the noise grew louder inside as he brought the engine to operating RPM. Abruptly, he picked up to a hover, maneuvering sideways until clear of the other parked aircraft. They stopped over the concrete runway, aligned with the markings, and began accelerating forward.

Seconds into the flight, Hoffmann knew it was a mistake.

Thirty feet above the ground, they encountered the first significant fog and lost visual contact with the ground in a quick and unexpected loss of outside references. He held the cyclic-control stick tightly, knowing he was overcontrolling with erratic movements, manifested in large changes in the pitch and roll of the aircraft. Rivulets of perspiration stung his eyes.

He fought for control—of the helicopter and his own mounting fear. The aircraft emerged from the billowy fog, and they saw the ground rising to meet them.

Hoffmann spoke through the intercom. "We're punching in."

Chapter 26

The soldier clumped noisily up the wooden stairs of the guard tower and dropped his heavy steel helmet on a makeshift table, next to the cold field phone with its wiring snaked across the floor. His name was Janko Hubacek; his home was in Prague. And he wished he were there now, instead of standing guard on the border, in a dark watchtower, waiting for the invasion that even he realized would never come.

"Wake up," he roared, directing the command toward the sound of snoring in the corner, regretting the volume of his own voice immediately—the effects of too much vodka remained oppressive after only five hours' sleep. "Your replacement is here. Be glad it isn't the watch commander who catches you asleep all the time."

"What can they do? Send me off on border duty?"

"Maybe they would shoot you."

"Even that would be better than this."

Janko Hubacek shrugged in the darkness. The soldier was

right; border detail was the worst duty he had known. Tedious. Annoying. Morale was the lowest he'd ever seen in the ranks, and even the nightly bouts of drunkenness failed to alleviate the boredom.

"Nothing will ever happen here," the soldier grumbled, groping in the darkness for his rifle, cursing loudly when he bumped into the edge of the table.

"It is a good thing for you it never does. By the time you woke up, this place would be part of Germany."

"Go to the devil."

Hubacek clenched his fists, then forced himself calm. Hitting the man would accomplish nothing beyond a momentary relief of frustration, not worth the consequences, he reasoned. Fighting among the troops had become epidemic, and measures were now being instituted to curtail it; but at the next relief, he would not be as kind in waking this guard. The soldier finally located his gear and departed, muttering inaudible obscenities.

Hubacek tested the field telephone by calling in to the central switchboard, then pulled out a flashlight and writing materials to continue the letter to his brother.

In twenty minutes, he too was asleep.

Wisps of cottonlike moisture enveloped the helicopter as Hoffmann pulled in power. The machine shuddered and started to climb. The brilliance of the searchlight slung beneath the fuselage was magnified by the cloud as they climbed up through it, and Hoffmann flipped the switch off. At eight hundred feet, with the aircraft firmly under control, he began a slow, climbing left turn and rolled out on a heading that pointed southeast toward Deggendorf.

At two thousand feet they broke out on top of the overcast, able to see scattered clouds above them and a low overcast below—a thin layer of ground fog mixed with scud. Minutes later they crossed the Vils River Valley and the visibility began to increase. Five miles farther on, the clouds below turned from the overcast to a scattered condition, allowing them to descend; from there, they were able to navigate by ground reference. Hoffmann relaxed, the first minutes of chest-tightening fear gone. Fifteen miles southeast of Hohenfels, he picked up the lights of Regensburg and turned toward the city, welcoming the sight. The clock on the instrument panel indicated 6:37 A.M.

They skirted the city, located the autobahn, and used it as the primary navigation feature. Soon the city was left behind, and they struck out into the darkness. Hoffmann concentrated on the world outside the cockpit, scattered points of light on the ground—not stars, he reminded himself—an easy illusion that could make flying in the darkness over sparsely populated areas a hazard. What was the medical term? Spatial disorientation. Strange that he would think of it now, when so much demanded his attention. A sign of fatigue.

The dim glow of Straubing's lights became visible in front of them. As the helicopter passed the town, Hoffmann looked southeast into a black void, aware that the easiest part of the flight was behind them. From here on, there would be no cities of any appreciable size to guide them, and finding the exact point at which to cross the border would require excellent nagivation from Ben Ari . . . and a generous dose of luck. The Israeli was tuning the navigation radios, again fixing the location as Hoffmann descended still lower, trying to get below radar coverage on both sides of the border. The steady beat of rotary blades kept them company as the miles slid by.

The Israeli recited ground features over which they should be flying as Hoffmann confirmed them; their teamwork in the cockpit steadily improved. They passed over the Danube, heading for the final checkpoint inside West Germany. On course. On schedule. To the east, the sky was becoming marginally lighter. Mountainous terrain rose east of the river, and Hoffmann slowed as Ben-Ari ticked off the names of the towns passing by only a hundred feet below. Grafenau, Schönbrunn, Mauth, Finsterau.

Finsterau!

They'd made it.

Hoffmann eased the aircraft lower until they were at tree-top level and picked up the heading Ben Ari called off, feeling the hard knot of anticipation and wariness in the pit of his stomach. He reset the timing hand of the clock for the first leg of the route, his attention momentarily concentrated inside, on the instrument panel.

When he looked up, the wooden guard tower filled the windshield.

Janko Hubacek rolled over, startled, grasping wildly for his rifle in the darkness. Half-asleep, he stumbled around inside the guard tower, knocking the field phone off the table in his panic.

The roar that had awakened him now receded to the northeast. A huge black shape was all he could make out at first; it had swooped in on a collision course, then swerved, missing the tower by only a few yards. Now the form was gone from sight, though he could still hear it in the early-morning stillness. He realized what it was: the whine of a turbine and the distinct slapping noise could be only one thing.

Hubacek switched on the flashlight to locate the field telephone. He cranked the handle.

"Guard Post Number Four, Hubacek. I think they started an invasion . . . yes, sir . . . I'm sure. I just saw the first helicopters . . . only one . . . but I heard several more . . . yes, sir . . . yes, sir . . . that is right . . . just a minute ago . . ."

"Where are those troops?" Anatoly Kusheloff ranted. Since arriving the day before, he had been a tyrant. Schellen watched it all with detached amusement; he despised both Russians.

"They should be here any minute, comrade," Kasimirov replied.

"That is not good enough. Call and find out exactly where they are and when they will arrive."

"It is not really necessary."

"Yes, it is! They should have been here last night."

"I told them to arrive before nine this morning."

"What! Those were not my instructions."

"As I told you, this may give away our plan. Bringing in reinforcements early may scare the Americans off."

"That is no longer your decision to make. I am in command now. Make the call."

Kasimirov would not back down from the bureaucrat. "You are not in charge of this operation until I am officially relieved by Moscow. I will make the call . . . but only in the interest of maintaining interdepartmental cooperation."

"You will make the call because I tell you!"

They were at an impasse.

Finally Schellen spoke. "Excuse me, gentlemen. It is about time for my morning walk. I would not want to be the cause of any further arguments concerning the details of your masterfully conceived plot." He retrieved his coat from the closet in the next room and left the house.

The cool, crisp air was invigorating as he stepped briskly down the walk toward the street, the German shepherd running ahead, enjoying the freedom of the open spaces. Schellen felt in high spirits this morning. Even a casual observer, had there been one on the streets of Zdikov at that moment, would have noticed. He laughed aloud as he turned north, away from the house.

He had outsmarted all of them again. Kasimirov would be left to explain how an old man had vanished from under his nose—an old man who knew all the transportation plans for the invasion of Western Europe, no less. Tonight, he would begin his journey into hiding. All of them—the Americans, the Russians, the East Germans—would have to carry on without him tomorrow.

His only regret was in knowing that he would not be around to take part in bringing together the two Germanys as one Fatherland, a dream now decades old. His own role was to have been a major one, and not being there to see the plan through to its conclusion would be disappointing. Other than transportation needs, he knew little of the military planning, but what he had learned was encouraging. It was feasible, especially with the Chinese promise of increased border activity half a continent away to divide Russian attention at the crucial time.

Thoughts of the previous day's fishing in the stream north of Zdikovec replaced those of the Fatherland as he walked down the narrow road toward the distant town. Off to his right, across the fields and beyond the hills, the morning sun lightened the eastern sky, but the clouds were still low over the mountains.

A high ridge towered over them on the left, parallel to their direction of flight, as Ben Ari called out his continuous instructions over the intercom. Still on the treetops, they reached the first checkpoint two minutes ahead of schedule and turned to the next heading. Eric punched the clock, resetting the small timing hand, and slowed the aircraft by ten knots to put them back on schedule. The fuel gauge indicated four hundred pounds—less than hour until burnout. It was enough.

Minutes passed.

Zdikovec came into view.

On the ground, Schellen heard a muted sound faintly resembling a flushed covey of quail. Seconds later he recognized it and the object from which it came—a helicopter turning sharply south a quarter of a mile away. It was coming directly at him, not more than twenty feet above the ground. Anatoly Kusheloff, seated at the breakfast table seven hundred yards away, heard the noise and came to the same conclusion as Schellen at exactly the same instant.

The Americans were precisely on time.

But they were one day early.

"There he is!" shouted Ben Ari, opening the quick release on the seat belt and shoulder harness. He reached down and grabbed the Uzi. "He's running. Land south of him, between him and the town."

Hoffmann was too busy to reply. With rearward movement of the cyclic control, he stood the aircraft on its tail. The airframe shuddered violently under the strain, slowing rapidly. As forward speed bled off, he kicked hard on the left pedal and lowered the nose of the ship at the same time. The tail swung right, and he planted the skids solidly on the road.

Ben Ari was out of his seat almost before ground contact, rushing in full stride at the overweight figure fifteen yards behind them. The Israeli stopped, fired a burst from the machine gun that killed the dog, then caught up to Schellen. He grabbed the German by the right arm, almost dragging the man down the road toward the aircraft.

Looking quickly toward Zdikov, Hoffmann sighted a black car about six hundred yards away, coming for them as it accelerated. He yelled at Ben Ari to hurry, but his words were lost in the noise of the turbine and main rotor.

The car was less than a hundred yards away when Ben Ari clammered aboard. Hoffmann already had the aircraft light on the skids, pulling in power rapidly before the cargo door closed. He lowered the nose of the helicopter as he increased the pitch of the blades, accelerating forward, keeping the skids barely off the ground. A shudder wrenched through the airframe, heralding the onset of translational lift. Shots ripped through the crew compartment.

Hoffmann became the first casualty.

Plexiglass from the pilot's door exploded through the cockpit, followed by the window shattering in the left door. His vision blurred. He closed his eyes instinctively, wiped a hand across his eyelids, and felt a gash above the right eye. Then his vision cleared.

Two hundred yards from the road, he climbed enough to clear a stand of trees and banked hard right toward the town, gaining momentum through the turn until the airspeed indicator danced back and forth over the red line at 120 knots. Zdikov flashed by the right door, then receded quickly behind them.

Ben Ari tied Schellen's hands behind him with a piece of nylon rope, lacing the running end through one of the small, circular cargo tie-downs attached to the floor. Then he plugged the headset into one of the two rear receptacles and keyed the mike.

"How are you holding up?"

"I can see," Hoffmann replied, again wiping blood from his forehead.

The Israeli moved to the jump seat just to the rear of and between the pilot and copilot stations. He picked the map off the center console, oriented it, and fixed their position. "Follow this valley for another three minutes . . . we should hit a hard-surfaced road running east–west. Turn right ninety degrees there, and follow the road for two kilometers."

"Okay . . . I've got the road dead ahead."

Ben Ari peered forward. "Come right ten degrees . . .

"There's a north–south valley coming up on the left," he continued. "We'll bypass it and look for the next one on the left . . ."

"I've got the second valley."

"Turn left there to a heading of . . . 170 degrees . . . and follow it for almost four kilometers."

". . . This the right one?"

"This is it . . . turn left."

Eric executed the turn, then followed the low ground until they crossed another hard-surfaced road and the Vitava River on the other side. Five miles to the border. Fourteen miles to touchdown.

"Turn right thirty degrees," Ben Ari was saying, "and stay on that heading . . ."

"We've got problems," Hoffmann said, pointing at the yellow master-caution light on the instrument panel.

"What is it?"

"Twenty-minute fuel light," he replied, glancing at the illuminated segment light.

"Freyung is a little less than twenty kilometers away. Could the circuits be faulty?"

"Maybe . . ."

"Border coming up in about one minute."

Hoffman could see the border guards and barbed-wire fences clearly now. The vibrations multiplied as he increased speed for the crossing.

Troops on the ground looked up as the helicopter went by them at over a hundred miles an hour, only fifty feet overhead. They were close enough that Hoffmann could see the surprise on several faces that peered upward from beneath steel helmets. So quick and unexpected was the sight of an aircraft coming from behind them that the machine was out of range before the first soldier got off a shot in the general direction of the target.

"There's Freyung at eleven o'clock," Ben Ari announced three minutes inside West Germany. The fuel gauge hovered a notch above the one-hundred-pound mark.

"I don't see it."

"Eleven o'clock . . . two kilometers, maybe less." Ben Ari

leaned forward and pointed. "Castle Wolfstein off to the right."

"Got it." The ship turned and started down toward the open field the Israeli indicated, the approach steep and fast. A precaution.

The skids hit the ground hard. The worst landing he could remember . . . but they were down. He shut off the fuel and battery switches immediately, without waiting for the engine to cool. The main rotor blades began to coast down slowly.

A car emerged from the woodline off to their right, crossed the open expanse of the field, and stopped outside the arc of the rotor system. Roy Locke, his clothes still damp, got out and ran toward them. Only then did Hoffmann allow himself the luxury of relaxing. He felt like he'd been strapped to the seat for a lifetime, though it had been only slightly more than two hours since they'd taken off from Hohenfels. Exhaustion swept over him; tension drained from his limbs. Ben Ari was talking to him from behind, but he barely heard as his eyes closely involuntarily.

". . . Hurry up. We'll be at the house Simon arranged in less than an hour; then you can sleep. Damn it, get moving!"

Chapter 27

"What is your name?"

   "Heinrich Schellen."

   "Where did you live?"

   "Berlin."

   "Where in Berlin?"

   "May I have a drink of water?"

   "The street?"

   "You know all this. Why must you continue to—"

   "The street!"

   "Dorfstrasse."

   "What was your position in the East German government?"

   "Minister of Transport."

   "What was your part in the plan called Dovetail?"

   "I never heard of it."

   "A lie!"

   "Please . . . may I have a drink?"

   "No. What was your part in the plan called Dovetail?"

   "I told you . . . I never heard of—"

"What did you do in the SS during World War II?"

"I was a supply officer in what you would call the Quartermasters, not the SS."

"You were in the SS!"

"I beg you . . . a drink."

"When you decide to tell the truth. Let us try again. . . . What is your name?"

"Heinrich Schellen."

"Where did you live?" . . .

Ben Ari continued with the questions as he had for the past three hours, since arriving at the house at ten o'clock that morning.

Schellen sat tied to a wooden chair in the middle of what served as the parlor of the secluded farmhouse outside Mühldorf, fifty miles east of Munich. Because he was blindfolded, he spoke into space, the words directed at his captors though he could not determine their exact location. The ropes binding him cut deeply into the flesh around his wrists and ankles, creating painful swellings.

The Israeli constantly circled the object of his questions, shouting at him from behind, from the sides; then whispering in his ear, keeping him off balance. Constant repetition of questions and the manner in which they were asked had long since worn through Schellen's resistance.

"What are you doing?" Hoffmann asked, when Ben Ari finally stopped and left the room

"I am interrogating him."

"It looks more like slow torture."

"I want him in the right frame of mind when we begin our trip. He must know that I will be merciless if he should decide to step out of line. When I allow him the basic necessities of life, he must know that he is totally dependent on me for his existence. When that happens, we will be ready. But it will take more time."

"It sounds like brainwashing."

"It is." Ben Ari crossed to the phone and dialed. It was answered immediately. "Simon?"

"Yes," came the reply.

"We have him. Can you contact Wiesenthal?"

"Whenever you say."

"We should be ready to move by morning, if you can set it up that quickly."

"I'll call you back this evening after six. Aki . . . I'm glad you got him."

Ben Ari hung up. He heard the East German call out. "At least tell me where I am."

"Silence!" the Israeli commanded. "You will not speak unless I tell you."

"Where am I?" A whining plea.

Reentering the room, Ben Ari said, "You are in West Germany—the first stop on your journey to Israel."

"*Juden?* You are Jews?" The voice cracked.

"Just one of us. Think about it. We know who you are . . ." He leaned over, close to the man, and whispered menacingly. "We know everything about you from the day you were born."

"I have done nothing to you."

"An Israeli court will judge that."

"You can't do this . . . my government will not allow you . . ."

"You are beyond the reach of your government. You are in the hands of justice."

"This is not justice."

"It is better than you deserve."

Schellen's breathing became rapid; he was hyperventilating.

"*What is your name?*"

"*Heinrich Schellen.*"

"*Where did you live?*"

"*Berlin. Dorfstrasse.*"

"What was your position in the East German government?"

The interrogation continued for another hour, until Schellen fainted from exhaustion. Ben Ari went into the kitchen, drew a glass of water, and returned to the room. He poured some down the throat of the unconscious man. Schellen awoke, coughing and gagging on the liquid.

"More. Please . . . another drink."

"When I am ready. . . . What did you do in the SS during the war?"

"I was a writer on Goebbels' staff."

"That was early on, and not the SS. What did you do later?"

"I was on Himmler's staff for a brief time."

"What did you do there?"

"I was responsible for transportation systems."

"Transporting what?"

"Everything . . . ammunition, fuel, clothing . . ."

"Jews?"

Silence.

"Did you arrange transportation for Jews to the extermination camps?"

"That function was performed within the section I was assigned to, yes."

"Is it true you were in charge of the section?"

"No."

"Do not lie to me. Were you in charge of that section?"

"Yes."

"Is it also true that Himmler himself awarded you a citation in 1942 for improving the existing system—increasing the number of Jews being moved by twenty percent?"

"I don't remember."

"I think you do. Did you make a trip to Auschwitz that year to discuss with the camp commandant methods of speeding up his end of the process? Methods to keep up with the increased numbers of Jews being moved there by your improved systems?"

"I don't remember."

"It was in early November."

"I have no memory of any visit there."

"Isn't it also a fact that during your visit you met every train that arrived and helped in the selection process?"

"I do not remember any . . ."

"Because you don't want to remember!"

"It was a long time ago."

Ben Ari's voice grew louder as he spoke.

"Do you remember a day at Auschwitz when you met the cattle cars from Warsaw, and made the selections of who would live and who would die among the children packed into the last car?"

"I have no memory of—"

"Do you remember me?" Ben Ari shouted. He ripped the blindfold roughly from the man. Schellen blinked rapidly, unable to focus.

"Look at me! Do . . . you . . . remember?"

"I have never seen you."

A calm came over the Israeli agent. "Yes, you have. But I was much different then."

"I swear . . . I do not know what you are talking about."

"Then I will refresh your memory." He pulled a chair in front of the East German and sat down.

"We were loaded onto the cars at a rail siding outside Warsaw. They put over a hundred of us in a cattle car, all children; none of us could have been over twelve years old. The soldiers told us we were going to a camp, like a farm, to get away from the rubble and the conditions of the ghetto. They said it was a fun place, out in the country. A place of fresh air and sunshine. Away from the rats, the disease, the hunger.

"It took three days to make the trip; most of it the train

spent waiting on sidings. It was cold, bitter cold. Exposure killed half of the children in the car before we ever arrived at our destination. Because we had been separated from our parents, and there were no adults in our car, many of the smallest ones were hysterical from the time the doors were closed and locked. By the end of our trip, the smell of human waste was so strong that everyone left alive was sick.

"We were given nothing to eat or drink.

"At the railroad siding outside Auschwitz, the train made its last stop. SS guards awaited us, many of them with dogs. When the doors opened, most of those left alive were so frightened they tried to run away. None who tried survived. The dogs caught them. I will never forget those black-clad monsters who stood there laughing as they let the dogs loose and yelled, *'Juden Kinder! Juden Kinder!'* I was only ten years old then, but the memory of that day is as clear now as anything that has happened since.

"The little girl who sat beside me during the trip was so frightened by the snarling dogs and what she saw them do to the kids who ran, she could not control herself. She tried to hide underneath the dead bodies of others. I thought I could protect her if I kept her with me instead of leaving her for the guards to find.

"She had no possessions except the torn dress she was wearing.

"When we got off the train to line up with the rest of the children, an officer came up to one of the guards and apparently told him to separate the boys from the girls, because that is what he began doing. The little girl saw this, and it frightened her even more. She cried. Another soldier slapped her across the face to make her stop. He was over six feet tall; she was half that. Still, she clung to me with all her strength.

"The officer saw this and returned, but instead of correcting the soldier or making him stop, he grabbed her arm and twisted it until she let go. She screamed and tried to grab my hand. When she wouldn't stop screaming, the officer hit her on the temple with his riding crop. She died in front of me, at my feet.

"But I survived.

"I did every dirty job imaginable at Auschwitz. Picking up clothes from the dressing rooms outside the gas chambers, carrying drinks to the guards at the crematorium, cleaning the grease traps in the guards' kitchen, cleaning their latrines.

"I became an animal.

"But I survived.

"I escaped a year later, along with about fifty other prisoners. Most of them were recaptured. An old Polish couple watched over me until a Jewish partisan group took me out of Poland.

"After the war, I was interned by the British in a refugee camp on Cyprus until the Palmach smuggled me to Israel.

"Does that do anything for your memory, Herr Schellen?"

"I have heard of such things but have never seen them for myself."

"Yes, you have!" The Israeli rose to his full height and stood over the German. "You are the reason I fought so hard to stay alive."

He paused and breathed deeply. Once. Twice.

"You were that officer . . . and the little girl was my sister."

He turned and walked from the room.

Ben Ari left the farmhouse without a word. Reliving that time now thirty years past had been agony, a form of self-inflicted martyrdom. At last he was free of the guilt. But he needed time alone.

And so he walked; across the fields, his head bowed, his eyes filled with tears.

When he returned to the house two hours later, it was past five o'clock, and nothing remained of the daylight on the Bavarian landscape. The tears of sorrow were replaced by a

grim determination to see Schellen returned to Israel for trial
and execution. Failing that, he would quickly—and gladly—
kill the German himself at the slightest provocation.

Locke and Hoffmann looked up as he entered. Hoffmann
rose and followed him to the room in which the German sat.

"Ask him about my father," the American said.

"There's no need."

"Why?"

"Because he can't tell you a thing. He knows nothing
about your father. Despite what your CIA friends told you,
he never commanded a POW camp." Ben Ari saw the look
on Hoffmann's face. "Did you expect anything they told you
would be true? They used you."

"What surprises me is that you would."

"Then you have a lot of learning to do."

"It would appear that way. You're a hell of a teacher."

"So I've been told."

"You knew all along I'd never learn about my father."

"I didn't say that. In the bottom of my rucksack you'll
find a folder inside a waterproof bag. It's the personnel record
you could never locate."

"Why didn't you—?"

"Tell you before? Because you might not have done what I
needed to get at Schellen."

"You think I would have backed out on you?"

"Yes."

"Then you have a lot of learning to do also."

"Perhaps. But I couldn't take the chance."

For the first time since meeting the Israeli, Hoffmann
perceived himself as Ben Ari's equal. He went to the nylon
rucksack, opened it, and retrieved the green bag. For a long
moment he held it, wanting to open the folder yet almost
afraid of what it contained; now that it was in his possession,
doubt surfaced. Finally, he took the file into the kitchen and
sat at the table.

Inside the folder was a picture of a young Air Corps lieutenant. It struck him as strange at first; he'd always pictured his father as a man older than himself. Seeing the face of one eight or nine years his junior made the moment awkward, the sensation vacant. The expected surge of closeness was absent. He felt somehow guilty.

He turned the picture over and picked up the service-history record. It listed chronologically all the major events in the brief career of Lieutenant Kenneth M. Hoffmann: induction, basic cadet training, primary flight, advanced training, bomber transition, leave, overseas assignment, stateside Christmas leave, return to England. None of it revealed the nature of the man. The next set of documents was copies of orders for every move, every school attended. A separate folder contained medical records; another held copies of pay vouchers.

The last documents in the file were carbon copies of flight-mission sheets on onionskin paper. Only eight slips were present, the last dated 23 January 1945.

Checking the clock on the wall, Hoffman realized he'd been absorbed in reading for twenty minutes. Ben Ari walked in and sat down across the table.

"This tells me nothing," Hoffmann said.

"I know, but there's a clue to where you can find the rest of what you've been looking for. Pull out the last onionskin, the one dated January twenty-third."

Hoffmann extracted the sheet and located the entry two lines below the heading.

BRIEFING: OPS 230545 JAN. - GREGORY KNIGHT

"You'll see there used to be a slash between the two names. On the day your father disappeared, he received his instructions from the man you found dead in Silver Springs, and the man who has been controlling this operation—planned to result in your own death."

"They were responsible?"

"You have to find that out yourself. There is something more important left to be done—something you must do. . . . Dovetail has to be stopped."

"But you have Schellen. That has to set it back until you, or somebody, can get them to call it off for good."

"Such things are not easily accomplished. Schellen has confirmed there are others in East Germany who can and will perform his function. The apparatus can be dismantled by only one person. That man is Knight."

"Go after him, then."

"As I said, that's not particularly easy . . . at least, not for us. Israel is currently walking a very narrow line in our relationship with the U.S.. This oil situation is causing a reevaluation of political necessities in your country, and there is a growing feeling in our government that some of your leaders are looking for a good reason—an excuse, perhaps—to dump Israel. We cannot afford to be caught openly dealing with the CIA at the Deputy Director level . . . for any reason. And, for our own sake as well as yours, we cannot afford to publicize this Dovetail."

"Who should—?"

A scraping sound, muted and barely recognizable as humanly induced; without conscious thought, Hoffmann pulled the pistol from his belt and aimed it in the general direction of the back door. Three shots rang out, sending the room into darkness an instant before the back door crashed inward. Hoffmann fired, and kept firing until the rounds were gone. A muffled scream reached his ears, then the sight of a form falling toward him, shapeless in the dark.

"Ben Ari!"

"Here." The voice came from the far wall, next to the window, followed by rapid gunshots into the field behind the house. "The second one got away. He'll be back." The Israeli produced a flashlight and shined it on the attacker's face. "Locke?"

"There's movement out front. Two cars, maybe three."

The front of the house was bathed in white from headlights. A pane of glass shattered, pierced by a bullet fired from outside.

"Ben Ari, we have come for you." The voice from beyond the darkness carried a heavy German accent.

"What do you want?" the Israeli called out, moving to the parlor with Hoffmann, resting his back against the front wall.

"No games, please. We want Heinrich Schellen."

"If you try to take him, you will force me to kill. I'm sure you're aware that I am prepared to take his life." Ben Ari nodded at Locke to cover the rear of the house.

"Then you and the American will die with him."

"We are prepared for that also."

No reply came. Seconds became minutes. Finally the silence was broken from outside.

"Ben Ari . . . we offer you a trade. Give us Schellen and we will give you the girl."

"Maggie!" Hoffmann yelled through the window. There was no answer. He looked to the Israeli. "They've got her!"

"Even if they do, we will not risk losing Schellen."

"Damn it, she has nothing to do with this! If they don't get Schellen, they'll kill her."

"They might."

"Schellen isn't worth it!"

"He is to me."

"If they have her, we trade. I'll fight you on this one. You can't take on all of us."

"Shut up, and use some common sense. They're most likely the Odessa. Even if we try to go along with them, they won't let us live."

"We can work that out once she's safe."

The quiet outside was pierced by a scream of pain, the loud slapping of flesh against flesh. They were beating her!

"Eric!" Her voice was filled with anguish.

"Maggie! Are you all right?"

"Don't let them hurt me again. I can't stand it anymore . . . please . . . help me."

"I want to see her," Hoffmann yelled. Unseen figures pushed the girl in front of the headlights. She stumbled, lost her balance, and fell. Her clothes were torn.

"Are you all right, Maggie?"

"I don't know," she moaned, barely audible. "They beat me . . . two, three days. Then they . . . don't let them hurt me any more." She sobbed; her voice trailed off to a whimper.

"Do we trade?" came the voice from behind the lights.

"Yes, we trade," replied Hoffmann.

"Ben Ari, we want to hear it from you."

"We trade," the Israeli replied after several seconds. "Let the girl come into the house, and we will release Schellen."

Another windowpane shattered, sending jagged pieces of glass through the room.

"We told you before: no playing games. Bring him outside. We will meet halfway for the exchange. We want both you and the American where we can see you."

"You have the advantage then. We will trade only if we bring our car around so our headlights are in your eyes, as yours are in ours."

More time passed while the Israeli's proposal was considered.

"Agreed. You stand in the doorway while Hoffmann drives the car around."

Ben Ari turned to Hoffmann. "They don't know about Locke. Both of you into the car with weapons. Come around the left side of the house. Leave the motor running and all doors unlocked. As soon as we have the girl, we'll make our break." He went to the German and tightly gagged him.

Then he untied him from the chair and bound his wrists behind him. "If you make one sound, one move I don't like, you're dead," he hissed. "Is that understood?"

Schellen nodded rapidly, his eyes wide with fright. The Israeli dragged him roughly toward the window.

"I'm coming out with Schellen in front of me."

Hoffmann and Locke went through the back door as the Israeli stepped out onto the porch. The car pulled up next to the house. Ben Ari sidestepped toward it, using Schellen as a shield. A lone figure pulled Maggie upright, causing her to cry out.

"Send the American forward with Schellen. I will meet him halfway with the girl."

Ben Ari leaned toward Hoffmann and whispered, "Keep him in front of you all the way . . . and keep your eyes open. Get back and get her into the rear seat of the car as fast as you can."

Hoffmann started forward slowly, his palms wet, his pulse rapid. He stopped when he judged they were almost at the halfway point.

Maggie was only a foot away when he caught the first scent of her perfume. She seemed under control despite the ordeal, though her eyes were disturbingly vacant. Her face was streaked with dirt, but unmarked. She leaned forward, clinging to him, and kissed him lightly on the cheek as her left arm went around his neck. Hoffmann retained his hold on the rope binding Schellen's hands. The four of them stood motionless.

Something was wrong.

The man behind Maggie was slowly pushing a small automatic forward underneath her arm. Hoffmann looked down and saw her hand clasp the pistol's grip, her finger entwine around the trigger. She pushed it into his stomach and whispered into his ear.

"Don't do anything unless I tell you."

"What—?"

"Don't talk. We're going to start back toward your car very slowly. I'm weak . . . you have to help me. Make them believe. Now, let go of Schellen."

"No."

She pushed the weapon farther into his stomach.

"You're one of them? You're with the Odessa?"

"We are Der Zorn." A cruel smile crossed her lips. "We must have Schellen—his money and influence, his knowledge. . . . I hated every minute with you in Bad Tölz. And I will have no regrets at killing you. Do as I say."

"You won't let me live anyway. But I can keep you from killing Ben Ari."

"He won't live long. A dead Jew in Europe is worth more to us than a hundred on the battlefield. This is the last time I tell you!"

From the corner of his eye, Hoffmann saw the abrupt movement of the man behind her an instant before the concussion shattered the quiet and thundered through his head. A bright flash blinded him, and he was thrown to the ground. Two more concussion waves passed over and through him as he groveled on his knees, barely able to see, the taste of dirt in his mouth. Maggie was only a few feet from him on her knees, her hands pressed against her face, trickles of blood coming from between her fingers. Glass from the headlights shattered in front of him as they went out in quick succession. Sights and sounds blended together in strange, bewildering patterns.

Ben Ari was kneeling over him, shouting words he could not hear; then he was gone. Around him there was pandemonium. Then he was running in the darkness; stumbling, weaving, direction meaningless. He felt himself being pushed, then felt the fabric of seat covers scrape his face.

He sensed the slamming of doors and the lurching of the car as it sped across grass fields and dirt roads, swinging wildly. At times he thought he heard Maggie's voice, and then others'——all unfamiliar. When he opened his eyes, the world outside was blurred, spinning madly; the sounds in his ears a raging cacophony. In his confusion, he tried to open the door and jump. Each time he was pulled backward and pinned to the seat.

Finally, too weak to resist, he slumped over unconscious.

Chapter 28

A muted hum of tires on concrete invaded the boundaries of his consciousness, thrusting, probing. His vision was still blurred. His head throbbed in rhythm with a pounding pulse. Voices intruded, distant and unintelligible. The pitch of the engine lowered as the car slowed and turned. The hum of the tires changed, replaced by the crunching sound of rubber on loose gravel. Finally the car stopped.

"He's coming around."

Hoffmann struggled weakly with the hands that held him, unable to move them, overwhelmed with frustration. At last he went limp and felt his arms grow unendurably heavy. He took several deep breaths, expelling the last audibly, praying the pain would leave his head.

"Easy," said the voice. "Take it easy. You'll be all right." A familiar face came into focus. Ben Ari. "Can you hear me?"

"Just barely." He felt incapable of speech, or thought. His tongue was swollen and numb, too large to form intelligible words.

"You had a rough go of it back there, and your ears are probably still ringing. They will for a while. It's going to take a few days for you to return to normal. Relax for now. We're at a *restplatz* near Ingolstadt."

Hoffmann massaged tense neck muscles with his left hand, slowly rotating his head full circle. "What happened?"

"We knew something was wrong when you didn't move back to the car. You were taking too much time, and we could see your grip still on Schellen. Locke used the stun grenades."

"They work."

"Very well, in fact."

Hoffmann closed his eyes again, resting his head on the soft cushion of the back seat. The pounding of his temples remained, joined by the realization of acute pain in his shoulder. "She was one of them," he said, his voice weary, subdued.

"We know. We saw her drop the gun when the first grenade went off."

"Is she . . . alive?"

"Does it matter?"

The question confused him. The day before, he had felt unutterably guilt-ridden when Locke revealed her disappearance following Edelmann's death. Her presence at the farmhouse had seemed infinitely miraculous. He had not seen the inconsistencies—until now. In Bad Tölz she had been afraid of him because he was a practiced liar, but in the dining room of the Munich hotel she had indicated otherwise. *You're a very poor liar. Does it have anything to do with this trouble you're in?* . . . He hadn't been listening! He was too engrossed in fabricating the story to explain his assault on the hotel chef. And she had not believed his story *before* the phone call from her father—not after, as explained in Deborah Mueller's apartment. Other questions surfaced now. Why had she gone to the Hofbräuhaus alone that night? He had not been professional enough, or sufficiently alert, to ask.

"Simon was working with them, too," Ben Ari was saying. "Only he and Aaron knew about the apartment in Bad Tölz."

"Why not . . . ?" He couldn't bring himself to say her name. "Why not her?"

"It could have been, but only Simon knew the location of the farmhouse." The Israeli paused. When he spoke, disappointment was evident. "Schellen is gone. I fired at him as the headlights were knocked out, but there's no way to be positive whether or not I got him. Alive, and in our possession, he could have verified Dovetail's existence. You and Locke are the last ones who can stop it now."

"I don't think I can do it."

"You can . . . and you will. In a few days, when you're recovered, you'll see it's true. When I came here, I was convinced you were incapable of completing the operation. But you proved me wrong, in every way. You're the type I'd fight to keep in my unit when I was in the Army. You can see this through. . . . And you know it has to be done."

"Sounds like the kind of speech you'd give somebody going on a one-way-only mission."

Locke turned from behind the steering wheel, looking into the back seat. "By this time tomorrow, we should be in Amsterdam. You can rest for a few days before we head back to the States."

"What are you going to do?" Hoffmann asked, looking at Ben Ari.

"First I'm going to Munich to settle the business with Simon, and try to pick up Schellen's trail. Neither will be easy." The Israeli exhaled slowly and looked past him out the rear window. "Then I'll go back to Israel. This is my last assignment—I owe that much to my sons. Even if I don't find Schellen, he'll spend the rest of his life looking over his shoulder for me . . . or somebody like me. Maybe that's worse than trial and execution."

"Deborah said you were a farmer. It's hard to imagine."

"After this? Maybe it is. It's what I'd prefer. I want to settle down, forget the past."

"I hope you make it."

"I will.

A car pulled from the sparse autobahn traffic and entered the *restplatz*, stopping twenty yards to their rear. A solitary figure got out and went into the bushes to relieve himself. When he returned, he leaned against the left front fender of his car and casually lit a cigarette. Three times a match flared in the darkness.

"My signal," Ben Ari explained. He turned to Hoffmann and grasped his hand in a firm grip. "For all our sakes, I hope you get through."

"Wait! I still have a lot of unanswered questions. She mentioned something called Der Zorn . . ."

"It means the Anger. Locke will explain."

Before Hoffmann could reply, the Israeli closed the door and walked through the darkness toward the other car. Seconds later, it pulled around the Mercedes and disappeared behind the treeline growing to the edge of the autobahn.

Chapter 29

Montreal.

Almost home.

Hoffmann knew the most difficult part of this particular leg of the journey was behind them when the big jet touched down, then slowed and turned onto a taxiway leading to the terminal.

After Ben Ari's departure that night in Germany, Locke had driven north to Hanover, then west toward the Netherlands. At daybreak, they stopped at a motel within the city limits of Osnabrück to rest and await nightfall before continuing. Three hours after sunset, they again struck out westward.

Locke was familiar with the narrow, sometimes overgrown back roads along the border and knew which passages would be checked only periodically by roving sentinels. Three hours after leaving Osnabrück, they crossed into the Netherlands on a dirt road through the Itterbecker Moor, a seldom-traveled path through the marsh used only by smugglers moving arms or drugs. Twice Hoffmann had to get out and push as the car got stuck. By the time they left Germany, his clothes were covered with drying mud and his feet were soaked, adding to his general discomfort.

At 2:00 A.M., they arrived in Amsterdam.

Locke drove to a downtown bar in a dimly lit district and entered alone, leaving Hoffmann in the car across the street. He was back in twenty minutes with the owner, who took them to a second-floor apartment situated over a camera shop several blocks away; a sparsely furnished single room, bug-infested and dreary. But Locke insisted it was safe—at least for a few days.

When Hoffmann awoke the next morning, the agent was gone.

Shortly before noon, he returned with a doctor, a solemn, middle-aged man who avoided asking questions while cleaning the gash above Eric's swollen right eye. The searing pain brought back memories of the flight to Zdikov.

During the next two days in Amsterdam, Locke arranged for passports and other personal documents under false identities. Reservations were made on a Friday-morning flight to Ireland, and at Shannon they boarded the Aer Lingus flight to Montreal.

Canadian customs inspectors passed them through with nothing more ominous than a few openly curious stares at Hoffmann's abrasions. They were minor irritations now, seemingly acquired in another, best-forgotten era of his life. Less than an hour after arrival, they registered at the Laurentien, overlooking Dominion Square.

"We still haven't talked about our next step," Hoffmann said as they left the elevator at the third floor.

"I know. Get cleaned up first, then I'll have a bottle sent up and we can talk. Bourbon all right with you?"

They walked down the hall and found the adjoining rooms; the arrangement had cost them an extra hundred dollars for the reservation clerk. It was a weekend and the hotel was a popular one, the man explained deferentially. The sight of cash removed the difficulty.

Twenty minutes later, after a hot shower, Hoffmann heard Locke's tap on the door.

"At twenty-eight dollars a fifth, you'd better enjoy this," Locke said, placing the partially empty bottle on a writing table.

"Where are you getting all this money?"

"I've got a few accounts stashed around for emergencies. The one in Amsterdam was part of a missile-guidance system on the F-111."

Hoffmann filled a glass with ice, then poured bourbon almost to the rim. The liquor burned his throat and caused a shudder. After a second, more tentative sip, he sat on the edge of the bed, facing Locke, who had reclined in a stuffed chair beside the dresser.

"I think we ought to split up tomorrow," the agent began, "to double our chances of getting through to Knight." Hoffmann stared at him without replying. "You don't agree. Look at it this way. They're looking for me; he made sure of that, and they'll get rid of me on sight. You'll be better off on your own."

"How? I don't even know what he looks like . . . or where he is. I don't know how to contact him."

"The best way is to go through the Madras intercept. It's an automatic telephone-switching terminal in Atlanta tied into another in Washington. The one in Washington is linked to a special terminal in Langley." Locke handed him a card. "Call this number in Atlanta and wait; after a delay, you'll hear the relays working first on one of the terminals, then on the other. When the phone goes dead the second time, it means they're tracing the call. Within about three minutes, you'll know whether or not they'll talk to you. If they don't want to, you'll get a recorded message saying the phone number is no longer in service."

"Why don't you just give me his home and office numbers?"

"I will. But the impact will be greater if you use the intercept. Only a dozen people in the world know about it."

"Let's keep it a two-man act, and you make the call. We can arrange a meeting with him together."

"Exactly what I'd want if I were Knight. We're better off doing it separately. With two of us working independently, our chances of getting through are multiplied."

"You say that, but the logic isn't there. I don't know how the Agency functions or how Knight thinks, how he reacts."

"Look, if we went together, he could eliminate us, without fear of somebody else to fill in the details and elaborate on the Schellen defection. The file itself might not stand on its own."

"Ben Ari could handle it."

"You heard what he said about the Israeli position. They're not about to admit their part in kidnapping and murdering an East German minister. That's political dynamite. My way is the only way."

Hoffmann debated. "How do I get in touch with you?"

"I have a sister in Charleston, South Carolina. She'll know how."

"If I get to Knight first, he'll want proof that we have his records."

"Take the last page of the Gregory staff study. I'll keep the rest of the file and secure it somewhere he can't reach."

"You plan to keep the file!"

"And you keep your father's military records. The Dovetail file has to be kept intact. Splitting it weakens our case; maybe destroys it." The agent saw cynical disbelief in Hoffmann's eyes. "I know what you're thinking. Trust me—I could have left you days ago in Amsterdam."

Hoffmann stared at him for long seconds, thinking of Ben

Ari's warning after Locke had joined them in Hohenfels. "You've got all the answers, don't you?"

"I wish I did. . . . I'm fighting for my life."

"So am I."

"Which is exactly why we have to split up and go after him from more than one direction. You've got the ability—I've seen you improvise."

Sitting motionless, Hoffmann studied the agent's face. The oblique compliment was meaningless, added only to distract him. How long ago had he begun looking for double meanings—hidden agendas—behind every statement, every action? "I'll need information, details. A crash course on inside information about the Agency—obscure particulars they wouldn't expect me to know."

"Such as?"

"Names and positions of people inside Langley. Phone numbers, if you have them. Organizational structures classified secret or above. You mentioned once before that the CIA had the largest fleet of commercial planes in the world—start with that."

"Nobody knows all the details of the air proprietaries—not even the Director, and certainly not Congress or the public. I can't help you much there; most of what I know is hearsay, or limited to personal experience on field assignments."

"A few details will be enough," Hoffmann replied, finishing his drink and deciding against another. He needed a clear head, and the liquor was already having more of an effect than he'd expected. "Go ahead."

"There are several proprietaries around the world: Air Asia, Intermountain Aviation, Southern Air Transport. I'm sure you're familiar with Air America from your days in Southeast Asia."

Hoffmann remembered. It was common knowledge that the CIA operated the mixed bag of cargo planes—mostly old gooney birds, from what he'd seen in Viet Nam. Their cargo and destinations were closely guarded information. The other organizations were unfamiliar to him. "Where did it begin?"

"In China, 1946, with CAT—Civil Air Transport. It was an offshoot of Chennault's Flying Tigers, who flew in support of Chiang Kai-shek before he was driven off the mainland. They followed him to Taiwan, where their headquarters are located now. Air America and Air Asia are part of CAT; it's been that way since the late 'fifties. Ten years ago, Washington sent a negotiator to Taiwan to discuss turning over CAT's passenger runs to the Chinese. He's still there."

"What's his name?"

"Alex Rodale."

"How much business is done over there?"

"Last year Air America had contracts with the Defense Department worth forty-two million—that's all I know, but there's undoubtedly more. They made a fortune during the buildup; it's a self-sustaining, profitable enterprise."

"Forty-two million?"

"That's the number I've heard batted around. But again, it's hearsay. The proprietaries are constantly selling, leasing, or trading aircraft among themselves, so it's impossible to keep track of their size of finances. What central coordination there is comes from the Executive Committee for Air—I've heard Ex Comm Air's proceedings are so classified the executive secretary is forbidden to keep minutes. By and large, each proprietary is allowed to live its cover as it sees fit."

"Any estimate of total worth?"

Locke smiled ruefully and poured another drink, allowing the silence to be his answer.

"Who runs this Ex Comm Air?" Hoffmann asked.

"The Agency's general counsel, Hyland Palmer. I don't know who else from Clandestine Services, the support directorate, or the executive suite."

The agent spoke casually, with an understanding of protocols and organizational structure that eluded Hoffmann.

"What is Clandestine Services?"

"It's one of the four directorates, reporting to Knight through the Deputy Director for Community Relations. It's officially called Operations. The other three are intelligence; Science and Technology; and Management and Services. Knowing that isn't necessarily earth-shattering."

"Give me something that is."

Locke thought for a minute, observing Hoffmann over the rim of his glass, his eyes cold and distant. It was almost as if the agent had suddenly remembered a vow of secrecy, probably recorded on a document buried somewhere in the bowels of Langley, similar perhaps to the one Hoffmann had signed for Carnahan. Promises had been broken; the signature meant nothing—to either of them.

"There was something that happened back in 'seventy," Locke was saying, reaching for the ice bucket and dropping two more cubes into the glass. The bottle's contents were rapidly disappearing; the agent's words were now slightly slurred. "It was a petition that some of the younger ones in Science and Technology got up, objecting to policies in Indochina. . . . It was after the Cambodian invasion. A couple of hundred signed it, including some from Intelligence. Word of it never got out."

"A rebellion in the CIA?"

"Not quite. Like I said, a couple of hundred. The State Department and other agencies had it worse—especially after every newspaper in the country got hold of it."

"But you say the CIA petition wasn't leaked. The media would have had a field day."

"Secrecy was tight. The protest itself was conducted in secret." Locke grinned, apparently finding the ludicrousness of the idea amusing. "The protesters were herded into the main auditorium at Langley and lectured on separating their personal feelings from professional requirements. It died after that—a quick and unnatural death."

"Somebody had to lead it. What happened to the organizers?"

"Don't know . . . except for two of them—both in the Office of Special Projects."

"Which directorate?"

"Science and Technology." Locke took a long pull on the drink and lit another cigarette from the stub he'd just finished. The agent was chain-smoking, filling the room with an odorous haze. "I remember one, because he was the captain of the bowling team, and he didn't show up for the next match against us."

"Why not?" Hoffmann asked, quaintly surprised at the notion of clandestine mentalities engaging in something so dull. "Was he canned?"

"Not until last year, after they had moved him two or three times. For a while he was assigned to the Comm Center, which reported to the Director—probably placed there so they could keep an eye on him. Not unexpected, since he was familiar with most of the Delaware corporations who were developing the next generation of sophisticated technology. The guy had a brain. He also had a big mouth. Apparently they figured he'd been weaned away from most of the really sensitive material; and the technology gets obsolete almost before it hits the field."

An idea formed, an improvisation; one of many he would need. But it was an important first step. He had to have the name, and Locke supplied it.

"Ojakaar. Dominic Ojakaar," he continued without prodding. "Everybody called him Domino, and that's how they listed him the phone book for his directorate. Had a lot going for himself until then."

Hoffmann changed the subject. "Diagram the organization for me," he said quickly, moving to the writing table and pouring another drink. Distracting Locke's attention was suddenly important.

"I don't know it all."

"Give me what you do. Anything will be a help." He retrieved a sheet of the Laurentien's ornate stationery from the top drawer of the desk and placed it in front of Locke. "After that, you can tell me about this Madras intercept."

"I already told you."

"Tell me again."

He picked up the bottle and poured Locke another drink.

Sharp tentacles of lightning clawed at the formless dark sky, briefly illuminating the tree-lined shore encircling Ouquaga Lake, outlining surrounding hills. Thunder crashed and rolled across the mountainous landscape, rumbling through the valley like a giant drumbeat herded by the wind. It was unusual for a thunderstorm to come up so late in the year this far north, but Hoffmann was beyond being surprised—by human or natural forces. Another bolt of lightning streaked across the sky, and from where he stood on the broad porch of Labruzo's cottage, he could see whitecaps forming on the lake.

He had called the lawyer two hours after extracting the information he needed from Locke. Assuming Labruzo's phone was tapped, he provided the number of a pay phone two blocks from his hotel, using a hastily conceived code based on an address familiar to both: a club in central Philadelphia.

"We went there my first night after rotating home," Hoffmann had said, without revealing the name. "Do you remember the place? The address?"

"Like it was yesterday."

"Copy this . . . it's a phone number. First number: add the first and second digits. Second number: multiply the second digit by two and subtract from the first digit. Third number . . ." The call had been too short to trace, and though the code was simple and probably broken easily, it would allow time to talk freely with Labruzo. Twenty-five minutes later, the lawyer called him from a corner tavern and arrangements were made to meet the following night at a gift shop in Alexandria Bay, on the New York side of the St. Lawrence Seaway.

He bought a bus ticket in Montreal, changed clothes in the men's room at the terminal, and slipped on the coat he'd stolen from a rack outside the Laurel Room at the hotel. In Ottawa, the coat was discarded in a trash dumpster behind the depot after the labels were removed, later to be scattered along the highway twenty miles southwest. He boarded a late-afternoon bus from Ottawa to cross the border.

Rain came in cold gray sheets, beating against the porch roof and pouring from swollen gutters. Hoffmann pulled his collar up and went inside, where the aroma of fresh-brewed coffee wafted from the kitchen. Labruzo placed a mug on the coffee table before pulling up an old, hand-painted rocker next to the cast-iron stove.

"That's some yarn," the lawyer offered, throwing another log on the fire and closing the small square door. "What's your next move?"

"I'm going after this Bill Knight."

He had told Labruzo most of the story as they drove the interstate from the Thousand Islands, through Syracuse as far as Binghamton. From there it was a short thirty-mile drive across back roads to the lakeside house. The peaceful setting reminded him of a cottage in the Ebersberger Forest, and at first his mind had been nervously active, looking for routes of escape, checking for signs of unwanted surveillance. Now the world was a hostile environment, the change in perception becoming surprisingly normal.

"I think you're in over your head," Labruzo said, testing the coffee. "An unbiased legal opinion. . . ."

"Over my head, maybe. . . . If I wanted a decent lawyer, I'd have gone elsewhere." He looked at Labruzo and arched his eyebrows innocently, comfortable with the easy banter, a special chemistry. "They forced me into this and left no alternatives, no escape. They have resources beyond even your wild imagination—I've heard about some of them."

"You want to take on that? In the clinches?"

"My desires don't fit anywhere in the equation. They were stripped away when I sat down at a conference table in Washington." He thought briefly about the meeting with Carnahan, the momentum of his life rapidly accelerating from the first words, the control of his destiny wrested from him and placed in the hands of others.

"Last night you said you needed a favor."

"Several," Hoffmann corrected. "First, I have to locate Nick Sadukas, the maintenance technician in my father's squadron. I got his name from the personnel records; he wasn't listed on any of the squadron rosters I dug up before this began. I want to know why—and I want to know where he is. All I have is that he was born in East St. Louis fifty-two years ago.

"I also need to find Dominic Ojakaar. Last known employer: the CIA. He could be living in Washington or a surrounding suburb; maybe working in government, or possibly one of the think tanks. His credentials are supposed to be outstanding."

"How soon?"

"Tomorrow night. The day after, at the latest."

Labruzo emitted a low whistle, shaking his head. "Not possible."

"It is. Maybe not for you. . . . How are things between you and your father?"

Wariness played at the corners of Labruzo's eyes; the lawyer's mouth drew into a tight line. "In general, we're still not speaking. Every time we do, the conversation eventually gets around to taking over his business. Don't think for a minute I'll go to him."

"I will. An introduction from you is required."

"Required!"

"Sorry, bad choice of words."

"It's worse than that."

Their conversation had taken a swift descent into dangerous ground, but Hoffmann knew he had no other choice. Time was critical. The longer he remained inactive, waiting for information and trying to avoid detection, the greater were his chances of *being* detected. Knight had all the resources. The only possibility for success rested on bold and immediate action, finding vulnerabilities sowing confusion. In his own mind, he knew their confrontation was a brutally unequal mismatch. But he had surprise on his side, to him the most important principle of this secret war. He would get what he wanted . . . even if it cost Labruzo's friendship.

He expected it would.

"I have to talk to him," Hoffmann said finally.

"About the information?"

"Yes."

"What else?"

"Just that. I shouldn't have brought it up, but you're the only one who can put me in touch with him."

Labruzo stared at him, no longer the easygoing young lawyer of the previous moment, his face betraying undisguised apprehension, suspicion. There was more. "You're lying. There's something you want; it goes beyond information. I can see it in your face, hear it in your voice."

Hoffmann breathed deeply and replied. "It's business . . . something you probably wouldn't want to be involved with."

"You're out of your damned mind! This is a bad joke, Eric."

"I'm dead serious."

"Forget it!" Labruzo said with emphasis, the tone of his voice carrying an ominous warning. Abruptly he stood and walked to the side window where rain pounded against the storm windows, driven by a fierce wind. "That kind of thing doesn't exist in the real world."

"Don't con me, Tony—I know better."

"You know nothing."

"I know that you owe me. If it hadn't been for me, you'd have come home in a body bag."

The lawyer turned to face him, his eyes wide and angry. "How damn long are you going to ride that?"

"Until I finish what has to be done. Contacting your father will be the last payment of the debt; and you'll do it." Hoffmann stopped, his face devoid of emotion. He had dreaded this moment like none other, knowing the results before he'd even seen Labruzo, rationalizing the means—hating himself for what he had to do. "I've been through a lot," he said apologetically.

"That's weak. . . . Damn it, everything you've said flies in the face of what I believe in, what I'm trying to do with my life." The lawyer sighed deeply, then walked to the stairs, stopping at the landing. "I'll set it up—the introduction."

"Thanks. You won't regret it."

"I already do. . . . This is it, though. Tomorrow, I'll drop you in Philly, and it's over. The debt is paid, and that's the end. Finis." Labruzo shook his head sadly from side to side. "I wonder whatever happened to the real Eric Hoffmann. . . . Pick any bedroom you want to crash in, but for the life of me, I don't know how your conscience allows you to sleep."

Chapter 30

Hoffmann finished typing the letter and pulled the sheet from the portable typewriter's carriage. It was the fourth and final copy, identical in content to the others he'd done the past four hours while seated at the table in the motel room.

Each was addressed to a different leader, and he made sure to indicate the others who would receive the message. The last was addressed to the Commander, U.S. Army, Europe; the carbon-copy list included the Chancellor of West Germany, the Prime Minister of Canada, and the President of the United States. A bureaucratic maze would delay and maybe shortcircuit most of the letters. Hurdles were expected; some would be blockades. But decisions at the lower end of organizational structures would inevitably involve superiors, people more likely to protect established careers and defer accountability to those still higher up. Somehow, at least one would get through. And one was enough.

It had taken him almost a day to compose the letter before he was satisfied with the content and wording. Now, as he read it again, he was confident it would have the desired effect. Some, maybe all of them, would at first consider it a malicious prank. But the facts included could easily be checked by intelligence networks, and that would lend credence to the accusations. If all went as planned, several heads of government would be in contact with each other in a matter of days, perhaps hours, after receipt.

After checking the final letter, Hoffmann went to the registration desk and, with the aid of a twenty-dollar bill, persuaded the young clerk to allow him the use of the copying machine. He made seven copies of the letter addressed to the President. Then he returned to the room, addressed the envelopes, and affixed postage.

At 10:15 A.M., he checked out of the room and dropped the letters in a mailbox two blocks away. Forty-five minutes later, he was sitting in a public phone booth at the Reading, Pennsylvania, airport. He deposited twenty cents, dialed the phone number in Atlanta given him by Locke four days earlier, and waited for the operator. Seconds later, he heard the first set of relays being activated. Over the next three minutes, the sequence described by the agent took place, until he heard the recorded message telling him the number was no longer in service. The trace had been made.

To the people at Langley, it looked like another of the infrequent nuisance calls. A wrong number.

Exactly one hour later, Hoffmann placed his second call through the Madras intercept, this time from a phone booth at the Lancaster airport. The sequence was repeated, and ended with the same recorded message.

Harrisburg/Olmstead airport was the location from which Hoffmann placed his next call, again one hour after the previous attempt. The sequence was repeated but the recorded message was delayed. He hung up and left before the first words came over the line.

Someone in Langley had finally caught on.

He crossed the Susquehanna River, headed west, then turned south toward nearby Capitol City airport. His fourth call was made twenty minutes after the third.

This time the sequence ended differently.

"Who is this, please?" came the male voice over the line.

"My name is Eric Hoffmann."

"And, where are you calling from, sir?"

"You know exactly where I am. That's part of the procedure."

"Beg your pardon?" The man's tone was skillfully apologetic, the voice passive, a role well prepared. "I don't know where you're calling from. . . . This is Mr. Jacobs with the telephone company in Atlanta, and we've noticed several calls coming into the same disconnected exchange here. Can we assist you?"

"First of all, I know you're not with Ma Bell. You're at Langley."

"Excuse me?"

"Obviously I know about the Madras intercept, so let's not fool around. Sometime within the next twelve hours, I'm going to call back. When I do, I'll expect you to have the unlisted phone numbers of each of the Joint Chiefs. That's home and business numbers, meaning I want the private lines used in emergencies—the red phones."

"I'm afraid you've made some kind of mistake here. If you'll tell me exactly who in Atlanta you're trying to reach, then maybe—"

"You know which numbers I want. Get them. I'm sure you need clearance, so you'd better get started. Call William Knight and tell him Eric Hoffmann knows about Dovetail and the intercept. If I don't get the numbers when I call, the information I have will be forwarded to the wire services and the KGB section chief in Berlin."

"Sir, this really is—"

"I suggest you contact Knight immediately. I have his number if you need it."

The pause on the other end indicated the message had been understood. Hoffmann hung up and quickly departed.

The phone was ringing in William Knight's Washington office when he returned from a late lunch. He sat down in the swivel chair and picked up the receiver.

"Knight."

"Sir, this is McLoughlin at the Langley Commo Center. We just got a call you should know about. It came through on Madras."

"Go ahead."

"Somebody named Hoffmann called . . ."

"Hoffmann! Are you sure?"

"Yes, sir. I played the tape back to make certain."

"Origin?"

"Several different places before we finally talked to him."

"Why did you acknowledge?"

"It was suspicious. All the calls came from public phone booths in airports at exactly sixty-minute intervals, on the hour, except the last one. The first call was from Reading, Pennsylvania, at 1100 hours local; then 1200 from Lancaster; 1300 from Harrisburg; and finally 1320 from Capitol City airport. The pattern indicated it was not the occasional wrong number we get."

"How did you handle it?"

"I cut in and told him I was with the phone company in Atlanta, but he didn't buy it. He knows Madras, and is trading on it to get the emergency phone numbers of the Joint Chiefs. He suggested I call you for clearance."

"Damn."

"That was my reaction."

"What else did he say?"

"That he'd release the information on Madras and some-

thing called Dovetail to the wire services and the KGB
section chief in Berlin if he didn't get the numbers when he
called back."

"Are you sure?"

"Positive. I can patch in the tape if you'd like."

"No, that's not necessary. Who else knows about this?"

"Just me and the shift supervisor. What do you want us to
do when he calls back?"

"Give him the numbers—but stall, and have somebody
give me his location on a separate line, no matter when the
call comes through. . . . And McLoughlin—"

"Yes, sir?"

"I want the original tapes delivered to me. Bring them
here yourself. I'll accept responsibility." Knight hung up and
paced the office, chain-smoking until his tongue burned and
the ashtray was full. How had this . . . amateur . . . gotten
to Madras? It had to be Locke—somehow the two were tied
together. Missing funds from the section chief's account in
Amsterdam had already been discovered, and from there it
was easy enough to reconstruct the flights to Shannon and
Montreal. But it had never occurred to him that his companion at the Laurentien was Hoffmann. It should have.

Especially after the disturbing call from Palmer first thing
that morning. Hoffmann had gotten to the counselor shortly
after midnight, requesting an interview with the assembled
Ex Comm Air. Palmer had handled it badly, exposing nothing of his knowledge beyond what Hoffmann had revealed,
yet apparently verifying what was said by dangerous, awkward silence. A matter before Senator Billingsworth's subcommittee had demanded his attendance most of the morning,
leaving no time to deal with the lawyer, and his afternoon
calendar was already crowded—Douglas Emory had seen to
that.

The senator from New Hampshire burst through the door
unannounced, the normally impeccable mane of white hair

slightly out of control, a harried look on his face which was now flushed crimson. He looked at Knight, then closed the door and walked across the room, pointing an accusatory finger. "You kept a file! Even worse, you allowed it to be stolen! . . . You fool, imbecile! Ruined! Everything—the plan, the timing . . . everything!"

"And your career?" Knight replied evenly.

"Yes, damn it! Thirty-five years in the Senate shot to rags. Because of you!"

"Calm yourself, senator, or you'll end up in Bethesda with a massive coronary." Knight calmly lit another cigarette and leaned back in his chair. "Also because of me, sufficient funds were made available for you to outspend each one of your opponents twenty-two of those years—or has that conveniently slipped your mind? And, Emory, don't ever burst in on me like that again. . . . Now, sit down and compose yourself."

"Compose myself! After the phone call I received?"

"From a Mr. Hoffmann?"

F. Douglas Emory's eyes rounded as if he'd been struck. "You knew! For heaven's sake, the man knows what we're planning. We can't go through with it now. I'm calling an emergency session tonight to cancel the project and see if we can't salvage something of our careers."

"Sit down, senator," Knight commanded, rising from the chair, his own face a threatening mask of anger. "There will be no emergency meeting, no saving of careers as you say. You're overreacting, and that's more dangerous than this Hoffmann, who thinks he's dealing from strength. But his strength is nothing, and we'll use his misconception to silence him when he tries to exercise it."

"You're a fool—he knows! As the chairman of our committee, I'm calling an end to the project."

"I'm afraid you're not in a position to do that," Knight replied. "We've only allowed you to think you were in command, a necessary expedient to salve an enormous ego that required constant stroking, because we needed your voice. You've been a figurehead, nothing more. The operational decisions have come from me. As long as you thought along the same lines as the rest of us, you were allowed to continue in the self-delusion of being the guiding hand. Upshaw and Shockley wanted to dump you six years ago, and there were times when your pompous vanity was almost too much for me as well. Now you'll follow orders instead of giving them. And you *will* do it."

Emory blinked in surprise. "You're insane! This Hoffmann plans on going to others outside our circle."

"If he does, the reception will not be a welcome one."

"Are you willing to take that risk? I, for one, am not."

"Because you've never had to face up to the tough decisions. We've insulated you from most of them, knowing you couldn't handle it. Even you don't know everything involved in pulling this off. Go back to your chambers and carry on as usual. There's a vote this afternoon on a compromise budget; be there, and conduct yourself appropriately. And remember, I can do far more harm to your precious career than this unknown, this Hoffmann. . . . Good day, senator."

Emory continued to stare at him, shocked beyond words or comprehension at the sudden revelation of his impotence. The phone rang.

Knight picked up the receiver quickly, glancing at the clock next to the pictures of his daughters on the end table across the room. A call from McLoughlin? So soon? Hoffmann must be impatient, another weakness to be used against him. The voice he heard was familiar, but unexpected.

"Hello, Mr. Deputy Director. This is Locke. You put out a memorandum on me a week ago. I'd like to talk to you about it. . . . That, and something called Dovetail."

*   *   *

Hoffmann headed south after making the connection with Langley, accompanied by a strange elation at the success achieved thus far. It was working: the confusion had begun. In a few hours, the pressure on Knight would begin to increase, and that would eventually drive him out into the open.

He crossed the Mason-Dixon line and entered Maryland, reaching Westminster just before three in the afternoon. On the new highway around the north side of town, he found a motel; next to the manager's office, a phone booth. He entered and dialed.

"This is Eric Hoffmann," he said when the intercept procedure was completed.

"You said twelve hours."

"I said sometime *within* twelve hours. Give me the numbers—you had everything within the first fifteen minutes."

"I'm afraid you overestimate us."

"And you're underestimating me. The numbers, please. You've got one minute . . . starting now."

"We weren't expecting you to call back so soon. It'll take me longer than that to pull them off the computer."

"Fifty seconds."

"Listen, I'm telling you the truth. We don't leave those things sitting around."

"Forty-five."

"All right . . . I've got them here."

"Spit it out. Quickly. You've got eight seconds per phone number."

McLoughlin recited each one rapidly as Hoffmann wrote. When he had the entire list, he hung up without acknowledgment. Minutes later, he was in the car, heading east through rolling hills of farmland, along back roads leading from one small town to another.

*　　*　　*

It was not quite dark when he finally stopped at a motel outside Aberdeen Proving Grounds. After registering and prepaying the bill, he ate at a diner a mile south, then returned to his room.

He had composed the message to be phoned to each of the Joint Chiefs, revised now as he jotted the essential points in outline form so no time would be wasted. Several rehearsals in front of the mirror refined his talk to less than three minutes.

Hoffmann sat on the edge of the bed, the phone in front of him on the nightstand, his handwritten outline next to the base of the instrument. He took a deep breath to calm his nerves, picked up the receiver, and dialed the long-distance access number. Seventy-five miles away, a special red phone rang.

"General Trumbull."

"Sir, my name is Eric Hoffmann. I was given this number by the Communications Center at Langley on the authority of Mr. William F. Knight, Deputy Director of the CIA. I'm aware that such procedure is unusual; however, the matter I am about to relate to you requires special handling. It concerns a clear and present danger to our national security. I request that you listen to my entire statement before making a decision on its merit or plausibility."

"Who do you represent?"

"I am not currently employed by the federal government, but I have worked for the Central Intelligence Agency in the recent past. Let me repeat: the matter I will describe affects our national security, and I request only that you listen to what I have to say before making any judgments. The fact that I obtained your private emergency extension from Langley, with proper authorization, should indicate this is not some joke.

"I am calling to alert you that a plan to reunify Germany is under way. The plan is called Dovetail and is being run by

Mr. Knight. It would appear that he is being aided by your Deputy Chief of Staff, General Shockley; Senator Emory; and others unknown to me. It's also possible that others at the Joint Chiefs level are involved." Hoffmann realized he was speaking too fast and attempted to slow down, inhaling deeply before continuing.

"I believe that if such an attempt were made by persons within our government—with or without the consent of the President—the Soviet Union would view it as an act of aggression, and that could lead to war. I believe it imperative that Dovetail be stopped and those responsible for it removed from their positions.

"The details of the plan will reach you within the next few days. A letter explaining what is currently known was mailed this morning to you and the other Joint Chiefs. The same letter was also mailed to the President, the Chancellor of West Germany, and the Prime Minister of Canada.

"If you are personally involved, then I suggest you disassociate yourself from Dovetail immediately and advise the others to do the same. If you're not, then I would hope you'll see to it that those involved are stopped before they take actions detrimental to the welfare of the United States.

"I'm calling your counterparts in the other services with this same message. You may want to consult with them on a course of action."

"And if I do nothing?"

"That is your decision. I'm sure at least one person will check into this matter, and when the facts become known in Congress, you may find yourself having to explain a reluctance to investigate a serious threat to our national security."

"Just a damned minute!"

"I don't have another minute, general."

"I want more information."

"It's in the packet I sent to your Pentagon office. Between

now and the time you get it, you might want to contact Mr. Knight to see what he says. . . . Good evening, sir."

Hoffmann depressed the telephone switch; he was still shaking, the receiver in his hand wet and slick. The alarm clock on the nightstand indicated the conversation had lasted slightly more than two and a half minutes.

He dialed the next number.

"Petit."

"Admiral, my name is Eric Hoffmann. I was given this extension by the Communications Center at Langley on the authority of William F. Knight, Deputy Director of the CIA. I'm aware that such procedure is unusual; however . . ."

Each call became progressively easier as the words flowed with practice. None of the officers seemed particularly upset over his accusations, a credit to their ability to function in time of crisis, or perhaps to years of self-discipline in presenting a stoic, self-controlled image devoid of personal feelings. Public display of emotion was bad form in the truly professional soldier.

The calls were completed in less than a half-hour, and though he was relatively sure no trace was possible, he didn't plan on taking chances. Movement was the key to survival. He checked out of the motel and paid the phone charges; minutes later, he was headed north on Route 40. Fifteen miles farther on, he crossed the Susquehanna River for the second time that day and heard an announcer on the radio cut in at the end of a song with an abbreviated weather report. It forecast a bright, cloudless day throughout the Chesapeake Bay area, with light southwest winds. It was exactly what he had hoped for.

Three hours later, after traveling south down the eastern shore of Maryland, he stopped at a roadside telephone booth below Salisbury and placed his last call of the day.

"Hello!" Knight's voice told the story of an agitated man beyond frustration.

"Hello, Mr. Knight, this is Eric Hoffmann. I take it you've been busy this evening."

"I almost have to admire your work. But it can't go on forever."

"It sounds like the Joint Chiefs have contacted you."

"I can handle them. You don't stand a chance, you know. Sooner or later we'll get to you."

"Actually, I've got a pretty good idea of my chances. But I've got something you want . . . something you need very badly. I'm willing to trade it for a guarantee of safety."

Knight laughed loudly, but there was a trace of anxiety in it. "You don't have anything."

"I think I do . . . and you know it. I visited Nick Sadukas in Chicago the day before yesterday. A tape and a signed statement attested to by three witnesses are now in my possession."

A long pause followed.

"Who the hell is Nick Sadukas?" Knight finally asked.

"You know exactly who he is—you've been sending him two thousand a month since 1964. Before that, it was a thousand a month."

"I don't know what you're talking about."

"If you'd prefer, I'll send copies of this to a few members of Congress and the wire services. You might be able to sidestep one issue, but I don't think you can survive both. And I think I've demonstrated sufficient knowledge of certain mechanics to make a meeting worth your whle."

"Maybe we should talk."

"I think that's a good idea. You have a sailboat tied up at a boatyard in Crisfield. Be there tomorrow morning at eight." Eric hung up before Knight could protest or suggest an alternate location.

It was done. The confrontation would come—at last.

By noon the next day, one of them would no longer be a threat.

Chapter 31

Crisfield. Self-proclaimed crab capital of the world. Gulls circled above the dock in the early-morning sun, squawking loudly as they dove to the surface and skimmed the top of the water before climbing skyward to repeat the cycle. It was chilly, and a thin mist hung over the quiet waters of the protected basin, the throaty screech of the waterfowl the only intrusion upon the tranquility of Joshua Wake's Boatyard. A solitary figure approached the wooden pier.

"Hello, Mr. Knight."

The CIA man stopped and turned rapidly in the direction of the voice, coiled to strike out, his hand going quickly to a shoulder holster hidden beneath the light brown corduroy sport coat. The old man who tended the boatyard looked at him tentatively from beneath the long bill of his fishing hat.

"Hi, Charlie." He relaxed.

"Don't usually see you down here through the week like this, leastwise not this time of year. How ya been?"

"Pretty good, I guess. And you?"

"Can't complain none."

Knight wondered how many times they had had this conversation, with the same questions and always the same responses. Usually he enjoyed talking to the old eastern shoreman; the easy banter about tides and fishing and local gossip helped to slow him down from the Washington pace, something the long drive from the city never seemed to do. But today the attendant and parttime commercial fisherman was an irritation.

"How's the fishing?" Knight asked, looking around, scanning the walkways leading to four parallel piers where more than half the slips were now vacant.

"Folks is catchin' a few rock and some blues now and then. Oysters startin' to come in pretty good now. Nothin' great . . . ain't like it used to be."

"Guess not," Knight said, hearing but not listening. There were a hundred hiding places in the large yard, others in the tall marsh grass surrounding it. A few work boats and most of the pleasure craft had been pulled in and put up on blocks for the winter—all offered concealment from which he could observe the entire scene and await Hoffmann's arrival. Isolating him would present no problems.

"There was a fella here lookin' for you last night," the attendant was saying.

"Who?"

"Didn't say. Kind of an odd sort. Showed up around ten, maybe a little before. Scared the you-know-what outa me. Said he was supposed to meet you, but told me he couldn't stick around." Charlie rummaged through his pockets and finally retrieved a crumpled scrap of paper. "Here it is. Fella said to hand you this . . . gave me ten bucks to deliver it. Easiest money I ever made."

Knight looked at the paper.

Crab Factory, Tangier Island, 9:00 A.M. Hoffmann

"Is this it?"

"That's all."

"Did he say anything else?"

"Nothin'. Just said to give it to you, and drove off back down the road." The old man scrubbed a whiskered chin with the knuckles of his right hand. "Right soon after he left, there was another fella drove up and started snoopin' around. Never seen him before, either. I was over on the other side of the yard. When I got over here, he was gone . . . so was his car. Checked all the boats, includin' yours, 'cause I thought he might be tryin' to steal somethin'. You still might want to check the *Pegasus* over pretty good . . . just in case."

"I'll do that. Thanks for the help, Charlie."

"Sure thing, Mr. Knight. Say, you goin' out this mornin'?"

"That's what I came down for."

"Looks like a good day for it."

"I'd say it was just perfect."

The sailboat rolled gently on lazy swells like elongated sine waves as Knight guided the forty-one–foot Morgan out through the protective rock jetty of the boatyard, pointing south of Smith Island into the bay. Usually he enjoyed being on the water, relaxing with the feel of the boat under his feet; the lower Chesapeake was his private retreat, and had been since he purchased the sailboat in St. Petersburg five years earlier. Today, because the island was only ten miles from Crisfield, he decided to leave the sails stowed and rely on the big Perkins diesel to motor the distance.

The reduced workload would also give him time to think.

Hoffmann had proved to be surprisingly resourceful. Using Madras to reach the Joint Chiefs earned him a grudging respect. More troublesome was what the young pilot knew about Sadukas.

Although Hoffmann's choice of Tangier Island as a meeting place was unexpected, it pleased the CIA man. Located in the middle of the bay just south of the Maryland–Virginia border, it was almost ideal for what Knight had planned—secluded, isolated from outside contact except the daily postal boat from Crisfield. There was no means of escape, no room to maneuver.

Fifty-five minutes after leaving the boatyard, Knight guided the sailboat to one of the deep-draft piers on the north side of the inhabited portion of the island. Off to his right sat several working boats, their long aft sections piled high with crab traps. An old waterman and his younger apprentice looked up from their chores of mending one of the three or four dozen crab pots stacked on the wooden pier; they glanced at the shiny white sailboat as Knight lashed it to pilings, then went back to work without a word of greeting. Outsiders were not to be trusted, their presence tolerated but not welcome. The descendants of the Parks and Crocketts had little use and no time for the prying ways of mainlanders.

Knight finished securing the Morgan and headed down the sandy path toward the crab factory. Minutes later, he cautiouslessly approached the building, a concrete-block and metal structure at the edge of the water only a few yards from the abandoned Navy runway. An old man sat on a wooden chair propped against an outside wall.

"Good morning," the CIA man said. The only acknowledgment was a wary, sidelong glance from beneath gray eyebrows. "I'm supposed to meet somebody here."

One eyebrow raised. Finally the old man spoke. "You be Knight?"

"Yes."

"Fella say you be comin' here." The words were barely intelligible, spoken in a dialect with its roots in Elizabethan English. The man withdrew a well-worn pipe from his mouth and pointed with the stem toward a small wooden building with gray paint peeling from the walls. It sat on the edge of an asphalt parking ramp, in the open, insuring approaches from any direction would be in view for the last thirty yards.

Knight crossed the open space quickly and went in.

"Welcome to Tangier Island, Mr. Knight. I'm Eric Hoffmann. You're five minutes late." Hoffmann sat on a swivel chair in front of two old desks that lined adjacent walls and met at right angles in the corner. His words carried the unmistakable ring of confidence; the Deputy Director of the CIA caused no fear in him. "It's about time we finally met."

Knight looked around the shack. It was only twenty feet square, and almost half the space was occupied by two restrooms. A small VHF radio transmitter sat on one of the desks, next to a black telephone. Except for those items and an oil-fired heater, the room was bare. "Mind if I smoke?" Knight asked nonchalantly.

"As a matter of fact, I do."

The harsh words caught him by surprise, and he hesitated a second. The phrase was a meaningless courtesy, employed more out of habit than because he cared what others felt. Knight smiled and lit the cigarette. "You want to talk or play games?"

"I want to stop Dovetail."

"That's beyond your capabilities."

"I hadn't planned on doing it myself. I thought I'd delegate that to you."

"Be serious."

"Believe me, I am." Hoffmann noticed Knight's quick glance outside. "We're alone. Nobody's going to interrupt. And if you're thinking about using your own gun, I suggest you listen before making a big mistake."

"I'm listening. But my patience is limited."

"Let's first talk about how you killed my father."

"That's ridiculous. Who said I killed your father?"

"This does," Hoffmann replied, opening the center desk

drawer and extracting the personnel file. He momentarily held it inches above the desk, then let it fall.

"There's nothing in there to indicate I had anything to do with his death. He was lost in combat."

"Part of the answer is there. You and Gregory briefed him the day he died. Gregory was the operations officer for the squadron. You were there on special assignment from the OSS as intelligence analyst. You were blackmailing Gregory because he had gotten some English girl pregnant and didn't want that to get back to his wife."

"You have a vivid imagination."

"Stick around; it gets better. On your instructions, Sadukas altered the recognition symbols on the tail of my father's airplane before the flight, and then you arranged a single-ship photo mission—for intelligence purposes. There was a lot of fear the Germans were using captured or rebuilt American and British aircraft to get past England's home defenses, so you rigged his aircraft to look like it was one of them. Then you planted the information in the daily intelligence summary so that RAF would be sure to see it. Apparently it worked. I suppose he was shot down by a British fighter."

"Sadukas told you this?"

"Yes."

"Let me see the statement. There's no deal until I have the original."

"He was too scared of you to put it on paper, but he was too scared of me to keep quiet. The tape and the document don't exist—they never did, but I needed something more than Dovetail to convince you to come here."

Knight smiled, an expression of relief and satisfaction, his worst fears gone. "You really are stupid."

"Maybe. But I haven't finished. I think I know why you killed him. Somehow he stumbled onto something about you he shouldn't have. What was it?"

"It's funny. You're a lot like him—he was a troublemaker, too."

"He knew, didn't he?" Hoffmann asked, the question more assertive than inquiring. "You were working on this plan to reunite Germany—or keep it from being divided—even before the war ended, before Yalta could take effect. That's what he found out—he learned you were subverting the agreement the Allies had reached, and he tried to stop you . . . you and whoever else was involved then."

"Yes, he knew!" Knight's face grew animated, distorting his eyes like those of a madman. "And now you think you can finish the work of your father—pick up the crusade and finish it. You fool! He was one of us!"

Hoffmann's world burst open, his whole being on the verge of exploding. *One of them!* No! He would not believe.

"You're a liar!"

"No, he was in it almost from the beginning. But he wasn't satisfied with a supporting role. He wanted more power, more authority. More money. He was *never* satisfied, and that caused concern. Twice in January of 'forty-five he flew couriers into Zurich to meet with emissaries from Dönitz, and each time he demanded larger payments. He was dangerous, too dangerous to be left alive."

Hoffmann stared at the man, his eyes glaring. "I don't believe you."

"Look at the file. The mission sheets are still there—photo-recon missions with no specific targets, only general areas of coverage. Not too wise in retrospect, but we were all new at this business—it wasn't quite the same as parachuting into France. There was a lot of wasted motion and thrashing around in the air war as available targets dwindled. With Gregory's help, the flights went unnoticed. I kept the records for personal reasons—they could have been sterilized if the need arose. It almost did when you started nosing around, contacting people who used to be in the squadron. I've had you under surveillance for a long time."

"You had him killed."

"Made the arrangements, yes. The changed markings were one contingency; giving the Luftwaffe his route of flight and ETA's was another. Actually, I don't know who finally got him.

"Afterward, we doctored the offical reports and quietly advised your mother he had been working for the Germans, to head off any ideas of an investigation—a probe that would cost her survivor's benefits and caused unnecessary embarrassment. It gave us time to clean up loose ends. After thirty years, there's no trace, no trail to follow."

"Except Sadukas."

"Not even him any longer—after you pointed the finger at him last night. His knowledge and deductions about what he'd done didn't surface until four or five years after the war. By then he had developed a strategy to make himself some extra cash, with minimum exposure to risk. That no longer exists. Nothing does, with Gregory and Sadukas gone."

"Neither of them appears on any of the old records."

"One of the loose ends we took care of after the war. Gregory was getting to be a problem, though. When he got shafted at the Pentagon, he started drinking too much. Even that wasn't too bad until the two of you got together."

Knight dropped the cigarette on the floor and stepped on it before continuing.

"When Schellen's supposed defection came up, I saw an opportunity to eliminate a number of problems at the same time. We've been working with Schellen since before the end of the war, and I knew he didn't really want to defect, but we had to make it look like we were going to try.

"Gregory was killed and the finger pointed at you so you'd be more likely to cooperate. There's still an open investigation, by the way, and you're still the prime suspect. We used you because you had some of the skills we needed . . . and you were another loose end. There were several alternative plans to insure you failed and were eventually eliminated."

"They didn't work."

"Not until now. But things are falling into place. Losing Schellen hurts a little, but we have a backup who can do his job. This little annoyance you've stirred up with the Joint Chiefs can be handled also—two of them are involved already. They convinced the others you were part of the lunatic fringe. It wasn't hard. And if you think the documents you sent will arrive, you're mistaken. You don't really think we'd allow mail to get through to such people without a thorough screening. The proper links have already been alerted— consignment to the burner is about as far as they'll go. Within the next month, Dovetail will become a reality. We're going to make it happen . . . and you can't stop us. Nobody can. Even if I were to die today, the mechanism would still function."

Knight gazed at him with contemptuous amusement. It had been so easy. Hoffmann's position had been weaker than he'd expected, the sole purpose of arranging the meeting to put finally to rest the unknowns about his father. Revealing the truth had simply served to confirm his superiority over the young pilot. Hoffmann could do nothing with the information now.

"I want Dovetail stopped," Hoffmann said.

"And if it's not, you'll make the file public, see that it's the lead story on every network and every newspaper in the country." The agent laughed mockingly. "There's no way you can get to the file—Roy Locke gave it to me last night, in exchange for a new identity and my promise he won't be harmed. You've got nothing, Hoffmann. *Nothing.* Without a deposition from Sadukas, you're empty-handed. You don't have a thing to trade—except your life."

Silence filled the room as they looked at one another across the short distance.

"I expected Locke would contact you eventually and make a deal," Hoffmann said at last. Swift dismay crossed the agent's face. "Truthfully, I have my doubts that anyone could be persuaded to believe what's in there in time to stop what you're doing. It took months before the true story came out on Watergate, and you're talking in terms of weeks or days before loosing something that goes beyond rational ability to comprehend."

"Bringing Germany together is far from that. It's a necessity."

"Desirable, I'll grant you. And, in a way, I'll agree with the principle. But not the method, or the timing. That's why you'll stop it."

"Because you desire it? You've added new meaning to the concept of criminal insanity as a defense. *I have the file.* And I have you." Knight reached beneath his coat and pulled out his weapon, the movement effortlessly rapid. "Suddenly, I'm tired of our discussion."

"So am I," Hoffmann replied. "But if you pull that trigger, you'll have killed your daughters—and yourself as well." There was an instant of hesitation, a look in Knight's eyes that was the confirmation hoped for, expected but not verified until then. Hoffmann continued. "That's right, your precious girls—one of them married to a doctor practicing in Houston; the other is a junior at the University of Wisconsin, Madison campus, living with some long-haired phys ed major you don't care for very much." He saw shock register, the seed of caution sown.

"You've got no right—"

"Just like you had no right to ruin Janet Hoffmann's life!" he roared. He could see the face—a woman old before her time, carrying the shame of something that never happened. No wonder she had avoided speaking of her dead husband.

Knight would pay for her misery. "They're in no danger as long as Dovetail is cancelled."

"You couldn't."

"Not by myself. Three days ago I visited a *padrone* in Chicago, a father with an abundance of Sicilian pride, and extravagantly grateful to the man who saved his son's life."

"Labruzo."

Hoffmann nodded, noticing a slight trembling in the hand that held the gun. "He put me in touch with another, a mechanic if you like, who has even lower standards of morality than you possess. His tastes are expensive, I should add. This morning, about an hour and a half ago, a telegram from you was hand-delivered to your daughter in Madison. I understand she was genuinely surprised at your sudden approval of her live-in boyfriend."

"You expect me to believe this?" Knight's face had flushed red.

"Call her if you'd like," Hoffmann replied evenly, lifting the telephone and offering it to the agent. "I know how much Dovetail means to you—it's your life's work. But how do the scales balance when you weigh it against their lives? And you're experienced enough to know you can't possibly protect them forever. They're important to you. A man like you needs something to keep things in some semblance of normalcy, otherwise you'd go crazy. Your daughters provide that—and I'm betting you're obsessively protective of them."

Knight's eyes had clouded over, appearing dazed, almost translucent. He had not expected this; the man before him bore no resemblance to the psychological profile prepared two months earlier. "I'll kill you."

"A very stupid move. The man who delivered the telegram is expecting a call at nine o'clock his time. That's less than an hour from now. If he doesn't hear from me by then, he has certain detailed instructions concerning her future, and that of your other daughter."

Knight looked past Hoffmann to the open area visible through the window.

"If you're looking for the agent who came over on the boat with you this morning, forget it," Hoffmann continued. "You might have noticed a fisherman at the dock when you tied up. He knows nothing about fishing, but he does possess other useful skills. He's already neutralized your man by now.

"Another thing—don't even consider trying to come after me later. The man watching your daughter today has been paid very well to finish the job if anything ever happens to me or my mother. He's also been promised five thousand a month just to check in with me every thirty days. As I said, his tastes are expensive. The bottom line is that it's going to cost you ten thousand a month to insure your daughters' safety."

"I don't have that kind of money."

"You'll find a way to get it. I'll give you an address—a numbered account in Zurich—where the money is to be sent on the fifteenth of each month. When I get it, half goes to the man who's now watching your daughter, and half goes to the wife of the man you and Gregory had killed. She deserves it, after what you've done to her life. If anything happens to either of us, the girls are dead. So are you.

"Now, let's talk about Dovetail. You will see that it's stopped . . . or the first payment, which is due in two weeks, will not be made. It's that simple."

"You're making a colossal mistake."

"And you're compounding it if Dovetail goes forward. Think about it. Or don't you care what happens to your daughters?"

"Shut up, damn you!"

"There's something else I want you to know. A lot of good, dedicated people inside the CIA would like nothing better than to see you fall flat on your face. They're watching you very closely, and they don't like what you've done to the Agency for personal gain and satisfaction. And they're willing to work with me to keep you in line. One of the things they told me about is a ship Howard Hughes recently had built for you. I'm going to see the press learns about it, to prove I have the ability to keep track of everything you do from now on."

"Just make sure you make that call to Wisconsin."

"But you haven't given me your answer on Dovetail. What's it going to be?"

Knight's face still registered numbed astonishment. The young man's strategy created a reversed advantage too unexpected, the possibilities too abhorrent. He nodded his head without speaking.

"Then I'll make the call. And I'll make an extra effort to stay out of trouble so my man gets his payment every month. I'm sure you appreciate that, since you've now got an interest in my continued wellbeing." Hoffmann reached for the radio transmitter, pulled it in front of him, then looked at Knight. "I also suggest you stop the murder investigation into General Gregory's death. At least get my name out of it."

A small, single-engine plane glided toward the runway beneath a high, clear sky, its wings rocking in the southwesterly breeze. It touched down on the runway, a spidery pattern of asphalt that told of many repairs through the years.

Hoffmann rose from his chair and pushed past Knight to the front door. He paused and faced the Deputy Director, feeling hugely, inordinately fatigued.

Hoffmann's right hand lashed out at the face in a blur, and he felt the knuckles of his clenched fist make solid contact with the side of the jaw. Knight's head snapped violently sideways as the blow sent him crashing backward into the wall. His knees buckled and he fought for balance, dazed, his eyes unable to focus.

"I wish I could tell you how satisfying that was," Hoffmann said, turning away and walking out toward the awaiting plane.

"Strange place to meet with your lawyer," Saxon said above the noise of the engine as Hoffmann climbed in and buckled the seat belt. Glad you finally took my advice. . . . You want to fly it?"

"No, you go ahead. My hand is starting to swell."

"Let me see. Hurt?"

Hoffmann smiled. "A little, but it felt damned good."

A puzzled look crossed Saxon's face as he opened the throttle and guided the aircraft across the small ramp.

The plane gathered speed and lifted gently off the ground halfway down the runway, its nose pointed above the horizon as Tangier Island slipped from view beneath the left wing. Hoffmann closed his eyes and enjoyed the taste of freedom.

Freedom.

Flying had always meant that to him, but his mental and physical reactions were now more keenly felt. He had fought for this freedom—and it had changed him, far more than he cared to admit. Half aloud, he said, "For those who have fought for it, freedom has a taste the protected will never know."

"What's that?" Saxon asked, raising his voice to be heard above the engine.

"Just mumbling something I remember reading on a wall plaque at a camp overseas. It didn't mean anything—at the time it didn't, anyhow." Out the right window, he could see the expanse of the Chesapeake stretching toward the horizon like a broad, peaceful velvet mat.

EPILOGUE

November 1974 was an unusual month.

To several different and seemingly unrelated people, it was one of those periods that got slightly out of control, a time when the cogs in the machinery of events inexplicably slipped or went out of sync, though the machine itself plugged along.

Senator F. Douglas Emory called a press conference late on a Friday afternoon to announce that his letter of resignation had been sent to the governor of New Hampshire, effective the end of the month. The reason: failing health.

Yuri Kasimirov and Anatoly Kusheloff were both recalled to Moscow. Statements by each were used to convict the other in swift, secret trials that saw both men eventually imprisoned for life.

Radio messages and telephone communications between U.S. Army units in West Germany were monitored in East Germany, and an attempt was made at analysis. No satisfactory conclusions were ever drawn; the myriad of orders and countermanded orders were beyond deciphering, the chaos apparently created by the many recent changes of command within the senior officer ranks of the U.S. Armed Forces in Europe.

In Washington, General Shockley abruptly announced his retirement and left the service two weeks later. No public comment was ever made concerning the absence of a formal retirement ceremony for a much-decorated officer.

By the end of November, message traffic between the United States and its army in Europe was back to normal.

On February 7, 1975, the *Los Angeles Times* ran a story on the *Glomar Explorer*, detailing its intended use as a spy ship to attempt recovery of sunken Russian submarines. CIA attempts failed to get the story scratched just days before publication.

On the following day, the *New York Times* ran a similar story, but it was buried on page 30, due primarily to the efforts of one senior CIA official. After that, it gained momentum, becoming front-page news across the country. A detailed report by a well-known syndicated columnist with a reputation for accurately exposing government secrets culminated in a national television broadcast on March 18.

Heinrich Schellen's whereabouts remained a mystery. It was not known for over two years whether or not he survived the October evening when Eric Hoffmann learned the effectiveness of the Israeli stun grenades. On January 20, 1977, a band of guerrillas attacked a mountain plantation in Peru, killing all occupants. The story received no coverage in the United States and only slightly more than a paragraph in most other papers around the world, if it was covered at all. The event was overshadowed by the inauguration of a new President of the United States.

Two days later, a message was hand-delivered to a farmer in Kibbutz Yad-Il. It originated from a Mossad agent in Paraguay and had been sent to an Israeli general in Tel Aviv.

After more than three decades, Akiva Ben Ari could try to forget the Holocaust.

On September 17, 1977, the body of William F. Knight was found floating in Chesapeake Bay, five miles from where his boat had run aground. A nine-millimeter bullet wound in his temple was listed as the official cause of death. Maryland authorities concluded that the death was a suicide, but a young lawyer of Sicilian descent periodically gets the case reopened.

The investigation continues as an open case.